# IN A NAKED PLACE

# In a Naked Place

## SHIRLEY ESKAPA

QUARTET BOOKS

First published in 2008 by
Quartet Books Limited
A member of the Namara Group
27 Goodge Street, London W1T 2LD
This paperback edition published in 2009

Copyright © Shirley Eskapa 2008

A catalogue record for this book
is available from the British Library

ISBN    978 0 7043 7179 8

Typeset by Antony Gray
Printed and bound in Great Britain by
T J International Ltd, Padstow, Cornwall

For

ROSEMARIE

*Grief twists us in many ways, but a mothers's grief is unquenchable.*

**1992**

After Lily's father left them for another woman, her mother banned all contact with him. In retaliation, he named his new baby after his own first child.

When the pattern was repeated, and Lily's adored husband Hugh left her, she swore that she would never allow their nine-year-old daughter, Amanda, to suffer as she had suffered when she had lost her handsome father to his young wife and *their* children. Accordingly, after she moved to London, she encouraged Amanda to spend every other weekend in Arundel with Hugh and Jane.

On the Saturday afternoon of Amanda's fifteenth weekend with her father, he telephoned to say that because she had a cold and slight fever, it would be best for her to stay with him until her temperature was normal.

'There has been an outbreak of chicken-pox at school,' Lily said. As a former nurse, the rarest complications of chicken-pox crashed into her mind. Encephalitis? Pneumonia? 'Two cases in Lily's class this week, I'm – '

'It's only a mild cold, Lily,' he interrupted in that tender, musical voice of his that had first attracted her to him, when she was an eighteen-year-old student nurse. He was a doctor at the same hospital, and exactly double her age.

'Are you sure?' Lily sounded doubtful.

'You know what to do when in doubt, Lily?'

'Worry!' she replied, laughing in spite of herself. She'd been hyper-anxious about Amanda since before she was born, and Hugh had deployed this private joke, as a kind of code of reassurance.

'That's right,' he said. 'Worry!'

Lily had no sooner put the phone down than she felt her whole body sink into a posture of despair. Two or three extra days without Amanda's comforting presence meant that the wasteland in which Hugh had left her would become even bleaker. She felt as if all her confused thoughts were happening in a language she could not understand. Desperate to escape a further attack of acute loneliness, she took up a pile of essays to mark. Thanks to God and Hugh, she had a teaching career which was meaningful to her. Because it was Hugh who, in that poetic way of his, had urged her not to allow her life to become simply a storehouse of abandoned dreams; she could become the teacher she always wanted to be. After all, had she not admitted to him that she had qualified as a nurse only to fulfil her mother's thwarted ambition? So she had taken Hugh's lead, and when Amanda was two years old she had enrolled at the Teacher Training College, where Amanda went to Nursery School while she went to lectures.

On Sunday, the day she now thought was the most heartless of the week, she went all out to keep herself busy. After a strenuous session at the gym, and scores of lengths in the pool, she and Magsie Henderson, the school matron and her new friend, met for a pizza. They talked about the paper entitled A Policy on Behaviour and Discipline that she had been asked to write for the *Educational Time*s. Of little education, but much wisdom, Magsie's insights were invaluable.

Later, as usual, their conversation turned to Hugh.

'I don't think I'll ever get used to the fact that my mother's best friend is now Amanda's stepmother,' Lily began.

'You've always said they'd been friends for ever,' Magsie said. 'But just how long was for ever?'

'Since my mother was pregnant with me,' Lily said with an air of puzzlement, as if this had only just occurred to her. 'I'm thirty-four now.'

'Then she's at least *fifty*-four,' Magsie said. 'She's even older than *me*!'

'In her fifties or not, she's really got it,' Lily winced. 'Men have always been attracted to her like bees to honey.'

Magsie leaned forward, and dropped her voice. 'They say when a man opens his trousers his brains fall out!'

They laughed that bitter, knowing laugh women reserve for the ways of men.

Later, at the end of the afternoon, driving home in the slow-moving traffic, looking in at the lighted windows in the gloom, Lily suddenly felt as if she were homeless. She wondered when, if ever, the phrase 'I want to go home' would stop echoing in her head. Back at the flat she doubted she would ever come to accept as her home, the feeling of foreboding that had been gathering all day gained pace. Calling Hugh was always painful, but her overwhelming need to find out how her daughter was got the better of her. If Jane picked up the phone, she would hang up; her throat seemed to close even at the thought of speaking to her.

Hugh answered. 'Amanda's much better,' he said. 'I'll take the phone to her.'

'Thanks, Hugh.'

'She's fallen asleep,' he said a few moments later. 'She's been reading *Tess of the D'Urbervilles* all day.'

'That's fantastic!' Lily said. 'It's way above average for a child of nine.'

'We've got a wonderful little girl,' Hugh's voice was warm with pride. 'I'll let you know if she can go home tomorrow.'

'Thanks,' Lily said. 'I miss her.'

'I know,' he said.

That night, sleepless, aching for Hugh's body, and yearning for the sound of his voice, she went to Amanda's room. There, between Amanda's fresh pink sheets, among her collection of fluffy puppies, it came to her that she was in danger of becoming as dependent on Amanda as her mother had been on her. She would have to guard against that. She had failed Hugh; she dared not fail Amanda. If she had measured up to his expectations of her, she would not have had to endure the shame of Hugh having chosen a much older woman over her. She understood, now, that she had put herself in a kind of isolation ward, where shame and guilt flourished. Perpetually overwrought, she was behind glass, in a sort of quarantine. She would have to make herself smash the glass to move on.

True to his word, Hugh called the next evening. 'She's better, her temperature has been back to normal for twenty-four hours,' he said. 'I'll bring her back to London after surgery tomorrow.'

'I'll have the day off tomorrow,' Lily said. 'My class has a geography field trip, so I could collect her myself at about noon.'

'Fine.'

'I won't come in. Ask her to watch out for me, will you?'

'She'll be ready and waiting for you, Lily,' he replied, his tone grim. Lily had told him that she would never again cross the threshold of what had once been her home.

Lily had won the school raffle for an aromatherapy massage at the local hairdressing salon, and considered cancelling the appointment she had made for the next day. If she did that, she would get to Amanda much earlier. But then, reminding herself of her resolve to move on, she decided not to change anything. She would keep to her plan to give Amanda lunch at that pretty inn overlooking the rushing waters of the River Arun. After that they would go to the bird sanctuary where she would photograph Amanda holding an exotic Amazonian bird for her Nature Study Project.

She straightened her back. What was more, she would accept the geography master's invitation to go with him to the Vivaldi concert at the Albert Hall.

Lily revelled in her massage. Responding to the mixture of honey, jasmine and lavender unguents, her tense muscles began to ease and, for the first time in months, she felt cleansed, somehow rejuvenated, ready, at last, to make a serious effort to begin again. She was well on her way to Arundel when she remembered she'd left her camera on the kitchen table. She turned back to fetch it. As always, she parked her Mini outside the modest apartment building in which she and Amanda lived. She had just got out of her car when one of her neighbours, Mabel Johnson, with much wringing of her hands rushed forward and blocked her path.

'I'm so sorry, so sorry – such a terrible, terrible, *terrible* thing – ' she wailed.

'What are you talking about?' Lily asked, panicked and horribly frightened.

'The caretaker let him in,' Mabel babbled. 'He's in your flat.'

Even as she spoke, Lily whipped off her high heels and ran up the cement staircase to the fourth floor. She had not yet reached the first landing when she heard the howling. Flying up the stairs she tripped and fell. Someone helped her up. The howling grew louder, still louder. An answering scream tore her throat. The moment Hugh saw Lily he stood up. 'It's Amanda,' he wept. 'Amanda.'

'She's not dead, is she?' Though her entire body shook, her voice was deathly calm. 'Not dead?'

'My fault!' The howling began again. 'Our daughter is dead, and it's all my fault!'

He tried to take Lily in his arms but she pushed him away so forcefully that he fell back.

'Encephalitis?' she rasped.

'No – a Rottweiler.'

'Rottweiler?' she repeated. '*What* Rottweiler? I didn't even know you had a *dog*! Amanda didn't tell me.'

'It was Jane's sister's dog and I wasn't there to save her – ' his voice cut off, and that roar began again.

Two police officers, a man and a woman, had driven Hugh to London. Margaret Stevens, the younger of the two, took Lily's hand and led her out of the living room to her bedroom. 'He so desperately wanted to tell you himself,' she said quietly.

*'Tell me! For God's sake, tell me!'*

Her body rigid, Lily sat on the edge of her bed. Kneeling in front of her, Margaret held both Lily's hands in a firm grip. 'The dog pierced her carotid artery,' Margaret said. 'Her life ended in seconds.'

'Where is she?' Lily demanded.

'At the Lavinian Hospital.'

'I must go to her,' Lily said, her voice jagged. 'I must go to the hospital at once.' She stood up, pulled the keys from her pocket, and turned to leave.

Margaret gently took the keys from her hand. 'I'm Margaret Stevens. I'll drive you.'

'Thank you,' Lily said. 'I must leave this minute.'

'I'll have a word with my colleague, and we'll be off.'

Margaret opened the car door and helped her into the car. A scent of lavender still clung to the seats. Lily sat still and stiff, her tightly clenched fists showing the white bones beneath the skin.

'How did it happen?' she demanded, her scratchy voice sounding as if it had come from another person in a distant place.

Uncertain of how to say what had to be said, Margaret Stevens did not answer immediately. The rain bucketed down, and she switched on the windscreen wiper.

'How did it happen?' Lily repeated.

Willing herself to sound matter-of-fact, Margaret explained that Amanda's stepmother had taken Amanda and the Rottweiler alongside the river, where dogs were allowed to run free. Jane had stopped to chat with some friends and Amanda and the Rottweiler ran on ahead.

Amanda was attempting to rescue a rabbit from the dog's jaws when he turned on her. Amanda's screams and the Rottweiler's growling brought everyone rushing to her. Before they reached her the screaming went silent. 'They were too late,' Margaret Stevens concluded. 'Once he'd punctured that artery, she never had a chance.'

'I should have been with her. I could have collected her earlier,' Lily moaned. 'But I went for a massage. I'll never forgive myself. Never, never, never!'

'You can't blame yourself,' Margaret Stevens protested.

Throughout that interminable journey, in the same tone and rhythm in which she used to recite 'Hail Mary' at the convent, Lily repeated, 'I wasn't with her. I should have been with her. I went for a massage. I'll never forgive myself.'

It was forty-five minutes before they arrived at the hospital. The mortuary attendants tried to stop Lily from going in.

'What *are* you talking about?' Lily demanded, her voice as sharp as broken glass. 'I was a head nurse at this hospital! Have you gone mad?'

Amanda's father, Doctor Hugh, was one of the most loved physicians at the Lavinian Hospital. They could not refuse her.

Lying on a stretcher, Amanda was unrecognizable. Her face had been torn apart, and her body savaged. Her shining red hair was now matted in what looked like a tangle of bloodied rope. It was six hours since the attack. The autopsy had not yet begun, and she was still wearing her shoes. Her right hand was intact. It was when Lily opened Amanda's fist, squeezed her eyes shut, and buried her face in the only undamaged part of her child's body that her own mouth was filled with rabbit fur. Her screaming did not stop until a hypodermic was plunged into her arm.

A week later, during a furious storm, they buried Amanda in the small churchyard that fronted St Nicholas, the church where they had been married, where Hugh had been a church warden, where Amanda had been christened, where she had sung in the choir.

Lily left immediately after the funeral and has not returned since. Even now, fifteen years later, she is unable to bear the sight of Amanda's grave.

**2007**

# CHAPTER 1

Christmas was, as always, a painful time for Lily Lidbury, Headmistress of Belgrave Hall. It didn't surprise her to know that the suicide rate rocketed on Christmas day. Not that a mother who has lost a child needs any particular occasion to remind her of her grief. Her eye fell on the bright colours on the large Christmas card the African children of Jabulani orphanage had made for her. After Amanda died, she had gone out to Jabulani as a volunteer nurse. She had hoped to lose herself, and perhaps even find a little solace in her nursing. She found none, but she did find the courage to endure. So it was that she came to lead a dual life working with some of the most underprivileged orphans in Africa in her vacations, and some of the most privileged school girls in England for the rest of the year. Living on two continents, losing autumn, sliding from an English summer into an African winter, Lily gradually found each day easier to bear – more so than she had ever dared hope. Grief did not let up its grip, but leading two lives of usefulness was gratifying.

Lily lived in the old servants' quarters, now the headmistress's flat, on the top floor. It was two days after Christmas and she was soaking in a hot bath when the phone rang. Instinctively, she answered it, only remembering after she had called out 'Belgrave Hall' that she was not supposed to be in London, but holidaying in the country.

'This is Benton Anderson, Savannah's father, calling Mrs Lidbury,' said a deep voice.

'But it must be the crack of dawn in New York!' replied Lily.

'It is. I thought I would have a better chance of reaching her before 10 a.m. London time.'

'I see.'

'I guess I just missed her.'

'You haven't, actually.'

'Oh – Mrs Lidbury?'

'Yes.'

'What a relief! My wife has a major meeting tomorrow, so we decided I should call. You remember Jodi telling you that she wasn't sure we would be able to bring Savannah to school before the new term starts?'

'Of course I do.'

'Well, I can bring her over, after all. She could start with you on Tuesday, if that's OK with you. We'd like to do all we can to make the transition easier for her. It's going to be extra tough for her to be the only new girl in the class when you say she's not up to the standard of the other girls.'

'Savannah is a bright child with great potential, but getting her up to standard will take rather longer than eleven days, I'm afraid. As I explained to your wife, American children start formal education so much later than their British counterparts. They cannot possibly have attained the same level.'

'School starts on January 19. If we fly after New Year's on Sunday, I could bring her to you on Tuesday, January 4.' His words came fast in a burst of enthusiasm. 'If she has four hours' worth of class for eleven days, that will bring her up to forty-four hours.'

Unthinkingly, she let more hot water into the bath. Who was this audacious man calling on such a day? The sound of running water travelled three thousand miles. 'Something wrong with the line?' he said. 'Sounds like some kind of static.'

Hastily turning off the tap, Lily said, 'A bad line.'

'The line is clear now,' he said. 'Tuesday at ten?'

'Agreed.'

'I understand you're making a major exception accepting Savannah at this time of the academic year?'

'Yes.'

'I'd just like to register my appreciation, Mrs Lidbury. My wife and I are very grateful.'

'Thank you.'

'Till January 4, then.'

'Yes,' Lily said, her voice crisp and definite. 'Give my love to Savannah! She's a super little girl.'

She put down the phone, and slid further under the water. Her heart was racing – Benton Anderson – Savannah's father. His voice had sounded warm, even strangely intimate. She had never met him, and could not understand why she was so pleased that it was he, and not Jodi, who had called her. She remembered Jodi well; little make-up, red hair pulled back from her face into a pony-tail, masculine suit and sensible brogues – all chosen, it seemed to Lily, to proclaim her status as a high-powered New York litigator. The Andersons were to be in London for a three to five-year stay. Benton was the president of the newly opened London office of Carlyle Klein Bank. Jodi's august law firm (at which she was a partner) had granted her leave of absence contingent on commutes between New York and London.

Lily got out of the bath and began to dry herself vigorously. There was no doubt that tutoring Savannah would be a challenge.

Belgrave Hall was one of the most prestigious girls' schools in England. Housed in an elegant Georgian town house, it stood proudly but gracefully across a leafy square in London's West End. Places at Belgrave Hall were hard to come by. Applications arrived at the school almost as soon as soon as a mother had the gender of the foetus confirmed. The school was always over-subscribed – every year there were more than two hundred and fifty requests for twenty-four places.

When Lily was appointed headmistress at the tender age of thirty-four, Belgrave Hall was more of an elitist refuge from reality than a rigorous but nurturing school. Within a week of taking up her post, Lily had changed the school motto from *Sanctimonia et patientia* (Purity and patience) to *Plenae spei fideique* (Full of hope and trust) and with that single stroke set about transforming the school's goal from turning out compliant ladies, to developing educated women.

Few teachers were as loved or as mysterious as Lily Lidbury. Lily knew the names of each of the one hundred and ninety girls, yet her legendary skill as a charismatic leader was nothing beside her gift for teaching. Worlds apart from her own education at the Sacred Heart Convent, the dimmest of children were inspired to try harder, while the intelligent ones were awakened to an exciting need to learn which shaded and sharpened their thinking for the rest of their lives. Her lyrical voice, surprisingly at odds with her air of authority, disclosed nothing of the working class accent that had been drilled out of her by the compulsory elocution lessons of her convent up-bringing.

Lily was not conventionally beautiful, but her vivid smile, straight nose, unusually high forehead and rapid graceful walk made for an arresting presence. Her gaze was direct, and even humorous, with kind, intelligent eyes that sometimes betrayed a private sadness. Addicted to impossibly high heels, her flair for combining vintage brocades, silks and velvets with the every-day look of Marks & Spencer shirts and trousers, was both economical and distinctive. Yet despite the fascinating specula-tion she provoked, not one of the parents, for all their fervent effort, ever came close to penetrating her inner life. Only the school matron, and her closest friend, Magsie – now a kind of surrogate older sister – knew the true source of her formidable strength.

She had been so desperate to keep the nature of her daugh-ter's horrific death hidden, that she had spun a web of secrecy around her entire life. She had given up her job at Warwick Comprehensive, discarded her married name of Challoner and adopted her maternal grandmother's maiden name, Lidbury. At Belgrave Hall she was believed to be a widow, bereaved at the age of twenty-eight.

Lily had been hurrying to the Carol Concert, the most important event in the school's social calendar, when she first saw Savannah waiting with Magsie in front of the Christmas tree in the school hall. Lily stopped still, drew a sharp breath, and paled. There before her was a nine-year-old girl, with a gleaming mane of red hair, and stormy sea-green eyes. She was the double of Lily's own daughter. Overcome by the resemblance, Lily was at a complete loss for words. What was more, Savannah was dressed in an almost identical green coat to the one that Amanda had been wearing the last time Lily had seen her alive.

'But who is this child, and why is she here?' she asked at last, an urgent, almost fearful note in her voice. Then, without waiting for the answer, she bent down to be of a height with Savannah. Gently stroking the waves of her shiny hair, and as if she had all the time in the world, Lily murmured, 'What a beautiful emerald coat you're wearing.'

'I got it for my interview,' said the anxious little girl.

'Your interview?'

'The school made a mistake with the date,' Magsie explained, waving the letter confirming the interview. 'Her mother dropped her here about ten minutes ago.'

'In that case, Savannah will have to come to the concert with me,' Lily said. She looked at the child and smiled wistfully. 'Would you like that, Savannah?'

Magsie watched as Savannah returned Lily's gaze. It was as though something was passing between them.

Given the circumstances, Lily had arranged to interview Savannah the following day, even though the school was closed on Saturdays. The doorbell rang exactly on time, and Savannah raced in ahead of her mother.

'She was in such a hurry to get to see you that she's been ready since early this morning,' Jodi explained, keeping her voice light and amused, as if she were not impatient – as Lily suspected she was – to get on with her morning without the impediment of her daughter. 'I've kept the taxi waiting.'

'I'm very happy to see you, Savannah,' Lily said emphatically. 'I enjoyed meeting you, and I'm glad you enjoyed meeting me.'

'You need Savannah for three hours, right?' Jodi looked at her wafer-thin Patek Philipe watch. 'I guess that means you want me back at twelve thirty?' It began to rain so furiously that they could hear the heavy raindrops striking the roofs of the cars hard, like pebbles. The cab driver honked loudly. 'Sounds like he's getting impatient,' she said, turning to wave at the driver through the open door. 'I'd better get going.'

On their way to the study Savannah asked, 'Why do you always wear blue?'

'What makes you think I always wear blue? You've only seen me once.'

'Because you're wearing blue now, and the long dress you had on yesterday was blue.'

'My word, you *are* observant.'

'Bronnie always tells me I notice too much for my age.'

'Bronnie?'

'Bronnie's my nanny.'

'Bronnie, that's short for Bronwyn isn't it?'

'Right,' Savannah said. 'Bronnie's Welsh, she says she hates London.'

'I'm sorry to hear that, because London is a very beautiful city,' Lily laughed. 'You'll love it, you'll see.'

Seated at the child-sized desk, her tongue tight between her lips in concentration, Savannah worked on her essay, 'My Family'. Later, while Savannah wrote her maths paper, Lily marked her essay. '*If I ran away my mom wouldn't notice for days*' she read. Children often wrote things like this if they were upset with their parents about something, but Lily thought it could be more than this. There was the beloved nanny, the mother's high-flying career, and – as she could see now – fingernails bitten to the quick.

When Jodi had returned to get her daughter, Lily explained that although Savannah was clearly very bright, it would be in her best interests to begin schooling with girls a year younger. The conversation followed a familiar pattern – Lily had clarified this many times before. 'Savannah's results are totally normal for her age and peer group. American children who start formal education so much later cannot possibly have followed a similar curriculum.'

'What about private tutoring?'

'If you could bring her back to London about ten days before term begins, I would tutor her myself,' Lily said, breaking her own rules. 'I am prepared to do this in exceptional circumstances.'

'Ten days early? No *way* can I leave New York,' Jodi replied. 'I'll be interviewing expert witnesses then. It's this case I'm working on – I'm heading up a large team of attorneys and millions of dollars are at stake.'

'Well in that case, you could take several books back with you, and Bronnie could help her with her reading.'

'Savannah talked to you about Bronnie?'

'Yes. She said Bronnie doesn't care much for our city.'

'That's right, Bronnie has refused to come to London,' she sighed. 'But Savannah doesn't know – we haven't told her yet.'

Lily wondered, now, what had made the Andersons change their minds. Something to do with the nanny, she thought. But whatever the reason, she was deeply pleased. From the very first moment she had laid eyes on Savannah, the child had dominated her thinking. Her startling resemblance to her own daughter was uncanny, but Lily was realistic enough not to delude herself that Amanda had come back to her. Yes, Savannah's likeness to Amanda was unnerving, but it was also strangely comforting.

*If I ran away my mom wouldn't notice for day*s – the sentence hung in Lily's brain.

Every child deserved a mother who noticed her.

Well, she would certainly go all out to make it up to her.

Clasping his hands behind the back of his head, Benton tilted his chair and leaned back, pleased with the result of his call to Lily Lidbury. He was still worn out from two days of hysterical scenes with Savannah when she had been told that Bronnie would not be with them when they moved to London. He and Jodi had concluded that it was essential to get Savannah to London as soon as possible.

Bronnie had confronted them with the news that she'd lost patience with prolonging the charade she was going to London with the family. 'The best way for all of us is to tell her the truth together. The alternative is for me to walk out and leave you to tell her. I couldn't live with myself if I had to go through New Year's and start the year dishonestly.'

It had been much worse than Bronnie had predicted.

An unusually quiet child, Savannah had immediately started screaming, 'No! No!' Shaking with sobs, she yelled, 'Don't leave me, Bronnie, you can't leave me!'

By the time Jodi and Benton left for work – they would both be late – Savannah's sobs were by no means exhausted. The terrible, primal sounds followed her parents all the way to the elevator, rose to an ear-splitting crescendo, and only stopped when the doors closed, shutting out the noise.

That night, after a huge effort to rearrange their schedules, Jodi and Benton returned home together. Savannah no sooner saw them than she began to sob tearlessly, shrieking, 'I hate you! I hate you! I hate you!'

Finally Jodi could bear it no longer. 'Can't you control her, Bronnie?' she snapped. 'You went to nanny school, didn't you?'

'If you knew your own daughter you'd know that she's

terrified!' Bronnie's small eyes glittered in her scarlet face. Her anger took hold of her, jostling against her sorrow and loosening her tongue, spilling truths she had never dared express. 'She's like your Lexus; you only use her on Sundays. It's the only time the three of you are together, and even then, only while you're on the way to your country club, where you dump her on some friend's mother or tennis coach.'

She spoke fast and urgently, dizzied by what came out of her mouth, but unable to stop.

'When did either of you two ever go to Parents' Night, or the school play, or any kind of school event?' she exploded. 'And I don't suppose either of you has given a thought as to what separating from Savannah is doing to *me*?' She answered her own question. 'Of course not! I've taken care of her for close on nine-and-a-half years – since I was twenty-two and she was only three months!' She swallowed unhappily, tears rising. 'I can't leave Bill – he said I had to choose between London and him.' Distressed almost beyond bearing, she said, 'I hate doing this to Savannah.'

The awful thing, Benton reflected now, was that Bronnie had spoken the complete truth. Savannah had never been at the centre of his or Jodi's life, and he felt as if he had spent more time with his daughter during these past few days than he had in all her life. He was shocked to discover that he hardly knew her; in a way she was like a godchild who had become a permanent house guest, whom he saw for brief periods during the week, when it was convenient to him. Bronnie had really got to the core of things.

By now it was five o'clock, and Benton returned to their bedroom just as Jodi awoke.

'Were you able to reach Mrs Lidbury?' she asked as she rolled over in bed, pushing her tangled hair back from her face.

'I was,' he said. 'Savannah will have her first lesson on January second.'

'That's a Tuesday,' she said, running her hands through her hair. 'I guess you should be the one to tell her?'

'I hadn't thought about that yet,' he said. 'She'll still be asleep when you go to the office so, yes, I'll tell her.'

'These last four days with Savannah have been so rough that I've been sorely tempted – ' her voice trailed off. A look of annoyance crossed her face. 'Oh no – Louisa Stacey's breakfast meeting in a little over two hours!'

Louisa Stacey was the CEO and creative genius of Wishes International, the multinational lingerie chain. A notoriously temperamental diva, encased in rhinoceros hide, given to holding meetings until 2 a.m. and now Jodi's *bête noire*, Louisa Stacey had been charged with stock fraud. Jodi was leading her team of defence attorneys. 'I need her like I need a hole in my head! But she brings in the bucks – big-time.' Casting a shrewd look at him, she went on, 'Speaking of which, I've decided to sell my Ericcson stock – '

Her vitality was too aggressive for him at that time of the morning but he said, 'Why not sell? No one ever lost anything taking a profit – except perhaps more profit.'

She was surprised he agreed. 'You're right on point, Benton. How about a piece of Bronnie's chocolate cake?'

'At this hour?' he said, noting the change of routine. As a rule, Jodi would be at the computer by 5:30. An hour later, they would join up, go for a jog in the park, when she would frequently take and make calls on her mobile. Benton would stop at Three Guys, his favourite coffee shop, for about fifteen minutes for breakfast, and Jodi would go on ahead.

He followed her into the black and white kitchen and watched as she set about making the coffee with the same efficiency with which she managed everything in her life – everything except Savannah. Sometimes, on those rare occasions when Jodi was with Savannah, but without Bronnie, she would seem uneasy, or bored – as if she wished she were some place else. Watching her now, he experienced the kind of secret pride that sometimes came over him when he believed a strategy of his had been successful. And his call to Mrs Lidbury had certainly achieved all that he had hoped it would.

Jodi took the black cups from the glass case and poured the strong coffee. She was beginning to question the accepted principle under which she had been functioning – that as long as it was legal, it was not required to be moral or ethical, or even just. Could these doubts, this heresy, be a symptom of the dreaded burnout that she had read about in the National Law Journal?

She had recently grown more resentful of the interminable stress and infighting within her own litigation department, the constant competition to bill the most. She was tired of her struggle against the old boy network, in which deals were often negotiated on squash courts, or in men's lavatories in court-houses and offices.

'Well, at least I won't have to deal with the men's room in London,' she thought to herself.

Still smarting after Bronnie's tirade, Benton said, 'Perhaps we should try to get to know our daughter a bit better.'

'I don't think I know *myself* very well, let alone Savannah,' she said, a note of surprise in her voice, as if the thought had only just occurred to her. 'I've never had the time to do that.'

Benton was amazed by her moment of introspection. He was about to say that he thought she had been avoiding herself since Savannah was born, but thought that would be unkind, and so checked himself. He had come to believe that she had replaced emotion with ambition, where there could be no space for sadness or joy or fear. It seemed to him that she was terrified of feeling. Perhaps this was because the maternal instinct frightened her so much that she had buried it under her drive and the intellectual challenges of her work. She could handle money – she couldn't handle emotion.

'Great cake,' he said instead. 'Bronnie outdid herself.'

Jodi continued, 'You know what, Benton, Bronnie was right

when she said we didn't give a thought to what separating from Savannah was doing to her.' She threw her hands up, ' I don't feel good about that. She adores Savannah, she's been a mother to her, and I've had the luxury of being free to do my own thing.' Her voice lowered, 'I don't think I'm mother material, but I'm going to try.' There was a feverish glitter in her eyes. 'I don't know how you'll feel about this, Benton, but I'm liquidating my Ericcson stock, and giving the lot to Bronnie.'

'When did you decide this?'

'A few minutes ago,' she said. 'It just came to me.'

'What's your total investment?'

'Twenty thousand.'

'Tell you what, Jodi, I'll match what you give her. Forty thousand would get her started on the property ladder. She could buy an apartment in Queens.'

'Great, ' Jodi smiled. 'You'll give her the cheque, then. Don't tell her about my contribution, OK?'

'Why not?'

'She'll go all emotional, and it'll embarrass the hell out of me,' she said. 'You haven't said much about your call to Mrs Lidbury. What did you think of her?'

'I liked the sound of her voice,' he said. 'Lily Lidbury could be the best thing that ever happened to Savannah.'

'And we can thank William Hardwick for our introduction to her.'

'True enough.'

She nodded. This connection with her law firm established that the London move was definitely *her* decision, too. Benton had been canny enough to know that any attempt to influence her decision would have been counter-productive.

Later, in hindsight, and in spite of the cataclysm that was to follow, she would neither blame him nor fault her decision. The plain truth was that she would never have agreed to move to London unless it had suited her.

Benton had known in advance that a Mercedes would be assigned to him for his exclusive use. The car and a driver, called Derek, were at Heathrow to collect him and Savannah. Derek's welcome, like his friendly dignified presence, had instantly infused Benton with a sense of being in the right place at the right time for the right reasons. Like a tour guide, Derek pointed out the famous landmarks of London all the way from Heathrow to their house on Eaton Crescent. Of course he wanted to know the name of Savannah's school in London. When he heard that it was Belgrave Hall, he told them that it was the school the Royals chose. 'Princess Margaret's daughter went there, you know.'

'Bronnie and I just love Princess Di,' Savannah said.

Derek turned into Wilton Place. 'And who, may I ask, is Bronnie?' he asked.

'My nanny,' Savannah answered sorrowfully. 'She's got a picture of Princess Di in her wedding dress.'

Sitting back and listening to his daughter's reply, Benton realized that from the moment they had boarded the plane, he had found himself observing her with more interest than he'd ever had before. He realized that he had rarely seen his daughter in a happy frame of mind. He felt an unexpected pang of regret and guilt for all the time he'd lost with her and, for a moment, he blamed Jodi for this. He corrected himself at once: as a baby-boomer and male feminist, he was not supposed to think this way. Fathers, he reminded himself, *shared* parenting these days. True, at fifty, he was twelve years older than Jodi, but that did not mean he was stuck in some 1950s fantasy where the men ran the world and the women ran the household.

Benton was pleased with the efficiency with which Carlyle Klein's London office had handled his transition. Everything from a smiling Filipino housekeeper called Opi, to a fully stocked fridge and even a cheque book from his London bankers, were ready and waiting for him when he arrived. What was more, his secretary had asked for and recorded significant dates such as birthdays, his wedding anniversary, even the school holidays as if this were as natural as having his home phone number in her computer.

A dedicated Anglophile who had always contrived to have British secretaries in New York, Benton was delighted with the gracious town house Carlyle Klein had rented for them. Jodi would certainly approve of the extensive equipment in the mini-gymnasium, the vast slate shower stall, and the freestanding copper tub in the middle of the master bathroom. But the knotty pine kitchen, living room with ornate silk drapes, chintz sofas, embroidered cushions, gilt mirrors and the mixture of ancient tapestries were quite the opposite of the minimalist style of their New York apartment. And the fact that what she considered a basic necessity – air-conditioning – was missing, would drive her crazy.

Lily was in the hall, pacing the worn black and white checked marble tiles, waiting for Savannah and her father to arrive. She drew comfort from the enduring school smell of gym shoes, chalk and pencil shavings; without the buzz and clatter of the girls, Belgrave Hall seemed as inert as a bank vault. During term the oak-panelled hall and stairwell resounded with the thuds of running footsteps, sending echoes right to the top of the fourth floor.

Over the years, the impressive sweep and grace of the staircase as it swirled into the entrance hall had become symbolic of Belgrave Hall. The staircase grew steeper on each floor, and its near-darkness meant that even in daylight the lamps were lit. Its elegance and grandeur inspired awe in all the girls. Tempting as it might have been, they would never have dreamed of sliding down the broad, smooth banisters – or indeed playing any sort of game. In any case, such behaviour – even talking on the staircase – was strictly against school rules.

Lily paused in her pacing to look at one of the portraits of the school's distinguished alumnae. The woman who gazed back sourly was an aristocratic Belgrave Hall old girl who now sat on the Board of Governors for the sole purpose – or so it seemed to Lily – of plaguing her. Natural enemies from the day they met, Lady Violet Anstey would never forgive Lily for raising the academic standards at the school. She opposed Lily at every turn, using her own forbidding personality and the power of the Anstey name to sway the Board. The woman had recently won a small battle against Lily and was enjoying her most recent success. It was the antiquated custom at Belgrave Hall for the girls to curtsy to the teachers at the end of every afternoon. Lily thought the practise was absurd and had proposed its abolition. But Lady Violet's voice had won the Board's approval, and Lily's proposal had been rejected.

Since her conversation with Benton Anderson, Lily had been working at fever pitch to devise an intensive education programme for Savannah. She was convinced that Savannah could reach the required standard in record time. She would insist on the old fashioned system of learning multiplication tables by rote: unless she knew the tables inside out, and mastered the art of applying them, she would remain at the bottom of the class. Since maths had not yet been part of her syllabus, her mathematical language was virtually non-existent. Savannah would also have to learn English currency, and measurements. It was a daunting task, an exciting challenge of the kind likely to inspire Lily to invent new teaching techniques.

It was raining steadily. Savannah, wearing her emerald coat, hurried into the school, followed by Benton and Opi. Benton introduced himself and Opi to Lily, who with a warm smile was welcoming Savannah. Reiterating his gratitude to Lily for having accepted his daughter, Benton asked about the tuition fee. Was it to be paid directly to Lily or to the school?

'Private or otherwise, Mr Anderson, there is no fee,' Lily replied. 'As a matter of fact, I never give private tuition.'

'We feel very lucky to have you teach Savannah,' Benton said. 'I brought Opi along, because she'll be collecting Savannah today.'

'I am delighted to have met you all, Mr Anderson,' Lily ended the conversation. 'We'll expect you at three o'clock, Opi.' Her air of authority was so powerful that like obedient children, Benton and Opi immediately turned and left Savannah to her studies.

Lily settled Savannah behind her small desk and handed her a fountain pen.

'Is this pen for me?' Savannah asked.

Lily nodded, and bent Savannah's fingers in the correct position for pen control.

The lesson went well. Clearly, she had not been wrong in her earlier assessment – Savannah was an ideal candidate for Belgrave Hall.

While Savannah was writing her timed essay entitled 'My Friends', Lily saw the small spot of red on the pale blue inside arm of her cardigan. She did not allow Savannah to finish the essay, but rested her hand lightly between the child's shoulders, and gently pushed the sleeve upward. A stab wound, probably inflicted with a pencil, was exposed among a scattering of older wounds. She had seen similar wounds before, when she was working in a psychiatric day hospital. Although Savannah was only nine, there could be no doubt that this was a case of self-harm. She dropped a kiss on Savannah's head, and told her that she'd be back soon.

Cleaning the wound as if there were nothing out of the ordinary about it, she said, 'This must have hurt a lot – when did this start, Savannah?'

Savannah did not meet her eyes. 'When Middy died.'

Lily went to the kitchen, selected a juicy apple, and sat down to read Savannah's essay, entitled 'A Terrible Event'.

It was the beginning of Christmas, Lily read, and the Christmas trees were covered in fluffy snow. Lucy loved NY, all the smells of the hot dog stalls, and cabs beeping at each other.

Her father came up to her. She knows something is wrong. He tells *her they are moving to London, England. He said that her nanny, the most wonderful person in her life, had to stay in NY with her cat, Snowy. Lucy's nanny loved Snowy more than she loved her.*

*So Lucy wished her nanny's cat would die. Then Snowy died. Now Lucy had a terrible secret in her life. She wished Snowy would die, and Snowy did die, so it was all her fault.*

Lily read the essay several times, and then picked up the phone and dialled Benton Anderson's number.

'I hope you won't mind my calling about Savannah?' she asked when she was put through to him.

'Of course not.'

'I'm slightly worried about her. It's something we need to deal with before the new term begins.'

'Oh,' said Benton, slightly taken aback. 'How about dinner this evening? I used to like Mimmo when I was here fifteen years ago – the restaurant is still there on Elizabeth Street, right?'

'It is, and it couldn't be more convenient. It's about a five minute walk from Belgrave Hall.'

'Eight o'clock suit you?'

'I'll look forward to it.'

Benton replaced the receiver slowly. The last thing he ever thought he would be doing was having dinner with Savannah's headmistress. True, she didn't really look like his image of a headmistress, she was attractive in her classical British way. He had only met her once, briefly, but he remembered her crisp accent especially well. He'd admired her light, bell-like voice that was so similar to that of the British actress, Celia Johnson, whom he and his father had been so passionate about. He had also liked her laugh, a chuckle that seemed to bubble from her tummy. And though she had been daunting, and very much the headmistress, he found himself looking forward to the evening, not only because he had nothing better to do, but because he liked the company of intelligent women.

He wondered what Mrs Libury had found 'slightly worrying'

about Savannah. He was glad to have the opportunity to invite her to dinner.

As for Lily, she was surprised by Benton Anderson's invitation. She'd thought that he would offer to meet her either before or after the lesson. But his response had been so quick, so spontaneous – so co-operative – that it would have been churlish to have refused. Hoping she was exaggerating the significance of Savannah's essay, she reread it yet again. She adored having Savannah with her. Already, after only four sessions, the child was so familiar, and looked so achingly like her lost daughter, that the present seemed to have been preordained. Yet the girls had very different characters: Amanda's inborn happiness had survived her parent's divorce, but there was an aura of deep discontent about Savannah. There had been other unhappy girls at Belgrave Hall, and though Lily had helped them overcome this, none of them had aroused anything like the powerful maternal feelings she felt for Savannah.

A soft rain was falling when she set out to walk the short distance to Mimmo. It made no sense to take her Mini. Belgravia was well lit, and the graceful magnolia-cream houses cast solid, comforting shapes in the gloom. Lily never tired of her area's loveliness.

Though she delighted in the touch of the rain against her face, in deference to her newly washed hair tied back with its usual blue velvet bow, she unfurled her umbrella and, with her hips swinging gracefully, walked rapidly, as she always did. It occurred to her that although she couldn't remember when she had last been to dinner with a man, her betrayal by Hugh had not left her with any bitterness towards men. In fact, she welcomed the company of intelligent men, even if she did shy away from getting involved in an intimate physical relationship with any of them.

Nor could she have been fairly described as cold; before Amanda's death she had known great passion and suffered for it. She now counted it as a blessing that her need for physical passion had evaporated like steam after rain on a hot day. For she'd had her fill of passion and it had turned toxic, and, like anyone who has ever had a severe dose of food poisoning, she was committed to avoiding the cause of it for ever. As she saw it, she was like the engine of a fully functioning aeroplane, but without wings there was no chance of either flying or of falling from the skies. As long as she was a good teacher and a respected headmistress putting her nursing skills to good use in Africa every summer, she would feel both fulfilled and safe.

By the time she arrived Benton was seated at a table at the back of the restaurant, close to the huge indoor tree under the skylight. A bottle of Krug champagne was cooling in a silver bucket. He rose as soon as he saw her, and moved forward to welcome her. She was at once struck by his abundant mane of white hair – she'd been so focused on Savannah when they first met that she'd scarcely noticed him. He was much taller that she'd thought; for all her authoritative air, she was shorter than average and tended to notice people's height. Soon he was pouring the Krug, and telling her that in '85, he'd spent many happy hours in this restaurant. He'd been with Morgan International Bank, doing financial work in the billions of pounds for Maggie Thatcher and the British Treasury.

'That was when I began to go grey,' he said. 'By the time I was forty, it was pure white,' he added, tugging at his hair so that it fell boyishly out of place.

His easy manner, powerful confidence and natural warmth roused her to a delightful awareness of her femininity.

It was not until the second course was served – they'd ordered *spaghetti vongole* – that smiling his mischievous, beguiling smile, he dropped the small talk and broached the subject of Savannah.

'Savannah's verbal scores are above average,' Lily told him. 'But most of the girls at Belgrave Hall are at least five years ahead of their contemporaries for spelling.' She paused. 'Did Bronnie have a white kitten called Snowy?'

37

'She had a black kitten called Middy. Bronnie was always taking in strays – there wasn't a cat in the neighbourhood who didn't know her.'

'Middy died suddenly, didn't she?'

'Middy was a he, not a she,' he said. 'He had feline infectious peritonitis. But why do you ask?'

'Because when I questioned Savannah, she told me the family did not have a cat,' she said, handing him Savannah's essay. 'I think you should read this,' she added.

A fast reader, he seemed to absorb it in a single glance. She watched his strong, male hand slowly fold the page before he handed it back to her.

'It's well written,' Lily said. 'What disturbs me is that a child her age would write so graphically. Did she say anything to you about this? Did you notice how upset she was?'

'I don't think she's ever been a particularly happy child,' he said. 'But when the cat died she and Bronnie were both hysterical.' The muscles of his jaw tightened. 'Bronnie took care of her – she's been more of a parent to Savannah than either of us.' He hesitated over his choice of words. 'She's a sweet kid, but there have been other problems. She's an only child, doesn't know how to share, I guess.'

'Savannah will actually learn to like sharing at our school,' Lily said. 'It's the sort of behaviour we encourage. I'm an only child myself.'

'Really,' he said. 'So is Jodi.'

'Anyway, Mr Anderson, you were about to tell me about Savannah's difficulties?'

'Well, after Bronnie made us tell Savannah that she wasn't going to London, she went so wild it was frightening. Hysterical tantrums.'

'Savannah must be heartbroken and, at the same time, angry about Bronnie. She evidently adored her nanny. All of which is very confusing to a little girl, Mr Anderson.'

'Benton.' He brushed his hand briefly across her wrist. His

shirt cuffs gleamed. 'Can't you call me Benton? I'll feel more comfortable if you do.'

'If you'll call me Lily – a lot of parents do, you know. Americans, particularly.'

'Lily,' he repeated.

'It's good you've told me all this,' she said. 'It explains a lot.' Then she informed him of his daughter's stab wound. 'As you can see from the essay, the poor child blames herself for Middy's death. I've seen this sort of irrational guilt lead to self-mutilation once before.'

'Oh, my God,' he said. 'This is really terrible news.' Reflexively looking for a possible solution, he asked, 'Do you think she needs a shrink, Lily?'

'Not yet,' she replied. 'I'm a qualified psychiatric nurse, and I've seen them blow things out of proportion.'

'You're a psychiatric nurse as well?' he asked.

'In my first incarnation,' she grinned. 'But don't worry, I've been a teacher for twenty years.' Her smile faded. 'Let's see how we get on before we see a therapist,' she said. 'If there's no improvement we'll think again.'

'I'll buy that,' he said. 'It makes sense.'

'Good.' She glanced at her watch, and following her signal he called for the bill.

They had put on their coats when he saw that Lily had muddled her buttons. Unexpectedly emboldened, he bent over her, placed his hand at her throat, tilted her chin, and tended to the top button under her collar. He remained with his face close to hers a little longer than necessary. Then, in a way he had noticed women liked, his eyes probed into hers. Her eyes locked into his, only for a second or two, but long enough to turn acquaintance into a sort of intimacy.

She turned away. 'It's raining again,' she said.

'You walked here, right? I'll drive you back – it's torrential out there. I'll bring the car to the door.' Moments later, he was back. He left the engine running, and the door open, and rushed in to help her out of the rain, which now fell horizontally.

He drove slowly. As unlikely as it seemed, he felt that a friendship had arisen between them, and was reluctant to leave her. 'That's some coat you're wearing,' he remarked. Complimenting women came easily to him – it was part of his warm, optimistic nature. 'Savannah says you loved her new coat.'

'I did. It *is* a very lovely coat.'

'She's a great kid,' he said. 'I'm mad at myself for all the time I've lost with her. And you know what? I'm glad we decided to come to London– if we hadn't, I don't think I'd have taken the time to know my own daughter. I feel kind of responsible for her unhappiness.'

'We'll get her right, I'm sure,' Lily said. 'She's such a beautiful little girl.'

'Jodi's always said her lips are as thin as a crack in a mirror,' he said. 'I don't think I'm going to tell Jodi about the pencil-stabbing – she'll rush her to a shrink. You know how one sometimes has faith in a doctor, Lily?' he asked rhetorically. 'Well, I've got all the faith in the world in you. I'm going to leave Savannah in your hands.'

'I'm certainly going to do my very best.'

'I know that,' he said. 'We're lucky to have you.'

'Just over here on the left is fine,' she interrupted as the imposing facade of the school came into view.

Benton began parking his Mercedes. 'Bronnie complained that we treated Savannah like a Sunday toy. And do you know what? She was right!' He brought the car to a halt and looked up. 'Hey, but this is the school.'

'Yes, that's right, I live on the top. Don't look so worried!' she laughed. 'It used to be the servants' quarters before the building was turned into a school, and now it's the headmistress's flat. It's really very comfortable. Why don't you come up and have a look?'

Immediately she had said it, she caught her breath, shocked. The words had escaped from her subconscious even before she could register what she was thinking. She rarely invited anyone to her flat, except Magsie, and here she was throwing the doors open to a man she barely knew. But there was no time to backtrack – Benton was already out of the car.

After unlocking the door, Lily switched on the light in the entrance hall, turned left, and with her usual speed began mounting the steep staircase to her flat. 'I hope you don't mind but you'll have eighty-four steps to climb!' she warned.

'Not at all,' he replied. 'It reminds me of when I once visited a friend in Cambridge. There were steps just like this right up to his rooms at Trinity.'

Her front door merely interrupted the staircase for there was no landing, and yet there was another set of steps to climb before they entered her flat.

She switched on the light. 'Do go in,' she said.

'Thanks.'

Striding into the room he took in the wide mahogany desk, the feminine drapes wrapped around the edges of the mirror above the fireplace, the books spilling from their shelves onto the worn oriental rug. When he turned around, he saw Lily standing beside the hall coat stand, her posture stiff, as though she didn't know what to do next. Calmly and silently he approached her, removed his own coat and hung it beside hers. Then he murmured her name, drew her to him, and kissed her.

Lily pulled away. 'No!'

'But Lily – '

'Please – ' A cry pressed against her throat, but she clamped her teeth, strangling it. 'Please go!'

He stepped back. 'Can't we at least talk?'

Trembling, she took his coat from the stand and held it out for him so that he could put it on. 'Let's pretend this never happened.'

He had no choice but to put his arms into the sleeves. 'Jeez, Lily,' he said. 'I don't know what to say. This is not like me at all. I've behaved like a schoolboy. I've been telling you things I haven't even known I've been thinking. I feel so close to you, so

41

grateful.' He shook his head wonderingly. 'I didn't know I was going to do this – I took myself by surprise. I'm really, really sorry,' he said, tugging at his hair.

'It was a lovely evening.' Her tone softened. 'It really was.'

Lily listened to his footsteps scurry down the stairs. She stood beside the coat stand and did not move until she heard the school door slam. Then, trembling, she poured a tumbler of whisky, took it to her bedroom, and lay fully clothed on her bed, neither of which she had ever done before. She wished she had let him kiss her; she could not recall when – if ever – she had been in such a pitiless state of arousal. She downed the whisky and hoped it would knock her out, and stop the pain of wanting him. The combination of champagne and whisky seemed to work. When she awoke, about four hours later, her body was calmer but her mind in turmoil. She undressed, showered, put on her nightgown and watched mindless TV, all the while quarrelling with herself for having allowed herself to be so attracted to him. She'd loved it when he'd touched her wrist and asked her to call him Benton. The heat of his strong male hand had made her imagine the heat of his body. *Was this why she'd invited him to have a look at her flat?* She hated herself.

During Savannah's lesson the next morning, her mind concentrated on teaching, yet did not succeed in obliterating the memory of the night before. She was relieved that there were no lessons on Sundays because she would have the entire day to begin to recover from the night before last.

Lily awoke before dawn, exhausted, but too agitated to attempt to go back to sleep. She took a quick shower, put on the warm tartan dressing gown Magsie had given her, and decided not to get dressed for the rest of the day. She was at her desk much earlier than usual for a Sunday morning, listening to the nine-year-old violin prodigy Katie Radcliffe's tape recording of Bruch's haunting Violin Concerto. She hoped Savannah and

Katie would become friends. Trying to keep her mind focused, she began writing the 11+ Common Entrance reports. Several girls had applied to three or four schools, which meant filling in different forms for each school. She moved on to plan dates for the school outings to the National Gallery and the Tate Modern, and then began to draw up a list of possible speakers for the School Birthday celebrations. But it was hopeless: her muddled mind couldn't come up with anyone remotely suitable. Agitated, she gave up.

Lily's body jittered. Physical activity would help; ironing would soothe her. She decided to iron the vintage silk dress she would wear to the school's Open Night. She rose from her desk to get it, but then, for no reason that she could understand, changed her mind and fetched instead the cardboard box in which Amanda's green velvet coat was kept.

It was all she had left of Amanda. A week after the funeral she had asked Magsie to send everything that could be associated with Amanda to her father. She kept the coat, though. Amanda had been wearing it the last time she saw her alive.

The box on her lap, she lifted the coat from its bed of yellowed tissue paper. She spread it on her lap, and stroked it as tenderly as she would a delicate child. Then, gathering the coat in her arms, she greedily pressed the velvet to her cheek, rocking gently, as if she were putting a baby to sleep. She sat like that, rocking to and fro, for a long while. She stopped abruptly. A memory of the dead rabbit's fur in her mouth reared in her mind. It made no sense, she thought. Amanda had lived in a hyper-civilized era of heart-lung transplants and cyber space, and had survived the threat of terrorists on the London streets, and yet she had been *killed by a dog*. 'Ludicrous!' she said out loud. 'Ludicrous!' She got up, folded the coat carefully and, telling herself to buy tissue paper, placed it back in its box.

She skipped lunch, and worked on until the end of the afternoon, when she stopped for a cup of tea. But all that effort – and even Amanda's coat – had failed to rid her mind of Benton. Nor could she stop herself from thinking that she might have missed an opportunity . . . A long-ago conversation with Magsie leapt into her mind.

'A young woman needs a man,' Magsie said. 'You mustn't lose faith in men just because your husband betrayed you.'

'What about you, Magsie?'

'I'm not young, thank goodness,' Magsie replied. 'Who was that poet who said "all passion spent"?'

'Milton.'

'That fits me exactly. No more of that chemistry, or whatever you want to call it, to bother me.'

'It's not men,' Lily said. 'I was so humiliated when Hugh left me for that slut that I lost confidence in myself.'

Which is as true now as it was then, Lily thought. And I also lost confidence because I was afraid to risk being hurt again. A recovering alcoholic has the courage not to risk a single drink, and I've been too cowardly to risk another relationship.

She finished her tea, and turned to the letters of thanks she had to write to those children who'd brought her Christmas gifts. Some parents had sent exorbitantly expensive gifts, such as a Hermès handbag, a Cartier diary and a Cartier wallet, a Chanel brooch and matching belt. All these would be sold to a resale boutique on Cheval Place, and the money given to Jabulani. Lily took the most trouble over the letters to the children from homes she considered 'normal', whose mothers had sent home-baked gingerbread Christmas tree biscuits, a slice of home-made Christmas pudding, a jar of home-made Cranberry sauce. Fortunately, there were children who came from backgrounds where parents were obliged, and even content, to live on a careful budget. It was this, Lily believed, which gave Belgrave Hall the kind of middle class stability on which its reputation depended.

At about nine that evening, when she'd almost come to the last of her letters, the entry-phone buzzer sounded. She went to answer it, and on the tiny black and white TV monitor, saw Benton clutching a huge bouquet of roses.

'Hello,' she said.

'It's me, Benton. I've come to apologize – '

'Oh,' she said. 'Benton.'

'Will you let me in?'

She pressed the button to open the school door. It was only then that she remembered she was still in her dressing gown. Her hands flew to her hair. The bow holding it in place had unravelled, leaving it hanging loosely on her shoulders. She was on her way to tidy it when her door bell sounded, but she went down to let him in.

Benton handed her the roses. 'I hope you'll forgive me,' he said.

'Thank you,' she said, 'They're very beautiful. I'd better put them in water.'

He followed her into the kitchen. 'I'm sorry I'm not dressed,' she said. She laid the scarlet roses on the kitchen table. 'Did you run all the way up all those stairs?'

'Yes,' he said. 'I haven't been able to get you out of my mind.'

Lily was silent.

He stepped closer. Then with confident familiarity (as she was later to recall) he pulled her toward him as naturally as if she were being reunited with a long lost lover and began to kiss her deeply.

Lily found herself prepared and unprepared, disbelieving, yet eager. Numbed nerve terminals, long entombed, suddenly ignited, speeding through every cell of her body. Then, he lifted her in his arms. 'Which way is your bedroom?' he asked.

'On the left.'

He carried her there, and lay her on the bed. Still wearing his coat, he slowly untied her dressing gown belt. Except for her knickers, she was naked. She watched him tear his clothes off, scattering shirt buttons. Next, he gently removed her knickers.

And yet, at dawn, gazing at him in his unguarded sleep, she stared at him, to make sure the night had really happened; but then, afraid of disturbing him, she feigned sleep. Soon she heard him stir, and she opened her eyes and smiled into his just as he smiled into hers, and in that shared smile they were again absorbed into one another.

Afterwards, he said, 'I understand you lost your husband?'

She nodded.

'Never remarried?'

'Never wanted to, and never will.'

'You're in love with your work?'

'I love working with children,' she said. 'In the summer I go out to Africa to nurse AIDS children.'

'You're one hell of a woman, Lily.'

'I work with children of extreme wealth at the beginning of their lives, and with children of extreme poverty as their lives are ending. Does this make me an extremist or does it give me balance?'

'Those kids speak English?'

'I speak a passable Zulu,' she said. 'The hospital is called Jabulani which, ironically enough, means hope,' she smiled. 'I love the name almost as much as I love Africa.'

'You're a complicated woman,' he caressed her cheek. 'I like that.'

'I really hope I'll be able to help Savannah,' she said. 'I seemed to connect with her the moment I met her.'

'She loves her classes with you. You've sure got magic with kids, Lily.'

'She's touched me in a way no other child ever has before.'

He tilted his head to one side, studying her. 'Seven days,' he said, 'we'll have seven days.'

'Yes,' she said, 'seven days.'


Lying in bed after he had left, breathing his powerful scent, the aura of his maleness was, it seemed to Lily, almost palpable. Her body exulted, but her mind cringed. *After having gone so long without a lover, how the hell could she possibly have leapt into bed with the father of one of her pupils and a complete stranger, virtually the second time she'd met him?* Ah, yes, during that transatlantic phone call his rolling confident voice had sounded warm, and perhaps even rather flirtatious. And now, in one misbegotten night, she'd jettisoned all the standards of a decent woman. She barely knew the man, and yet she'd been more abandoned, even wild, with him than she had ever been with Hugh. For that matter, she'd scarcely known herself last night, either – embarrassed, during torrid love scenes, she would avert her eyes, and yet with Benton, dispossessed of herself, all constraint had fallen away, vanishing like mist on a bathroom mirror. Benton's energy, and the power he radiated had charged her own frozen sensuality back to life.

Late that afternoon, tense with guilt and self-loathing, she took one of her leisurely scented baths. Switching on the fluorescent lights she examined her body in the full-length mirror behind the bathroom door in a way she had not done for years. The memory of the night before was in the stretch of every muscle. She was pleased to see that apart from a slightly thickened waist, her astonished, jubilant body looked as if it belonged to a nubile teenager. And she thought of his waist, his almost unnaturally slim waist, his tightly muscled torso, his heroic shoulders and his narrow hips. Her hips were narrow, too, and she was as grateful for that as she was for her firm breasts. He had gloried in them last night – they were still slightly reddened by his stubble. She felt a sudden tenderness for her body.

And then her gaze locked directly into her own eyes. She saw a glow in them reflecting a night of lovemaking. She'd not realized, during her long bout of chastity, just how starved of flesh she'd been until last night.

Incredibly, Benton's scarlet roses had survived the night without water. Lily took this to be an omen, but of what, she couldn't say.

So began a magical seven-day stretch of erotic euphoria for Lily. Her life was now given over to the Andersons; the nights to

Benton, the mornings teaching Savannah. Afternoons she spent taking the girl to museums or theatre matinees, or baking scones and gingerbread men. Lily had found that the happy, comforting scent of baking was a wonderfully effective way to get close to a troubled child.

It was while they were waiting for the chocolate cake to cool that Lily raised the subject of Bronnie's cat's death. 'Tell me, Savannah, did you think, really think Middy died because you had wished her to?'

'*It was my fault!*' Savannah began to weep. '*It was all my fault!*' She wiped her eyes with the edge of the floor-length apron Lily had made her wear. 'No one knows, nobody knows – I wished – I wished – '

'Come here, Savannah – I want you to sit on my lap and listen to me very carefully. If someone was horrid to me I could wish they had a raging toothache – that would be fantastic – but do you think that would happen?'

Savannah shook her head.

'We can say our prayers to God to make someone better, but He certainly wouldn't grant a wish to make someone suffer and die.' She stroked Savannah's cheek, 'Do you understand that?'

Her eyes glowing with trust, Savannah nodded gravely.

Listening to the rain drumming against the tiny window above the sink, a pang of alarm rose, making her throat feel dry and parched. *I've had Jodi's daughter on my lap, I was in bed with Jodi's husband last night – what, I ask myself, what do I think I'm doing? Going against my nature? Or is this my nature?*

She stood up. 'It's time to ice the cake,' she said.

Because time was too short, Lily and Benton quickly settled into a routine. He would have a light supper with Savannah and would not leave for Belgrave Hall until she was asleep. He would arrive at Lily's at about nine and then, as a sensuous prelude to making love, they would have ciabatta bread, cheese and a bottle from the case of Montrachet he'd sent to her.

Waiting for him on their last evening together before Jodi arrived in London, the wind rattling against her attic windows had made Lily switch on her gas fire. The artificial, lifelike flames brought a golden glow to the vivid room. The amber couches and armchairs, with their plump, burnt-orange cushions made of hand-woven fabric from Africa, mingled easily with the brightly beaded Zulu baskets filled with purple azaleas. Soapstone sculptures of mother and child, Brancusi-styled African masks, paintings of the African bush and watercolours of English gardens crowded the walls. Lily looked upon the room as a sanctuary, and, despite its jumble of colour, there was an ambiance of serenity.

'Beautiful,' Benton said, caressing a wood carving of a pregnant woman. 'Simply beautiful.'

'It was given to me by the matron at Jabulani.'

'What do you do during half term?' he asked abruptly.

'Catch up like a good bureaucrat.'

'When were you last in Paris?'

'Two years ago, when one of our parents sponsored a tour for the girls of Year 5.'

'Half term goes from February 18 till February 28, right?'

'Right.'

'Jodi is taking Savannah back to New York.'

'So Savannah told me. She's so happy she'll be seeing Bronnie again.'

'I'm taking you to Paris with me.'

'Is this an invitation or a command?'

'Both.'

'I accept unconditionally.'

They laughed together. They loved to laugh in unison – it had become a joint physical act, as intimate as sharing bites of the same apple, and as comforting as a quick public caress might have been.

He passed his fingers through his hair, and it fell boyishly out of place.

'It's a habit of yours,' she said, dropping a quick kiss on his forehead. 'I love it when you do that.'

'My hair?' His smile faded. 'I guess I began that when my hair grew back after my mother just about had it all *shaved* off as a punishment. I'll tell you about it one day.'

'There is so much I don't know about you,' she murmured.

'And there's a lot I don't know about *you*,' he said. 'There's a lot I haven't asked, because I sensed you didn't want me to.'

'That is true.'

'But I'm going to ask you in Paris.'

'And I'm going to tell you in Paris.'

*So this is the way an affair continues*, she wanted to say, *with a timetable to give it the illusion of a future*.

For years, longing to dream of Amanda, Lily had begged, prayed that a dream would come to her that she could remember in her waking hours. Though her prayers and pleas had been to no avail, she had never given up hope. But tonight, when she finally fell asleep, it was to dream of lying stomach to stomach with a little girl breathing rhythmically and in unison, saying in a hoarse but musical voice, 'I'm the mother, you're the child, I'm the mother, you're the child.' When she awoke, she was ecstatic, but shocked to acknowledge that whether the child had been Amanda or Savannah, she could not say.

In the early hours of Monday morning, three days before the new term was to begin, the intimate world Lily and Benton had made for one another was suspended, and their real lives began again.

Magsie, bronzed and glowing with health, returned from her son's farm in New Zealand, relieved and delighted to be back in the big city again. Jodi arrived in London, apprehensive and somewhat resentful at leaving New York and the foundations of her life.

At 9:30 that morning, the teachers returned to Belgrave Hall for three training days, as recommended by the Department of

Education. This term there would be lectures on extending the more able student, coping with children's allergies and new techniques for managing dyslexia.

On the third day The Bees – an enthusiastic committee of chic and dedicated, mostly American mothers, quite a dominant force to be reckoned with – held an informal meeting about the Daffodil Ball, the first benefit they were organizing for Jabulani, which they all referred to as 'Lily's orphanage'. This was the first time they had been involved in a fundraiser that would not benefit Belgrave Hall. The meeting over, Courtney Hunt took a vase of crimson peonies to Lily's study. The Bees made sure that the school hall and Lily's study were always decorated with beautifully arranged fresh flowers.

'Thank you, Courtney,' said Lily.

Smiling rather too broadly, but sighing inwardly, she managed to conceal her sharp dislike of The Bees' ambitious chairperson, Courtney Hunt. Courtney was as boastful of her industrialist husband as she was of her own talent for steamrollering over everyone to get her own way, thereby achieving the brilliant results her kind of ego demanded. As the wife of the legendary Charles Hunt who'd recently turned around Synthetics, the giant contraceptive and surgical equipment conglomerate, Courtney's dogged abrasiveness had – as one parent remarked drolly to Lily – clearly been caused by a birth defect. Never one to let bygones be bygones, she couldn't resist mentioning, at every opportunity, her 'surprise' at Lily's refusal to accept her and her husband's generous offer to 'financially secure' the two front pews in the school church, so that their friends and family could be guaranteed good seats at the carol concert.

'Magsie told me there's going to be a new girl in Tiffany's class,' said Courtney. 'She must be mistaken.'

'You must mean Savannah Anderson.'

'I wasn't told that anyone was leaving.'

'That's because no one *is* leaving.'

'In that case there'll be twenty-five girls in the class.'

'Correct.'

'But Belgrave Hall never allows more than 24 to a class!' Courtney protested. 'This is irregular, isn't it?'

Lily shot her a hard look. If your husband weren't the chief sponsor of the ball in aid of Jabulani, I'd throw you out of my office, she thought. 'Unusual, yes,' she replied, her tone sharp. 'But hardly irregular!' Then, unable to contain herself, she added, 'Are you questioning my authority, Courtney?'

'I guess you have to make exceptions,' Courtney placated. 'Is Savannah the girl you had on your lap at the carol concert?'

Lily gave a cursory nod, shifted her papers on her desk, and rose from her chair. 'Thanks again for these delicious peonies,' she said.

At 8:25 on Thursday morning, hidden behind slatted blinds, waiting for the school bell to sound, Lily took her customary ten minutes to watch the playground filling with children and parents – the parents huddled in groups gossiping about their holidays, the girls dashing everywhere, yelling and laughing, delighted to see their friends again. She loved looking at their faces, so alive and wreathed in smiles; she loved the mass of their violet uniforms. This year, looking for Savannah, she scanned the playground more keenly than usual. She had no doubt that her instructions had been followed. Mrs Trubshaw would have introduced Savannah to her form mistress, Miss Worthington, who, in turn, would have taken her to the playground to find Tiffany Hunt. After her disagreeable encounter with Courtney the day before, she'd decided that Tiffany should be asked to look after Savannah.

Ah, yes – there Savannah was – her flaming red hair disciplined by Opi, no doubt, into two thick plaits.

Minutes later, the assembly bell sounded. Deeper than the crude, shrill ring of the average bell, the melodious Belgrave Hall bell reminded Lily of the Romanesque church bell of Santa Maria Gloriosa dei Frari in Venice. A muted ring called the monks from the adjoining monastery to prayer whilst the Belgrave Hall bell called the girls to lessons, play and home time. No one knew the exact history of the bell, but several had tried to update it, insisting that contemporary schools needed a contemporary sound. Lily had resisted, and the distinctive bell stayed.

The silence as the girls entered the hall was expected to be absolute, but on the first day of a new term they found it difficult to control their excitement. Lily could hear and feel it rippling through the whole building.

They rose as soon as they heard the clatter of her high heels entering through the swing doors at the back of the hall. The clamour and the laughter subsided, but it was not until they heard the commanding clap of her hands that the odd giggle stopped and silence fell.

'Good morning, girls.'

'Good morning, Mrs Lidbury.'

'Goodness me, you sound as if it's late at night, not first thing in the morning! Come on, wake up, where is your energy and pizazz – you sound bored stiff. Do it again with much more spark and conviction,' said Lily with an imperious lift of her chin.

'Good morning girls.'

'Good morning, Mrs Lidbury!' the girls chorused, enthusiasm and humour in their voices.

Except for the first day of a new term, or after half term, Lily held her assembly on Friday mornings. This was a time when the girls and the headmistress could be together without the constraining presence of a single member of staff. It made for a more intimate connection, Lily believed. She wanted the children to feel her passionate conviction that life could be wonderfully funny at times, and would recount stories of her own school-days.

Today she told them about the grim, frightening atmosphere of her school when she was young, one of their favourites. 'We children all knew that we were very *unwelcome*. They made us feel that it was our fault we hadn't been born with reading, writing and arithmetic already in our brains! If you got your tables wrong, if you made a mistake with your spelling, your knuckles got punished with a thick wood ruler. Now, girls, I ask you, was it our knuckles' fault that we didn't know our tables?'

'No!'

Gusts of giggles followed.

'At my school giggling and laughing were against the rules. You were punished for that – you were sent into silence for a whole day, and had to write what you needed to say! But here, at our beloved Belgrave Hall, we like you to hear you laugh, just as we like to know you are trying your hardest to do your best for your wonderful school and for yourselves.

'You can recognize a Belgrave Hall girl as soon as she enters a room. Now, do we have the straight backs of the girls of Belgrave Hall?' As always, the suddenly perpendicular backs of the four-year-olds in Reception brought a tinge of laughter to her voice. 'Are your shoes polished? Is your collar straight? You really can't use your brains if your collar isn't straight!'

'And, now what does every single Belgrave Hall girl know?'

'Unless you are polite and kind you cannot have an educated mind!' the girls sang out in unison.

'Today, on the first morning of the Winter Term, we are going to end assembly differently. Our Belgrave Hall prayer will not be said by me. As you all know, it is very unusual for a new girl to join our school in the middle of the academic year. Therefore, to make her feel absolutely welcome, I have invited Savannah Anderson to come to the stage, to read our Belgrave Hall prayer. Will you please come forward, Savannah?'

Blushing, Savannah made her way to the stage. She stood beside Lily, and in a clear voice read the prayer that she had practised reading with Lily. 'Please God bless all the sick and suffering children in the world, and wrap them and the girls of Belgrave Hall in Your love.'

'Thank you, Savannah! Well done!' Lily exclaimed loudly. 'And now girls, would you all join me – ' Aghast because she was about to suggest applause, Lily stopped abruptly. Improvising quickly, she told Savannah to leave the stage.

She nodded in the direction of the Year 6 girl poised at the piano, and the children filed out to the strains of Beethoven's 'Für Elise', which would be played over and over until the hall emptied.

Watching the four-year-olds looking like mini-soldiers on parade, Lily felt a sharp pang of gratitude that she was lucky enough to be at the head of this secure, happy and quite unique community to which she had whole-heartedly given herself, and without which she would she would be utterly lost.

At the same time, however, she was afraid of herself, of the runaway euphoria bordering on carelessness which had almost propelled her into calling for a round of applause for Savannah, because she had read a *prayer*! It would have been as crass as applauding a Sunday sermon. Worse still, it would have shown a lack of judgment, a flagrant disrespect for convention and, as a result, her authority as a headmistress could have been dangerously compromised.

She was aware – but did not altogether accept – that she was in danger of destroying the entire edifice of her life. So she chose the desperately perilous way, and retreated into denial, where it seemed safe.

## CHAPTER 2

After five long weeks in London, Jodi found herself idly calculating the number of hours it had been since she left New York. Each day seemed to last too long, as if time itself had swollen. Sometimes she felt as if she were trapped in a theatre, watching an unendurable and interminably boring play in a foreign language, helplessly waiting for the intermission before the last act.

Apart from those weeks of depression she'd suffered after Savannah's birth, Jodi had no experience of how to handle great blocks of unencumbered time. Used to working seventy hours a week, these London hours, weighted with emptiness, crowded in on her and forced her to acknowledge that she had no inner life. Without the ruthless cut and thrust of her work she was dislocated, an empty husk, an alien in an alien land, finally estranged even from herself.

She'd always been too energetic for loneliness, too busy for friendship and, although she was unaware of it, too fearful for introspection.

Confused and bewildered, she'd been giving serious thought to resigning from Hardwick, Murphy and Ford. But then if she did that she would miss her profession, where careers, and millions of dollars hung in the balance every day, all dependent on her drive and dedication, her cunning and her skill as a litigator. How could I possibly think of abandoning my profession? *But it wasn't a profession any more. It was business and billing hours and competing to be the biggest rainmaker.* And yet here she was, once an intrepid woman who spoke in absolutes, without a trace of indecision, now lost in a maze of doubt and inconsistencies. She had lost not only her purpose, but her sense of direction as well. She had lost her way.

She shook her head, as if she might dislodge this tangle of thoughts. She seemed to have acquired an immense capacity for complication.

Where once, during her brief visits as a tourist, she had found London quaint and enchanting, she now found it stagnant and dangerously antediluvian. Even a routine visit to a Harley Street doctor – she needed a prescription for her chronic insomnia – had been an affront to her sensibilities. The doctor's office was nothing more than a crumbling, unhygienic and germ-ridden apartment. Worse still, she was examined on an ancient leather couch, covered with a dark moss-green towel instead of hygienic disposable paper, and the doctor's pin-striped suit was unprotected even by anything as rudimentary as a white coat. London, she thought, was as uncivilized as its disorganized arrangement of streets. Her house, for example, was on Wilton Place, yet the owners called it Eaton Crescent. She was convinced that for as long as she was deprived of the reassuring night sounds of a New York skyscraper – elevators, air-conditioning, honking taxis – she would be forced to depend on noxious soporifics.

And it was all made worse by Benton's huge – and in her view, incomprehensible – affection for London life and for Belgrave Hall.

'You're taking the British way of doing things as a personal insult,' Benton said.

'But surely you agree that it's absurd that Savannah has to curtsy to Miss Worthington when she says goodbye every afternoon!'

'It's a long-standing custom,' he laughed. 'It began when the girls had to learn to curtsy to the Queen.'

'But can't you see that it encourages the girls to buy into a kind of traditional role and culture that generations of women have fought to discard?'

'It's a charming survival of an earlier, more polite age, a

British way of teaching the girls to have respect for older people, as well as good manners,' he smiled.

It was most unlike him. 'It's sexist, Benton!'

'So what?' he snapped. 'Savannah's happier than she has ever been!'

She couldn't argue with that – it was an incontestable fact.

This morning Jodi was going to a school event called Form Presentation. The project the children were working on was called 'Experience Different Cities', and Savannah was going to give a talk on New York. The parents of all twenty-five girls in Savannah's class had been invited to watch the performance, after which coffee and Magsie's scrumptious shortbread were to be served.

Benton had spent hours coaching Savannah for the presentation speech on New York that she was to give. Although she was meant to speak for no longer than five minutes, she had in fact prepared a talk for fifteen minutes. 'But it has to be a secret, Daddy,' she insisted. 'I want to surprise them.'

'But didn't your teacher give you a guide time?' Benton asked.

'No,' Savannah lied. 'I also want to be the one who gives the last of the speeches.'

'But why, honey?' Benton asked. 'Why the last and not the first?'

'Because everyone remembers how a movie ends, so they'll remember me best,' she replied, a coarseness in her tone.

'Ambitious, like your mother,' Benton laughed.

'But surely they'll remember you best if your talk is the best,' offered Jodi.

'Oh Mom!' Savannah snapped. 'That creep Katie gets on the stage to play the violin when the parents come in *and* when they leave. Just because she can play the violin, she thinks she's the greatest!' She tossed her head in agitation, her heavy thick plait swinging forward across her neck. 'She's a real cry-baby. You should've seen how she cried when she lost her stupid bow, and someone found it in the cloakroom broken – she went kind of crazy.' She turned to her father. 'Let's tape my speech again.' Kicking off her shoes, she climbed on to his desk.

Jodi had decided to arrive at Belgrave Hall exactly on time. That way she would be spared those moments of small talk from which she would be painfully excluded anyway. Her forthright but misguided attempts to introduce herself to the mothers who waited for their children in the playground – 'Hi! I'm Jodi Anderson' – had been met with an aloof chill, an only just perceptible irritation, an icily polite 'Oh Hello,' and the women had continued with their conversations. It had been all that was needed to freeze Jodi in her place as an outsider who should not even dare to think of entering their territory, nor hope to infiltrate their group.

Jodi stepped into her Armani trousers. She noticed that they had become almost baggy. Though she had always been slim, all those work-outs in their basement gym appeared to have sliced off at least an inch. Her newly tightened muscles represented her only achievement – tight muscles at the expense of a loose brain, she thought grimly.

She still smarted at the memory of a particularly hurtful re-buff she had experienced, three weeks earlier. One typically rainy London morning, she dropped in at Oriel, a nearby bistro, for a cup of coffee. The place had reminded her of the bistros she had visited in Paris with her parents when she was eighteen, the year before they were killed on their way to the country club. The tiny tables, the wicker chairs, the air thick with smoke and the aroma of wine and strong coffee, and the waiters in their starched white floor-length aprons with purses in belts around their waists. It threw her into a time warp, and she felt lonely and vulnerable.

Then the unexpected yet thoroughly familiar sound of her beloved New York accents made her turn around. When she saw that one of the voices belonged to Courtney Hunt, one of the parents whom she'd first met at a doctor's office, she had spontaneously – even joyously – rushed over to talk to her. 'Hi, Courtney,' she said. 'I'm Jodi Anderson. We met in Dr Setchell's office.'

'That's right,' Courtney replied.

'I'm Verine,' the other woman put in.

'Hi, Verine,' Jodi said.

'Jodi is Savannah's mother,' Courtney told Verine.

'Oh, the girl Mrs Lidbury accepted in the middle of the academic year – Lily Lidbury's *pet*,' Verine said snidely, 'you must be very important.'

Stung, Jodi summoned a smile. 'I guess Mrs Lidbury thought Savannah would be a credit to the school,' she said.

There was a silence.

Courtney turned away from Jodi. 'Charles only gets back from Tokyo at six, so he won't be able to make it,' she said to Verine.

Not knowing what else to do, Jodi stood with them for a while, before muttering, 'I'll be off, then,' and picking up one of the newspapers Oriel kept for guests, she returned to her table.

She'd told Benton nothing of the incident – telling him would only have diminished her. How could she admit to having allowed herself to feel humiliated by a couple of jealous airheads?

Brooding over the rejection now, thought Jodi, was even more humiliating than the incident itself. She shook herself free of it. Checking her appearance in the mirror, she felt satisfied with her square-shouldered, slimmed-down look of a successful New York executive. But she reluctantly had to admit that attending the Form Presentation would be less of an ordeal if she were accompanied by Benton. She found herself resenting him on two counts: firstly, because he claimed a major meeting prevented him from attending, and secondly because dismayingly she *needed* him beside her to make her feel less insecure. After all, he was the one who'd made such a big deal about Savannah's speech, so why the hell wasn't he coming?

It was all so confusing. Benton had never seemed as pleased or as confident as he was now. She wanted to call him, but couldn't – the smallest risk of appearing like a clinging wife was so abhorrent to her that she was loath to ask for his emotional help. A moment later, powerless to stop herself, she bypassed his secretary, and called him on his mobile.

'Benton Anderson.'

'What time is your meeting?'

'What's wrong?'

'Nothing. Just answer my question.'

'Ten-thirty. Why?'

'There's still time for you to get to the Form Presentation.'

'You know I've got the Kingston merger – '

'I need you to be with me, Benton.'

'But that's impossible! You *know* that!'

'It'll be easier if you're with me – I can't face all those mothers on my own – '

'What d'you mean, you can't face all those mothers?'

'If you don't come with me, I won't go either.'

'What?' he yelled. 'You'll ruin Savannah's day!'

'Can't be helped, I guess.'

'What's got into you, Jodi? Savannah's happier than she's ever been.'

'Do you think I don't know that?'

'You're behaving like a spoilt, selfish bitch!'

'Just what do you mean by that?'

'Like after Savannah was born!'

Jodi hit the red button and cut him off.


Jodi's stomach churned. She felt crushed, and at the same time, furious. Her post-partum depression was something they never mentioned. A long-ago problem had been solved, and was irrelevant to their present lives. Benton wouldn't have dared speak to her like that in New York. Her head raged. I'll leave him. I'll get Bronnie back, and Savannah and I will live in New York and visit him during school vacations, she thought. But this would mean that London had defeated her. Besides, she couldn't deny that Savannah was happy at Belgrave Hall. But the fact that Benton had changed, that he was different from the man she'd known, was more disturbing.

Had London's mysterious alchemy turned him from professional banker to professional father? Impatient now to get the morning over and done with, Jodi looked out at the low forlorn sky, made iron-grey by the absence of a weak winter sun, and decided she would need a raincoat if she were to walk to the school. Then she set off at a brisk pace. Determined to avoid the possibility of turning up even a few minutes ahead of time, she stopped off at the Chocolate Society, a delightful shop selling its own brand of delicious chocolate. She inhaled the aroma for a moment, let her discipline go and ordered a hot chocolate. She sipped the steaming drink and stared into space. Yes, she mused, Benton definitely had changed. She couldn't fathom why he had dredged up that distant phase in their lives, but she wouldn't ask him. As far as she was concerned, it had become a forgotten memory, and she was determined to keep it that way.

The Form Presentation began with the light, happy sound of Bach's *Bourée*. The violinist must be Katie, Jodi realized. The child really was unbelievably talented; it made Savannah's jealousy understandable.

Although there were more women than men in the audience, there were at least ten fathers. Child-sized chairs were arranged against the back of the hall and when she took her seat along with the other parents, she avoided eye contact, determined not to make even the smallest friendly approach. She'd made up her mind that there was absolutely no way that she would stay for coffee and 'scrumptious' (how she disliked that word) shortbread biscuits afterwards.

Each girl delivered her lines faultlessly, but hardly any paused for breath. Their performances were adequate for girls of their age, self-conscious and rigid. These were girls especially chosen by their form mistress because they were never given big parts in plays and concerts and had never been asked to read for one of the church services which took place during the school year. Fortunately the girls themselves did not seem to realize this.

When Savannah stepped forward, with such confidence and such a loud, clear voice, she made the other girls appear duller than they actually were. She wore red, white and blue striped gloves, and her left hand, rising above her head, held the American flag, while her right hand rested smartly against her heart.

Jodi shifted in her seat. *Savannah's going to overrun her time allocation – not one of the other children's speeches lasted more than five minutes. She must have lied when she said no time limit had been given.*

'I live in Manhattan – an island in New York City, and I am going to tell you about it. Manhattan means island of hills. You can't help loving Manhattan, a vertical city, where the streets and avenues are lined by mountainous buildings . . . '

As her speech came to an end, she switched on the tape recorder she'd concealed in her pocket. When the triumphant sound of Liza Minelli singing *New York! New York!* burst into the room, she signalled the audience to sing along with her, and almost everyone joined in. Then she bowed, and the applause she'd been waiting for quickly followed.

Clapping enthusiastically, Lily rose to her feet. 'Well done, Savannah!' she called out. 'Bravo! Bravo!'

Aware of Courtney and Verine's loud exchange of whispers, Jodi began to make her way toward the children.

Before filing out of the hall to go back to their lessons, the girls were allowed to join their parents for a few minutes. 'You were wonderful, honey,' Jodi said, stroking her hair. Around them parents and children were embracing one another, and she put her arms around her daughter, and tried to hug her, but as usual, Savannah stiffened and drew away.

63

'I wish Daddy was here,' Savannah said. 'I got the longest applause, didn't I?'

'You sure did.'

'Longer than Katie's?'

On her way out, Jodi stopped to thank Miss Worthington. 'It was a great show,' she said with a false smile.

'Thank you,' Miss Worthington replied. 'The girls worked hard. Savannah's speech took rather longer than we had rehearsed, however.'

At that moment Lily joined them. 'Good to see you, Mrs Anderson,' she said. 'Savannah *did* take longer than the others, but then she showed great initiative and terrific confidence. If we can channel her energies in the correct areas, we're going to do great things with Savannah.' A circle of parents rapidly collected around her, clamouring for attention. 'We're all very pleased with the way your daughters are developing,' Lily said, including them all in her remark.

Declining Miss Worthington's offer of coffee, Jodi walked briskly away, as if she were in a great rush. But Magsie, carrying a tray of her famous shortbread biscuits, stepped forward, deliberately blocking her path.

'Morning, Mrs Anderson,' she said, her voice rather too hearty. 'Will you have one of my biscuits?'

'Can't stop, I'm in a desperate rush.'

'It was a beautiful Form Presentation, wasn't it?' Magsie persisted irritatingly, obviously determined to delay her escape.

'The girls did a great job.'

'I watched Savannah very carefully. She was clever enough to snatch extra time for herself.' Magsie's disapproval clung to her like the smell of garlic. 'There's more to your daughter than meets the eye, isn't there, Mrs Anderson?'

'What does that mean?' Jodi snapped.

'Some things have to be seen to be believed, Mrs Anderson,' Magsie replied meaningfully.

This insult was not lost on Jodi. Pale with suppressed anger, she turned on her heel and marched out of the room. Although the cold air and sharp wind stung her face and cut its way inside her coat, she did not go home at once. Distressed by Magsie's remarks – Jodi too felt that Savannah had gone a bit far, much as she hated to admit it – she walked aimlessly through the streets of Belgravia until she reached Victoria Station. She went in and stood in the vast concourse, wondering how she had come to take refuge in this huge, refuse-littered train station. It was there – among the homeless and the anonymous, breathing in the smells of pizzas, burgers, coffee, cement and damp clothes – that it came to her with sudden clarity that her daughter did not like her. She couldn't blame her. She had never really liked herself, either. Jodi felt strange and wretched and empty. She wished she could walk away from herself for ever.

Fifteen days, and she would be back in her increasingly beloved New York. Not knowing what to do, or where to go, she took herself to WH Smith, bought a Coke and copy of the *International Herald Tribune,* although one had already been delivered to her door, and sat at a table. She ignored the disgusting pools of someone else's milky coffee, and hid herself and her sudden tears behind the newspaper.

Jodi had no memory of when she had last cried.

Through her tears, she now realized just how much she wished Benton had accompanied her to the Form Presentation. Alone among those mothers, she felt nervous, amorphous, invalid. But if he'd been at her side his mere presence would have been enough to validate her to herself. It was then that she understood that she, Jodi Anderson, the famous New York lawyer, had, incredibly, come to feel not only redundant but somehow useless.

It was inconceivable to her now that she'd even courted the idea of giving up the legal profession. Her career, she recognized, was both her alibi and her opiate.

'What an obnoxious child,' Lady Violet said to Lily on their way to the governors' board meeting.

'Obnoxious?' Lily echoed.

After arriving too early for the meeting – on purpose, Lily suspected – Lady Violet had called in to see her. Told that Lily was at a Form Presentation, she decided to pop in to the school hall to see how the girls performed. Lady Violet was like a recurring low-grade fever in Lily's life. Thin as a church spire, Lady Violet's sharp profile had reminded Lily of a narrow teapot, as narrow, she thought, as the shape of her tiny, interfering mind. Now looking unblinkingly into Lady Violet's suspicious eyes, she said, 'I can't imagine which child you find obnoxious.'

'You know, the *American* one,' Lady Violet replied. 'The girl you allowed to read the school prayer! The girl who took twice as long as everyone else with her speech about those ghastly skyscrapers. Quite frankly, I am disappointed in *you*, Mrs Lidbury.'

'I'm sorry to hear that,' Lily responded. 'May I ask why?'

'As Headmistress, your reputation for fair-mindedness is a byword for what Belgrave Hall has come to stand for. And yet when you saw that American child over-running her time like that, you did nothing to stop her.'

Lady Violet is absolutely right, Lily thought. I'm not thinking straight – I'm becoming everything I don't want to be. I've lost my moral compass! But she said, 'As you know, Lady Violet, I go all out to encourage originality and individuality in all our girls. And I was impressed, I must say, by the way Savannah limited her talk on New York to a description of a vertical city of sky-scrapers.'

'Miss Worthington seemed put out,' Lady Violet insisted. 'She thought it extremely unfair on the others.'

'I was pleased with them *all*, this is a particularly outstanding year.' Curbing her anxiety, Lily went on, 'They're very competitive, of course, but however competitive they may be, they are above all a contented, caring group of girls. Savannah is a new girl, she only started this term and not at the beginning of the academic year, and has adapted to the new system extremely well.'

'Precisely my point, Mrs Lidbury – Belgrave Hall does *not* accept children in the middle of the academic year!'

'Actually, Lady Violet, it is thanks to *you* that Savannah Anderson is at Belgrave Hall. Indeed, I believe it was William Hardwick who asked you to set up an interview for Savannah.' Benton had reminded her of William Hardwick – a rush of longing for him assailed her.

'Wonders never cease,' Lady Violet's expression twisted into a grimace of a smile. 'Wonders never cease,' she said again.

This, Lily believed, was one of those small unexpected moments of one-upmanship that make life sweet. Not that anything would stop Lady Violet from interfering with the running of the school; Lily had lost count of her numerous objections. She'd fought Lily over the school uniform, the curriculum, the Assemblies and the school rules. Childless and proud of it – neither she or her tax-consultant husband had wanted to add to an already over populated world – Lady Violet, daughter of the Earl of Galridge, and a Belgrave Hall old girl, had been born with an undying faith in her own superiority, but without any of that easy, aristocratic grace which made others of her class so attractive.

The meeting was well under way when Lily glanced up from her notes and found her gaze trapped by Lady Violet's malevolent stare. It was then that she knew that her brief moment of triumph would exact an enduring punishment. Lady Violet would make sure of that.


The mindless giggling of two nine-year-old girls was driving Jodi crazy. She'd given them lunch and was now serving them chocolate ice cream.

'You inviting Katie to your party?' asked Savannah, her voice suddenly taking on an imperious quality that made Jodi stop and listen.

'I'm inviting all the girls in our class, silly,' Tiffany giggled. 'My mom said I had to.'

'Well if you invite her, I won't come.'

'But my mom will make me invite her, I'm taking all the invitations to school on Monday.'

'Your mom isn't mailing them?'

'She doesn't need to if I can take them.'

'So, you don't have to give one to Katie. Your mom won't know, will she?'

'No.'

'Do you want me to come?'

'Of course, silly!'

'Well I'll only come if only you promise not to invite her.'

'Okay.'

On the point of taking Savannah to task over this, Jodi managed to stop herself – it would be counter productive to discuss the matter in front of Tiffany. As soon as the girls had gone down to the basement gym to play table-tennis, she stacked the dishes in the dishwasher and made herself a cup of strong instant coffee instead of the real thing. She remained in the kitchen she so deeply resented for its inefficiency, and slowly sipped her coffee. In her real life, in New York, there wasn't a spontaneous moment in her day. Yet now, though it was still, unbelievably, only the middle of the day, she switched on CNN, saw that it was reporting sports, and switched it off at once. Horrified to find herself speculating on how the dishwasher came to be invented, she impatiently turned to a large envelope that had been delivered with the noon mail. It was the *Yoga Journal* with a yellow tag pointing to the article written by Paul Chalmers, a senior partner in her law firm, and a *cum laude* graduate of Harvard Law School.

Rereading the article, Jodi was aware that she'd become vulnerable to the kind of things she would barely have noticed before – the aloof chill of the mothers at school, the pointed remarks of someone like Magsie, the invisible bands of barbed wire that Savannah appeared to have erected against her, but not against Benton. Precisely what it was she was afraid of she could not say. She knew only that she'd never been as fearful as she was now. When the shrill buzzer sounded as urgently as a fire alarm – another of the things she hated about this house – she jumped in fright, and had to force herself to go to the front door.

An Indian woman in a scarlet raincoat was on her doorstep. Tall and majestic, her skin was golden and shining, her smile serene. But it was her luminous, dark eyes with their knowing, intelligent look which dominated her appearance. 'I'm Bandrika Chatoo,' she said in a singsong voice. 'Sorry, I'm ten minutes late, I know, but the traffic was horrendous.'

'I think you've come to the wrong address,' Jodi said.

'You're not Anne Curtis?'

'No.'

'Oh, my word, I'm supposed to be giving her a yoga lesson!'

There was something in the woman's kind and friendly manner that made Jodi feel at ease.

'This sure is a weird coincidence, I was reading the *Yoga Journal* when the buzzer went.'

'We say there are no coincidences,' Bandrika Chatoo said earnestly. 'This *is* 29 Eaton Place?'

'29 Eaton *Crescent*. These streets are crazy – three names on the same street on the same block!'

'Well, that underlines my point about destiny,' Bandrika smiled. 'May I come in and use your phone? I'd like to let Mrs Curtis know that I'm on my way.'

'Of course. I'm Jodi Anderson by the way.'

Bandrika Chatoo followed her into the library, made her call and with an embarrassed laugh, turned to Jodi. 'Well it seems there was a medical emergency. Mrs Curtis has had to take her mother to the hospital.'

'Can I offer you a cup of coffee?'

'A glass of water would be most welcome.'

'Evian or Perrier?'

'Evian, thank you.'

69

'The *Yoga Journal* I was just reading is on the coffee table,' Jodi said as she removed the Evian bottle from the small fridge concealed behind a door of fake books she so disliked. 'And what's probably one of those coincidences which you say are not coincidences, this is the first time I have ever even *looked* at a yoga magazine. What's more, the article I was reading is about *lawyers* taking yoga classes, and I'm a lawyer.'

'What seems to be coincidence is the face of destiny,' Bandrika quoted as she might quote the Bible. 'Our mind obeys what our fate says.'

'I'd like to explore this,' Jodi replied thoughtfully. 'In fact I'd like to take a few classes with you.'

# CHAPTER 3

It was Lily's sixth Saturday morning lesson with Savannah since the beginning of term. In all her years of experience among all the many hundreds of children she had taught, she had not encountered anything like Savannah's stern determination to succeed. And she was convinced it was not so much success as victory that the child craved. Not yet ten, Savannah was shrewd enough to be content in a class of girls a year younger than she, where she could excel, rather than with her own age group where she would be mediocre. Already it was clear that if Savannah, like most children, needed to conform, she did not also need to be ordinary, and it was this that won Lily's respect.

She longed to discuss this with Benton. But both had kept to their agreement, neither to see nor speak to one another until they were to meet in Paris which was still twelve long days away.

'Mrs Lidbury, do you remember the poem we read last week?' asked Savannah.

'Of course, one of my favourites.'

'Would you like to hear me say it – I mean tell it, I know it by heart.'

'I'd love to.'

Listening to the poem, Lily marvelled at the way Savannah's voice had gone from lifeless to lively. She too, knew the words by heart and found herself listening to Savannah as she would listen to music, when she'd hear the sound of the moment and yet anticipate the next phrase at the same time. No longer a drawl, her New York accent reminded Lily of a swiftly floating bubble, and there was usually a hint of laughter while she talked. She had adjusted her voice to the slow rhythm of the poem, but as a rule she spoke quickly, as quickly as Lily herself spoke.

As soon as the poem ended Lily rushed to hug her. 'First I'm going to plait your hair and then we're going to bake those chocolate biscuits I told you about.'

'Chocolate chip cookies?'

'We do not call them cookies, we call them biscuits.'

'*Biscuits*,' Savannah chimed with laughter. 'Chocolate chip *biscuits*.'

Soon they were in Lily's kitchen, finding mixing bowls and a wooden board, and before long the scent of chocolate was in the air. Savannah mixed the dough, chatting on about Bronnie and the kind of chocolate frosting she could make. She had seen her eat a whole big bowl of frosting, and once, 'Bronnie even made a white chocolate frosting especially for her cat, and I ate loads of it too.'

Savannah's essay on Bronnie's cat flashed into Lily's mind, and her pulse quickened. Fortunately, over these past weeks, during PE lessons and netball practise, she had discreetly checked Savannah's uncovered arms for any sign of self-inflicted wounds. She needed confirmation that her words of comfort had helped the child to feel less disturbed and less angry. She breathed more easily – if the self-mutilation had continued she would have been compelled to resort to psychiatric help.

They were about to remove the biscuits from the oven when the buzzer sounded. 'That'll be your mother.' Lily raced to answer the entry phone. 'I hadn't realized how late it was.'

Savannah followed her. 'She's early,' she said.

The TV monitor showed Benton.

'It's you!' Lily said. 'We're not quite ready, Mr Anderson. I hope it won't put you out too much.'

'My wife couldn't make it, she asked me to come instead,' Benton said. 'I'll come up if I may.'

'Of course.' Lily pressed the button to open the door.

'I'll run down and show Daddy the way,' Savannah said.

A minute later, Benton and Savannah were in the kitchen.

Lily's chest felt constricted and she realized she'd actually been holding her breath ever since she'd first seen him on the entry phone monitor. It was not until she had removed her oven gloves and they had formally shaken hands that her breathing returned to normal.

'The time simply flew,' Lily said.

'Tempus fugit?' he grinned.

'Tempus fugit?' Savannah repeated, puzzled.

'Latin for "time flies",' Benton smiled. 'I'm showing your teacher that I know a bit of Latin.'

'Oh Lord, the biscuits will be burnt,' Lily said. She dashed back into the kitchen with Benton and Savannah following close behind. Moments later the perfectly baked biscuits lay invitingly on the cooling rack.

'I trust you'll allow me to have one?' Benton said.

'I'm waiting until they are cool enough to eat,' Savannah announced.

'OK, honey.' He turned to Lily, 'My wife went off with Bandrika at the last minute to a lecture, so she asked me to come and get Savannah.'

'Bandrika is her yoga teacher,' Savannah put in swiftly.

'I'm glad you could come and get her, Mr Anderson.'

'Benton, remember? Last time we met you agreed to call me Benton if I called you Lily.'

'I *do* remember the last time we met,' she said.

Making an effort to regain a semblance of equilibrium, she told him that Savannah could probably go up a year to Y5, but preferred to remain where she was.

'I sure am proud of her,' Benton said. 'I was planning to take her to lunch at a place called Mimmo. You may know the restaurant?'

'I recently had the *most* memorable evening of my life at Mimmo.'

'Would you care to join us?'

'I would love to, but Magsie and I are lunching together. She's made her fantastic *ragout*. She'll be up here with it in about fifteen minutes or so.'

'Another time perhaps?'

'Magsie always makes much more than we can possibly need – she's not a typical Scot as far as her cooking is concerned,' Lily said with a laugh. 'Why don't you and Savannah join us for lunch here in my kitchen?' Oh God, Lily thought. I'm being stupid again!

'Please Daddy, say yes, say yes!'

'Why thank you Lily, we'd just love to do that.'

'May I help you set the table, Mrs Lidbury?'

'We'll both help,' Benton said. 'Meanwhile, I'm dying for one of those cookies.'

'Biscuits,' Lily corrected automatically. 'Just one, mind, or you'll spoil your appetites.'

She was longing to touch him; was starving for his touch, her self-control slipping perilously. 'You know where the cutlery is Savannah,' she said. 'So you get on with it while I ask your father to help me get the wine from the storeroom. He'll have to move some heavy boxes, so we'll be as quick as we can.'

And then they were in the dark storeroom with the door firmly shut, her body straining against his. Lost in the kind of lust she had never before experienced, if he had not been holding her in his arms with her mouth clamped to his, she would have fallen. At last, they drew apart, and she handed him the bottle of wine. Then they straightened their clothes, and he went to the bathroom to remove her lipstick from his lips while she returned to the kitchen. She then called Magsie on the intercom to ask her what sort of pudding she had in her freezer because they had unexpected guests.

It was years since Lily had sat down to a real meal around her kitchen table with a man. Benton had taken off his blazer, and his tight black cashmere sweater tucked into his jeans emphasized his slender waist and called attention to his broad shoulders, intensifying her longing for him, making her feel both elated and afraid. The scent of chocolate mingled with Magsie's clove-infused *ragout*, the cinnamon apple pie was warming in the oven. The fruity whiff of wine and the ripe aroma of Stilton and (at least as far as Lily's heightened senses were concerned) the musk scent of Benton's cologne, turned the kitchen into a sensuous garden.

If having exceeded what she called her 'normal glass of wine' had made Magsie more garrulous than usual, it had done nothing to diminish her distrust of Savannah. The appearance of Savannah, or rather, the way Lily had reacted to her haunting resemblance to Amanda, resurrected the never entirely dormant fear bordering on terror that had been with her ever since she had found Lily after she had taken that near fatal overdose. 'Do I strive to remember or struggle to forget?' Lily had asked. It was then that Magsie moved in and took over, nursing Lily through those demented weeks. Now, declaring that 'apple pie without cheese is like a kiss without a squeeze', she insisted on serving both at the same time.

'By the way, I bumped into Mrs Ratcliffe this morning,' said Magsie rather too casually, her eyes on Savannah. 'And she told me that the Royal School of Music has decided to enter Katie in the British Young Violinists of the Year competition.' Observing Savannah's eyes narrow and her face redden, Magsie smiled. She felt oddly vindicated; all the doubts she'd been harbouring about the child seemed justified.

'That's wonderful, Katie will only be nine next birthday,' Lily exclaimed with pride. Turning to Benton, she added, 'Katie is an adorable child. A highly talented musician and bright academically, too.' She picked up the small yellow pad and pen that she always kept within reach. 'I must ring her to congratulate her,' she said, rapidly writing a reminder to herself.

'I guess she's the one you told me about, the one who cried when her bow had been broken?' Benton asked Savannah.

Savannah shrugged, 'Yes.'

'I heard about that bow,' Magsie cut in swiftly, her voice sharp.

'You've got a new photograph, Mrs Lidbury,' Savannah said. 'Can I have a proper look at it? I love brides.'

'Of course you may,' Lily said. 'Bring it to the table, and then everyone can see it.'

'She's beautiful,' Benton said. 'Who is she?'

'Her name is Lindiwe, and I'm extremely proud of her. She was a very sick girl when she came to Jabulani five years ago.'

'Is that her grandmother?' asked Savannah.

'That's Matron,' Lily smiled. 'She's my boss, and she's very strict. I've known her for years, and I've never heard anyone call her by her first name. But strict as she is, and large as she is, you should see her singing and dancing for those sick children. There's no band or anything like that, but her singing is all the music she needs, and the children laugh and laugh.'

'Maybe I'll see her one day,' Savannah said. 'Can I have another cookie, Mrs Lidbury?'

'Yes, Savannah, you *may* have another *biscuit*.' Lily answered. Unable to resist teaching, she added, 'In England we say *may I please* have another biscuit, remember?'

'May I please have another biscuit, Mrs Lidbury?' Savannah repeated obediently.

'You certainly may,' Lily said.

Magsie felt uneasy – she could not bring herself to like this child, leave alone trust her. But Lily obviously adored her, and Savannah in turn worshipped Lily. And yet she could not pinpoint what it was about Savannah that so undid her. Granted, she wasn't the first child to have been jealous of a particularly gifted child like Katie. Could it be that it was not so much Savannah's personality as the effect she had on Lily that she feared? Now, watching her with Savannah, she could not help feeling that at some primal level Lily was trying to recreate the happy nuclear family which still she blamed herself for having lost. Magsie was the only person who knew that this outwardly strong, dynamic headmistress was inwardly as fragile as a dewdrop.

It was because Lily smiled at Savannah with the same wide, proud maternal way she used to smile at Amanda that Magsie was filled with such foreboding. Besides, she'd noticed the way Lily's eyes softened when she looked at Benton. She castigated herself for thinking like a suspicious, nosy woman – Lily would never even contemplate a relationship with a married man. More a fear than a suspicion, the possibility stubbornly persisted. She knew that if that possibility ever became a reality, Lily would lose everything that mattered to her.

With the chocolate biscuits wrapped in tin foil in a Harrods bag that dangled from Savannah's hand, she and her father made their way home. She was so engrossed in exuberantly hop-scotching on the pavement that she narrowly avoided colliding with another pedestrian.

'Aren't you Savannah Anderson, the American child who took too long over her speech?' the woman asked.

'That she is,' Benton said. 'I guess you saw the show? I missed it, but I heard she was great.'

'I happened to be at Belgrave Hall for a governor's meeting, so yes, I did indeed see the Form Presentation.' Looking at Savannah with distaste, she added, 'And that is precisely how I know you went over the time.'

'Benton Anderson,' Benton said. 'You're Mrs – ?'

'Lady Violet Anstey,' she corrected.

'I've been baking biscuits with Mrs Lidbury,' interrupted Savannah.

'Baking *biscuits*? With Mrs *Lidbury*?'

'Mrs Lidbury's tutoring me, right? And she said she would reward my good work one day and bake cookies with me.'

'Biscuits,' Lady Violet murmured involuntarily.

'Biscuits,' Savannah repeated politely. 'I got an A for my English essay today.'

'Today?'

'I'm very proud of Savannah, she has a three-hour session

every Saturday morning with Mrs Lidbury and instead of complaining, she can't wait to get there,' said Benton.

'I see.'

'And now, Lady Violet, if you'll excuse us?' Benton offered his hand and she had no alternative but to take it. 'I expect I'll see you around the school, Lady Violet.'

'I expect you will, Mr Anderson,' she replied spinning on her heel to leave. 'Good afternoon, Mr Anderson.'

But Savannah put out her hand and stopped her in her tracks. Compelled once again to shake a proffered hand, though somewhat mollified by Savannah's curtsy, Lady Violet said goodbye again and hurried away.


Lily read the same paragraph of the essay she was trying to mark several times and gave up. Work, her safety net, was letting her down; she hadn't taken in a single word.

*I don't know what's bad enough for me to call myself,* Lily thought, echoing what her mother used to say after recovering from a drinking binge. *Kissing a married man in my storeroom with his daughter only one or two metres away.* She buried her face in her hands. *First I invite him to lunch, and then I haul him into my storeroom. A shameless stupid cow, that's me. And yet I was drowning in him . . .*

Dizzy with the shame of longing for him, she decided the only solution was a cold shower. She might even wash her hair, and get back to marking those essays.


Irritated because the intercom in her flat rang too loudly and for too long, and because she'd only just stepped out of the shower, Lily wrapped herself in a towel, and went to answer it. Lady Violet was on the entry-phone monitor.

'Lady Violet?' she said.

'I need to see you.'

Hearing the urgent note in her voice, Lily immediately activated the electronic button to open the door. 'I'll be down as soon as I can,' she said. She wrapped her wet hair in a towel, and was reaching for her bathrobe when her door-knocker sounded like a roll of drums. Tying her bath robe closed she reluctantly went to open the door.

'I've been walking up and down Eaton Row for at least an hour pondering whether or not to come up and see you,' Lady Violet said breathlessly, with an air of grievance.

'This sounds like a major emergency.'

'In a sense it *is* just that.'

'I hope I may be of help,' Lily said. 'As you can see I've just washed my hair, but do come in.'

Lily's wet hair felt sticky and her scalp tingled and needed a further cold rinse. When they were in the sitting room, she pointedly adjusted the now soaking towel turban. 'What seems to be the problem?' she asked.

'I was unaware, Mrs Lidbury, that you gave private lessons.'

'Oh,' Lily responded neutrally.

'Surely it's unseemly and unfair for a headmistress to single out a child for *private* tutoring?'

Lily met her accusing stare head on, but remained silent.

'It gives the child an unfair advantage over the others – it diminishes the required distance between pupil and headmistress which inevitably leads to a certain familiarity and indeed, ultimately, to *favouritism*.' She flung out her arms with a superb gesture of disapproval. 'To give extra lessons at the school would be unprofessional and leave us open to abuse, criticism and misinterpretation. It could be suggested that the teacher was under-teaching in order to teach a pupil after school for financial gain.'

'Financial gain?'

'Your fee.'

'There is no fee,' Lily smiled. She guessed that Lady Violet had bumped into Benton and Savannah. 'Mr Anderson has donated a substantial sum to our school for the latest computer technology.'

'It would have been nice if I'd been told about that.'

'We've written you a memo – the computers have only just been ordered,' Lily said. 'As you know, Lady Violet, there are discrepancies between the British and American systems. I'm helping Savannah reach our requirements.' She paused. 'I am, as ever, totally committed to the excellence of teaching so that it benefits all the girls.' The smallest sliver of a smile softened her tone. 'As a Belgrave Hall old girl, Lady Violet, you ought to know what this school stands for.'

In spite of herself Lady Violet smiled and quoted the school motto, *'Fide Spes Nostra Ubique.'*

'I'm glad we understand one another.'

'Goodness me, I've kept you with a wet head of hair!'

'It'll dry soon.'

Though they parted on diplomatically friendly terms, Lily was now going to have to be more wary of Lady Violet than she had ever been.

Lily towel-dried her hair. She returned to her marking, but still found it impossible to concentrate.

Lady Violet had never crossed her threshold before today. Surely her unexpected visit was an omen, a message, a warning to her to stop this Benton madness. She knew she shouldn't join Benton in Paris. And yet, she reasoned, if just once they had this time together, this temporary reality, knowing that it wouldn't ever happen again, they could break it up and go back to their real lives, and never see one other in an intimate way again. Or so she thought.

# CHAPTER 4

'*Monsieur vous attend.*'

The receptionist at the Georges V hotel in Paris slid Lily's passport back to her. A porter smoothly materialized, picked up her small tote bag and led her to the elevator. Within less than two minutes they were on the second floor and the porter was ringing the bell of an ornate gilded door. Even before she could hand him the carefully folded twenty Euro tip in her pocket, the door opened and Benton took over. The porter melted away and she reflexively let out the breath she had not known she had been holding. A laugh, more of relief than of joy, broke from her. Benton chimed in, took both her hands in both of his and moved a step away from her. They stared at one another until the laughter had run its course. Then she was enfolded in his arms. He covered her with kisses, murmuring, 'We made it' over and over again.

It was only when they drew apart, somewhat self-consciously, that she saw they'd been standing in the entrance hall of a sumptuous suite. He'd filled the living room with roses, and led her into it now. As he slowly poured their favourite wine, he started apologizing because he'd realized too late that it had been very indiscreet of him to have had a chauffeur waiting, her name held aloft, at Charles de Gaulle Airport, announcing her arrival to the world.

'I must admit I thought of that, too,' she said, accepting her wine. 'Here we'd gone to elaborate lengths to ensure secrecy – it only takes one slip up to ruin a perfect crime – but to tell the truth I was thrilled to see my name, it seemed such a generous thing to have done.'

He raised his glass. 'To us,' he said.

'To us.' Her voice sounded hoarse; it was too many years since she'd found herself so close to tears. She swallowed hard. 'Today your eyes are exactly the same colour as Savannah's.'

'The colour you call sea green,' his half grin appeared. 'And yours are very clear today. Blue, ice blue eyes, I'd say.'

'But not cold, I hope?'

'No,' he said emphatically. 'Never cold.'

'I'd hate to have cold eyes.' A look of apprehension marked her face. 'Cold eyes – my mother's eyes.'

'You never talk about your mother.'

'I can't,' she shook her head. 'That would be too difficult for me.'

By way of an answer, he moved closer to her, took her hand between his hands, kissed her closed eyes tenderly, but slowly and lengthily until erotically possessed, she covered his hands with hers and brought her mouth to his.

In common with all new lovers, they were fascinated by what it was that had drawn them to one another. The whole thing would have been extraordinary, they reasoned, even if they had not come from such different worlds, but the fact that they were such an unlikely liaison made it even more momentous. Like two people who have narrowly escaped a catastrophe together they chatted incessantly, and their talk spilt into the early hours, until, exhausted, they fell asleep mid-sentence. Each morning they seemed to wake simultaneously, begrudging the hours lost to sleep.

On the first morning, Benton awoke with a stiff neck. They'd had less than five days together, but already had acquired a delicious sense of sharing – a sense of *our* – such as *our* favourite wine, *our* favourite music, *our* dinner at Mimmo.

But inevitably, at this happy stage at the beginning of their affair, their talk would return again to their initial impressions of one another over their first transatlantic phone call. Each had experienced an awareness of the sound of the other's voice so deep that it had instantly been imprinted on their memories, permanently recorded and as primal, they believed, as a mating call, their long-gone youth notwithstanding. Finding one another was a gloriously mysterious marvel. Surely they were mature and experienced enough and practical enough not to be fool enough to fall for this sort of wild, wanton fusing of hormones and souls and bodies? Was there something mystical about their union then? Of course not, neither went in for that sort of thing.

Had either, she wondered, had a premonition, a warning of an imminent *coup de foudre*? 'Well, perhaps,' she said, answering her own question.

'In what way?' he asked tenderly.

'Our first phone call of course. There was a moment when the line was unclear.'

'I remember,' he leaned over her to trace the outline of her lips. 'Rushing water sounding like a running faucet.'

'That's exactly what it was. I was letting in more hot water. It was nine o'clock in the morning, and I was in my bath, listening to Chopin's powerful second sonata, remembering that Sir John Mansfield – you know, the conductor whose daughter is at our school – had told me that he was convinced that Chopin had written it expressly for lovers. And then you called and I turned the volume down.'

'And you didn't know that you were speaking to your prospective lover.'

'But I knew I wanted to meet the owner of that voice,' she chuckled, snuggling her knee against his. 'That low, rolling sensuous voice.'

'And I've been crazy about a voice like yours since I was sixteen,' he confessed. 'My father and I both had a crush on Celia Johnson – it was about the only thing we had in common. We loved the way she spoke. And you have that same clarity, Lily-bud. To tell the truth I think I fell in love with you as soon as I heard your voice – I remember thinking how sexy it was.' He smiled that impish smile that she adored, 'I also remember feeling much happier – even excited – about moving to London after I put the phone down.'

She wound her arms around his neck and said in an urgent hush, 'I don't think I know how to cope with this much happiness.'

'You know what, Lily? We're going to have a very late break-fast this morning. Very, very late.'

Two hours later they were at Le Deux Magots leaning over the tiny round table, hands lightly entwined, waiting for the waiter to bring their order.

'I'm certain Savannah has completely stopped punishing her-self,' Lily said.

'Punishing herself?'

'About Middy's death – '

'You told her that wishing someone would get a toothache doesn't mean they will get a toothache, right?'

'Savannah must have believed me – there's no sign of any more mutilation.'

He rested his hand on her thigh. 'You know why I'm so glad you called me to tell me you were slightly worried about Savannah?'

'Because I fell into bed with you with unseemly haste – '

'You're such a genius in bed, Lily-bud. I can't imagine how you went without it for so long.' He drew her to him again. 'Savannah adores you, you know. You've made such a difference to her life.'

She wanted to tell him that something beyond understanding had passed between them the moment she and Savannah had met. She couldn't say what it was; she knew only that it was as if the very presence of Savannah had unlocked the gates of her soul. She ached to tell him about her own child, but was too broken, and too shamed by the manner of Amanda's death to even say her name.

They had just been served hot chocolate croissants when a large woman, clearly an American, of indeterminate age with vivid synthetic black hair worn like a helmet, marched purposefully toward their table. Clutching his napkin, Benton rose to his feet at once. 'Well if it isn't Peter Hamilton!' she exclaimed in a high authoritarian voice. 'Fancy running into you in Paris of all places.'

Lily observed him turn visibly pale.

'Mistaken identity,' he said politely.

The woman clapped her hands over her face. 'I'm mortified,' she said, backing away apologetically. 'I could have sworn you were Peter Hamilton.'

'That woman really upset you, didn't she?' Lily turned smilingly toward him, but the laughter to which she was so prone froze in her throat. Benton appeared to be staring fixedly, an expression of helplessness mixed with horror in his rigid gaze. She rested a sympathetic hand on his knee.

'She could have been my mother,' he muttered agitatedly, dabbing his lips with his napkin, making no attempt to disguise his distress. 'Same voice – God, what a resemblance!' A sudden grimace darkened his face. 'It's taken me all these years, as a matter of fact, until this very moment, to come to the realization that I married Jodi because of the woman I most disliked on this earth, my own mother!' He set his cup down forcefully in its saucer, 'You're shocked, right?'

'Nothing you could say could ever shock me.'

'Jodi was the opposite of my mother. She was calm. You could never tell when my mother would fly into one of her terrible rages. But you could always count on her to take every opportunity to put in the wounding word, the toxic remark. She persecuted my father who, as she quaintly put it, married up, just as she'd married down.' He fiddled with his hair, and his familiar lock fell across his forehead. 'But it is only now, it's only since you and I – '

'Since you and I turned into us?'

'Since we turned into *us*,' he repeated. 'It is only since then that I've gotten to understand that Jodi owes her calm to her congenital coldness.'

'You were going to tell me all about your mother and that dreadful haircut.'

'It's such a horrible story, Lily-bud,' he said hesitantly. 'I don't think – '

'What was she like?'

'As a mother?'

Lily nodded.

'She was the sort of mother who liked to shock. She would tell everyone that all children – but especially her own – bored her. She was famous for the Sunday lunch parties she gave for her powerful friends. She never included me. But one Sunday, a guest brought a boy of about my age, so I was invited.' His tone was subtly ironic. 'After everyone had left – we were still standing in the hall – she asked me if I'd enjoyed the pie. She said she'd baked it herself. I said it was great. Then she told me that I'd just eaten George, my pet rabbit. I started crying No! No! No! I began to run toward the vegetable garden to look for George, and crashed into her precious Steuben umbrella stand. Glass was everywhere. By then I was sobbing. I was already at the door when she yelled that I was an *idiot, it was a joke, she was only teasing me!* Then she laughed as if she had said something terribly amusing. I can still hear the sound of that laugh.' He covered his ears with his hands for a moment. 'The next day she marched me off to the barber. She had him cut my hair so close to my skull that I looked almost bald.' He stopped and gave a stiff smile. 'This is not something I talk about.'

Lily had shut her eyes involuntarily. The memory of the rabbit fur in her dead daughter's hand had grabbed her, like a sharp pain. Now she opened her eyes and looked into his. '*Why?*' she asked. 'What on earth could have made her do – '

'She said she it was to teach me a lesson,' he interrupted, his voice bland.

'A *lesson*!' she repeated. '*What lesson?*'

'Not to be a cry-baby!' He smiled suddenly. 'And manners!'

'How old were you?'

'Twelve.'

'This is monstrous,' Lily said. 'We hear all sorts of accounts of abuse at school, but this – ' Lily rolled her eyes to the ceiling. 'That you actually *believed* her says it all.'

'She took great pride in telling people that kindness was not one of her particular aspirations.'

There was a silence.

Lily's head whirled; so many colliding thoughts blurred her mind. 'I think we should go back to our hotel,' she said, increasing the pressure of her hand on his thigh. 'They'll have done our room by now. Middle of the morning or not, middle of Paris or not, we're going back to the hotel.'

'We've seen nothing of Paris, I'm happy to say – we've hardly left our room.'

'If it didn't have to be cleaned, we wouldn't leave it at all!'

So they returned to the hotel and their room was clean, and the linen fresh. She removed the cream brocade quilt swiftly, and then turned the crisp linen sheet back.

'I just want to hold you,' she whispered over and over again. 'I need to hold you. I'd decided not to come to Paris – I nearly, nearly didn't come, you know.'

'I knew you'd have doubts,' he said. 'But I also knew you *would* come.'

The roaring of a chill mid-winter wind outside somehow infused them with an even deeper warmth.

Towards ten o'clock that evening, Benton's mobile phone rang. He looked at Lily, raised his eyebrows quizzically, and answered it.

'Benton Anderson.'

'Benton – the roses are beautiful,' Jodi said, her tone enthusiastic. 'Thanks for remembering.'

'Remembering?' he echoed. 'It's Jodi,' he mouthed silently to Lily.

'You're not fooling me for one minute, Benton Anderson, pretending you didn't send those red roses for our anniversary.'

His secretary, Penny, must have organized it. She'd obviously taken it for granted that this was the sort of thing he liked to do. Hastily changing the subject, he asked for news of Wishes International.

'We'll win,' Jodi said dryly. 'It'll cost mega-bucks in fines, but it'll be a whole lot cheaper for the company if no one goes to the slammer.'

'I'm losing you – I'm running out of juice,' he lied. 'I'll get back to you later, OK?' Then, so she would believe his battery was flat, he switched the phone off.

'It's our anniversary,' he told Lily with a crooked grin. 'Penny took it upon herself to send Jodi roses from me.'

The mention of a wedding anniversary made Lily miserably aware of her own shameless betrayal of Jodi. 'Thoughtful of Penny,' she said dryly.

'I guess,' Benton replied.

They'd had room service and the left over sauce of *poule au riz au saffron* had congealed on the plate.

'I'll get rid of this,' he said. The room service table on wheels was easy to push. 'And then we'll go back to bed, OK?'

They made love again and once again eventually collapsed into sleep.

But a thought tearing at the edge of Lily's mind broke through and jolted her awake.

What if the woman with the helmet-like hair who had mistaken Benton for someone else had been one of the school mothers or grandmothers? The very possibility sent her into a spiral of panic. Perhaps they had already been seen together? And she'd loathed herself when she'd heard Benton lie to his wife on their wedding anniversary. What in the name of hell was she doing here? Nauseated by her wanton recklessness, and her brazen indifference toward Jodi, she rushed to the bathroom, and turned on all the taps to drown out any sounds that she might make. When the retching at last stopped, a tidal wave of reality hit her, and she knew she had no choice but to leave at once.

With only the light coming in from the bathroom, she packed quietly. At the high-pitched mechanical sound of the closing zip, Benton awoke. Instantly alert, he switched on the bedside lamp. 'What's going on?' he asked.

'That woman who thought she knew you – '

'What about her?'

'She could have been someone I knew – '

'You're not thinking rationally,' he said. 'She didn't know either one of us!'

'But she *could* have been one of the school grandmothers,' Lily spoke in an urgent hush, 'in which case I'd lose everything that matters in my life.' A tiny hammer banged in her chest. 'I've got to get out of here now!'

'It's not even six a.m.!'

'I've just got to go – ' She crossed the room and began punching in the security code of the hotel safe. 'I'm taking my passport. I'll get the early morning flight.'

'I'm coming down with you – '

'No! We could be seen together.'

'I'll call the front desk and tell them you're checking out.'

'That's hardly necessary,' she protested. 'Besides, it will make it seem so sordid.'

He jumped out of bed and took her in his arms. He began to kiss her, but she forced herself to pull away from him.

'Meeting in hotels is dangerous for me,' she said. 'I'll call you from London.'

Suddenly ravenous, Benton called room service and ordered coffee, croissants and quince jelly. Lily's 'what if' talk had hit a raw nerve. He knew where she was coming from; she was head-mistress of a great school and was having it off with the father of one of her students. There would be hell to pay if she were found out. He wouldn't look too good, either. Jodi would sue the pants off him, and he wasn't ready for that right now.

Discretion, as Molière said, is always in season, he reminded himself. Yet both he and Lily had thrown discretion to the winds as if they had no need of it. If he wanted to go on with Lily, he'd have to find an apartment where they could be private. It was complicated, having an affair – nothing at all like those delicious, casual fucks he was used to. But the sex with Lily was something else, kind of mind-blowing and beyond perfect.

Something about Jodi had changed. When she'd called him as he was on his way to the airport, she'd told him that she wanted to hear his voice. She'd never said anything like that before. Friends rather than companions, they'd had the security of knowing they could count on one another. If Jodi rationed their sex life it wasn't that he turned her off, it was because of her chronic shortage of time. He understood that, and made his own arrangements; there was no scarcity of women keen to make sure he wouldn't be deprived. Perhaps this time – because it was so different with Lily – she'd sensed that he had another woman in his life? He had an urge to speak to her, but it was just after midnight in New York. What the hell, he'd call her anyway – if he woke her, she could always go back to sleep or do her meditating.

So he called her and she said something about thinking of calling him, too. She told him she had bought cushions for their apartment, and they talked about stuff like that, and he was sure she hadn't caught on to what was going on. But he would rent an apartment anyway. He rather liked the idea; he never would have thought of such a thing before Lily.

# CHAPTER 5

At the same time that Lily and Benton were in Paris, Jodi and Savannah were in New York. Clutching a bunch of white daffodils, Bronnie had been at Kennedy Airport to meet Savannah and Jodi. They had hugged and kissed one another, but it was a calm reunion; they all behaved as if they'd only been parted for a few days. Savannah immediately took the flowers from Bronnie, and handed her the beribboned package containing most of the biscuits she and Lily had baked. Bronnie already knew about the cookies called biscuits. Savannah had written to tell her she was bringing them to New York.

Jet-lagged, Jodi went directly into her meeting with her client's insurance company. The meeting was tense and hostile, and went on for longer than she had planned. She left feeling stressed out, her shoulder muscles locked in an ever-tightening vice. She fell asleep in the taxi, and the cabbie woke her when they reached Park and Eighty-Eighth. When she stumbled into her apartment, she found a note from Bronnie telling her that they had already left for her new trailer home in Queens where Savannah was to stay until they returned to London.

Still tense the following morning, Jodi put on a pair of loose drawstring pants and set about the yoga stretching exercises to help her relax. Before Badrika had returned to her Ashram in Southern India, she had skilfully introduced her to the gentle art of meditation. Now, seated cross-legged in the lotus position, a measure of serenity came to her, and she contemplated her home with cool objectivity. Like the rest of her apartment, the living room embraced the current vogue for minimal chic – but now, with her new view of the world, the furniture struck her as cold, without character or colour.

Chosen by their designer, the huge neutral abstract canvases that hung on the walls lacked any life, as if the artist had styled them both to measure and to match. The room had been meant to be restful, but Jodi now thought it was as soulless a window display in a furniture store.

Whether it was New York or London, it seemed to Jodi that she had lost her identity and her direction, and belonged nowhere; she was a stranger in her own home.

Rudderless and lonely, she experienced an urgent need to speak to Benton, to hear his voice and though it went against the grain to seem so . . . so clinging, she gave in to herself and phoned him. She remembered his meeting in Paris, called his mobile, and reached him on his way to Heathrow.

'Benton Anderson.'

'I'm calling from our apartment.'

'What's gone wrong? The plumbing again?'

'Everything's fine,' she laughed. 'I wanted to hear your voice.'

'You wanted to hear my *voice*?'

'I also wanted to tell you that you were rude to me,' she said, taking herself horribly by surprise. She'd had absolutely *no* idea she was going to mention this.

'I was rude to you?' he repeated. 'How was I rude to you?'

'You said I was a spoilt bitch, like I was when I had that depression after Savannah was born.'

'I remember now,' he said. 'I shouldn't have said that, and I'm sorry I did.'

'That's OK.'

'They're calling my flight.'

'Have a good flight,' she said. 'I hope the meeting goes well.'

'Thanks.'

I shouldn't have admitted that I needed to hear his voice, she thought, but I'm not as lonely as I was before I called him. But I *am* lonely, and I *am* in my home town. I was never like this before London.

She left the living room to go to her bedroom. Except for

Bronnie's daffodils (which looked trapped, rather than arranged) in a Steuben vase, the place seemed uninhabited.

Five years earlier, when they'd moved to this apartment, their celebrity decorator had banned all photographs from every room except the bedrooms. The decorator had outlawed the Andersons' participation in his creation, and since they both were under pressure at work, it was easier to leave the hassle of decorating and moving to him.

Now, observing how aseptic it looked, she felt like a trespasser. She decided to distribute a few framed photographs to make it feel like a home in which people lived. She went to her desk to choose the photographs, and defiantly placed them about the room. Searching for photographs of herself and Benton, she came upon the photograph of her parents, in the original ivy frame given to her when she went to Columbia University. It was so long since she'd looked at it that she had the eerie sensation of seeing it for the first time. Her father, smiling hugely, was wearing his black tie and her mother, smiling falsely, was dressed in a cobalt blue designer ball gown.

She placed the photograph on the glass coffee table, and decided to take it with her to London. The photograph used to stand on the antique desk she'd squeezed into her living room that was so tiny that she'd been compelled to choose between a desk and a couch. She had settled for the desk partly because it was the only piece of furniture she had wanted to salvage from her father's bankrupt estate, but mainly because it was large enough to house her many files. But when the decorator decreed that the antique desk would be as out of place in 'his' apartment as a Rembrandt in a room of Picassos, the desk had gone.

She was pleased she had told Benton she needed to hear his voice. She would never have said anything like that to him before Bronnie had read them the riot act. But then at that time – before London – she would hardly have had the need to hear his voice.

Her mind reeled back to the long overdue analysis of their

lives that had resulted from Bronnie's overwrought outburst, the day she'd forced them to confront the truth of themselves as parents. They had admitted that they had married for the same practical reasons as they had become involved in the relationship. Pragmatism, they believed, was more durable than love and passion. They shared the same likes and dislikes, the same ambitions, the same lifestyle. Leisurely Sunday mornings reading the *New York Times* had steadily evolved into a shared habit, so though Benton had kept his apartment on 62nd Street, he had moved into Jodi's apartment on 54th Street because it was nearer her office, and therefore more sensible to live there. Their mutual need to be sensible connected and cemented their lives. When, in spite of the contraceptive coil, Jodi had become pregnant, though they recognized that this conception was not the result of wild passion but of a calm and mutual attraction, the idea of a termination was, for different reasons, surprisingly repellent to each of them. While Jodi could not bear the notion of ending a foetal life, Benton was excited by the beginning of a life. And from this it followed that they might as well have a wedding – about sixty guests at the Metropolitan Club, of which they were both members.

Benton carried himself with a certain languid assurance. Tall and immaculately dressed in custom-made suits, and with a weakness for cashmere sweaters, he had the amused, easy air of a young man with old money who was entitled to the highest aspirations. Neither kind nor unkind, but always polite, his friendly, optimistic nature exuded warmth – Jodi, like everyone else, felt comfortable with him. Since Benton was eminently suitable as a husband, it did not occur to Jodi to consider whether they were well suited as a couple. Jodi's pregnancy, it seemed to Benton, merely underscored her suitability. They readily fell into the roles of a New York power couple, fitting their lives around their careers, each enhancing the image of the other.

Both Jodi and Benton had been born to elderly parents, of

similar patrician backgrounds. Synonymous with steel, the illustrious Anderson name rang out with a clear and powerful glory, but Jodi's once distinguished family name, Witley, had been unexpectedly sullied. While she was a student at Columbia University, her parents were killed in a car crash. In the ensuing legal wrangles, it was revealed that their huge capital had been replaced by an even huger debt. Her mother, a cold-hearted socialite, was well known for her lavish spending, in particular her penchant for jewels. The real shock, however, was the discovery that her adoring father, an executive television producer, whose hobby was to take her to lunch, and lavish her with imaginative gifts, also had a secret gambling hobby which included betting on Wall Street. Unknown to the family, he had risked more than he had in Libertas, a failed insurance company. The family was ruined. Two weeks after their combined funerals, at the beginning of spring break, nineteen-year-old Jodi attended a meeting in the conference room at the prestigious law firm (where she was later to make partner after only eight years) in charge of her father's affairs. Three attorneys, all men, all wearing more or less identical three-piece suits, like military uniforms, faced her. The corporate lawyer gave her the bad news – her father not only had huge debts, but he had long ago managed to raid his daughter's trust, and left her with nothing, not even life insurance.

Jodi was devastated. Looking around for a friendly face, she asked why Professor Hardwick, her father's former room-mate, wasn't at the meeting. She was informed that the senior partner, who was also an adjunct Professor at Columbia Law School, had no time for minor estate matters.

The humiliation of going from being a spoiled, wealthy only child, to an impoverished only child of a bankrupt father, combined with her anger over her father's deception, propelled her into finding loans for college tuition as well as a part time job, working nights as a hotel receptionist. Later, she came to see all these hardships as fortuitous – without them she would not have become a frantically ambitious trial attorney with a zealot's determination to succeed. Nor would she now have the unchallenged reputation of being one of the most brilliant New York litigators in the field of white-collar crime. The pent-up emotion and grief at her parents' sudden, tragic deaths drove her on with unwavering determination.

Benton had been a student at Harvard, and though Jodi knew he was not as driven as she, he was unshakable in his ambition. In his early years at Carlyle Klein, he'd been in the office at least six days a week, often working until past midnight. But since he'd been elevated to vice-president, the hours had loosened up, and he rarely worked at weekends. As a banker, he was charming, calculating and, above all, sensible. As a trial lawyer, Jodi was succinct, brilliantly clear and above all, sensible.

Then Savannah was born and Jodi, to her eternal horror, found the very notion of a sensible approach impossible. Sleep was the only thing in the world she wanted, but Savannah kept her awake with crying that only seemed to stop when her unforgivably wakeful baby slept.

Unlike most of their friends, Jodi had decided to take care of the baby herself. Instead of the expected radiance of new motherhood, however, she was dominated by her obsessive preoccupation with her own mother. She could not stop herself from hearing, in the whirl of her mind and above Savannah's seemingly endless sobbing, the sound of her mother's voice, repeating, 'You're all guile and no guts, my girl,' followed by and clashing with, 'Don't bother about what is fair or unfair, know the rules!' It came to her that there was only one way she could put a stop to her mother's smug voice and the baby's tears, and escape from the crushing weight of water closing over her head, and that was to load the baby into the car and drive, at speed, into the same high brick wall her parents had smashed into. At that stage she had thought of her daughter as 'the' baby, not 'my' baby. So she had put the baby in the Moses basket in the front and, if the battery of the car had not been dead and the superintendent of the building had not come upon her sobbing in her car in the below-ground parking lot, that was exactly what she would have done.

Benton now hired a maternity nurse. Jodi's postnatal depression was diagnosed and successfully treated at Mount Sinai hospital and by the time Savannah was eight weeks old, Jodi was safe in the savage world of litigation again. It was then that Enid Hardwick, aware of Benton's fondness for everything British, found a trained Norland nanny and Bronnie entered their lives. And with Bronnie's expert ministrations, Savannah's nightly sobbing ceased, and she became a more cheerful child.

A sour whiff of cabbage drifted into the room, interrupting Jodi's reverie. As part of her detoxification program she'd been fasting, drinking only lemon water for the past two days. Today she introduced cabbage soup into her diet. Soon she would add rice and spiced lentils. She was now a committed vegetarian, for both health and ethical reasons, and had been ever since Bandrika had shown her that documentary on battery chicken farming.

Suddenly, three different bells sounded simultaneously. The phone rang, the doorman buzzed on the intercom and the kitchen fire alarm screeched – the cabbage soup was burning. She took the phone off the hook and was spooning the burnt cabbage into the garbage disposal when the doorman arrived with a lavish bouquet of red roses arranged in a crystal vase. She realized she had forgotten their tenth wedding anniversary. And Benton had obviously forgotten to tell his secretary that in New York all their floral arrangements were restricted to the neutral shades of white.

She looked at her watch – it was four o'clock – ten o'clock in Paris – Benton was probably still in a late meeting, but she decided to call him anyway. They chatted briefly. His battery was running flat, and he barely mentioned their anniversary, but wanted to know how her case was progressing. His conversation had been stilted, as if his mind were on something else.

In the middle of the morning of Jodi's third day in New York, her irritable bowel symptoms returned, forcing her to acknowledge that she was still letting the business of law take over her body. Even so, she was well pleased with the way things were going. It had been a huge struggle, but the behind-the-scenes deal-making by the team of warrior lawyers she'd assembled had – thanks to her Machiavellian tactic to blame consultants from Wharton and HBS – succeeded in staving off an arraignment.

Returning from the ladies' room, she knew her overall strategy had been brilliant. Get in bed with the prosecutors, the government investigators, do the power lunch with the greedy lawyers, and make the deal. Let the CFO take the rap and, if necessary, go to jail. Her client would be free, free to keep the Park Avenue penthouse, the summer house in the Hamptons, the jet, the chalet in St Moritz, the yacht and the Impressionist collection. She, however, would be a prisoner of her conscience.

On the way back to her apartment that evening, she realized that she wasn't looking forward to spending time there. On impulse she asked the cabbie to take her to Bloomingdales. It was seven o'clock, but it was Thursday and the store would be open until nine.

Within thirty minutes she'd acquired several kelim cushions, two kelim rugs, two lamps, and six candles all in the colours of the sunset. After the doorman had helped carry them into the apartment, she unpacked and placed them in the living room. She lit the candles, switched on the lamps and the room sprang to life. It lost its daunting look of opulence, and was less forbidding, almost ordinary, the kind of room in which they could make love, she thought, surprised by what was going on in her mind. She went about the room, adjusted the position of some of the candles, and found herself doing something else that surprised her – she was humming the aria from Puccini's *Madame Butterfly*. She couldn't remember which aria it was, but that didn't seem to matter.

This is our anniversary present, she thought. She considered ringing Benton to tell him what she had done, but it was only about six in the morning in Paris. About ten minutes later the phone rang, and it was Benton on the line.

# CHAPTER 6

Even though Lily's heart had been overturned, and her soul had come apart during half term in Paris, her security was in the musical sound of the girls' good morning at Assembly. There was a time when the school board, and Lady Violet in particular, had urged her to conform to the pattern of most headmistresses and relinquish her role as form mistress to Y6, the last year of the Junior School, when the Common Entrance exams would determine the educational future of each child. It was then that the senior school would be decided. But for Lily, life without the art of forging a significant relationship with each of the twenty-four girls in her role as their form mistress would have been unthinkable.

By 9:05, Lily had taken the form register, and attended Assembly where, to her delight, Savannah's red hair had flashed out at her. Now she was behind her desk, busily sorting papers and arranging her day. She would not meet with Savannah's form until 3 p.m. when she would take their English lesson.

Although she'd been in her study by 6:30 a.m., and had already noted the names of those who'd left messages, the answer phone's flashing red button indicated several new calls since then. Courtney Hunt, the first of several scheduled meetings of the morning, arrived at ten past nine, predictably punctual to the second.

'Charles and I have given it a lot of thought,' she began. 'And though it's not our idea, but Tiffany's, we want her to take the St Paul's entrance exam.'

'Miss Worthington and I talked about this just this morning.'
'Why?'
'Because you'd mentioned it to her,' Lily said patiently. 'Miss Worthington feels that Tiffany is a rather shy little girl – '

'She'll grow out of that!' Courtney protested. 'She's set her heart on St Paul's.'

Why, Lily asked herself wearily, must parents always insist on saying it was the child's choice? St Paul's was considered the equivalent to gaining a place at Oxbridge, Harvard or Yale. Dealing directly and firmly with aggressively ambitious parents was more testing than teaching. 'That's odd,' Lily answered tactfully. 'St Paul's is a huge school – about six hundred and twenty girls and,' she tapped her teeth with her pencil and went on, 'Tiffany's shy fragile spirit is more suited to a smaller school where she could be nurtured, and made to feel special.'

'She doesn't think so,' Courtney countered, her face reddening. 'She's definitely set her heart on St Paul's.'

'The environment has to suit the child as well as the academic standard. Sensitive girls do not usually thrive in a larger school. A smaller school would be less – ah – strenuous for her.' She thought it kinder to say 'strenuous' rather than 'academic'. The truth was that Tiffany was close to the bottom of the class. 'In any event, she may not pass the St Paul's entrance exam.'

'We've thought about that, of course. But Tiffany is the type of personality who can take failure in her stride.'

'Do you regard failure as a learning curve – a process that will lead to something beneficial?'

'We don't mind if she fails – we'll take it as an exercise.'

'*You* don't mind,' Lily repeated. 'Does that mean you think failure is a good thing to learn?'

'Well we feel it's important for our daughter to be able to take on a challenge.'

'But if the outcome is clear – if failure is guaranteed, a child as sensitive as Tiffany could well have her self-esteem gravely damaged.'

'Tiffany will have private tutoring in every single subject,' said Courtney, raising her harsh voice. 'American mothers believe in encouraging ambition. Unlike the British, we don't see ambition as a dirty word!'

'Now Courtney – ' Lily began.

'I bet if Tiffany's name was Savannah Anderson, she'd be good enough for St Paul's!'

'And just what do you mean by that?'

'Oh, everyone knows she's your pet!'

'You and I know each other so well, Courtney, that I'm going to pretend you didn't say that.'

Lily had been about to suggest that a consultation with an educational psychologist might be helpful, but Courtney's remark had thrown her off course. She knew that Courtney had her own interior radar – her long tongue was her antenna always at the ready to scent whatever sliver of gossip was available. Could Courtney have seen her in Paris? With the suddenness of a virus, she was hit by a bout of reality mixed with guilt – what she was doing was not only shameful, but reckless. She was flirting with catastrophe. Now, to mask the panic that gripped her, she said, 'Much as we love your daughter, we will not be able to support her application to St Paul's.'

'After eleven months of solid tutoring, her exam results will be all the support she'll need,' Courtney snapped, 'I believe you're on our table at the ball. Charles is away right now, but he'll want to debate this with you then.'

'I'll look forward to that,' Lily pushed her chair back and stood up. 'First day after half term,' she said. 'I'll have to ask you to excuse me; things are rather hectic I'm afraid.'

'Sure thing,' Courtney replied, masking her exasperation as best she could. 'I'll leave you to your busy schedule.'

Courtney left, but her aftertaste lingered. Lily's moment of panic subsided. She and Magsie would discuss this later, she knew.

Thinking of Magsie made her feel guilty. She had always hated deception, but now after having led Magsie to believe that she had gone to Paris to attend a series of meetings on AIDS in sub-Saharan Africa, she had become the kind of duplicitous person she despised. Mercifully the day was too crowded for regrets. Her next appointment was with a teacher from a neighbouring school – three members of staff had resigned because of a personality clash with the new head. Even though Belgrave Hall had no vacancy, Lily showed her round the school. She was back in her study, listing her agenda for the forthcoming staff meeting, when in stormed Jasmine's mother, the well-known news presenter Tara Styles, who was a single mom with a skeletal figure and an aggressive attitude. Needless to say she had not made an appointment – she never did. She launched into a tirade about netball practice – because it was restricted to girls in the team, those without a natural aptitude were discouraged from developing.

'My daughter needs confidence and it's shattering for her when she can't excel at anything,' Tara Styles complained. 'At this age she should be encouraged to aim for the sky.'

Lily saw that this was another of those moments when she was obliged to lay down the law. 'You have to realize, Mrs Styles – '

'*Ms* Styles.'

'As I was saying, Ms Styles, you have to realize that just as we are a highly academic school – do not forget that is why you chose us – we are equally competitive when it comes to sport.'

'I fail to see the point of what you're saying.'

'*If* you'll allow me to finish, Ms Styles,' Lily cut in sternly. 'Your daughter can happily play in the internal matches, for example, when we have house matches and form matches, but when a Belgrave Hall team plays other schools it must be the best we can find. I'm sorry, but I feel as strongly about this as you do. There are many knocks in life, and craving for something that can never be is detrimental to your daughter. I'm sure we can find an alternative activity in which Jasmine can shine.'

'That's all well and good, Mrs Lidbury,' Tara Styles shrugged, 'but I'll have to have another think about all this.' Pointedly looking at her man-sized watch, she picked up her Vuitton briefcase, rose from her seat, and left hurriedly.

There were still a few minutes left before break ended, enough time to peer through the slatted blinds, which allowed her to be invisible, and catch a second glimpse of Savannah that day. One of the tiniest four-year-olds tripped and it was with no small measure of pride that she watched Savannah comfort the child and help her to her feet.

Absorbed in planning the points for discussion at the staff meeting the following day, the relatively new sound of her mobile phone startled her. She answered it at once, 'Belgrave Hall.'

'Mrs Lidbury, I presume?' said Benton amusingly attempting a British accent, but with little of his daughter's gift for mimicry.

'It's *you!*'

'I guess you got that right, Lily-bud. It most certainly is me.' His voice was both vigorous and sensual. 'Guess what? I've found a bunch of physiotherapists for us.'

'What are you talking about? I don't need a *physiotherapist!*'

'The last time I saw you – in Paris – you told me that meeting in hotels was too dangerous for you, remember?' he said with a hoarse chuckle. 'The good news is that I've located a building on Sloane Street with offices for doctors, dentists, physios – you name it. There are dozens of plausible reasons for going into that building, but only one compellingly private reason for you to come see me in this cute little apartment I've just rented for us.'

Her throat closed; she couldn't speak.

'Hey, Lily-bud – are you there?'

'Benton, you are *brilliant!*' she said.

'How about five-thirty today?'

'I don't get out of school until six tonight – I have a meeting with the head of the music department, and then Magsie and I are having a quiet meal together.'

'Her unforgettable *ragout* again, right?'

'She hasn't told me,' she laughed. It was time to look through the blinds, and she left her desk and crossed the room to the window.

'I know you're a busy lady, Lily-bud, but I don't think I can wait too long. The building is called Bryce House and it's on 515 Sloane Street, Flat 12.'

'I can but try.'

'I can make Wednesday or Thursday at six o'clock, OK?'

'Super,' Lily replied. 'You have yourself a Wednesday date, Benton,' she went on hurriedly, 'I can't talk now – I'll get you on your mobile later.'

The bell rang, ending the break.

The day flew. In addition to attending to the everyday, but often unexpected, administrative chores, she'd given her own class, Y6, an English lesson. She'd then assessed the reading progress of the five-year-olds. It was always rewarding to witness their delight at suddenly realizing that they could go from sounding out each word to discovering that the words told a story. She'd also supervised a music project for the seven-year-olds. As usual, her day was a continuous balancing act laced with a sense of permanent emergency.

Towards the end of the day, about an hour before she was to see Magsie, she was again attacked by a feeling of guilt and even treachery, for having failed to entrust her with the secret of her complicated liaison, a liaison that was as unlikely as it was forbidden. Though the reason for her silence eluded her, she suspected that her own shame, mixed with Magsie's disapproval, would disrupt the magic and, worse still, eliminate the mystery. Magsie would be sure to point out the pitfalls, the dangers and the risks – and would no doubt remind Lily that when she'd been matron at Warwick Comprehensive, the maths teacher had been fired – sent away in disgrace – for having had an affair with the mother of one of the students. Lily was not ready to face either the reality or its consequences. If she thought about the future at all, it was to dream vaguely about the three of them – Savannah, Benton and her somehow living as a family somewhere, some day.

Was she in love? Magsie would want to know. Well, *was* she?

Love, as she now remembered it, was like trying to distinguish between the bad and the worse. The bad, the breath-stopping uncertainty, the grinding despair of an enthralling obsession. That had been the legacy of her former faithless husband, the revered and saintly doctor who'd annihilated her reason and stolen her soul, and turned her from loving him to hating him. Since Magsie knew, and had even shared, the worst of her history she was certainly entitled to ask if this, indeed, was love.

At seven o'clock that evening, Lily went down to Magsie's basement flat to join her for dinner. Magsie had made an early, romantic marriage which had been satisfactory rather than happy. It was because her husband, Tom, had found it impossible to hold down a job that she'd taken up a post as school matron in the first place. But she'd stood by him, and handled her private disappointment with him and nursed him through his long and losing fight with renal failure. She'd had her fill of romantic love, but had frankly admitted to Lily that she was more content without it than she'd ever been with it, for it was the death of the hope for romantic love which had endowed her with the gift of inner peace. This, perhaps, was why there was something soothing about dining in this minute kitchen – it was like resting in a capsule of serenity wrought by Magsie's calm, and her loyal pride in their warm friendship. Lily handed Magsie the beautifully wrapped scent she'd bought hastily at Charles de Gaulle airport – 'I did no real shopping in Paris,' she said apologetically.

After thanking her enthusiastically, and because it was a wonderful surprise, and also because she hadn't expected anything at all, Magsie, with an exclamation of satisfaction, gave her a small package in return. Lily opened it slowly, taking great care not to spoil the glittering wrapping paper, which she knew Magsie would probably want to use again. It was an enlarged photograph of herself with her arm about Katie's shoulders. It had been taken on the day of the Form Presentation, and Lily remembered hugging both Katie and her violin. It was one of those rare, happy photographs which capture a smile of supreme joy, turning a commonplace photo into an arresting image.

Brushing away Lily's thanks, Magsie offered her a glass of wine, and before long, a plate of steaming lamb *ragout* had been set in front of her. Magsie served herself and went on to gossip about the children and their parents and pets as if they were all members of her own extended family. Her observations were invaluable to Lily, for she'd an accurate way of divining which child might be facing parental strife, struggling with sibling rivalry or subtle bullying. Indeed, it was Magsie who'd solved the mystery of why it was that bubbly little Rebecca Carter had become suddenly quiet and withdrawn. Her marks had fallen and as the staff and her mother had observed, she was obviously too distressed to be able to concentrate on her work. Magsie had been checking the window in the cloakroom when she overheard two eight-year-olds talking about how sad Rebecca was because her mother was in love with another man and was getting a divorce. 'The innocence of children does not make them any less efficient at spreading gossip,' she told Lily. 'To believe that children are wholly innocent is to believe in a fairy tale,' she added. 'We all have to do whatever it takes to put the poor child's mind at rest.'

The practise of deception had come with surprising ease to Lily. Although she glossed over Magsie's questions about those non-existent AIDS meetings in Paris which she was supposed to have attended, there were several moments when she came alarmingly close to telling Magsie about Benton.

'To think I'm going to be at the same table as Courtney Hunt at the Daffodil Ball,' Lily said, steering the conversation away from what dared not be said. The first fundraising extravaganza in Belgrave Hall history, the Daffodil Ball would also be the first gala event of that kind Lily had attended for fifteen years. 'The one good thing about being at the main table is that – ' Lily stopped herself just in time. She'd been about to say that the

Benton Andersons would be at a different table. Instead, she said, 'What *am* I going to wear?'

Magsie jumped out of her chair, 'Believe it or not, Lily, I think I've got exactly the right dress for you, right here in my cupboard,' she said. 'Hold on a minute, I'll go to my bedroom and unearth it.'

Lily was amused and a little sceptical at Magsie's pronouncement, but by the time Magsie returned, Lily had loaded the dishwasher and carried two glasses of wine to the cosy living room.

'Can't think when I last looked at this dress,' Magsie said. 'But it's been safely inside this plastic cover for more years than I care to remember. The zip may be stuck for all I know.'

But the zip opened easily. A moment later, Magsie held up a silk evening gown.

'I think you've seen this dress before,' she said.

Still holding her glass of wine, Lily jumped up and flung her arms around Magsie. 'You've kept it all this time,' she said. 'All this time.'

'Waste not, want not, I always say,' Magsie replied tartly to conceal her own emotions. 'It will fit you I'm sure. We'll have a glass of wine and then you can try it on if you want to.'

'I'd love to,' Lily said.

Magsie hooked the evening gown back to front over the door, and sat back and took a long meditative sip of wine.

Magsie's collection of school photographs and newspaper clippings dominated the room. Everywhere there were photographs of girls on horses, on skis, on beaches, and cuddling pets. A few were of Belgrave Hall old girls showing off their new babies. Some had been given to her in frames, while other unframed photographs had been placed under the glass of her dressing table. Her bedside table was cluttered with several photographs of her son and his partner in New Zealand, one of Lily and Princess Margaret, another of Katie playing her violin. The uncluttered nightstand at the far end of the room was given over to an enlarged snapshot she had taken of Lily and Amanda wearing identical coats of emerald velvet. Magsie had chanced to catch them during a moment of shared laughter, their heads thrown back, and their lips curved in wide smiles of pure happiness. At first Lily averted her eyes. Then she crossed the room and picked up the photograph and though she knew it well, stared at it as greedily as if she had never seen it before.

Magsie watched her, but only for a moment, before turning her eyes away, unable to bear the sight of Lily's grief – the eternal, soul-violating grief of a dead child's mother.

'The duplicate of that photograph is still in the frame you're holding, Lily,' Magsie said.

Lily flinched.

'You asked me to keep it for you in this very frame, remember?'

'I remember,' Lily replied. 'Amanda really does look like Savannah, Magsie, doesn't she?'

Half furious, half despairing, a profound sorrow shook Magsie.

The unaccountable anxiety she'd been feeling for Lily all evening turned to fear. '*Dear God, Lily,*' she ranted inwardly. '*You've got it the wrong way round. It is Savannah who looks like Amanda, you idolize her!*'

She had told Lily that she had seen Savannah hide Tiffany Hunt's ballet shoes, and she had also informed her that Savannah had invited Isobel Midgeley home for tea, and then left her stranded at the school saying her mother had cancelled the date, but Lily had made excuses and moved on to talk about other children's problems. Magsie sighed. This was one of those times when she had the unnerving sensation that Lily was bewitched.

'Perhaps you would rather not try on the dress?' Magsie asked Lily. 'You've gone as quiet as a grave.'

'Have I?' Lily replied. 'Sorry – I've been reminiscing, I suppose.'

'It's getting late – if you're going to try it on you ought to put it on now.'

'I didn't mean to keep you waiting, but the dress took me back to another time in a long gone world,' Lily said, following Magsie into the bedroom. 'I thought I'd asked you to give the dress to Oxfam when we moved to Belgrave Hall.'

'So you did,' Magsie laughed. 'But I couldn't find it in my heart to part with it. I always hoped – ' her voice trailed off. 'I don't think you've gained an inch these past fifteen years,' she added, busily helping Lily into the dress.

By the time the dress was on, and she had freed the zip which had caught Lily's flesh, the bow holding Lily's hair had un-ravelled, leaving it hanging loosely on her shoulders. Lily looked different, Magsie thought, puzzled. She seemed troubled. Magsie was confident that the dress could now be classified as vintage. Actually it was she who'd persuaded Lily to go in for vintage clothes when they'd moved to London, which had been, as Lily said over and over again, an inspiration. Because second hand clothes had been reasonable at that time, and because she found that by mixing and matching long skirts with stylish flowing jackets and fussy or simple blouses, she could get away with fewer clothes. Besides, the abrupt and unexpected change in her life-style which had flung her from married to unmarried, had left her feeling an outcast, a remnant from another time, and some-how better suited to the clothing of the past. Now, standing before the mirror, in a figure-hugging dress, she saw that she'd been transformed, temporarily metamorphosed from the gracious to the glamorous.

'I don't look at all like a headmistress, do I, Magsie?' she said, staring at the sexy woman she'd become since Benton had come into her life, a woman as sexy as the dress.

'That you don't,' Magsie emphatically agreed. 'You look too young for one thing.'

'But, Magsie,' Lily protested, 'I was a headmistress at thirty-four.'

'As if I didn't know, Lily,' chided Magsie. 'Anyway, I think you look beautiful in that lovely dress. But those square shoulders look as if they've been made for a big footballer. Never mind, I'll soon put that right.'

'I can't tell you how grateful I am to you for looking after it for me,' Lily said. 'Savannah will just love it, I know!'

The joy faded from Magsie's face. *Now is the moment to say what has to be said. Now!* 'There's something I've got to tell you,' she said, fixing Lily with her wise eyes. 'Savannah, I'm sorry to say, is not what you – '

'Oh Magsie,' Lily interrupted. '*Please* don't spoil things! Savannah's voice is even beginning to sound like mine and she's actually changing her handwriting to look like mine! I'm thrilled with the way she's developing.'

It was an incontrovertible fact that Lily was the sister Magsie had never had. Her heart swelled with the weight of love for her dearest friend, this surrogate younger sister, and her resolve cracked like an eggshell and she said nothing.

Lily broke the silence.

'You're a star, Magsie,' she murmured enigmatically, 'a real star.'

Later, much later, when it was too late, Magsie would learn – or more accurately, suffer – the terrible consequences of her silence.

# CHAPTER 7

Over the past five years, every other Tuesday afternoon during the school term, all three members of the unofficial core committee of The Bees met for lunch at San Lorenzo, the long-standing trendy restaurant on Beauchamp Place. Annabelle Arlington was English, the other two were New Yorkers, ex-pats living like adult orphans, without the advantages and disadvantages of an extended family. So, as resourceful as only New Yorkers can be, they turned themselves into a close and trusting unit, closer and probably more trusting and certainly less fraught than relationships bonded by blood.

They had met when their children were no more than toddlers, and became friends because they'd all been successful career women who were now professional mothers by choice. None of them experienced a moment of regret at having left high-powered careers, and all were grateful to the school for providing an acceptable outlet for their considerable skills. It was no exaggeration to say that some parents at Belgrave Hall saw their daughters as by-products of their own ambition, a priceless badge of entry to this vibrant school community of powerful connections. Working for the good of Belgrave Hall was not only a means of shedding their heavy burden of anonymity, but also served to justify their privileged lives by giving to those who were less fortunate.

Like her mother and grandmother, Annabelle was a Belgrave Hall old girl. Though her family lived in their ancestral home less than an hour out of London, on those rare occasions when she was invited, usually to lunch, her parents would invariably make her sign their visitors' book; so effectively she was without the support of an extended family. She gladly embraced the friendship of the two Americans, who shamelessly relied on her to guide them through the maze of bewildering British customs, such the meaning of the Honourable title, wearing hats to weddings, not bragging about your kids, not looking pushy or as if you are trying too hard, and the standard absence of introductions at parties.

Though inclined to be shy, Annabelle nevertheless taught them how to accept expecting nothing from those bewildering titled mothers of the inherited aristocracy, who deliberately dressed down and who believed that allowing their titles to appear on The Bees' letterheads more than made up for the work they left to the lower orders to do for them. Since Annabelle qualified as one of their own, it was she who extracted the major gifts for the auction. So far she'd garnered firm offers of a shoot in the wilds of Scotland (where valuable business connections were unavoidable), tickets to the Royal Enclosure at Ascot, including lunch with one of the lesser Royals on Ladies' Day, and a week's fishing from Lord Kilmarny on Loch Erne. She was still anxiously awaiting confirmation of two seats in the Royal Box for the Wimbledon final. The Americans would bid fast and furiously for that particular privilege, and so it was bound to reach an astronomic figure.

It was four days since they had met at the collagen specialist and their identical puffed lips further strengthened their bond. Right now their skills were heavily concentrated on organizing the Daffodil Ball – in aid of Jabulani – which was to be held at the Dorchester. There were only six weeks to go so, as Annabelle put it, 'things were getting a trifle hectic'. They made much of the fact that by happy coincidence all three were in their thirtieth year when they met, the Chinese year of the dog, and attributed their harmonious relationship to that. If there is any accuracy to the Chinese horoscope's precept that personality traits are determined by the year of birth, then this group would be classified as Crusaders. With their shared positive characteristics of diligence, honesty and devotion, and the negative qualities of self-righteousness and tactlessness, they were, as they often liked to say, ample testimony to its validity.

Since all their daughters sang well enough to be included in the choir which was to sing *We are the Children of the World* at the champagne reception preceding the ball, there would not be even a glimmer of competition to disrupt their long-standing, generally harmonious relationship.

Verine Joseph, a former journalist, was in charge of the ball's public relations. She was fresh-faced, healthy and outgoing with a glowing sense of humour and endless energy and Lily saw her as a typical all-American determined to be considered an inspired hostess, a connoisseur rather than a mere power-spender, a committed mother, and an ideal wife.

Courtney Hunt often looked as if she were blushing, her face scrubbed clean and her hair usually still damp after her mandatory twice daily visit to the gym. A former corporate lawyer relentlessly scaling the social ladder and much given to name-dropping, Courtney had still not forgiven Lily for having refused to back Tiffany's application to St. Paul's. Lacking most social skills except for self-confidence, Courtney was convinced that she knew what 'made people tick'. Speculating on the private life of Lily Lidbury had become one of her more irritating habits. Like all congenital gossips, she was endowed with an overdeveloped sense of curiosity. Not surprisingly the table seating plans fell under her jurisdiction.

Verine and her husband Edward were a gregarious and confident couple who shared the same athletic good looks which made them seem like siblings. They openly and courageously admitted that their lives centred on the school, and confessed that they dreaded the day when their daughter, Olivia, would leave Belgrave Hall and go to senior school. They both believed that Belgrave Hall gave them a sense of belonging, as well as a sense of commitment, and they looked forward to every school event from sports day to the carol concert the way some others look forward to a Buckingham Palace garden party. Verine brought her Hermès notebook to their Tuesday meetings; the decor of the ball was entrusted to her. The other two relied on their BlackBerries.

'Did you happen to notice Savannah Anderson at the Princess Margaret Ballet Day?' Courtney asked.

'Sure, I saw her,' Verine drawled softly, in that deep Southern accent the English found so sexy. 'But I hardly noticed the kid. I was too busy looking at Lily. That vintage cobalt-blue suit of hers is to die for.'

'She has tremendous style,' Annabel said. 'Fabulous *posture*. She carries herself like a model.'

'I hear she gets all her vintage things at Steinberg and Tolkien on the King's Road,' Courtney said. 'Expensive – I wonder how she – '

'No she doesn't,' Annabel interrupted. 'Lily gets her things at the Hospice charity shops.'

'I guess I forgot that vintage is another word for second hand,' Courtney said with a sly grin.

'But Courtney, you haven't said what was so special about Savannah at the Ballet Day,' Verine said.

'She was handing out the ballet programmes!' Courtney replied. 'Favouring Savannah again. It's always a girl from Y6 who gets that honour! And instead of the usual tradition of having one of the finalists present the bouquets to the judges, she chose Savannah! I don't know what she sees in that girl, do you?' Without waiting for a reply, she rushed on, 'Lily's looking very good lately, sort of glowing.'

'She's always been very attractive,' Anabelle said.

'I don't care what you say, there's got to be a man in the background – she's too attractive to live like a nun!' Courtney insisted. 'She's too secretive. We don't even really know where she gets her clothes from.'

Annabelle flushed. Courtney never loses an opportunity to knock Lily, she thought irritably. And yet she knows about the bursary Lily arranged for Laura when the Bedfords had money problems, and she knows how she got Bill Edwards to go to AA. But since Lily declined the Hunts' cheque for those front pews, Courtney's been engaged in some kind of one-way feud with her. 'I *do* wish you wouldn't go on about Lily the way you do,' she said.

'How can you trust a woman as secretive as Lily?' Courtney persisted.

'I think we should get down to the business of the ball,' Verine said. 'So far, everything seems to be going swimmingly.'

Courtney immediately reported the positive responses from *Hello!* and *Tatler,* whose editors had considered the guest list sufficiently star-studded to merit mention and would even send a photographer or two. Verine had assembled a team who, faithful to the concept of daffodils as the school emblem, would convert the ballroom into a simulated meadow of daffodils. The Bees' energetic effort selling tickets had paid off – they were practically sold out, Verine reported. 'Stelios Tsakiraki,' she went on triumphantly, 'has invited ten couples as his guests and has actually bought two whole tables.'

'There is something so creepy about that man,' Courtney said with a shudder. 'Even his smile is phoney.'

'He's a real misogynist,' agreed Annabelle.

'He's asked to sit next to Lily,' Verine grinned. 'I told him she'd be delighted.'

'Was it his request or your suggestion, Verine?' Courtney asked, her voice sharp.

'He's on his own, she's on her own and two singles make a couple,' Verine giggled.

'So it *was* your idea,' Courtney snapped.

'What's got into you, Courtney?' Verine asked, puzzled. 'Lily hasn't been to a dance for years – it will be just great for her to have a partner. The school's taken over her entire life, and it's not healthy for her to be so focused on the school and the girls.'

'But the school *is* her life,' Annabelle said in a firm but kindly tone.

'Well, lots of fathers find her very attractive, probably because she's so enigmatic and professional. Personally, I think they're all petrified of her,' Verine laughed.

'I wouldn't be at all shocked if she surprised all of us,' Courtney paused to pluck at the Medusa button on Verine's jacket. 'Versace,' she murmured, caressing her own Gucci cashmere suit. 'Women like Lily have lots of secrets,' she went on. 'Take it from me, I've seen it all before and I'm never wrong.' She thumped the table so hard the cups clattered in their saucers. 'She's having an affair with a married man!'

'That's ridiculous,' Verine objected, switching off her smile. 'She despises women who break up marriages. She calls them praying mantises.'

'Greek men don't see women as threatening,' Courtney pronounced. 'Stelios Tsakiraki is *not* married. He'll definitely enjoy trying to seduce her.'

Annabelle turned on her furiously, her delicate face blotched with anger. 'Well, he won't have a chance in hell with Lily!' she exploded. 'You're never short of a negative opinion on Lily, are you, Courtney Hunt?'

At that moment she answered her mobile phone, and the others thankfully turned to the tricky question of who to invite to the give the main address – Lily, the headmistress, or Lady Violet.

# CHAPTER 8

Lily's reluctance to reach her rendezvous with Benton did nothing to slow down the clicking of her high heels as she wove her path through the dark slashing rain. It seemed to beat upon her heart, as she made her way to 515 Sloane Street that late winter's afternoon. She resented the irresistible force riding roughshod over her resolve either to cancel their meeting or simply not turn up. Normally fully in command, she was furious with herself for allowing the cravings of her body to dominate the demands of her mind. Though she ached for him with all her being, she was ashamed of imagining what it would be like to touch him again. But she held her head high as she strode past the Royal Court Theatre, glancing only briefly at the people sheltering under the awning, eating and smoking at Oriel's pavement tables.

What was she doing? She could easily turn back but something stronger than her doubts was pulling her on, and she could not shake her mind loose of it. Not far to go now, but how could she do this? She knew it was an absurdly dangerous situation to find herself in. Above all, it was wrong. And she was so ready to criticize morally indefensible behaviour in others. Maybe this was God's way of teaching her a brutal lesson. She was just like the rest. She was no better than Jane Kale.

The harsh exterior of 515 jarred. It seemed to her to subtract from the quiet elegance of Sloane Street, where she sometimes liked to window shop. She pressed button number twelve. The answering buzzer squealed, and she found she had to push hard against the heavy door before it opened. She took the stairs to the third floor; there was a greater chance of meeting someone who knew her in the lift than on the staircase.

Even as she stood lingering in Benton's delicious kissing, she could not help thinking how preposterous it was that she was here in this pretty flat, in this vast, restful living room – which clearly was some stranger's much-loved home – purely for the purpose of going to bed with another woman's husband.

'Well,' he said, when they drew apart. 'What do you think?'

'It's not what I expected.'

'What *did* you expect?'

'I don't know what I expected,' she laughed, embarrassed. 'But this is quite charming.'

'It was the first apartment the realtor showed me, and I took it at once,' he said, pouring the champagne he'd opened before she arrived. 'The bedroom's something else.' He handed her a glass, 'To us,' he said, raising his glass. 'The owner knocked out walls and converted four rooms into two.' He took her hand, 'Come see the bedroom.'

'It's positively huge,' she laughed. 'And so pretty. It looks as if it belongs to a romantic woman in her early thirties.'

'You got it!' he exclaimed. 'That's exactly what the realtor told me.'

Equally as large as the drawing room, it was far and away the most feminine bedroom she had ever been in. A glamorous four poster bed, draped in deep fuchsia French brocade, stood at the far end of the room. The covers had already been turned back – no doubt by Benton – and the pink bed linen was crisp and freshly made up. The walls covered with small delicate pink roses matched the curtains, and gave the room the old-fashioned look of a country house. Light years away from everything she had ever known, it was all part of the magnificent unreality of having an affair.

As always he released her hair from its restraining velvet bow and very soon they were naked and making love. And yet, though her body ardently participated, it did not entirely succeed in disconnecting her from the quarrel of clashing questions warring in her disapproving brain. Because she should not have been there, in that flamboyantly feminine bedroom, between sensuous cotton sheets with another woman's husband. Then suddenly, and mercifully, though astoundingly, her body's chemistry took charge and the rest of her world fell away.

A screaming electronic alarm jolted them both awake.

Snatching it up, Benton switched it off. 'I set it before you arrived,' he apologized. 'What a *murderous* sound!'

'What's the time?' she asked dreamily.

'*Shit*! It's only 6:30; I meant to set it for 7:30. I've got a major dinner at the Ivy tonight and I figured 7:30 would leave me time for a shower and a chat,' he scowled. 'What a fucking idiot I am.'

'What a perfectly dreadful expression, Benton,' she said. 'I can tell I'll have to re-educate you and teach you a wider, more interesting vocabulary.' A smile lit her face, 'But I must admit your sort of vocabulary sounds much better with an American accent.'

And then, as if she had said something excruciatingly funny, they doubled up with the kind of laughter that can only flow from the deepest sensual satisfaction.

Another contented silence fell, and he dropped a tender, thoughtful kiss on her high forehead.

'I certainly hope Jodi won't do the same kind of number she did the last time we dined with a major client.' He shook his head and ran his tongue in agitation over his lip. 'She went on and on about the mysticism and serenity of the East. Here they were, typical big-time city types with matching wives, and she starts giving them all this embarrassing kind of crap that there can be no joy without sorrow.' He shook his head angrily, 'But when she said she'd embarked on a long search for the golden keys to unlock her spiritual gates – ' he paused, and gave a irritated shrug. 'What do you make of that?'

'They might well have found Jodi refreshingly different,' she said, careful to be neutral, and determined not to allow a single negative word about Jodi to escape her lips.

A thin laugh came from his throat. 'Sure it was different, Lily-bud, but there was nothing fucking *refreshing* about it!' He'd cringed with embarrassment, and so had his clients. In case it hadn't been bad enough watching them flash horrified glances at one another, he'd had to endure the expression of evangelical ecstasy on her face like a nun in a movie experiencing a divine vision. This had never been her style, he asserted. If ever there was a pragmatic realist, it was Jodi Witley Anderson.

Changing the subject, Benton traced the outline of Lily's lips with his finger and said, 'I've got a set of keys to this apartment for you, Lily-bud. It's ours for three whole months. I've rented it until the end of June.' He rumpled her hair. 'I'll go take a quick shower.'

By the time he returned, Lily was in her robe and making the bed. He drew her to him, wrapped her tight in his arms and told her that they didn't need to make the bed because the apartment came with daily fresh linen and maid service. He'd meant to show her round the place, the state-of-the-art music system especially, but then he hadn't meant to fall asleep either, so he hoped she would look around before she left. She had the keys now, and could come and go as she pleased. He'd had a whole lot of fun, buying things for their time together; he'd put stuff in the fridge, and though as a rule he hated shopping, he'd loved every second of it.

Benton hadn't exaggerated when he said he'd bought a 'whole lot of stuff'. The under-counter chrome fridge was crammed with champagne and white wine, out-of-season strawberries, peaches and even the cherry tomatoes to which she'd said she was addicted; smoked salmon, Gruyère, and huge jars of plump green olives had been neatly placed on the shelves. The freezer was stocked with tubs of her favourite vanilla and chocolate ice cream. An inspection of the chrome cupboards lining the walls revealed that he'd remembered her weakness for Japanese crackers and had thought of everything – from potato crisps to cereals and Japanese crackers and cashew nuts. The cupboards told her that he'd gone as far as to shop where she shopped, and had dropped in on Charles of Belgravia for luscious out-of-season peaches, Jeroboams for natural cheddar, and the French *boulangerie* Poilâne for croissants.

Lily felt as if she were suspended above the real world, where right or wrong didn't exist. Distinctly at odds with her own frugal material needs, the extravagance which seemed to come naturally to him was so flattering to her, that she did not feel quite herself, as if while she was with him or thinking of him, she was a fictitious Lily who found herself doing the sort of things she never would have dreamed of contemplating. And so here she was in this fairy-tale flat, wearing nothing but a cream silk robe, carrying a pack of Japanese crackers and her glass of unfinished champagne to a pretty bedroom, and climbing back into a sensational bed simply for the fun of it. She felt deliciously wicked, lying on the bed, sipping champagne, with nothing to do, without comprehension tests to mark, lessons to prepare, or reports to write. She was blissfully free to reassure herself that she would break it off at the end of term when she would go to Jabulani in the summer. For a few precious moments her guilty conscience was on hold. It was a treat she allowed herself – like bingeing on chocolate and forgetting about calories.

In the manner of such things, within only a few meetings a settled pattern evolved – she would arrive before him and stay on after he had left. She would bring nibbles from Harrods food hall, but they would always gravitate to the bedroom and never once sat in the living room. As soon as she arrived, she would slip into her robe, and on rare occasions when he was there before her, she would find him in his robe. Their joint secret, separate life seemed to require a different way of dressing – without all the outer trapping of undergarments, with nothing other than the sensual silk of a loose robe to come between them and their own hungry bodies.

One Thursday afternoon, watching the snow gently falling against the wide window, she was aghast to hear herself question whether he made a habit of this kind of thing.

He lay beside her, propped on one elbow. 'What sort of thing?' he asked.

'Affairs.'

'If you're asking me if I've been faithful, the answer is no,' he said with one of his mischievous smiles. 'But a real full-blown affair? Again the answer is no. This is a first for me. Does that surprise you?'

'I honestly don't know.'

'To tell the truth, I never even wanted to have anything as complicated as an affair. But in my world it would have been considered kind of weird if I hadn't done the odd bit of fooling around.'

'Do you think Jodi knew?'

'Of course she didn't! She didn't even give it a thought – '

'You sound very sure of yourself, I must say.'

'That's because there never was any doubt in Jodi's mind that my career was any less important to me, than hers was to her. For one thing that meant that there was no actual physical time to have an affair. Which is why there was a time she used to set the alarm at dawn on Friday mornings so we could make love.'

'How *very* organized!' she laughed.

'I guess sex was never a major priority for either one of us,' he went on thoughtfully. 'Even at the beginning, even before we were married, it was never a big thing, sort of necessary, but not vital.' His free hand caressed the nape of her neck. 'As a matter of fact, Lily-bud,' he continued, 'she'd had lots of guys in her life before me with whom – to quote her words exactly – she went to bed frequently and with frigid intensity!' His eyes lighted into a winning grin. 'No satisfaction in it for her. She said it wasn't like that for us. But back then she was trying to behave as crudely as most of the men she had known.'

'How sad,' she said. 'The very definition of uncreative sex.'

'True,' he said, 'though I've never thought of it in those terms.' He spread out his hand, 'Don't forget, I was forty-one when we married. I'd sowed my wild oats by then. Screwed my brains out.' He looked at her quizzically. 'But you? What happened in your life?'

'I was nineteen when we married. My husband was thirty-seven. But he was the first and only man in my life. Until – ' she broke off.

'Until?'

'Until you,' she said.

'Until me? You've got to be kidding!'

'Well yes, perhaps I am,' she said with an embarrassed laugh.

'What was he like? I'm curious about what sort of guy you married.'

'When I married him I thought he was the kindest man I'd ever known. Deeply dedicated to medicine, an excellent doctor, and I met and married him the year I won the Nurse of the Year gold medal.'

Every word is the truth, yet it is all a lie. Now is the time to tell him about Amanda, about what happened to her. But he doesn't even know I had a daughter. Now is the time to tell him everything. I've been waiting for the right moment, this is the right moment.

Instead, she heard herself ask, 'Have you been to bed with Jodi since you and I got together?'

'Yes,' he said shortly. 'But I pretended it was you. Do you mind?'

'How can I?' she protested. 'I've got no right to mind!' *But I do mind*, she thought, *I mind terribly.*

'I guess I'd better tell you how it happened?'

Her curiosity overcame her, and she nodded in spite of herself.

'I was in bed watching the news, getting madder and madder at the way Jeremy Paxman was haranguing Gordon Brown, when Jodi came in, switched off the TV, and said she'd something important to tell me. She said that she was embarking on a

course of purification for thirty days. No food until the evening –
nothing but water during the day, complete celibacy for one
month. The next moment, in the same breath, she suddenly
dropped her robe. She had nothing on – absolutely naked. Not at
all like her. She was brazen – kind of mocking, like taunting.' He
sounded puzzled. 'I responded not out of desire, but because . . .
well, because I had to prove that I wasn't impotent.' He looked at
Lily anxiously, hoping she would accept this explanation.

'That's one problem we women do not have,' she chuckled.
'I read somewhere that there is no female equivalent in any
language for virility – not that you have any problems in that
area,' she added. 'Anyway, how long has Jodi been a yoga
enthusiast?'

'The yoga bug hit her about six weeks back, I guess.'

'Nothing like the zeal of a new convert – '

'Couldn't have come at a better time for me.' He corrected
himself, 'For *us.*'

An easy silence fell, much to Benton's relief. After a while, he
said, 'A girl of nineteen with a guy eighteen years older – ' A
small grimace of distaste crossed his features. 'Were you happy
with him?'

'I worshipped him.'

'Doesn't mean you were happy.'

'*I* thought I was – ' Afraid she might say too much, Lily
stopped short. Besides, she didn't like the way the conversation
was tending.

'I guess he was a kind of father figure.' He sat up suddenly.
'Was he good in bed?'

'I don't honestly think I knew what that meant until you
taught me.'

'The funny thing is I believe you.'

'You got it right, Benton. In some ways he was a father figure
to me,' she said slowly. 'I couldn't really let myself go – '

'But you let yourself go with me, don't you?' he whispered, his
hand slowly travelling from her neck to her breast.

Then he locked his mouth on hers, and soon the silky insistence of their bodies' rhythms took over, and for a blissful moment, all memory – and all guilt – evaporated.

She could never afterwards understand how she could have revealed some of her innermost secrets to him, and yet hold silent as the grave about Amanda. The right moment had been given to her, and she had squandered it again. It made no sense to her.

# CHAPTER 9

When Jodi awoke, the dream was still heavy inside her, as disturbing as a foetus. She lay quietly in their London bed, with Benton beside her, recalling or, rather, re-living the dream. She did not want it to leave her, just as once – as she now realized – she had not wanted to let Savannah leave her either, afraid that when her unborn child spurned her womb, she would be bereft. And yes, as it turned out, Savannah's birth *had* left her unforgivably and unnaturally grief-stricken, which was probably responsible for that terrible post-partum depression she had gone through. And yet it was only now, thanks no doubt to her yoga-inspired insights, that she had at last come to understand what ought to have been obvious to her doctors – that *she had never wanted her pregnancy to come to an end.* All of which had eluded the team of medical experts who'd descended on her as if she were a specimen in a Petri dish on which they could test their pet theories on brain chemistry.

She lay completely still, watching Benton asleep. Suddenly, taking herself by surprise, she bent over and fleetingly kissed the touching lock of white hair sprawling across his forehead. That he was wearing his beloved navy-blue and white striped silk pyjamas made by Gieves and Hawkes, who were, as he would be quick to say, shirt-makers to Prince Charles, made her smile. A sensation of peace drifted over her, and she left their bed gently, so as not to disturb him. When the shower, another of those lacklustre British products, yielded its irritatingly slow trickle, but failed to provoke even the smallest ripple of annoyance in her, she smiled to herself again. She was getting on top of her intolerance of everything British.

But instead of sprinting down to the state-of-the-art gym in the basement and its array of slimming chrome instruments, which now reminded her of a sophisticated torture chamber, she made her leisurely way to the sparsely furnished attic storeroom she'd taken to calling her 'meditation space'. It was six weeks since she'd been skilfully introduced to the gentle art of meditation. She was still amazed at how easily, even willingly, she had been able to suspend and empty her mind of all thought for a protracted period of time. She had never for one moment realized that she had been carrying the wound of loneliness all her life, but now that she had come to believe, as Bandrika had taught her, that loneliness is the opposite of aloneness, she was no longer lonesome.

An hour later, when she joined Benton and Savannah in the kitchen, Opi was serving breakfast. She found this ordinary domestic scene surprisingly moving. It was then, strengthened by the air of contentment flowing among them, that she decided to schedule a meeting with Savannah's headmistress.

On March 15th, the morning of the school birthday, it was as if summer had arrived early. Bright white daffodils, the school flower, were everywhere, and in such abundance that you could not help smiling. Thousands of white daffodils festooned a huge arch as you entered what had once been the large, bleak school hall. Soft grey evergreen branches provided a natural framework to which The Bees had added arbours and pots to create focal points. It was like a wilderness, under tight control. Mirrors had been placed in strategic positions to reflect the arbour from all corners of the room. Flowing in glorious profusion, the white blooms were a perfect expression of restrained English exuberance.

The scent was sweet and fresh and invigorating. Daffodils were in every office and every classroom. Girls wore small bunches on their chests, in their hair, some plaited, others with coronets. Even the staff wore the flowers. The tradition of wearing daffodils to celebrate the school's birthday had begun almost 130 years earlier, when Belgrave Hall had celebrated its first birthday. The headmistress, a fierce and gifted teacher, had chosen the daffodil as the school emblem not only because it was her favourite flower, but because its simplicity seemed to symbolize the girls' innocence.

Lily was putting the finishing touches to a huge vase of daffodils standing in the centre of the table in her study. She was quite startled when her internal phone rang . . . It was Miss Trubshaw, asking her to check her diary – a parent needed an urgent appointment. No, Lily told her, today was totally impossible – she would see nobody on the school birthday. Exceptionally, however, she had agreed to see Jemima Stark's parents who would be with her in a few minutes. The Starks had a problem finding the money for the school fees, and she was hoping to ask one of the banker parents to help out. 'Could you let the parent know I'd like to see her tomorrow morning?' she asked.

'Eight o'clock, as usual?

'Eight o'clock,' Lily chuckled. 'Who is the parent?'

'Jodi Anderson.'

Lily shuddered and she rang off. Frantic to find out if Benton knew why Jodi wanted to see her, she called him at once. (She was never to know quite how she'd got through that interview with the Starks, but would remember, later, to ask Benton if he would help.)

Unable to reach him, she carried her mobile into the church and only switched it off after the birthday thanksgiving service began. Light-headed and now dizzy with panic, she longed to rest her throbbing head against the pew in front of her. *Why did Jodi want to see her?* Gripped by an uncontrollable fear, she had to force herself not only to remain in her seat, but appear to be following the service. She glanced around the church and smiled and nodded, but scarcely took in anything of Father Milton's address, or the words of the guest speaker, Dame Tessa Aldington, a Belgrave Hall old girl, or even Katie's inspiring performance of Viotti. And though she saw Savannah's vicious movements as she wrenched the daffodils from her hair on hearing the first sublime notes, and then stripped them of their petals, not even this could distance her from the anguish of knowing that she was on the terrifying brink of her own catastrophe.

The service ended and there was a buzz of excited whispering and pushing as the girls filed out of the church to be given their traditional birthday bun. Once in her study, she immediately called him again, and left yet another message. Because school ended earlier than usual on the school birthday, the afternoon was overloaded with meetings.

Several times during those long, tedious and in the main useless meetings, she compulsively punched the redial button of her mobile phone. The phone rang and rang, and even though the phone was on automatic dial, she would not disconnect until she heard 'This is the voice mail of 08101-742-55' – just in case she'd dialled the wrong number. At the same time, she toyed with the idea of claiming a headache and cancelling the traditional school birthday dinner with Magsie. But she simply had neither the nerve nor the heart to let her down. Over these past fifteen years she and Magsie had fallen into the habit of dining on *pot-au-feu* and red wine, Rioja Marques de Romeral, on the night of the school's birthday.

Fifteen minutes before she was expected, she had a real and raging headache. Who could blame her if she cancelled? She picked up the phone and dialled Magsie's number. 'Magsie?' she began tentatively.

'Dinner is almost ready, ' Magsie responded enthusiastically. 'See you in five minutes.'

'That's what I was calling you about,' Lily said. Her resolve fell away. 'I may be a few minutes late.'

'It won't spoil,' Magsie replied. 'Come when you can.'

So Lily took two paracetamol, covered her eyes with lint saturated in a cooling cucumber lotion, and flung herself across her bed.

Ten minutes later, as she entered the kitchen, the scent of cloves, cabbage and leeks filled her nostrils. Magsie had set the table with a white linen cloth and had already poured the wine into the sturdily stemmed balloon glasses. She bustled about happily, and served her *pot-au-feu*, which was pronounced delicious. Soon Lily's headache began to lift, and she felt a bit better. Every now and then, she hit the redial button, waited for the answer phone message and clicked off. About the third time this happened, Magsie asked if it was anything urgent.

'These people got me to promise I'd call them tonight, and they're not even there,' she lied.

'People are so inconsiderate,' Magsie said sympathetically. It would never have occurred to her to doubt anything Lily said.

'Sorry, Magsie, I'll just have to keep trying,' Lily apologized. 'I'll give it a rest for a few minutes, and try again.'

'I'm afraid, Lily, I have something important to tell you,' Magsie said portentously. 'It's about Savannah. It's something I wish I didn't have to tell you. It happened in church this morning.'

'Sorry to interrupt you, Magsie,' Lily said, rising from her chair with an apologetic smile. 'I must go to the loo – will you excuse me for one moment?'

She left the kitchen in a rush. Thank goodness her mobile phone was in her pocket. The moment she reached the bathroom, she turned on both taps to drown out the sound and tried Benton's number again and got the answer service. Washing her hands hurriedly, she caught a glimpse of herself in the mirror and, flinching at the sight of her anguished eyes, quickly turned away. She dreaded the thought of meeting Jodi tomorrow, and it showed.

'Are you feeling all right, Lily?' Magsie asked anxiously. She had recently been through the menopause, and thought Lily might be just at the beginning of it. 'You look a bit flushed to me.'

'I feel fine, thank you,' Lily replied rather too heartily. 'You were telling me about Savannah – '

'You know where I sit in church, don't you? It's beside – '

'Of course I know where it is, Magsie,' Lily interrupted. 'You sit in it at every school function!'

'Savannah was sitting in the next row which meant she was directly in my line of vision, so I couldn't help watching her any more than I could help seeing her ripping, and then destroying, every single daffodil that had been so lovingly plaited into her hair!' She paused, thrust her face deep into her hands for a moment, and continued, 'Then, during Katie's prolonged applause, she shut her eyes and pulled her thick plaits over her ears to block out the sound.' A spasm of disgust crossed her face, 'I watched her shred every single petal. She must have felt me watching her for she suddenly looked up, and stared at me. It was not her eyes which made my stomach burn – they were as unreadable as ever – but her smile,' she shuddered visibly. 'I wish I could forget it, I wish I'd never seen that smile, that false smile – ' Her voice dropped. 'I can't get that smile out of my mind.'

'You are making far too much of an issue over a smile, Magsie,' said Lily, her tone acid.

Magsie leaned forward and grasped Lily's wrist so tightly that her watchstrap bit into her flesh. 'That kind of smile could make an atheist believe in the devil,' she muttered.

'You've never liked her, have you, Magsie?' Lily asked rhetorically, but angrily. 'You took against her from the moment you saw her – '

'I wouldn't say that,' Magsie cut in feverishly.

'But Magsie, you *know* you did,' Lily said tartly. 'You're not as objective as you think you are,' she continued implacably, 'you don't like the child, and that's a fact. You never forgave her for the way she played with that damn hamster – what *was* his name? I'm simply too agitated to remember.'

'Bertie.'

'Bertie,' Lily repeated. 'Anyway, you didn't really allow yourself to get to know her, did you?'

'I wouldn't say that.'

'Personally, Magsie, I think you're being very unfair. Savannah may have her faults; she's only a child, no different from anyone else. You really do have a bee in your bonnet about Americans – you know you have! She has as much right to be at Belgrave Hall as anyone else. In fact she, more than most, needs our understanding and care. She arrived here feeling terribly isolated, having had to leave her wonderful nanny who was really a mother to her. She must have felt totally rejected by her own mother whose main concern was herself and her career.'

'But Lily, the child is deeply troubled – you can see that much, surely?'

'Of course I can, but it's nothing we can't handle – this type of situation is one of our strengths. With love and kindly discipline we could make all the difference to her life and her attitude. She must be crying inside and very angry and bewildered because of the way her own mother rejected her. Our pastoral care is recognized as much as our high academic standards – you are the last person I thought I would have to appeal to for sympathy and understanding.' Lily pulled in her cheeks and then blew a deep breath as if she were recovering from a blow, and went on, 'I'm sure that Savannah senses your dislike of her, and this will certainly not help her to overcome her problems.'

*In all our years together*, Magsie thought, *this is probably the most important talk Lily and I will ever have*. 'If I hadn't sensed that she was a deeply anguished child, I would have made an example of her – as I would of anyone else – and told her to pick up every shredded petal at the end of the service.'

'That kind of sensitivity is so very typical of you, Magsie,' Lily said with great feeling. 'You've always been the first to recognize when children are really sad. But if you'd allow yourself to see her for what she really is, you'd see that underneath her hard exterior is someone who is loving, and extremely vulnerable.' She leaned forward again, but this time only rested her fingers for a second on Magsie's arm. 'I've seen her for what she really is, and now whenever I'm with her, I feel – ' Her voice trailed off.

Magsie stared at her. There was something oddly different about her expression – a mysterious air, one that she couldn't quite decipher. Uncertain of what to say, she said nothing.

Lily closed her eyes. 'Savannah gives me something, Magsie.' She opened her eyes, and partly pleading, partly triumphant, said, 'She has reunited me with my soul.' She picked up her mobile phone and, murmuring that her head was killing her, held it to her forehead as if it were a cold compress.

Magsie sprang to her feet. 'You'd best take two paracetamol – I've got this bottle right here.'

'I took two just before I came down to you.'

'You should have cancelled,' Magsie said.

'I wanted to see you.'

'Let me help you upstairs. You ought to go straight to bed,' Magsie ordered. 'I'll put you to bed myself.'

'You don't need to put me to bed,' Lily laughed faintly.

'I'll just take you upstairs then,' Magsie insisted.

Partly because she knew she had little choice, but mainly because she was frantic to try to reach Benton again, Lily capitulated and allowed Magsie to see her home.

Although she had given up any real hope of reaching him, she hit the redial button the instant Magsie left. All the same, when she heard his answer service respond, she almost wept with disappointment. She undressed quickly, and put on a comforting pair of warm, fleecy pyjamas and went to bed. Her mind slipped from its agonizing speculations on the purpose of Jodi's impending appointment to Magsie's annoying outburst. It had been hard not to be rude to her, and, were it not for the respect and affection she felt for the only woman who had her unequivocal trust, she would not have been able to control her temper. If it was true that Magsie was her eyes and ears, it was also true that, as she herself had admitted, she had an unfortunate tendency to 'take against' someone for no identifiable reason. This had already happened with nervous, fussy Miss

Trubshaw whom Magsie had disliked on sight, and with the athletic, masculine gym-mistress, Miss Hodkin. She'd been right about Miss Hodkin, who terrified the children, and wrong about Miss Trubshaw, who was an excellent secretary. She'd had an unerring instinct for spotting bullies, and children who were secretively facing horrendous and heartbreaking family difficulties, but she was not only wrong about Savannah but way out of order as well. Why, it was almost as if Magsie was jealous of her affection for Savannah.

There was only one way not to think about this, and that was to take a sleeping pill. Then she remembered that she had thrown out the few she had because they had gone well beyond their expiry date. Her headache returned, and spread to her cheeks. Deciding on a hot toddy, she made herself a pot of tea, added a dollop of honey and a double measure of Royal Salute whiskey – a Christmas present from one of the parents. She poured it into an outsize pottery mug, microwaved it for one minute and carried it, together with a pile of Year Six extended project essays, into her bedroom. She would mark the essays in bed, a practice she was much given to anyway, and sip her hot drink from time to time, and take refuge in the most effective of all therapies – her work.

For once, though, her unfailingly successful therapy was ineffectual, and she gave up even trying to concentrate. She longed to scream her anguish out loud, but instead listened to the silent sound of an inner scream echoing inside the chambers of her swirling brain where sirens now shrieked. Sleep continued to elude her. At last, desperate to obliterate all thought, she crushed three paracetamol tablets into a powder and, though the stated dose was no more than two at a time, she took all three at once, and finally fell into a troubled sleep.

Jodi had arrived early and was waiting in Lily's study when she returned from giving her English lesson, her arms loaded with the essays she would mark that evening. Apart from the odd glimpse of Jodi on those Friday half-days when she collected Savannah because Opi had that day off, Lily had not really seen her since Savannah's performance at the Form Presentation.

Lily could hardly hide her amazement at the change in her. Where was the chic, sophisticated woman she'd first met? Jodi had gone very ethnic – her tailored, mannish look had been exchanged for a long wide skirt, a matching chunky sweater and a canvas shoulder-bag in earthy shades of saffron and brown. Bangles covered her arms, large silver filigree hoops dangled from her ears but, most startling of all, her mane of red curls had vanished.

'I guess you're surprised by my change of style,' Jodi said, smiling her new enigmatic smile that so irritated Benton.

'Well, yes, you certainly do look different,' Lily replied. 'You've cut your lovely hair.'

'Benton hasn't seen it yet – I only had it cut this morning.' She wound a short lock around her finger. 'It's lighter, and much more comfortable this way.'

'It suits you,' Lily lied. 'But you can always let it grow if you want to.'

'It's kind of hippyish,' Jodi murmured. 'But it's so much simpler to dress this way.'

Wincing inwardly, because she couldn't bear the small talk, Lily changed the subject. 'We're all very satisfied with Savannah's progress,' she said with more than her usual enthusiasm. 'She's certainly adjusted very well to English life and the English academic system.'

'She just loves your school.'

*My* school, Lily noted nervously. Just what is she getting at – why is Belgrave Hall suddenly *my* school? But she said, 'It's always gratifying to hear that a child is happy at school.'

'She hated her last school,' Jodi said. 'I never did understand why – I was very happy at Spence myself.'

'Oh, yes, of course. I'd forgotten you were a Spence old girl,' Lily replied, making a great show of checking her notes, forcing herself to endure the suspense of this inane small talk for a few more moments.

'Were you happy at your school, Mrs Lidbury?'

'No,' Lily replied, distracted. Assumptions and questions hurtled through her mind. Why *Mrs* Lidbury? Weren't she and Jodi on first name terms? The whole thing was absurd – here she was, having an affair with this woman's husband, deeply knowledgeable about her most private, intimate habits and attitudes, and unable to remember whether or not they were on first name terms! It seemed safest to assume they were. 'Lily,' she said abruptly.

'Sorry?' said Jodi, mystified.

'Oh goodness,' Lily laughed nervously, feeling foolish. 'I meant, do call me Lily.'

'Lily,' Jodi smiled. 'That's a lovely name. Did you know in China the day lily is an emblem for motherhood? But to the Hindus the water lily is the symbol of the maternal womb from which the sun rises. On the other hand, Christian lore has it that the lily sprang from Eve's tears when she was expelled from the Garden of Eden and learned that she was pregnant. And then there's the Madonna lily which turned from yellow to white the day the Virgin Mary stooped to pick it up.'

'My goodness,' Lily interrupted, her patience worn thin. 'Where did you come by all this – uh – incredibly interesting information?'

'Bandrika Chatoo, my inspired and inspiring yoga teacher,' Jodi replied earnestly. 'She's given me a new perspective on my profession. Law and Justice, she believes, are not of the outside world, but of the spirit.' With much clattering of her bangles, she gathered up her shoulder bag. 'No two flames are alike,' she said, as if she were reciting a well-known principle in law. 'For example, we've just been talking about the lily as a fragrant symbol of purity, and yet the jungle lily whose bloom weighs up to a half-pound, and gets as hot as 108 degrees inside, has a stench so powerful that it could put a skunk to shame.' She stood up. 'The Sumatrans call it the voodoo lily, but it is also known as the sacred lily of India, or devil's tongue.'

This was too much for Lily. She picked up her notebook and, once again, pretended to consult it. 'According to Miss Trubshaw's notes, you have a problem. How can I help?'

'I don't know exactly how to put this,' Jodi said awkwardly. Her voice trailed off uncertainly. She seemed to lapse into a private contemplation of her own.

Lily watched her, and though her heart hammered in her ribs, she decided not to rush her.

'I feel a failure as a woman,' Jodi said.

Here comes the drama, Lily said to herself, the whole catastrophe. And I deserve it all – every syllable of it. Desperately casting about for something to say, she managed no more than a sympathetic noise.

'That's because I'm a failure as a mother,' Jodi said. 'I don't think my own child likes me.' She paused and swallowed. 'Savannah does not want to come with me to New York for the three-week Easter vacation.'

'Is that all?' A laugh of relief started in her chest, but she disguised it with a simulated fit of coughing.

'Isn't that *enough*?' Jodi returned, apparently affronted.

'My dear Jodi, you really couldn't be more wrong,' Lily said, deliberately sounding like an authoritative headmistress stating an unbreakable rule. 'The exact opposite is true – Savannah's decision to stay in London sounds quite normal to me. Indeed, it proves successful parenting – she's obviously not a neurotically clinging child, but feels secure enough to remain in London without you.'

'What you say is logical,' Jodi answered. 'But there's more to it than that.'

'You must remember that Savannah had a huge change in lifestyle only a few weeks ago. She had to leave friends, teachers and her nanny behind. She must have felt utterly bewildered by the move.'

'All that is true,' Jodi conceded. 'But her father will be at work all day and though Opi is very nice, and she and Savannah get on well, she isn't really important to Savannah in the way that Bronnie was. Even if Opi gave her all the attention in the world, it would never be enough.'

'Why on earth not?'

'Because, coming from Opi – whom she doesn't really respect – it would be worthless to her,' Jodi explained. 'You see, Bronnie knew how to control her,' she sighed. 'Savannah can be . . . difficult.' She hesitated and arranged her hands in the shape of a tent and brought the tips of her fingers to her chin. The five silver and amber bangles Lily had counted on each wrist clanged against one another.

'As I said earlier, we're very pleased with Savannah,' said Lily, hastily sorting through her papers. 'I've been working on the girls' reports and even though it is not complete, I'd like you to see my comment on Savannah.' She gave an encouraging smile and handed the report to Jodi.

> Savannah is highly focused and is determined to make up lost ground due to differing academic backgrounds. Verbally, Savannah is above average with a well-developed sense of humour which can be most entertaining when used at the appropriate time.
>
> Her academic ability is very evident in the speed with which she assimilates new ideas. Savannah has a great deal of untapped potential.

'Anyway, you'll be leaving your daughter in very good hands. You can go to New York with a happy heart – Magsie and I will be delighted to keep an eye on Savannah.'

'That's very reassuring. I feel much more comfortable about the whole thing,' Jodi said. 'Only, I have the sense that Magsie's not too crazy about Savannah.'

'But Magsie simply adores all the girls, and they adore her.'

'No two flames are ever alike,' Jodi said again.

Once again, Lily noted the profound change that had come over Jodi. As she watched, Jodi's expression shifted dramatically, her clear intelligent gaze abruptly took on an ecstatic glow, as if she had been transported to a higher plane and was hearing celestial music.

Jodi had no notion of the commotion her appointment with Lily had caused. Going to see the headmistress was, in her view, one of her better decisions. But though she had not exaggerated when she had said she felt a failure as a mother, life was not nearly as stressful as it had been before they left New York. Jodi shuddered as she remembered all those wild tantrums Savannah had put them through, and all those cruel – but true – things Bronnie had said about the kind of mother she was. But now, thanks to yoga, an inner peace was already taking root within her. Under Bandrika's gifted tutelage she was learning the art of patience, and she believed that, given time, her relationship with her daughter would take on a healthier dimension and eventually flourish into friendship.

Her maternal instinct was not strong enough to strangle her, nor weak enough to destroy her child. Though it had not inhibited her from vigorously pursuing her ambitions, it had made her take this three year pause from her successful life as a litigator, and move to London, largely because she believed it was her duty as a mother to keep the family under one roof. Of course, as she now admitted to herself, she had been smart enough and lawyerly enough in her negotiations with Benton and with Hardwick, Murphy and Ford, to arrive at a deal to continue with Louisa Stacey's defence and only return to New York for brief periods when her physical presence was essential. Paradoxically, therefore, Savannah's decision to stay in London was the perfect solution. As a good trial lawyer Jodi would neither reveal faults nor disclose details until it suited her. Accordingly, she had not mentioned that she could not have taken Savannah to New York anyway – Bronnie had let them down, and there would be no one to take care of her. Bandrika and yoga had certainly transformed Jodi's experience of 'being', but it had not diminished her guile and instinctive strategic cunning.

It was with all this in mind that she called Bronnie in New York.

'I've got two minutes flat,' Bronnie said when she heard Jodi's voice. 'I'm on my way out.'

'Savannah won't be coming with me to New York.'

'I've already told you I won't be here,' Bronnie said.

'But Savannah doesn't know that,' Jodi said, her voice level. 'I didn't tell her because I didn't want her to know that you'd be letting her down,' she went on pleasantly. 'A lie by omission I guess.' A negotiating trick sprang to her lips – she would ask Bronnie for her advice, 'Do you think I'm doing the right thing, Bronnie?'

'Sure you are,' Bronnie replied. 'Haven't I always said Savannah's extra sensitive?'


'Had a good trip, sir?' Derek, the Andersons' driver, asked. 'The weather report said it was snowing heavily in Geneva.'

'Took off exactly on time,' Benton said.

'By the way, sir, I've got your new mobile phone for you. Collected it from the bank this afternoon,' said Derek, stretching an arm over the back seat to hand the neat cardboard box to Benton. 'I gather yours got lost, sir? A cabbie told me the other day that 60,000 cell phones are left in taxis every three months or so.'

'That figures,' Benton replied, not pleased with himself for having lost his phone.

'By the way, sir, Mrs Anderson called on the car phone with a message for you. She said she won't be joining you at the Ivy tonight as she's got the opportunity of being in the presence of a very major gooroo.' His South London accent mocked the word 'guru'.

'Right,' Benton snorted.

'She said to tell you she had a major meeting with Savannah's headmistress at school today. She will discuss it with you tonight. At least I think that's what she said. I wrote it all down, I'll read it to you at the next traffic light, if you'd like me to sir?'

'Don't worry, Derek,' Benton said in a tone that signalled the end of conversation. 'I've got the gist of it – '

Following his immediate decision to call Lily, he began dialling her number, thought better of it and stopped. No matter how urgently he needed to speak to Lily he was damned if he was going to call her in front of an avid audience of one.

He waited a few moments then asked to stop at a gas station for the men's room.

'Hi, Lily-bud,' he said when he at last got through. 'What the *hell* is going on here?'

'Good evening,' Lily replied in a clipped tone to indicate that she was not alone. 'Would you hold one moment please? Forgive me, Mrs Patterson, but I'll have to take this call.' Walking briskly away from the group of parents she said, 'Sorry – PTA meeting, but I can talk now, what's – '

He did not allow her to finish, 'I've had a message from Jodi,' he cut in brutally, 'saying she had a major meeting with you this morning.'

'Who told you that?' Lily teased.

'Derek.'

'What happened to your phone? I went ballistic trying to reach you all day, and all Monday night until Tuesday morning when Jodi came to see me.'

'Why?'

'Why what? Why was I so frantic?'

'Of course not,' he replied. 'I want to know why she came to see you.'

'Savannah doesn't want to go with her to New York. She wants to spend the holiday in London.'

'That's *all* she came to see you about? To tell you Savannah is not going to New York?' His voice dropped, 'I almost had a heart attack when I heard she'd had a major meeting with you, but that she would not discuss it with me until after dinner.'

'*After* dinner?'

'She's going to listen to what Derek rightly calls a gooroo.' The plumbing flushed noisily.

'Where on earth are you, Benton?' she asked.

'In the men's room. I couldn't talk with Derek's ears flapping.'

The plumbing screamed again. 'I can hardly hear you,' she said. 'Let's talk in the morning.'

'Tomorrow will be hectic, but I'll be free between four and five,' he said. 'Could we meet at Sloane Street? This is kind of an emergency.'

'I'll be there,' she replied and switched off the phone.

The scope and strength of Benton's reaction to the news that Jodi had had a meeting with Lily had constrained him to face up to the consequences of what he was doing, of the potential damage this affair could do to him at the pinnacle of his career. His formidable talent as a negotiator had been solidly based on his infallible instinct for assessing risk, and there was clearly no way of denying that he was knowingly and, it seemed, deliberately placing his career in a precarious position. He was well satisfied with the present way he was managing his life, and if Jodi's current obsession with yoga was hugely irritating, it was also – at this phase in their marriage – hugely convenient. Lust exerts a fearsome power. Right now, in the throes of the most profound and unlikely sexual attraction of his adult life, he wanted things to stay the way they were. He wanted his affair with Lily to remain the constant hope at the centre of his life that it had so rapidly become, no more and no less than he wanted his marriage to continue. At the same time, however, he sensed that innocuous as it was, Jodi's visit with Lily had already brought about a subtle shift in the way things were.

For her part, Lily too felt that things had changed. The panic in Benton's voice had been unmistakable. He had obviously

143

concluded, when he got the message about Jodi meeting with her, that there had been some ghastly sort of confrontation. Like the seriously ill, she and Benton had turned to denial to banish reality. But Jodi's visit, or, more particularly, their reaction to it, had shocked them both into an unfortunate meeting with reality. Which meant that though it was only just short of three months since it had all begun, they were now compelled to go in to a series of 'What if' questions. What if they were found out? What would the consequences be? Lily would not only be dismissed, but would lose her home – the grace and favour apartment at the top of the school building – and the press and the parents would for ever after refer to her as the disgraced former headmistress, Lily Lidbury. And Benton – what would become of him? Would he lose his job as vice-president of Carlyle Klein? She doubted it. Bankers were no more supposed to excmplify human decency than they were expected to be paragons of virtue like a headmistress or a priest. But whatever the effect of the scandal on her relationship with Benton might be, it was important only in so far as it would affect Savannah.

*Savannah* – this magical child, of whom she could never see enough. This beautiful child, with the distant sea-green eyes, framed by russet lashes, set in a perfectly shaped face, augmented by high cheekbones, and made even lovelier by a dazzlingly persuasive smile, and who'd come into her life like a sense of summer.

But then, it seemed she could never see enough of Benton, either.

In these new circumstances, not surprisingly, they both arrived at 515 Sloane Street at exactly the same time the next afternoon. By now Benton had discovered the back entrance in Pavilion Road, so they entered the building through different doors, but reached the front door of their flat simultaneously. For the first time ever, as if to symbolize the change that had come over them, they did not immediately undress and slip into their cream silk robes and head for the bedroom. Instead they lit the lamps against the rain-darkened afternoon, and actually sat in the vast, cheerful yellow drawing room, sipping their usual Montrachet. It was a relief to discuss the fear that had seized them because she'd believed a confrontation was in the offing, and because he'd been certain that one had already taken place.

They sat across from one another in comfortable sun-yellow armchairs, like any ordinary, busy couple who had dedicated an hour of their time to debate a major domestic decision, such as buying or selling their house, or acquiring a new car. In the end they concluded that because Jodi would soon be in New York, they would make the most of this unexpected gift of time without her.

'I can't get over what you've done for Savannah,' Benton said. 'When I think of the time you told me she was self-mutilating,' he added with a shudder, 'well, I'm just so grateful to you, Lily-bud!'

'She is a happy child,' Lily agreed. 'And a very good mimic, too. The other day I overheard her mimicking me – the girls were in fits of laughter.'

'How long do you think Jodi's altered state of consciousness will continue?' he asked. 'You've seen this sort of thing with one or two mothers before, haven't you?'

'One can't tell,' Lily said. 'It could vanish in an instant, or it could last for ever.'


A week after her meeting with Lily, Jodi received an urgent summons to return to New York ahead of time. Lily's reassuring words made it all so much easier for her to leave on the next flight. It meant that she would not be in London for the Daffodil Ball fundraiser, which she'd been dreading anyway.

She was closing her suitcase when Savannah burst into her bedroom.

'Opi told me you're going to New York but it's not true, I know it's not,' Savannah stormed. 'It's the Daffodil Ball.'

'I know honey, and I'm sorry about that, but – '

'I knew you wouldn't go to the ball,' Savannah interrupted. 'That's what you always used to do – say yes and then change your mind.' Her voice broke, 'Every mother is going except you. You're always different. You make *me* different!'

'But honey, I have to go – it's my *work*!' Jodi protested again. 'I can't understand this – you didn't even want to go to New York with me, you – '

'But that was *after* the Daffodil Ball,' Savannah replied bitterly. 'You said you and Daddy would be with Tiffany's parents, you said you would wear your blue dress, you said you would! Now Katie's mom will bid at the auction for Darcy Bussell's dancing shoes. Now she will get them for her. Katie will play her violin at the ball *and* get the ballet shoes. She gets everything she wants without even trying. Her mother never lets her down.'

'But honey, I had no idea the ball was so important to you.'

'It's your fault the other girls are laughing at me. I saw them giggling at your crazy clothes. Why don't you look like the other mothers? No, you've got to be different! They are all *cool*. Gucci bags and Jimmy Choo shoes and Calvin Klein jeans and Valentino sunglasses. They go to Michaeljohn or Nicky Clarke for their hair – you let that stupid yoga teacher cut yours – it looks a mess!' Savannah stopped and sighed. 'Why can't you make friends with the other mothers? Tiffany's mom had a mom-and-daughter lunch party at the Berkeley and I was left out,' she said, her voice rising. 'Daddy also wanted you to be at the ball because of his work – I even heard him say that to you! I hope you stay in New York!' She ran from the room. 'I *hate* you!' she sobbed. 'I *hate* you!'

Bewildered, Jodi remained where she was and did not follow her daughter. It was at least a minute before she could bring herself to mount the two flights of stairs to Savannah's room. She knocked on the door, calling, 'Let me in, honey.' She tried the door – it was locked.

Savannah's sobbing stopped abruptly. 'Go away,' she shrieked.

'Go away! I hate you!' The sobbing began again, rose to a howl and then dropped.

'I'm sorry, honey – I guess I should have known you cared so much about the ball,' Jodi said. 'I'm going to sit right here outside your door until you let me come in. Please, honey, please let me talk to you.'

Now that Savannah had stopped sobbing the ensuing quiet seemed ominous. After a while, Jodi again pleaded to be let in. A nameless fear took over, and in a breaking, half-sobbing voice she called out, 'Let me in, Savannah honey, please open the door.' She rested her head against the door and gave way to a fit of weeping.

Almost immediately, there was the sound of the key turning in the lock. Dropping to her knees, Jodi put her arms around Savannah and for once, because she was not rebuffed, began to cry again. She wept against her child's breast. When she felt Savannah patting her back, she made an enormous effort and pulled herself together.

'This is the first time in my whole life that I've seen you cry,' Savannah said gruffly.

'I'm sorry honey,' Jodi said. 'I was just upset.'

'Would you like to lie down on my bed, Mom?'

'That's a great idea, honey.' Jodi slipped off her shoes and climbed onto the footstool and then lay on the giant, elaborately canopied bed she'd always disliked. 'You look pale,' she murmured. 'Why don't you get on the bed and lie down beside me?'

Savannah stared at her for a long moment. Her cheeks were heavily flushed and swollen, her plaits had come undone and her hair fell thick and lopsided over one eye. She pushed it back impatiently, and Jodi saw that her usually unreadable eyes looked puzzled, even pained. Then she bent down, slowly unlaced her sneakers and gingerly, and rather thoughtfully, climbed onto the footstool. Holding her body stiff, she allowed herself to lie down on top of the bed beside her mother. There was nothing spontaneous, Jodi noted. Her daughter's every

147

movement appeared to have involved a decision. Steeling herself against yet another rejection, she summoned the courage to put her arm under Savannah's rigid shoulders, and was allowed to draw her close, cradle her head on her shoulder and actually stroke her hair and cuddle her. They lay quietly together like this and it was at least a minute before Savannah, her body still taut, pulled away.

'I've got to do some homework,' she said.

Jodi saw her eyes go vacant again, and though she was uncertain whether Savannah was being truthful, she took the hint and heaved herself off the bed. Next term, as soon as possible after the Easter vacation, she would make sure that Savannah took yoga classes. Hadn't Lily already said they had a yoga teacher for Year 6 to help the children to relax before the 11+ exam? She brightened suddenly. She would ask Lily to suggest yoga classes to Savannah – the child's body was so rigid that it was close to snapping. 'I love you, honey,' she said, surprising herself. 'I love you very much.'

'I've got loads of homework.'

'Well, I'll leave you to it, then,' Jodi said. 'Let me know if you need any help.'

After leaving her child's room, she instinctively made her way to her meditation space – the thought of the peace she always found in that converted box room was enough to calm her. But she had sensed a vulnerability in her daughter, a vulnerability so dark and so deep that it was almost awesome. And she suddenly understood that it was this feeling of helpless sadness in Savannah that had made her so unreachable – and so aggressive – for so long.

She turned to Bandrika's Eastern wisdom for help. *One must know that one is ignorant before one can begin to know.* She would have to learn what she assumed other women knew instinctively – she would have to learn how to be a mother.

# CHAPTER 10

Lily's mood jangled – she was profoundly exhausted – the kind of exhaustion that brings nausea with it. She always felt like this at the end of term. The last week of every term was fraught, bulging every minute of every hour with too much to do. At present she was at a stage where she just could not see how she could get through everything. No sooner were reports written for entry into senior schools, 11+ examinations, interview techniques debated, results out, 4+ testing completed, than she was faced with end of year reports for every girl at Belgrave Hall. Her mind was overloaded – this was always the term she dreaded most – she had, at least, to try to pace herself. There was little time even to talk to Benton; seeing him was almost out of the question.

Meetings with parents whose daughters had failed to be offered a place at Belgrave Hall were unfailingly gruelling. Sometimes the parents were so distressed that it took her back to her nursing days, when she'd had to break really tragic news, and then try to comfort the bereaved.

She was deciding what to do about a bright but troublesome child when Katie Ratcliffe's mother arrived, without an appointment, insisting that she had to see her on an urgent matter.

A former ballerina, Harriet Ratcliffe moved with the natural grace of a cat, but the austerity of her expression immediately let everyone know that she did not take kindly to intimacy. She wore her hair in the traditional bun of a ballerina, and her arched brows were those of a ballerina, too. Although she was the mother of a child prodigy, she expected no extra attention from Lily, and only communicated with her when she required permission for Katie to have time off from school for an audition or a recital. Widowed when Katie was only four months old, she always dressed in black, and whenever she gestured, as she did now, her large topaz ring would invite comparison with her hard gold-flecked eyes. This ring was the only piece of jewellery she owned – but for a small locket, everything else had been sold to pay for Katie's education.

'Katie would never forgive me if she found out that I'd come to see you. She so desperately did not want me to come that I promised her I wouldn't. But it's not the concert, nor even Katie's music that I've come to see you about,' Mrs Ratcliffe said, her stern voice strained with emotion. 'She's in bed to-day, couldn't, or rather wouldn't, get up to go to school.' Her mouth set into a taut, sarcastic half smile. 'Behaving like a prima donna,' she muttered, unable to contain her irritation. 'She's been having this terrible problem at Belgrave Hall – it's been going on since practically the first day of the term.'

'I'm glad you came to see me,' Lily said. 'I wish you'd told – '

'I've only just found out about it,' Mrs Ratcliffe interrupted, clenching at the material of her tailored trousers. 'It's been so bad that I had a terrible job to get Katie to go to school on the day of the school birthday – she said she just did not want to give a performance. And yet she played so perfectly and so movingly.' Breathing heavily, she went on, 'Anyway, I *made* her go – talked to her about stage-fright, and even though she got that helpless, dismayed expression, I didn't have the wit to see that it had nothing to do with her violin. She's being *tortured* – the girls leave her out of parties, whisper and snigger in a sly, nasty way, so she'll know they're talking about her! She was the only girl Tiffany Hunt didn't invite to her birthday. It was a disco party at Claridges, in the Royal Suite, too! She saw the girls passing around the photographs of Tiffany's fantastic birthday cake – a huge pink castle!' She winced, and her eyes went as hard as dead leaves. 'She doesn't know what she's done to make the most popular girl in the class, the new girl, *hate* her so much.'

Lily tightened her lips. Her working class origins reared up – she despised these birthday extravaganzas, and considered them to be merely a showcase for mothers to flaunt their finances. The girls grew up with false expectations, and a feeling of superiority that would not equip them for the future. 'Did Katie tell you who it was?' she asked.

'Savannah Anderson,' Mrs Ratcliffe burst out. 'And she hasn't only gone about this by indirect means to get the other girls to go against her – she's done terrible things herself. You remember when Katie's violin bow was found broken – just before she had to give that little recital to welcome the new parents? Katie has no doubt that Savannah was responsible – '

'I can't imagine any of my girls would possibly – '

'That's just the point,' Mrs Ratcliffe interjected. 'Katie told me Savannah is your favourite. She says you are always putting your arms around her, that you smile at her all the time. That's why she's so certain you'd never believe her – that's one of the reasons why she begged me not to see you! She's always been an obedient girl.'

'Katie's enormously talented, and, like all great musicians, deeply sensitive, so your reaction was perfectly understandable.'

But Mrs Ratcliffe seemed not to have heard her. 'It's ruining her career and the black rings under her eyes are getting darker and darker and she needs to look angelic when she performs.' She stood up, and resting both hands on the desk, thrust her head uncomfortably close to Lily's face. 'That child's got the other girls to call her 'Ratty Ratcliffe' – I can't take this, do you hear, I can't stand by and see my child's talent and future fame getting destroyed like this!'

'Please, Mrs Ratcliffe, let me – '

'*No!*' Mrs Ratcliffe said, rage edging her voice. 'You will just have to let me finish what I have to say. You have a moral responsibility to protect innocent children from being taunted and bullied – especially one with an artistic temperament, who is as highly strung as Katie.'

'Mrs Ratcliffe – '

'I never use the word "prodigy" in front of Katie – I say "privilege" instead. She will be compelled to practise and solve musical problems every single day of her life, but to become a star she must have a normal time at school.'

Immediately outside Lily's study a PE lesson was in progress. The teacher's commands and the happy, spirited laughter of the girls seemed to be an unfortunate intrusion. Lily knew the windows were tightly shut, but her study appeared to be acting like radar, picking up all the sounds and movements of the school. Today there were music exams, and the strident chords of a violin, not quite in tune, penetrated the room. Thinking this might be particularly offensive to Mrs Ratcliffe, Lily leapt up from behind her desk and pulled her chair toward her, so that she could sit beside her.

'Mrs Ratcliffe, I am totally horrified by what you have told me, and very upset for you and for Katie.' Laying her hand on Harriet's stiff arm, she went on, 'I can only apologize that this type of behaviour has not been checked. I regard school as a place where no harm should come to any child, especially a child like Katie, a child who is sensitive and kind.' She insisted that she would put an immediate end to such disgracefully unacceptable behaviour.

'Leave it to me, Mrs Ratcliffe,' she concluded. 'When Katie comes back to school, everything will be as it should be. Thank goodness you came to tell me about this.' She stood up. 'I'll do everything in my power to put this right, Mrs Ratcliffe,' she said. 'Believe me, I will.'

'The really damaging consequence of all this is that Katie has been neglecting her violin,' Mrs Radcliffe sighed. 'I've had to resort to drastic disciplinary measures to get her to practise.' She glared at Lily, and went on, 'I'm sure you have no idea of the hours and hours I spend, supervising practise. I've sacrificed everything for Katie's career.'

As soon as Mrs Ratcliffe left, Lily wrote a brief note on her complaints. Then, for the benefit of her staff, she listed relevant details of Savannah's background: Lily read it through once, observed with relief and satisfaction that she'd actually been objective enough to note ten points, and marched off to Savannah and Katie's classroom. The instant she swept into the classroom the children rose to their feet, smiling. But there was no answering smile from Lily, nor did she tell the girls to be seated. Instead, she turned to Mrs Worthington and asked to be forgiven for disturbing the lesson. Then she whipped round to face the class, ordered them to sit down and told them to be very quiet, please, because she had something extremely important to say to them.

During the long uneasy silence that followed, Lily's eyes darted from face to face. The back wall of Year 4's form room was covered in the Viking shields made by the girls as part of their project work, but this was not the time to praise them.

'At the moment I am *very*, very cross, something you rarely see,' she began. 'As you all know, Katie is at home ill. And why is she ill? Because she's extremely unhappy at school – extremely unhappy at *this* school – Belgrave Hall. I cannot believe that any girl at this school could be so unkind, so cruel to someone in her class, that she would make them become so frightened and scared that they would have nightmares and plead not to be sent back to *this* school, *our* school, Belgrave Hall.

'Poor Katie felt that no one cared for her – that none of you wanted to be her friend. And some of you – ' she threw up her hands – 'some of you have called her Ratty Ratcliffe. I will not tolerate this kind of cruel teasing.

'You had better realize how badly you have *all* behaved. And I hold you *all* responsible for this – every single one of you. Now you have all been told what this has done to Katie, I must ask you all not to say a single word of any of this to her. I rely on you totally, and I know I can trust all of you to be very kind to her, and make her feel that Belgrave Hall is the kind of school we all want it to be – a school where the happiness of the children is as important as the exam results.'

Here Lily paused dramatically, and slowly took a few steps closer to the girls' desks. During these few moments of acute silence, the harsh sound of pelting raindrops added to the tensions in the room. Now, with a spare, measured expression that cut through the girls like a knife, she advanced still closer. She told them that she relied on all of them to show Katie love and affection. 'If this doesn't happen immediately,' she added ominously, 'I will take very serious action – even to the extent of asking those of you who do not co-operate to look for another school.'

There was a loud gasp. Even Miss Worthington paled. Lily apologized once again for having interrupted the class and strode from the room. Now that she had spoken to the class she felt calmer, for she had no doubt that the girls would rise to the challenge and go out of their way to make sure that Katie would not only be included during playtime, but made to feel special. In her experience children of this age would not query what she had said. They would react without deep analysis of the situation and would be spontaneous in their support of Katie. The girls were innocent, they did not generally have malicious motives – the look of horror on their faces had told her that they were oblivious to Katie's pain.

Savannah, of course, was a different matter, and here again Lily knew that she had no way of avoiding the painful necessity of making her realize that she had changed the atmosphere of the class. She could not tolerate bullying of any sort whatsoever.

After lunch, during their silent reading period, Lily returned to the Y4 form room, ostensibly to collect the files. At the same time she had casually asked one of the girls to take a letter to the bursar, another to deliver a message to the gym mistress, and still another to return one of the books to the library. Finally she asked Savannah to help her carry all the class files to her study.

With Savannah at her side, she made her way along the corridor where Year 4's jewel-bright illuminated manuscripts decorated the walls. It was on the tip of her tongue to discuss this with Savannah who was artistic and had spent hours on her project. Instead, she stopped to look at Year 6's 'Finding the Area of Odd Shapes' and Year 3's 'Parts of the Human Body'.

Lily seated herself behind her desk, and Savannah sat down on the chair facing her.

'Stand up, Savannah – I haven't asked you to sit down,' Lily said sharply.

A shocked expression of pain and bewilderment crossed Savannah's face, but she rose to her feet immediately.

'When I spoke to your form this morning, I didn't tell them that Mrs Ratcliffe had said *you* were the one who was behind all the bullying,' Lily said. 'I have tried to help you in every way, and I am totally amazed and disappointed by your disgusting behaviour. We do *not* tolerate bullies at Belgrave Hall.'

'But Mrs Lidbury, I – '

'Do not interrupt!' Lily responded sharply. 'Don't you see that by being unkind to Katie you let me down? I have told your form, and you, many times that you must all be kind to each other. If someone feels that they have failed, give them love and support. If someone is successful – or talented, like Katie – congratulate them.'

'I sent her a special card when she won that competition,' Savannah protested.

'I am glad to hear that, Savannah,' Lily said. 'But someone told me that during her performance, playing at the school you were busy yanking the petals out of every single daffodil in your hair.'

'That was because Opi braided my hair too tight – it felt like the strings of my tennis racquet, and the daffodils started to itch.'

'My goodness, that must have really hurt,' Lily said sympathetically, and her throat swelled with gratitude. *Magsie was wrong – she had a tendency to be too critical, anyway.*

'Katie says you tell girls not to sit next to her – '

'That's not true, I asked her to sit next to me on the coach when we went to the Science Museum.' Savannah's lower lip quivered, and the next moment her body shook with dry sobs.

Unbearably moved and longing to comfort her, Lily jumped up and dropped a kiss on her head. 'Well, perhaps I've been too hard, Savannah,' she said quickly. 'I should have heard your side of the story first.'

'I always lend her my things if she forgets something.' Her voice breaking, she continued, 'The other girls are often mean to her.'

'In that case, it's up to you and me to make Katie happy,' Lily said. 'I totally rely on you to help me, to be my ally in fact.'

'Ally?'

'It means you'll be my partner, my friend,' Lily explained. 'And it will be our secret.' She lowered her voice to a theatrical whisper, 'But it can only be our own special secret if you *promise* not to tell anyone anything about it.'

'I promise I won't tell anything to anyone about it,' Savannah echoed.

That night, though drunk with fatigue, the image of Savannah's shoulders shaking with her pitiful, silent sobs refused to allow her to sleep. The incident had forced her to see Katie with greater clarity and she was now unhappily aware of Katie's unsmiling face, of the nervous way she jumped and startled when she was spoken to, of her habit of always looking as if she was thinking of something else. Her face was blank, impassive – it was rare for Lily to have no discernible reaction from a child. Katie could make her violin sing and soar; yet she was monosyllabic. Lily had always assumed that this was due to the innate sadness that seemed to define all musicians. Now, with her new objectivity, she questioned whether the fact that Katie contributed nothing to classroom discussions was because she had no original ideas, or because she never had to think for herself. *I never use the word 'prodigy' in front of Katie –I say 'privilege' instead.*

Perhaps Mrs Ratcliffe was too demanding? *Katie has to practise and solve musical problems every single day, but to become a star I insist that she has a normal school life*. But separating home life from school life was not as easy as separating the yolk from the white of an egg.

Isolated by her musical genius, Lily had thought Katie was a loner by choice, but perhaps the other children saw her as an oddity – an outlandish misfit to be avoided, if not ignored. For example, Mufti Day, each November, was the only day in the year when the girls were allowed to come to school in street clothes instead of uniforms. Unfailingly, however, Katie's smocked flowered muslin dress and black patent leather pumps set her apart the rest of her form who followed the current fashion of jeans and colourful boots. Could it be that Harriet Ratcliffe kept her daughter like a four-year-old so that she would look even younger for longer on the concert platform?

And then it struck her that it was because she had allowed Magsie's subjective judgment to influence her thinking, to intrude upon and cloud her own objectivity, that she had been unfair to Savannah. There was no doubt that a smiling child like Savannah was now, was a natural leader, willing other children to flock toward her with the ease one usually only associated with adults. Clearly, she had got things wrong – it was Katie who was jealous of Savannah and not the other way around.

Sickened with the realization that she had unjustly condemned Savannah because she'd had the audacity to believe that the child was jealous of her admiration for Katie, she gave up all hope of sleep, and went down the eighty-four stairs to her study in the empty school. Bucketing rain fell and she listened to the slash of tyres against the wet street, and opened the curtains and stared at the beams of headlights streaming down the street. After a while she went to her desk and turned to the three sheets of headed paper waiting to be checked. The papers summarized the results of the 4+ admission tests designed to select which little girls would be admitted to Belgrave Hall. Ranging from three-and-a-half to four-and-a-half, according to their month of birth, the children were tested in groups of eight – those born in August, for example, would be in a different group from those born in January. At that tender age, three or four months make a huge difference in the level of performance.

More than two hundred and fifty applicants for only twenty-four places meant an endless stream of letters and phone calls from parents, and frequently from every single powerful friend a parent could muster, hoping to influence her decision. But it was the rejection letter to sweet little Jade Hunt's parents that caused her the greatest anguish. Jade, the youngest child, was enchantingly pretty, her disposition could only be described as angelic, but her academic ability was well below what was required for Belgrave Hall. The really awful thing was that her sister, Tiffany, was in the same form as Savannah, and the Hunts, like most parents, believed that if one of their daughters was at the school, the others were automatically guaranteed a place. Yet Lily had often stressed that this was not the way things worked at Belgrave Hall. So she wrote the letter by hand, and put it in her pending file. She had neither the courage nor the heart to send it yet.

She also knew that they and other similarly upset parents would write to the board of governors. This meant that Lady Violet would once again bring up the vexed subject of enlarging the school even though she knew that doubling the intake would dilute academic standards and destroy the structure, the tradition and spirit of Belgrave Hall. Lily's hand-picked teachers certainly agreed with her, and as long as she was Head, Lady Violet would have a fight on her hands.

'Mrs Lidbury?'
'Yes.'
'Mrs Ratcliffe.'
Lily would have recognized that melodious voice instantly,

but did not say so. There was something about the woman that had made her uneasily aware that she was not the most benign of mothers.

'Oh good morning, Mrs Ratcliffe,' she responded. 'How is Katie today?'

'That's what I'm calling about – I hope I'm not disturbing you?'

'You're not disturbing me in the least, I assure you.'

'I wanted to tell you that Katie is a lot happier today. Savannah invited her to spend the day with her on Monday, and because she's been practising really hard, I decided to let her go.'

'A very wise decision – I'm glad you did that.'

'Sometimes one has to make an exception.'

'Thanks for letting me know, Mrs Ratcliffe. I very much doubt there'll be any further trouble, but if there is, you must tell me about it at once.'

Lily's pulses rang with simple gratitude and happy surprise. The truth was she had no idea what she had expected of Savannah. Surely the girl's spontaneous act of generosity should not have taken Lily by surprise – she should have expected the best, and not the worst, of the child. Plainly she was as guilty as all those others, like Jodi and even Bronnie who had let the poor child down. Lily had been told that Savannah rarely cried, but she'd cried yesterday when she'd been accused of cruelty. It was for this reason that Lily suddenly recalled the precocious look of overwhelming sorrow on Savannah's face, the way her entire body had rocked with her sobs when she had thought her beloved Bronnie's photograph which she'd taped inside the lid of her desk had gone missing. After Lily had found the photograph that had somehow got entangled with Savannah's geography project book, she'd studied it carefully. A tall obese woman, with frizzy orange hair and wide, fleshy matching orange lips smiled mournfully into the camera. It was impossible to judge her age – she could be as young as twenty-five or as old as forty-five.

'She made her hair orange,' Savannah said proudly. 'She wanted it to look like mine.'

'She's got a lovely smile,' Lily said kindly. 'You must miss her a lot.'

'I wish she was here,' Savannah's voice faltered. 'She didn't come to London like she told me she would. I guess she didn't love me that much,' she said sadly. 'So now it's like she died.'

Lily's mobile phone rang, wrenching her to the present. It was Magsie, excitedly calling from Chelsea Antique Market to let her know she had seen the perfect handbag for the Daffodil Ball. It was a real bargain – it would cost hundreds of pounds if it were new – and she wanted to know if she should buy it for six pounds. Laughingly, Lily agreed. Magsie really is like a devoted big sister to me, she thought. Unexpected tears of gratitude for all that Magsie meant to her pricked her eyelids. She would have loved to tell Magsie of Savannah's generosity, but that would have entailed telling her about Mrs Ratcliffe's visit. For reasons that might have been beyond her, or that she preferred not to face, that visit was something she most assuredly did not want Magsie to know about.


'The last time I went to a ball was more than fifteen years ago,' Lily said to Magsie over a pizza at Olivetto, their favourite Italian restaurant, where the pizzas were primary, and the décor secondary. 'It's quite ridiculous, Magsie, but as head of school I can hardly fade into the background or refuse to dance with anybody, and I'm dreading it. You've got to teach me, maybe it will all come back. Don't smile, I'm deadly serious.'

'You don't need a teacher, but I expect you could do with some practise.' Magsie smiled like a pleased child. 'When we get back to school tonight, I'll bring my portable CD to the entrance hall and we'll have a go, and you'll quickly find you haven't forgotten.' She sipped at her wine and went on, 'In Edinburgh, we used to go ballroom dancing at least once a week, the way some people go on a weekly visit to the pub.' Her eyes glinted with nostalgia, 'We'll have fun practising, I know we will.'

'I'll tell you what's made all this even worse for me,' Lily's lip curled with contempt. 'Courtney Hunt popped in to tell me that that odious Stelios Tsakiraki will be collecting me to take me to the Dorchester. I told her I'd prefer to go under my own steam, but she quite sharply reminded me of all that man has given toward making the ball such a resounding financial success. She also mentioned that Stelios Tsakiraki is the sort of man who would take it as a deliberate insult if I didn't accept.'

'He's the one who made you hand over his daughter's prep diary, isn't he?'

'He certainly is,' Lily's eyes darkened. Stelios Tsakiraki had used that diary in court, showing that his wife's signature rarely appeared. The fact that she had not checked Olympia's prep on a regular basis had counted heavily against her in the divorce court, and his wife, Tina, from whom he was now separated, had not been allowed to take Olympia back home to New York. 'The custody battle still rages on!' Her usually good-natured expression hardened. 'Stelios Tsakiraki is the only really spiteful man I have ever met.'

When they returned to Belgrave Hall, Magsie quickly collected her portable CD player and took it to the hall. The music began, rising high above the empty staircase. Light on her feet, and confident, Magsie guided Lily with soothing instructions. Lily's body was rigid, and for once rather clumsy. They were an ill-matched pair, but soon the younger figure relaxed and began to move in a fluid rhythm. Twirling and swaying to the music, they suddenly broke into relieved laughter. Dancing was like riding a bicycle – automatic and enjoyable after years of abstinence.

'I'll be right here, in this hall, waiting with you, when Mr Tsakiraki comes to collect you,' Magsie said. 'If you would like me to?' she added.

'That would be perfect, Magsie,' Lily laughed. 'Just perfect.'

So it was that when Stelios Tsakiraki rang the bell the next evening, Magsie opened the door to him. After having been formally introduced she helped Lily into the flowing midnight blue velvet cape that was as glamorous now as it had been in the thirties.

'Did I hear you right when I heard you say Magsie was your closest friend?' Stelios said as his black Porsche pulled away. 'I thought she was the school matron.'

'Magsie Henderson and I have been close friends for more than fifteen years, I'm proud to say,' Lily replied, nettled. 'She's one of the most important people in my life.'

'You're a very tolerant woman, I see,' he chuckled, hoping to sound both amusing and patronizing. 'The way Magsie was carrying on with your wrap anyone would have thought you were a debutante instead of a *mature*, beautiful woman.' Drawling through his nose, he went on, 'Stunning dress you're wearing. Very sexy, too sexy for a debutante.'

Her irritation turned into active loathing. She despised him for his exaggeratedly high collar, his overpowering aftershave, his obviously counterfeit ultraviolet tan, and she loathed him for the sneering curve of his fat, lewd lips, but it was his crude attempt at flirtatious familiarity that made her flesh crawl.

'Belgrave Hall is so fortunate in having a group of parents like The Bees,' she said, pointedly ignoring his clumsy attempt at amused intimacy. 'They've worked tirelessly for this ball.'

'Gives them something to do,' he sneered. 'Keeps them out of mischief.'

Seething, Lily smoothed the folds of her cape and made no reply. The man repulsed her, made her body crawl. He appeared not to have noticed her silence, and went on talking about his school days at Harrow with one of his compatriots, King Constantine of Greece.

Benton saw Lily before she saw him. She had an aura of mystery about her, he decided. Her slight smile was suggestive of an exciting secret, and in all the world it was he and he alone who knew that he was her secret. As always, a velvet bow at the nape of her neck held her long flowing hair in place, but she was exceptionally striking tonight – her dress, spilling like water, suggested the turning of tides.

Lily was one of the last to enter the ballroom but as she walked to the main table she was dismayed to see that Stelios Tsakiraki standing conspicuously behind her chair. Everyone was seated and she felt as if all eyes were on her. She held her head up and smiled – only Magsie would have recognized that her smile did not reach her eyes. As she sat down his hand snaked across her shoulders and down to the small of her exposed back. He felt her recoil and smiled to himself – he would soon have her eating from his hand – he believed all women were the same. He was over-attentive, leaning over her, continually touching her hand as if she were his property. She turned her gaze away from him toward the closed ballroom doors.

'Who or what are you looking at?' he demanded irritably. 'A sexy woman like you shouldn't be so uptight, you know.'

She ignored his comment. 'The choir are about to come in,' she remarked, making it plain that nothing else was of interest to her.

At that moment, fortunately for Lily, the choir entered the ballroom, and the buzz of pre-dinner chatter fell silent. The children's crisp uniforms and smiling faces, and their neat formation were, she reflected, a real credit to Belgrave Hall. The guests turned their chairs to face the children; many had heard the choir perform before, and those beaming parents whose daughters were in the choir had to struggle to remain in their seats. Lily had chosen *We are the Children of the World*, a dramatic song, perfect for the evening, and as the children sang, many mothers were in tears. They ended to enthusiastic applause, and though they smiled happily, they were well rehearsed and held their positions.

The applause was still ringing in their ears when Katie lifted her bow to the violin so expertly cradled under her chin. The violin came to life as she played a haunting gypsy dance especially composed for the evening by the Russian violin teacher at Belgrave Hall. No other sound was heard. Even the Dorchester staff stopped still, listening to the incredible soul-searching chords, a professional, mature performance by an eight-year-old girl. When the bow finally went slowly to her side, the silence continued until Benton rose to his feet. Everyone followed him, and the parents, the choir and even the hotel staff joined in the standing ovation.

Katie bowed several times; then, even though the ovation continued, she went up to Lily's table and curtsied. The applause grew still louder, and it was a long while before the hall quietened, and the choir and Katie filed out of the ballroom, followed by their parents.

Smiling triumphantly, Katie's mother went to say hello and goodbye to Lily. Naturally, she was taking Katie home – she had to be up and practising at dawn the next morning – but she wanted to thank Lily for having resolved the difficulties, and making it possible for her to be the kind of child she ought to be. But she particularly wanted to stress that Savannah's invitation to Katie to spend the day with her after school tomorrow had made her 'really, really happy'.

During dinner Stelios continued to touch Lily's hand possessively, and made sure that she could not speak to the man on her left. His smooth low voice was meant to be seductive. From time to time he stroked the nape of her neck and when the ebony ring on his little finger got tangled in her hair once too often, she could no longer ignore what he was doing. 'Do not touch my neck like that,' she said, exasperated. 'I'm sure they taught you better manners than that at Harrow!'

'You sound just like a spinster,' he laughed unpleasantly. 'But you don't fool me – you're actually a sexy doll who can't wait to be serviced.'

'Were you happy at Harrow?'

'Of course.'

'Well then, unless you want to give a good school a bad name, you should not tell people you went to Harrow,' she said, her voice brittle.

'Now control yourself, my girl,' he said, clutching her wrist. 'Because your kind of sexy banter really turns me on.'

Oh God, how I loathe this man, she thought. She looked at him with a brief hard gaze. A few seconds later she felt easier – the waiters were at last distributing the pudding, and a plate was set in front of her. She looked at her *Surprise de Chocolat Parfumé au Grand Marnier Sauce Caramel* and laughed with relief. Dinner was now almost over, and as soon as the auction ended and she'd given her speech she would make her escape. She would circulate – that was her job, what was expected of her. She would linger at each table but eventually she would seat herself at table 14, Benton's table. Sally Greenwood would be delighted to move to the main table as she'd been desperate to be on the ball committee, but the committee had been formed months before her daughter joined the school.

At last the auction began, and the air grew yet more festive. The parents reminded Lily of a huge extended family on a magical holiday of laughter. Most of the women were wearing identifiable designer dresses – Prada, Armani and Dolce & Gabbana shrouded these narcissistic, never-aging, putative leaders of London society. In hilarious accord they felt free to bid absurd prices to tease the prize away from other families. Wild shouts of encouragement, screams of delight and hoots of laughter rang round the vaulted, mirrored ballroom. Bidding was addictive, auction fever was high, and each table was ready to outwit the other. Their friendly rivalry was for the eventual benefit of the children of Jabulani, but, in fact, this rivalry was of a piece with their competitive personalities. The Christie's auctioneer who had donated his services to the evening understood the crowd well enough to know exactly which area of the room to target. He knew the soft-hearted Greek community would want to leave with the gigantic teddy bear dressed in the Belgrave Hall uniform. A week's stay at a fully staffed holiday home in Maine, a diamond-studded Cartier watch, and dinner for twelve 'prepared in your own home by the executive *chef de cuisine* of the Ritz' far outstripped the shooting, fishing and golfing prizes. But when the signed ballet shoes of Darcy Bussell came up, Benton took them all on, and his was the final bid which won the shoes Savannah coveted.

Lily's speech followed ten minutes later. A microphone had been set up at the main table, but because the thought of being associated with Stelios Tsakiraki was not to be borne, she quickly arranged to give her speech from the bandstand. Though this meant that there was a roll of drums and things would be far more theatrical than she would have liked, anything was preferable to being beside Stelios Tsakiraki.

Lily left the bandstand to thunderous applause. Stelios stopped her before she reached her seat. Bowing ostentatiously low, he kissed her rigid hand. Meanwhile, the dancing had begun and she accepted his invitation to dance with as much grace as she could manage.

Taking advantage of the romantic music, he held her too close, moving his body against her so that she would be sure to feel his erection. Pulling away from him, she stopped dancing. 'I'm rather dizzy, I'm afraid,' she said. 'All that champagne's gone to my head. I'll have to go back to my table.'

Faking solicitousness he immediately took command, put his arm around her waist and led her off the dance floor. 'Of course, you ought to sit down at once, my dear. We'll go back to the table.'

They'd hardly been seated when Verine, giggling, turned to him. 'My bestest dancing partner hasn't asked me to dance yet?' she said, playfully taking his glass from him.

Stelios rose unsteadily. 'If you'll excuse me, Mrs Lidbury?' he said to Lily, befuddled.

'Of course,' she replied smiling with relief. 'It will be fun to watch you two.'

The next moment Benton was at her side, 'Would you like to dance?' he asked formally.

Lily thanked him equally formally, and he took her hand and guided her to the dance floor.

They did not dance cheek to-cheek, nor lean up close, but gave themselves to the music, and melted into one another, their movement as fluid and as fluent as if they'd been dancing together all their lives. She felt heat from his arms, felt his strength, and was more than ever aware of his body, his after-shave, his smile.

They'd been dancing for less than five minutes when a slightly tipsy father cut in. 'May I have a turn?' he asked boyishly. 'I've always wanted to dance with a headmistress.'

This seemed to set a pattern. Several men followed suit, and Lily was whisked away and whirled around the dance floor, some-times awkwardly, sometimes expertly. But when Benton saw the fourth father – a spectacularly clumsy dancer – energetically heaving Lily and himself about, he decided it was time to rescue her. Once again, despite the space they deliberately left between one another, their bodies merged in perfect rhythm. Lily longed to give herself up to this bliss and to shut her eyes, but for the sake of propriety kept them wide open, yet was oblivious, even so, to everyone except Benton. Which was why when Stelios Tsakiraki came up to her, it was such a hideous surprise.

'*If* you don't mind, Mr Anderson,' he snarled, taking Lily's hand from Benton's shoulder, 'I believe *I* am Mrs Lidbury's escort for tonight.'

Because an ugly scene appeared to be in the offing, Lily thanked Benton for the dance, managed to smile up at Stelios and moved into his arms. Stepping back for a moment, he cocked his head to the left, and seemed to be greedily un-dressing her in his mind's eye. After a few endless seconds, he crushed her body against his, and began to dance. 'Nice tits you've got there,' he whispered, tonguing her ear. She stiffened and arched her spine away from him but it didn't help. His hand spread octopus-like on the small of her back and she smelt his whisky-breath on her face and shuddered. 'I saw the way that you danced with that anorexic, wooden scarecrow,' he said, baring his teeth in a semblance of a smile. 'What you need, my girl, is a real man. How long is it since you've had a good fuck?'

Lily stopped dancing, but instead of releasing her, he held her still tighter, now grinding his hand into her back.

'You are vile,' she said quietly but distinctly.

'Bitch!' he growled, tightening his grip and bruising her right hand. 'You're nothing but a *fucking* poisonous bitch!' Then he pinched her body so painfully that it took her breath away.

An uncontrollable white-hot rage engulfed Lily, and, using all her strength, she plunged the sharp tip of her pointed shoe into his shin and kicked so hard that he groaned out loud.

He gave a yelp of pain. 'How *dare* you!' he snarled. 'How dare *you* insult *me!*'

'Insult *you!*' she cried scornfully. 'You're nothing but a walking disease posing as a human being!'

Now his temper flared so out of control that in one quick fluid movement he struck her face with the palm of his hand. The sound rose up and cracked through the music and the chatter and the laughter like a pistol shot.

Then, before anyone had a chance to react, he turned and scurried away. A few women screamed. Seconds later, people gathered round her, their faces shocked and bewildered. Everyone stopped dancing and a huge pall fell over the crowd. People lowered their voices as though they were at the scene of an accident. Benton had slipped out to the men's room, and so knew nothing of what had happened. When he returned he sensed that something had gone wrong. For a moment he thought he had blundered into a different room. The mood had changed, the buzz had gone. The festive electric atmosphere had died, and small groups stood around as if attending a funeral, murmuring among themselves. The orchestra played on dispiritedly. He felt the hairs at the back of his neck stand on end, and immediately asked someone what had happened.

'Mrs Lidbury was *punched*!'

'*Punched*?' he echoed, stunned.

'Stelios Tsakiraki slapped her in the face!'

His one thought was to get to her. Striding quickly, he pushed his way toward her. Once again she was seated at the main table, the imprint of a palm clearly visible on her left cheek. She was smiling up at the sea of faces, urging everyone to go on with the fun, assuring them that she was quite all right, really she was, it was just one of those things that happen in life.

'I think I should take you home,' Benton said.

'I would agree to that but only on one condition,' Lily said, waving an admonitory finger, 'that everyone starts dancing again. It would break my heart if this glorious evening came to an abrupt and unpleasant end.' Rising to her feet, she went on, 'Please, Verine and Edward, won't you help me and go back to the dance floor?'

'Sure,' Edward responded, 'if you'll be super-nice and go home.'

'I'll not leave one minute before the dancing begins again,' Lily said, regaining her authoritative role as headmistress. 'To let aberrant behaviour destroy a beautiful evening would distress me greatly.'

Everyone obeyed, as she knew they would. Someone had the presence of mind to fetch her cloak and, consciously holding her head high, she left the room.

They did not speak until they were in his car. 'You do realize you'll have to return immediately,' she said.

'Of course,' he replied. 'What happened?'

Though her teeth were on edge, she chuckled. 'I think I called him a disease, I remember saying something even worse, but I've forgotten what it was.'

Benton glanced at his watch; at one o'clock in the morning,

the more or less empty streets meant that Belgrave Hall was no more than eight minutes from the Dorchester.

'I want to call Magsie and tell her what happened, Lily-bud,' he said.

'Okay.'

By the time they arrived, about four minutes later, Magsie had thrown a coat over her nightgown and was already on the pavement.

The moment the door had closed on him, Lily's face became distorted by pain. It was only then that Magsie noted the white weals across her flushed face. Now Lily allowed herself to submit to Magsie's soothing words, and gratefully accepted her help. Once she was in bed, Magsie hurried down the stairs to fetch one of the cold compresses she kept in her freezer for emergencies. She was back again with astonishing speed. Gently applying the compress to Lily's swollen face she saw she was still bristling with disgust.

'Don't worry my darling, you're here now with me, Magsie, you don't have to think of dignity. But, Lily darling, I know you too well – I can imagine how you continued to smile, to make light of what had happened. It's a wonder you allowed Benton to bring you home, I'm sure.'

Now Lily gave way, tears rained down her face, stinging her cheek. She pushed the compress away, and lay very still, her fists clenched, too weary and too drained to try to stop the tears, or even to dry her eyes. Seated beside the bed, Magsie leaned over to protect her burning cheek from being further irritated by salty tears, and gently dabbed her eyes.

'What a disgrace to humanity Stelios Tsakiraki is,' Magsie exploded. 'A *bastard*, that's what he is, a *swine of a bastard*.'

'All this – ' Lily hesitated, ' – this horror can be put to good use. It will count heavily against him in the custody hearing. I'll be happy to co-operate – even if it means some awful publicity for Belgrave Hall.'

'You'll have Lady Violet to contend with.'

'I know,' Lily agreed.

When Lily at long last fell asleep, Magsie tiptoed to the unlit drawing room and lay on the couch. A distant thunder rolled, the rumble drew nearer and a streak of lightning lit up the room and a heavy rain began again.

Then all at once she had a flash of insight. Though it had all been over in the twinkling of an eye, she remembered a tender brushing of Benton's lips against Lily's wounded cheek that had been nothing like chaste. Everything suddenly fell into place – Lily's urgent mobile phone conversations, her abstracted, dreamy air, her obsession with Savannah . . . *The child is a sense of summer, please Magsie, please don't spoil things.* The feeling of foreboding that had long been troubling her gathered pace.

Lily is the sister I never had, Magsie said to herself. And Savannah is the daughter Lily once had. Loving Lily as a sister was safe and respectable, Lily's loving Savannah as a daughter was misguided and dangerous. The sound of steady rain had always comforted her, but she was not comforted. After the events of tonight, nothing would ever be the same again, she thought.

The first person Benton saw when he returned to the Dorchester was Lily's *bête noire*, Lady Violet. There she was, in regal purple velvet, bearing swiftly down upon him, her darting eyes in the face Lily said reminded her of half a teapot, expressing rage and concern. There was no way of avoiding her. The last and, fortunately, only time he'd met her was on the sidewalk after one of Savannah's Saturday morning sessions with Lily. He remembered her sour disapproval over Savannah's baking lesson.

'I hadn't expected you back so soon, Mr Anderson,' she said. 'How is she?'

'Magsie's taking care of her.'

'What a dreadful ordeal for her,' she remarked, making a scandalized sound. 'That awful man vanished with the speed of a hired assassin. One or two men would have dealt with him outside, I'm sure.' He watched her face which was unreadable. 'I must say I certainly admired the dignified way Mrs Lidbury conducted herself.'

'I guess she's a true Brit,' he said with a tight smile. 'Stiff upper lip.'

By then they were surrounded by groups of outraged parents, some curious, others worried, all anxious to know how Lily was. But it was mostly the men who talked of suing the bastard, of laying a charge against him, of the need to bring back the lash, of teaching the coward who slunk away like a frightened rat the kind of lesson he would never forget. A woman Benton had never met suddenly took his hand and led him to the dance floor. 'Mrs Lidbury told us to carry on dancing,' she giggled. 'The fun must go on,' she said.

'You're right, I guess,' he agreed courteously, summoning a laugh. 'The fun must go on.'

But it was the devil's own job keeping up appearances at this time and in this way. He longed to be with Lily and he was sure she needed him as much as he needed her.

It was said that you could set your watch by Magsie – she opened the school gates at precisely seven forty-five each morning, exactly ten minutes before the arrival of the children and the teachers. This morning, as usual, the traffic warden who took delight in confronting the Belgrave Hall parents in an aggressive and threatening manner was already on the scene. However there was nothing he could do about the two legally parked cars outside the school. Magsie called out a greeting to the two fathers doggedly testing their daughter's spelling, wanting to feel that for at least five minutes they were participating in their daughters' education. Today, astonishingly, she found Lady Violet waiting, majestic and immaculate in her trench coat, the tips of her ears made scarlet by the chill wind.

'Good morning, Lady Violet,' said Magsie as if there were nothing out of the ordinary about this early morning visit.

'Mr Anderson told me how you looked after Mrs Lidbury last night,' Lady Violet replied briskly, handing her an envelope. 'I came to thank you, and to ask you to give this note to her.'

'Certainly, Lady Violet – '

'I don't want to disturb her myself, but no headmistress or, indeed, any woman should ever be subjected to violence. I'm filled with admiration for the way she maintained her dignity. She has my full support whichever action she decides to take. It's a good job she has you to look after her, as I know you will, and it's a good job it's the last day of term.'

'I'll give it to her at once. So far she hasn't mentioned anything about future action, but she'll be glad of your support, I'm sure.'

'It's the least I can do,' Lady Violet replied stiffly. 'Disgraceful behaviour – I can't think when I was so appalled.' She shook her head. 'Disgraceful man.'

'I only hope he'll have the sense not to send his daughter to school today,' Magsie said worriedly. 'The other children will have heard about it, and – '

'There's no telling what an animal like that will do,' Lady Violet interrupted. 'Tell Mrs Lidbury I send my love,' she added awkwardly.

Once again Magsie raced up the winding staircase. Because Lily had expected trouble and not sympathy from Lady Violet, she wanted her to have the letter as soon as possible.

Lily read the note. She made no comment, but held it to her burning cheek for a moment. Then, murmuring, 'There are times when reading is believing,' she handed the note to Magsie. 'Well Magsie, what do you make of Lady Violet? This is one of those times when you can't tell me you're not surprised.'

'But I'm not in the least surprised,' Magsie retorted, after reading the note.

'*Magsie!*'

'Lady Violet had already told me of her feelings on the matter, and she was visibly upset, I can tell you.'

'Oh, so she does have emotions after all.' The tiniest suggestion of a smile appeared at the corners of Lily's mouth, 'I've always thought she regarded all emotion as vulgar as wearing see-through blouses. It seems I've done her an injustice all these years.'

'It just shows you,' Magsie said. 'We think we know someone and then we find we don't know them at all.'

Lily shuddered inwardly. Magsie's commonplace observation filled her with foreboding. *She might just as well be talking about me*, she reflected. *If it ever gets out about Benton and me everyone will say they thought they knew Lily Lidbury but they didn't really know her at all . . . It had taken a Stelios Tsakiraki to sniff out the truth. . .*

At seven fifty-five, as she did every morning, Lily arrived at the staff room. Everyone turned as she entered; many remained quiet, but voluble Miss Worthington, undeterred as ever, flung her arms round her neck saying, 'I just hope he hasn't got the affront to come here this morning. He needs blacklisting from every school in London. That man's a real creep – I've always said so – he has cruel eyes and probably beats his poor wife. No wonder she left him – a lucky escape, if you ask me.'

A murmur of support arose as they crowded round her. Her facial swelling was obvious yet she smiled and appeared serene as she thanked them and said that such a trivial affair should not be blown out of proportion. Stelios Tsakiraki would enjoy being the centre of gossip, and she would not allow him that satisfaction!

Miss Trubshaw came in to report that the Tsakirakis' housekeeper had telephoned to say that Olympia would not be at school.

Striding toward her classroom, Lily rapidly organized her thoughts. If the news had spread to the staff so fast, the children would certainly have heard about it. She was right, of course. She found that though their eyes were wider, their concern and horror more obvious, the children, like Miss Worthington in the staff room a few moments earlier, could not contain their questions. To regain control of the classroom she raised her hand and silence, as usual, followed quickly.

She had no intention of beating around the bush. Children preferred – and deserved – honesty.

'You obviously know what happened last night. Just think how one silly thoughtless action can almost destroy a wonderful evening – but, believe me girls, that did *not* happen. The most important part of last night was the wonderful Ball that your parents organized to help Jabulani.

'I was so proud of the choir and of Katie. The music that you provided was the best part of the evening – a very happy, successful evening. It's important in life to dwell on the good things and to cast aside inconsequential things. Inconsequential means things that are not important.

'I need your help now, girls. Silly gossip is not encouraged at Belgrave Hall, so I want you to be mature and sensible and only discuss the good points of the ball.

'As you can see, I am very well – I had a super time at the ball – your parents were simply wonderful.

'Now let me take the register, and then we will go to assembly.'

As she made her way to assembly, an aura of shock hung in the air. The news that their headmistress, the invincible, unchanging mainstay of their school life, had been physically attacked by a Belgrave Hall father threatened their safety and left their world, where everything was black or white, good or bad, happy or sad, crumbling around their ears. The girls' anxious stares followed her as she passed them by. She smiled and gave a crisp 'Good morning' and strode ahead, the skirt of her favourite 1920s green and cream velvet dress swirling about her ankles. She stepped on the stage and, projecting normality and calm, took assembly in the usual way. She added a few words about the success of the Daffodil Ball, Katie and the choir's magnificent performance.

She returned afterward to her study and busied herself with the mass of paperwork that unfailingly cropped up on the last day of term. Her cheek burned and she touched it gingerly.

But something made her look up.

Unsmiling and silent, Savannah stood at the threshold staring at her. Then, when she became aware that Lily had seen her, and because she waved a brightly wrapped package, as if she were showing it to her, Lily asked her what it was.

'It's a present for Magsie,' Savannah said. 'My mom called to say she'd bought this antique black lace scarf for her. It arrived by FedEx so I could give it to her before we break up.' A look of intense anxiety crushed her face. 'Are you sure you're OK, Mrs Lidbury?' she asked. 'Everyone is so worried, kind of frightened.' Her face suddenly crumpled, and she broke into sobs. 'How could anyone hurt you, Mrs Lidbury?'

'It's sweet of you to care about me, Savannah dear, but you could help me by being my personal messenger, telling everyone that I'm perfectly well, that it looks much worse than it feels.'

Reassured and feeling important, Savannah went skipping off.

Forcing her mind away from Stelios Tsakiraki, Lily returned to her paperwork, ignored the flashing electronic eye of her answer phone and, apart from a brief conversation with Benton on her mobile phone, took no other calls.

She looked up and again found Savannah staring at her.

It was only a matter of seconds before she dropped her eyes and Savannah ran away, but in that fleeting moment she noted a disturbing change in her. There was nothing childlike about the sagging shoulders or the drooping mouth set in the bitter lines of disappointment. She had long sensed that there was a part of Savannah which was, and perhaps always would be, beyond her grasp.

Folding Jodi's precious lace gift in tissue paper, Magsie heaved a big sigh through pursed lips and puffed cheeks. Owning an antique Chantilly lace collar in black silk was beyond anything she could have possibly imagined. She'd actually seen a similar cravat at an exhibition, when an expert in lace-making had told her that the French Revolution had temporarily closed the Chantilly lace industry because so many of the lace makers had been sent to the guillotine. It amazed her that a woman as tough as Jodi Anderson had remembered that she had a small collection of antique lace.

Jodi had heard about her passion for lace only once, and that was on the day she'd been to talk to Lily about going to New York without Savannah. Magsie recalled how different Jodi had looked from the first time they met; she had scarcely recognized her. Jodi had stopped to admire the collar she was wearing and she'd told her about her modest collection of lace collars and added that several of them had been given to her grandmother during her brief stint as a lady's maid. She'd told Lily at the time that Jodi's behaviour appeared to have softened along with her clothes, and thought no more about it.

Her mind went in a familiar pattern from past to present, and she admitted to herself that she'd probably been too harsh with Savannah a few minutes ago. But she'd had an awful fright when she'd unexpectedly caught Savannah snooping in her flat, standing beside the door dividing her bedroom from her little living room.

'What on earth are you doing down here, Savannah?' she had demanded, blocking her way.

But Savannah had faced her boldly, not in the least fazed by her open display of dislike. 'My mom FedExed a present for you from New York,' she tossed her head and went on, 'I put it on your bed –'

'As you very well know, Savannah, my bedroom is strictly out of bounds.'

'I put it on your bed as a surprise.'

'Oh, well, thank you,' she replied ungraciously. Then, ashamed of her churlishness, she placed her arm round the child's shoulder. But Savannah stiffened under her touch and slid past her and out of her flat.

She had been around children all her life, and believed she'd a sixth sense about each and every one of them, but she could not recall ever having experienced anything like the feeling of dislike and distrust of a child that she had for Savannah. She also knew that this antipathy was mutual.

Throughout the following week, the slap that had sounded like a pistol shot reverberated like one. Lily found the publicity even more humiliating than the event that had caused it.

The headmistress of a preparatory school for the elite, a strict disciplinarian as uncompromisingly opposed to political correctness as she is to corporal punishment, has refused – for reasons best known to herself – to discipline or to press charges against one of the more virile of the rich and powerful fathers – nameless for legal reasons – who struck her at the society fundraising school ball held at the Dorchester.

Of all the press accounts, and including a rather vicious cartoon, this was the one which most annoyed and distressed her.

# CHAPTER 11

Harriet Ratcliffe was in no doubt that since her daughter and Savannah had turned into best friends, Katie had become an even more brilliant violinist, playing with a natural emotional involvement, performing at the level of an acclaimed professional. It was for this reason that she agreed to invite Savannah to accompany them on their two-day visit to Paris for Katie's audition with the great Maestro du Four. Disturbingly mystified, and somewhat resentful of Savannah's positive impact on her daughter's life, Mrs Ratcliffe studied her as closely as if she were a complicated road map she could not quite decipher or trust.

Despite her distrust, after less than an hour on the train she found herself amused by the child's quick, feisty and careless confidence. Her head and hands moved in rapid, theatrical gestures as she spoke, and there was a constant hint of laughter in her voice. At the drop of a hat she could take on the cloak and guise of anyone she chose – her impersonation of Lily left them helpless with laughter.

Savannah had a charismatic personality, an electrifying presence, Harriet Ratcliffe decided – difficult to define, but endlessly intriguing. She was always noticed. Either you were drawn to her flame-red hair and amazing green eyes, or to her infectious laugh which rippled melodiously and lit up her face.

For all that, it was clear that Savannah needed to be the centre of attention, and though she joked about Katie's violin and had christened it 'Fiddle-Faddle', Harriet Ratcliffe had an inexplicably uneasy sensation.

Harriet had devoted herself to raising a prodigy. Thwarted in her own ambition, she'd channelled all her drive into Katie, spending hours urging her to greater and greater heights. It was when Katie turned three that the Suzuki lessons began, and the merciless stage mother in Harriet was unleashed. Because the founder of the Suzuki Method held that talent could be learned, Harriet took this to mean that nothing less than total obedience to a punishing regime of practise would do. It was not only a question of making certain that Katie's talent would grow and grow, but if only for the sake of her future stardom, she had to try to bring a dimension of balance into the life of a child who was confident and fulfilled on stage, but sullen and unhappy in ordinary life. Relentless disciplinarian though Harriet was, this was one of those rare occasions when she was forced to be less than honest with Katie – she was too afraid to take her to Euro Disney where, to impress Savannah, she might insist on riding on one of those terrifying roller coasters which would be unwise before her audition. So she lied and said no tickets were available.

She could not, however, get out of taking the girls to the Eiffel Tower.

Waiting for the bill at the restaurant at the Eiffel Tower, Savannah suddenly announced that she needed to go to the bathroom.

'I'll go with you,' Katie said quickly.

'Okay.'

'Perhaps you'd better wait for me to take you?' Harriet Ratcliffe suggested nervously.

Savannah responded with a giggle. 'No one is going to eat us, you know.'

On their way back to the restaurant, Savannah suddenly stopped.

'I dare you to look over the edge Katie,' she said seriously.

'I don't want to.'

'Go on, don't be such a baby.'

'Heights make me go all dizzy.'

'Scaredy cat, scaredy cat, scaredy cat,' Savannah taunted. 'Don't you want to be my best friend?'

'I do,' Katie was close to tears. 'I do, I do want to be your best friend.'

'Well, if you don't do what I tell you to, you can't be my best friend,' Savannah scowled. 'Your mom's waiting – we'd better go.' She stalked ahead but stopped for a moment, tossed her head, and said scornfully, 'I knew you couldn't do it – I knew you were a coward.'

When the two girls returned to the restaurant, the bill had only just arrived. To make Katie laugh, Savannah imitated Lily, 'When you enter a room everyone should know where you have come from – Belgrave Hall girls are unmistakable! Remember that, girls – unmistakable!'

Katie and her mother laughed helplessly, and there was no trace of hostility in the air.

The next morning, after breakfast, the girls returned to their bedroom. The audition was at eleven o'clock, and Katie wanted to go over her piece once more. She picked up her violin and tuned it, and the moment she began Savannah saw that she was transformed, scarcely recognizable, her concentration on her playing shut out the entire world, and she knew that Katie had forgotten all about her. She was as invisible as if she were in another room. Hurt because she felt excluded, and somewhat put out even though she had known that she would be left alone during the audition, she watched and waited until Katie had lovingly laid her violin back in its case and snapped it shut, before breaking the news that she had something important to say to her. Still immersed in her music, Katie replied absently, 'Something important? What?'

'You can't be my best friend.'

'Why?'

'We made a rule, remember? You didn't take my dare – if you don't do what I tell you to do we can't be friends.'

Katie's face fell. But this time, much to her own and Savannah's surprise, she bit down hard on her lower lip and successfully stopped the flow of tears. A small victory, and because she had, for once, conquered her own tears she felt better about herself. Her manner changed abruptly– a flush of angry humour lit her eyes. An unexpected titillation of danger danced upon her mind. 'I've got a surprise present for you. It's in the *armoire*, hidden inside my new cowboy boots.' She tapped her violin case, 'I've got to get to my audition – '

'Why don't you call the closet a closet?' Savannah called out petulantly, already inside the *armoire*. 'I can't find it – I can't see anything.'

'It's right at the back, Savannah,' Katie responded, her voice bright. 'Hang on, I'll help you,' she said, moving quickly toward the cupboard.

The next moment Savannah heard the outer door slam shut.

'Let me out this minute!' Savannah roared. 'It's dark in here.'

'Don't worry, I won't lose the key,' Katie said sweetly. 'Mummy said we'd be back in an hour, remember?'

Beating frantically at the locked door, and sobbing with rage, Savannah began to call for help. But the room was in a wing of its own, much too far from the reception for anyone to hear. It was dark and cramped; there was no air, only a strong smell of mothballs. By now hysterical and breathless, her fists painfully bruised, she no longer had the strength to continue hammering at the door. Soon she was crumpled on the floor, like a discarded rag doll. She could not believe that weak, timid Katie could have done this to her. She was not used to being beaten by kids of her own age. And Katie was even younger than she! She would tell Mrs Lidbury about this. Mrs Lidbury would see what this great genius of a violinist was really like inside. What Katie had done was dangerous, and Mrs Lidbury was always warning everyone not to do silly, dangerous things that could get out of hand. Hadn't she herself mimicked Mrs Lidbury on this very subject? A Belgrave Hall girl looks before she leaps – a Belgrave Hall girl is sensitive to the needs of others – a Belgrave Hall girl does not act in a rage to pay someone back because she knows those things will rebound and hit her in the face.

Thinking how sad Mrs Lidbury would be if she died in this suffocating black closet with only a tiny bit of light, she wept with abandon until exhausted, but then, soothed, she drifted into sleep.

Savannah's intuitive perception that while Katie played the violin she, Savannah, no longer existed was entirely correct. As soon as Katie and her mother set out for the audition, Savannah vanished from her mind. After she'd performed the flowing melodious first movement of the Mendelssohn Violin Concerto the maestro judged her to be a 'musician of unimaginable depth overwhelmingly intuitive about her playing, her unique tone pure and powerful and her style perfect.' Caught up in his praise, she didn't remember about Savannah until she was a block away from the hotel. Panic-stricken, she broke into a run.

'Katie, what is it? Are you ill – are you going to be sick?' her mother added anxiously, running alongside her.

'I did something terrible to Savannah and I forgot about it!'

Harriet grabbed her wrist, 'Stop running for a minute and tell me what you did,' she ordered in a tone that brooked no argument.

'I was teasing her when I said I'd only be back in an hour. I meant to lock her up for only five minutes – '

'Lock her up?' her mother repeated. 'Where?'

'In that big cupboard.' Tears streaming down her face, Katie began to run again. Minutes later, when they burst into the hotel room, all was dismayingly quiet. Katie fumbled with the lock.

'It's stuck!' she cried. 'I can't turn it.'

Harriet Ratcliffe pushed her daughter aside, but the key refused to turn.

'*Savannah!*' she called out, shrieking. '*Savannah!*'

But there was only silence.

Shaking, Harriet Ratcliffe rushed to the telephone and called the front desk – 'Room 207 come at once. *Vite! Vite!*'

The terror in her voice was so acute that the concierge left his desk and ran to the room. By this time both Katie and her mother were sobbing.

'But, Madam,' he said, 'you must tell me what is wrong.'

'A child's locked inside the *armoire*,' Katie said through her sobs.

'*Merde!*' he said in a loud whisper as he struggled with the key. 'It is the other little girl, not so?'

He stopped for a moment, made a cartoonish gesture, gave a Gallic shrug, took a small screwdriver from his pocket and inserted it in the little ring in the old-fashioned key, and turned it and opened the door.

Savannah held her breath, hid a sneer, and lay in a heap on the floor.

Later, Harriet Ratcliffe could have sworn that Savannah had been awake all the time, but had simply refused to answer, whether to punish them or because she was ashamed of her swollen, tear-stained face, or a bit of both, she could not say. Although Harriet knew she would never forgive Savannah for the cruel way she'd bullied Katie, she could not help admiring her for the brave and even generous style with which she'd handled her own humiliation at Katie's hands. And she was shocked by Katie's unexpected cruelty.

'It was scary,' Savannah said over and over again. 'Scary – black and so dark, but I knew I was lucky because there was a long crack on the side of the closet and I saw a streak of light, like a magic wand, and I knew I'd be saved.'

Horrified by what she had done, Katie constantly sought reassurance that she had been – and would continue to be – forgiven, and went as far as to take the gold locket she wore round her neck and beg Savannah to accept it.

'You've always liked it, and I'll only know you've really forgiven me if you let me give it to you.'

Harriet hated the idea of Katie giving her locket to Savannah.

Apart from her topaz ring, the locket was the only piece of gold jewellery she owned – everything else had been sold to finance Katie's education. But she had been frightened by all she had read and heard about the psychology of prodigies forced to live precociously in an adult world, before they even had the language to think in adult terms. And so to help preserve the positive effect on Katie's talent of her friendship with this witty and perhaps wicked child, she reluctantly allowed her daughter to barter her locket.

Much as she distrusted Savannah, she could not help feeling some sympathy for her. It was the expression of sadness on Savannah's face while she was looking at the satin-bound baby album in which Katie's history had been recorded that had provoked this unwelcome sense of sorrow for the child. It had been much easier when she'd felt nothing but hatred for her – sympathy obstructs judgement.

The two girls had been giggling over the tiny hospital tag that had been clamped around Katie's wrist when she was born. A little later they had come upon the snapshot of Katie taking her first steps – 'You were eleven months and two days,' Savannah had called out from the caption. 'When my school asked my Mom how old I was when I began to walk she couldn't tell them because she didn't remember.'

Harriet had immediately, if clumsily, changed the subject. Though she'd no recollection of what it was she'd begun to talk about, she remembered Savannah's instantly unreadable eyes, the dull, flat sound of her voice, and the unhappy droop of her shoulders.

Still, she certainly would have preferred Katie to have a different friend, and would bide her time before putting an end to this friendship.

# CHAPTER 12

On a Tuesday morning, ten days after the ball, Lily was behind the wheel of her little Mini on the way to Arundel, the peaceful market town from which she had banished herself all those years ago.

It seemed odd, but strangely fitting – especially after having been at the centre of the recent scandal – that the only person in the world who knew she was on her way to Arundel was the man who had so grievously betrayed her, Hugh Challoner, her ex-husband. This was one of those times when she was a mystery even to herself. She could not understand why she felt guilty of deception, of playing truant, simply because she'd told no one where she was going. It made no sense – after all, Savannah was in Paris with Katie, Magsie was in Manchester attending a lecture and exhibition on the history of lace and would only return after lunch, and Benton was at a meeting in Geneva.

It was not until she reached the Downs on the Dorking bypass that she realized she had been travelling for almost an hour. There, the road seemed to cut a swathe through a mass of fire-red rhododendron bushes. Though she would rather have been anywhere but under a murky sky on the road to Arundel, the gently rolling chalk hills in this most wooded county of England somehow soothed the unpleasantness of the past week.

A little further on she swung off the London road, and drove through narrow lanes under an emerald canopy of trees. She stopped the car at the edge of a meadow. Though from the perspective of a city woman it was madness to wander alone in the depths of the country, she took off her high-heeled shoes and ran towards the sparkling stream. It was there that she and her husband and daughter used to picnic. Sometimes, Amanda would sing, her sweet pure chorister's voice rising high into the air. Now, like a sudden wand of light, a sparrow landed on apple blossom. She watched it until it flew off, and then wrapped her arms around a familiar oak tree and laid her face against its calming trunk. Then, beguiled by the carpet of primroses, she dropped to the base of the tree and seated herself on the weathered log she'd once known so well.

The sound of peace echoed in her ears. Surrounded by the fresh green of the still tender leaves, she breathed in the air of innocence and serenity where everything was still. Here, in this haven of tranquillity, the tumult of emotions that had been raging ever since Stelios Tsakiraki had slapped her began to quieten.

Never one to deceive herself, she faced the fact if Benton and Savannah had not come into her life, she would not now be breaking her long-standing oath never to see or speak to Hugh again. The truth was that it was as much Savannah as the alchemy of physical attraction that had after years of chastity induced her to open herself to Benton, and while she blessed Savannah for having brought Benton to her, it was unforgivable that she was now the other woman.

Impatient with herself, she got to her feet, picked up her shoes, and marched back to her car. There was no point, she chastised herself, in blaming Stelios Tsakiraki for the inner pandemonium devouring her. She knew that it was Hugh's phone call, or rather, her response to his call that had so thoroughly unnerved her.

Hugh's dawn call had awakened her from a nightmare. When she had answered the phone and heard his breathless voice saying, 'Amanda's father, don't hang up,' she had at first thought that her dream had shifted focus. Then, as the voice went on, 'I'm dying, Lily, I've only a few days left,' she realized she'd awakened into, and not out of, a nightmare.

'Are you there, Lily?

'Yes.'

'Please, Lily, don't hang up! Please!'

'I'm here.'

'I'm on continuous oxygen.'

'Heart failure?' she asked. The hospital had called three times over the past year about his heart attacks, but each time she'd angrily told them not to call again, she wasn't interested.

'That's why you must see me,' he responded breathlessly. 'For Amanda's sake,' he added, his breath coming in effortfully, 'help me to die in peace.'

'I'll be with you on Monday.'

There was a silence. 'That's the day after tomorrow,' he said finally in a hoarse and stretched voice. 'Can you not come sooner?'

'I'll be with you in three hours,' she said.

Now behind the wheel again, steeped in the memory of the private torture she had endured when she'd been imagining Hugh and Jane naked in bed together, she was scarcely aware that the storm had broken. It was only when the headlights of the oncoming traffic rushed at her that it occurred to her to switch hers on. Her mind reeled back to that animal jealousy, that patchwork of vicious criss-crossing emotions made up of disappointments, betrayal, shame, rage and overwhelming grief that had possessed her after Hugh had abandoned her. Looking back at that time she felt a surge of pity for that naive girl who had believed she had become a tragic wasteland just because her husband had left her for another woman.

Suddenly the full splendour of the hillside Arundel Castle appeared like a picture from a medieval fairy tale. Like the bridge, the river, the church and the cathedral, the castle merged into the countryside as naturally as if it were rooted in the land on which it stood. It is a truism, Lily reminded herself, that one should never say never. For here she was breaking her vow never to return to Arundel again, driving up the winding High Street dotted with quaint little antique shops on her way to the white Regency house in which she'd thought she would live for ever.

As she parked her car she saw a mass of daffodils in the window boxes she'd erected.

Aware that she was observing herself as if she were someone she'd once known, she sounded the brass dolphin-shaped knocker they'd bought at the Arundel Antique Market. She had the weird feeling that little in the house with the beautiful bow windows would have changed since she'd last crossed its threshold, that terrible day she'd left with nothing but her own and Amanda's clothes.

Hugh and Jane's relationship had not survived the accident. Paralysed by his grief, Hugh had abandoned their plan to move home and stayed where he was.

A slim fortyish man of middle height in a white uniform let her in. The navy stripe on his epaulette told her that he was a staff nurse.

After introducing himself, Jim McKenzie murmured that his patient was on continuous oxygen and that morphine was being administered via a drip.

Following him down the corridor she saw that the framed landscapes and portraits Hugh had painted in his free time were exactly where she had placed them. The obviously new carpet was almost the identical shade of lemon they had chosen together. She felt a rush of relief when she wasn't shown upstairs and into the bedroom they'd shared. Instead, the nurse led her into Hugh's study, now converted into a fully equipped hospital room, where he lay propped up in his electronic hospital bed. A giant oxygen cylinder fed a narrow plastic tube into each nostril. A heart monitor was connected to his chest, a plastic bag led from a catheter into his bladder, and saline and glucose flowed into his veins. His desk had been moved out, and an easel holding a large painting shrouded in a fresh white sheet stood in its place, probably, she thought, because he had asked to see one of the many unfinished landscapes he'd painted.

'I'll leave you then,' the nurse said. 'I know the doctor wants to be alone with you.'

Again that strange feeling of unreality, of observing herself from a great distance, took over. She moved to the bedside of this white-faced, bloodless shadow of the man she had loved to such excess and, making a huge effort, kept her expression bland, and took his cold, clammy hand in hers.

His hair was snowy white, no longer thick and luxuriant, but long and thin. His skin stretched across his cheekbones making his nose too prominent; the weight loss had turned him into a skeleton. She withdrew her hand, moved a chair closer to his bedside, seated herself, and took his hand again.

His shallow and rapid breathing was loud and rasping. 'Thank you, Lily,' he said simply. 'Thank you for coming in time.'

'I wish it could have been otherwise.'

'Very proud of you, Lily,' he murmured. 'Read a lot about you.'

She squeezed his hand lightly. 'Thank you.'

'This is the last time I'll ever ask you to forgive me, Lily – ' he began. 'I haven't even wanted to forgive myself.'

'I forgave you a long time ago,' she lied. 'It wasn't really your fault,' she added truthfully. 'It was her fate to die like that, and my fate, and yours too, to lose her like that.'

Tears rolled down his emaciated cheeks. 'Fate?' he whispered. 'Fate?'

'That's right,' she said. 'Fate.' A sigh shook her. 'I still believe that she was better off dead, than to grow up and become a mother and lose her child the way I lost her.'

'I think I can understand that.'

She gently tightened her grip on his hand and dried his eyes.

'I have something very important to give you,' he said, his voice so weak that she now had to strain to hear him. 'I wanted you to have it while I'm still alive, because I wanted to see you see it.' The effort of speaking exhausted him. Slipping into her nursing mode, Lily immediately adjusted the oxygen dial.

Too weak to raise his arm, he directed his eyes towards the easel. 'Pull back the sheet,' he said.

She moved towards the easel, and withdrew the sheet as slowly as if it were a shroud.

A small cry started in her chest. '*Oh my God*,' she whispered. '*Amanda!*' Clutching her throat, she took a few steps backwards and stopped. She felt all the blood drain from her face, felt she might fall. The shock of seeing Hugh's frail, corpse-like figure was nothing compared with the shock of seeing her child's soft smiling sea-green eyes filled with innocent wonder, staring at her from the canvas. She stepped closer – her hand moved across the canvas as if she were blind, seeing with her fingertips. Her eyes travelled to the edge of the painting. Instead of the usual artist's signature, he'd signed it: 'for Lily – Hugh'. The poetic background of a lonely, stormy sky, of light and colour with the sun shining through clouds in patches, infused the painting with an aura of serenity and sadness made still more poignant by the compassion behind those smiling eyes.

Wrenching herself away, she returned to Hugh's bedside and, kneeling beside him, rested her head partly against his wasted chest. He touched her face gently, and for a long timeless minute, they comforted one another.

Then, lifting her head, and with her palms supporting her chin, she said, 'It's very beautiful – you've captured her essence.'

'I stopped working on it two years ago. But it's not finished.'

'It's perfect.'

'I tried painting her as I imagined her to be when she was growing up. But it couldn't work, of course,' he said slowly. 'Because she did not live to grow up.'

Silence flowed back into the room.

'I think I know what you mean.'

'Will you take her home with you?'

She kissed his cold, clammy hand. 'Yes,' she said.

Beads of perspiration stood on his forehead. She got up, rapidly rinsed a cloth in cold water, squeezed it quickly, and laid it on his forehead.

'Thank you, Lily,' he whispered. 'I think I stayed alive to see you see her.'

'There's a new American child at school who looks uncannily like her,' she heard herself say, the words tumbling from her mouth. 'I wish I had a photograph of her to show you.'

'What's her name?'

'Savannah.'

'Savannah,' he repeated weakly, a knowing look in his otherwise lifeless eyes. 'Always remember then that she is not and never can be our daughter, Lily – ' he paused and a painful silence settled over him. Suddenly, obviously in great distress, he lifted his head off his pillows. 'Could be dangerous,' he murmured. His head sank back, and his fingers found the electric bell pinned to his pyjama top.

Nurse McKenzie appeared at once.

'She does want Amanda,' Hugh muttered.

'Didn't I tell you she would want her, Dr Challoner?'

He gave a weak nod.

'You'd better to go now, Lily,' he whispered. 'Nurse McKenzie will bring it to your car.'

Less than two hours after she had arrived, she was on her way back to London. There was a distant roll of thunder as she left, and though the wind moaned in the trees, the rain held off. Too distraught that morning, she'd not been able to eat. Now she found herself ravenous, even faint, and longing for a glass of white wine. It was rare for her to need a drink, and though she certainly needed one now, she could not leave the painting unattended, so she drove on and did not stop until she reached Belgrave Hall. She carried the portrait up the stairs and then, when it was safe in her bedroom, she collected the easel. Next, though it was only three in the afternoon, she poured herself a large whiskey; still undecided what to do with the portrait, she sat at her dressing table and slowly sipped her whiskey and hoped the answer would come to her when the glass was drained. But when there was no answer, she set the empty glass on her night table, still uncertain what to do.

Dismayed by her indecisiveness yet unable to contain her restlessness, like her mother before her, she resorted to pacing the stairs. But where she had eighty-four stairs, her mother had only twenty. If physical exercise is an antidote to depression, she reflected grimly, then turning to the stairs was one of her mother's more positive legacies to her. Now marching up and down, she was reminded of the humiliation, the deceit, the acting, the punishing fear of being exposed to ridicule and pity if anyone found out about her mother's drunken stumbling and falling during one of her binges when she was fixated on climbing up and down that set of rough splintery stairs. The remembered sound of her mother's repetitive warbling of that crazily terrible nursery rhyme pierced her consciousness. *Goosey, goosey gander, whither shall I wander . . . I took him by the left leg and threw him down the stairs!* The worn, winding stairs of Belgrave Hall began to calm her and, like a stab of unexpected pain, she remembered how pacing the lemon-carpeted stairs had been the only way to soothe Amanda's terrible earache when she'd been a toddler. Now, as then, she counted each step, and by the time she reached one thousand she decided that she would look at the portrait once more.

She returned to her bedroom, fitted the portrait on the easel and slowly drew off its white sheet. Peering at it closely, she gently traced the outline of the rosebud lips. Then, to get it into a better perspective, she turned her back to it and stopped a few paces away. But the portrait, unexpectedly reflected in the mirror, caught her off guard, and she found she could not face those hauntingly compassionate though smiling eyes, and then pulled down the sheet to shut out the light. *Cover her face; mine eyes dazzle: she died young.* These lines from Webster's *Duchess of Malfi* sprang out of a long ago memory.

She lifted the covered canvas off the easel, and rested it against the wall of her cupboard, behind her long skirts.

An hour later her mobile phone rang.

'Hello,' she answered drowsily.

'Don't tell me I woke you, Lily-bud?' Benton sounded concerned.

'I must have fallen asleep – I'd no idea I was so tired.'

'Has the swelling all gone?'

'The cheek has returned to normal, I'm happy to say.'

'I'm at Heathrow.'

'Heathrow?' she repeated.

'The deal was concluded, so there was no point in staying, right?'

'Did it go your way?'

'Sure did, Lily-bud.' He laughed like a pleased child. 'Anyway, I bought us a dinner at Geneva Airport from Caviar House. All your favourites, beluga, Reblochon cheese, *viande sèche, pain de campagne.*'

'Gosh, Benton – '

'Savannah, as you know, is with Katie, so you and I are going to have a private, intimate little dinner in our Sloane Street apartment.'

'Great idea – what time?'

'I'll be there in thirty-five minutes – max.'

'See you.'

A few moments earlier she'd planned on a long hot bath, tea and toast and strawberry jam, after which she was going to watch the box and try to drop into mindlessness. Now she wanted nothing more than to escape from her flat, from the portrait and from the aftermath of her meeting with Hugh. And the miraculous thing was that now that Benton was in her life, now that she had been seized and shaken by love, she had parted with her self-sufficiency; she could lose herself in him, and in his body, and what better escape could there be?

By the time she arrived at 515 Sloane Street, he was already in his robe and setting the table. She deposited a kiss on his head and went off to get out of her clothes and into the silk robe that was like a balm to her skin. She saw with surprise that he'd not only turned down the bed but laid out the robe as well. His thoughtfulness was like the dawn, and she breathed it in and basked in it.

She returned to the table to find that the candles in their crystal candlesticks had already been lit, casting hoops of brilliance around the wine glasses. Chunks of bread lay in a basket, silver cutlery and a bottle of chilled champagne stood on the table. She went into the kitchen to help him, and he took her in his arms, left the tin of beluga he'd been about to open, and kissed her deeply and lingeringly. Soon his kissing sprang into urgency, and he half carried her to the living room, and laid her on the couch. His hard, masculine body, now so familiar, so trusted, slipped into hers and for a few blessed minutes the past and the future vanished and only the present existed.

Later they put on their silk robes again, and went to the table. Though they had not been alone together since the ball they didn't mention it. His tender lips stroked her cheek, and made her more than ever aware of his sensitivity – he knew she didn't want to talk about it. She was tempted to tell him about her day, about Hugh, about her dead child, but she held quiet. She courted the idea of showing the portrait to him if only to get his reaction to Amanda's resemblance to his own daughter, but for fear of being disloyal allowed her idea to go no further than a harmless flirtation. Disloyal? But to whom? To what?

So to save herself from divulging those intensely private though all-consuming prisms of her life, she began, at last, to talk to him about her own mother.

Lily had no doubt, now, she told Benton, that it was that powerful motivator, misguided guilt, that had made her take up nursing purely because her mother's own nursing ambitions had been thwarted. It was years before she realized that it had been easier for her mother to live through Lily instead of with herself.

'But, Lily-bud, aren't you mistaking compassion for guilt?' Benton asked reasonably.

She considered this for some moments. 'It's true I was very sorry for her,' she said slowly. 'Desperately sorry, in fact.'

'Well, then, you're underlining my point, right?'

'Not quite.' She looked pained. 'It was weakness and not compassion that made me allow myself to be manipulated. The very thought of disappointing her was not only excruciating but sinful.' She made a movement of discomfort. 'I hated illness, medicine, and, most of all, I hated death. The preparation of a dead body was repulsive to me – the smell of death made me retch – '

'It's a wonder you ever got your head straight.'

'I'm telling you things I've never even told myself.'

'It's not healthy to keep things locked up inside of you.'

'As *you* well know, Benton,' she said quickly, smiling inwardly – she did not regret one word she had said. But, she warned herself, these kinds of confidences could be dangerous and could make a mature woman delude herself that she was *entitled* to have fallen as hopelessly in love as a besotted teenager. 'Any news from Jodi?' she asked abruptly.

'There have been some major new developments in the case she's working on. Right now she's not needed in New York – '

'She's coming back to London earlier?'

'No,' he said with the mischievous half-grin she found so sexy. 'She's going to a yoga retreat in upstate New York.'

He leaned toward her and with the edge of his finger began to stroke her eyebrows. She shut her eyes, and he traced the outline of her nose over and over again and then, his touch as light as an eyelash on her lips, prolonged the moment until he finally kissed her with the fierce intimacy of a jealous lover. At the precise second when she could bear it no longer, he stopped.

'Let's go to bed,' he said. 'I want you to spend the whole night with me. We haven't been together since Paris.'

Wakened by the scent of coffee, she padded over to the bath-room, brushed her teeth, washed her hands, combed her hair, applied a light lipstick from her small store of cosmetics and then went to the kitchen.

'Out of bounds, Lily-bud,' he said. 'I'm serving you breakfast in bed.'

He appeared carrying a tray loaded with coffee, orange juice, and toasted bagels taken from the freezer. He laid the tray on her lap, and then got in under the blankets beside her. She poured the coffee and handed it to him.

'Great coffee,' he said. 'I guess we shouldn't leave here much before ten. It's only seven now, and the headmistress of Belgrave Hall should not be seen walking out of the building this early.'

'My sentiments exactly,' she chuckled. 'I'm glad I stayed – it was lovely to wake up in this beautiful bed.'

'Who is Hugh?' he asked.

She put down her coffee.

'You called out to him in your sleep – "Hugh," you said, "Oh Hugh." ' He smiled. 'Was it Hugh you called, or you?'

'Hugh is the man to whom I was once married,' she said woodenly.

'Of course, your late husband.'

'My *ex*-husband.'

'Oh – '

'I saw him yesterday. I suppose that's why I was talking about him in my sleep.'

'*Yesterday*,' he said, clearly stunned. 'You saw him only *yesterday*?'

'I had not seen or spoken to him for fifteen years – ' Her eyes travelled vacantly round the room and finally met his. 'He's dying,' she said. 'Progressive heart failure.'

'Don't tell me about it if you don't want to.'

'That's what I love about you,' she said. 'Your sensitivity.' She felt a cold, hard thump in her heart – this is the right moment – tell him now, tell him about Amanda *now!* But she said, 'A few months after my mother died, he went off with one of her best friends.'

He was aware of something hard and self-wounding in her that he'd never seen in her before. 'That must have been rough,' he said.

'They don't know anything about this at school,' she bit her lip. 'Magsie's the only one who knows,' she added wanly. 'You see, I'd been living in Arundel, and I'd expected to live there for the rest of my life, but I moved to London because I wanted to be anonymous.' She cleared her throat. 'I was lucky to find Belgrave Hall. I have Magsie to thank for that – she saw the post advertised and persuaded me to apply.' She sighed, 'I'd been *indescribably* hurt – but the pain was somehow more endurable or, I should say, less unendurable, if I kept myself wrapped in a bandage of anonymity.'

'You must have been married to one hell of an idiot, Lily-bud,' he said quietly.

'I got over him,' she murmured. 'It was – ' She tried to speak, but her throat closed, achingly. Not a word would come.

He drew her to him and, rocking her in his arms, sprinkled tiny kisses on her head, and she shut her eyes and tried not to think. After a while he said reluctantly, 'Don't consider me unfeeling, Lily-bud, but I've got to go. It's the big one – the Cornhill Group meeting.'

'Of course – you told me about it,' she said, feeling reprieved. 'You'd better hurry.'

She did not begin to dress until he had left. She put on her clothes like an automaton. She felt dazed, because she'd been on the edge of telling him about Amanda, but once again had failed to seize the moment. She went to the bathroom to splash water on her face and tried to make sense of her silence. Though she was an excellent secret-keeper, she was not by nature secretive. This silence, this secrecy about Amanda had made survival possible. After that tragically small coffin at the funeral, she had not once visited her child's grave. Yesterday, in Arundel, though she had gone as far as stopping her car beside the churchyard, she had gone no further. How, then, could she talk about her dead child to anyone who didn't know her? Magsie, of course, knew Amanda, but even so, it was painful to speak of her – sometimes a whole year could go by without as much as a mention of her name.

Lily had only been home for about ten minutes when the phone rang. She knew it would be Magsie – she'd been contemplating calling her to tell her about Hugh and the portrait. She answered it at once.

'Good afternoon, Magsie,' she said.

Delighted laughter followed. 'You must have been thinking of me.'

'I was about to ask you to come up and have tea.'

'I found something for your birthday at the fair,' Magsie replied happily. 'I'm giving it to you well in advance – you'll love it.'

Even before Lily had poured the tea, Magsie had taken the unwrapped gift from its bag. She held up a vintage blouse of gossamer black lace lined with layers of grey chiffon.

'It will go so well with your grey flannel skirt,' she said.

Lily thanked her, held it up to the light and pronounced it beautiful, then she carefully put it back in its used supermarket bag and poured the tea.

'It's true vintage,' Magsie proclaimed enthusiastically.

'You're right,' Lily murmured. 'It is perfect for my flannel skirt.'

A distant siren screamed, and Lily got up impatiently and went to the window. Hunched, wordlessly shaking her head, she remained there a long while. She seemed to have forgotten Magsie was with her.

Eventually Magsie broke the silence. 'What's troubling you?' she asked abruptly.

Lily quickly returned to the kitchen table and sat down. 'Does it show that much?'

'To me, it does.'

'I went to see Hugh yesterday.'

There was an audible intake of a very deep breath. 'How is he?' Magsie asked.

'He won't be with us much longer.'

'You did the right thing, Lily.'

'It was awful going back to that house again, Magsie.'

'He's not in hospital then?'

'They've converted his study into a hospital room – everything else is almost exactly as I left it – same copper vase of fresh daffodils on the hall table, new carpet, same colour – even those amateurish window boxes I'd made myself were still there.'

'It was big of you to go.'

'He got me on the phone himself – he was breathless,' she said, wincing. 'Anyway he begged me to see him, to help him to die at peace with himself.'

'How awful for you.'

'It wasn't only that,' Lily sighed. 'He had something he wanted to give me – ' She hesitated a minute and then seemed to make up her mind. 'It's a portrait of Amanda – fantastically, miraculously lifelike – he's been working on it for years.' She shrugged bravely, 'It's beautiful, very beautiful, but I can't actually live with it.'

'Would you like me to look after it for you, Lily?'

'Oh, Magsie, would you?' she smiled with grim melancholy – 'I thought of that . . . I just didn't know what – ' she broke off, muttered, 'It's too hurtful to me, Magsie – I can't . . . I just can't *bear* to look at it.'

'Where is it, Lily?'

'In the bedroom cupboard, behind the skirts. It's wrapped in a sheet.' She closed her eyes for a moment, as if she were praying. 'I'd love to know what you think of it, Magsie.'

Magsie was already on her way to the bedroom. The cupboard door creaked, and then there was a long silence – the seconds moved slowly. Lily had thought she had her life arranged, under tight control, impenetrably shielded behind permanent ice. But the portrait had blasted all that away. For the millionth time, the billionth time, she thought: my daughter died.

'It's more than lifelike,' Magsie said as she came back into the kitchen. 'It's alive,' she added huskily, unashamedly wiping her eyes. She sat down on the wing chair facing Lily. 'I could do with a drink after that.'

'What would you like?'

'A stiff Scotch.'

'At three in the afternoon?'

Magsie nodded.

'I'll join you, I had one myself at exactly the same time yesterday,' she said. She got up and poured two glasses.

Magsie took a long draught. 'I see what you mean – it's so alive, it's frightening.' A huge sigh shook her. 'It's Amanda,' she said, awed. 'Amanda.'

'She looks like Savannah, doesn't she?'

This was the second time Magsie would have liked to correct her – *it's the other way round, Savannah looks like Amanda.* 'There is a definite resemblance, the red hair, the shape and even the colour of the eyes, but Amanda's expression, the light in her eyes, the light of love, of compassion, and laughter is entirely different from Savannah's,' she snapped.

'I'm not yet ready to live with it,' Lily said, pointedly ignoring Magsie's negative comment. 'One day, perhaps, I'll get used to the idea – ' she floundered. 'But not yet.'

# CHAPTER 13

Jodi's daring strategy had paid off.

There was only one person who knew about the extent of her Machiavellianism and that was Mike O'Dowd, the cynical, talented private investigator whom she had hired so secretly that she had gone as far as to pay him in cash. Even if she had been able to trust anyone at Hardwick, Murphy and Ford, how could she have let anyone know what she had done when she had no logical explanation, nor even a smidgen of hard evidence, that could have justified hiring a PI to investigate the private life of the prosecutor, Cindy Fritelli? She had taken this drastic step because she'd twice observed the way the ambitious Cindy Fritelli had momentarily shut her eyes when the notorious Lloyd Brook's name had cropped up.

A devoted husband and father of five who taught Sunday School, Judge Brooks was being pilloried by the media for having attempted to conceal his affair with Elaine Meredith, the twenty-two-year-old graphic designer who had disappeared. But though Cindy had closed her eyes for no longer than the flutter of an eyelash, Jodi had within that same instant felt – rather than thought – that Cindy must be locked into some sort of obsessive relationship with the reputedly kinky judge.

In the new landscape of her only recently discovered soul this was unacceptable practice. But in the landscape of a litigator it was (as a distinguished attorney once wrote) *'almost routine for lawyers to cross the lines of the acceptable, the ethical, and, more rarely, the legal'*. But it seemed to Jodi that this was the only sure way she could act in the best – and winning – interests of her client, whose innocence or guilt was no more relevant to her as a litigator than was the cause of serving justice. In her business, winning was everything. She would quit her profession with an inglorious conscience, cloaked in a blaze of glory.

Accordingly, she invited Cindy Fritelli to a private lunch meeting at her apartment. Over coffee she handed her Mike O'Dowd's series of photographs, some of which showed her rubbing cocaine into the judge's gums. And then, without malice or mercy, she advised Cindy to dismiss the Government's case against Louisa Stacey on the grounds of insufficient evidence. It was simple and safe – no one questioned a prosecutorial decision to dismiss when there was a shortage of evidence.

Soon after that she sent an impersonal memo to William Hardwick informing him that, due to insufficient evidence, the case against Louisa Stacey had been dismissed.

But would she have been so reckless, she asked herself, if her vicious need to win had not been conquered? For the commanding urge to prove that she could be as confrontational as a professional boxer – whether or not it was necessary – was at last strictly under her own control.

Paradoxically, however, her victory over justice had been so startlingly profound that Professor Hardwick took the unusual step of visiting her in her own office to congratulate her. But where once this would have led to a state of exhilaration, she was as unmoved as a lover who has become bored, and even irritated, by the one who'd aroused so much passion for so long.

'You're at the height of your legal intelligence, Jodi.' Professor Hardwick allowed his enthusiasm to show. 'Getting the prosecutor to drop charges on the grounds of insufficient evidence has prevented tens of millions from being shaved off the stock.' He looked at her questioningly. 'You've changed your style of dress?'

She did not bother to reply. She was tempted to tell him that she had long known that winning a corporate case had everything to do with the price of the stock and nothing to do with justice. She flirted with the idea of confessing that she had succeeded because early in her career she had dispensed with idealism and accepted that the business objectives involved in commercial litigation reduced the concept of a belief in justice to an absurd embarrassment. Instead, she said, 'I meditate.'

'Of course you do,' he responded. 'We couldn't be attorneys if we didn't seriously meditate. To meditate is to think, to anticipate the unanticipated, to prepare for the most remote of possibilities.'

'That is not what I'm talking about,' she said.

'Just what *are* you talking about?'

She threw out her arms and her bangles clattered. 'Look beyond events, dissolve into infinity, and be in the moment.'

He gave a false laugh. 'The spiritual path is recognized by the constitution – ' He got up and straightened his tie. 'Well my dear, speaking of moments, as you'll be hearing at the dinner in your honour tomorrow night, Hardwick, Murphy and Ford look upon you as the woman of the moment.'

Wondering why it had all become so meaningless, she told him she had already sent her regrets: 'I'll be dining at the Mantra Retreat in upstate New York,' she smiled.

In spite of himself, he smiled back. Now that she dressed in this sort of soft, womanly way she had become rather pretty. Strange, he had known her all these years, but he'd never really thought of her as a woman. He'd seen her as a female student, and later as an unfeminine female litigator, but not as a woman. There was a time, he reminded himself, when she had claimed that she was not one of those mothers who was weighed down and diminished by the maternal instinct. Ah, well, all this crazy yoga stuff proved that she was an ordinary woman after all. Damned good litigator, though.

'You women are unpredictable and inexplicable,' he said. 'Declining a partners' dinner in your honour for a yoga retreat!'

'In litigation there really is a winner and a loser,' she replied. 'I guess I'm just not brutal enough to be a constant winner.' Her eyes glistened with tears. 'Didn't you teach me that if you believe in a client's innocence you are less effective, because you sacrifice your objectivity?'

'Which is why you're such a damned good trial lawyer.'

'Well, Louisa Stacey is guilty as all hell!' she cried furiously. 'You know it, and I know it, and we both know that she deserves to be locked up and the key thrown away. Instead the board's insurance will pay our fee, her flamboyant lifestyle will continue, and she won't even remember the name of the poor bank manager who threw himself out of a building because of her fraudulent manipulations.'

'You're permitting your fine legal mind to be distorted by scruple!' the professor retorted.

'Conscience in the legal world has become as outmoded as chloroform in the medical world,' she snapped. 'Honesty and principle are as inconvenient and as irrelevant as truth. As far as white-collar crime is concerned, we attorneys look for victory rather than justice. And, because a huge monetary fine takes the place of justice, the fine is seen as a victory.'

'Your reasoning is both improper and unproductive,' he protested. 'You acquitted yourself brilliantly, so much so that several highly respected big-time corporations have already requested you to lead the team for Hardwick, Murphy and Ford to act for them.'

'Victory won at the cost of morality,' she said. 'I'm going to the yoga retreat to do all I can to rid my body of noxious toxins,' she half whispered. 'Would that I could do the same to purify my soul.' She fiddled with her bangles. 'These past three weeks of late nights haggling over negotiation strategies have drained me dry.'

'Well it worked, didn't it?' he said. Determined to make allowance for what he saw as her eccentricity – she wasn't the only successful female trial attorney to dress outlandishly – he added, 'I'm proud of you, Jodi. You've more than justified my faith in you. I've seen you grow from a bright, mono-minded student into an outstanding litigator.' Warming to his topic, he continued, 'Your intuitive sense of legal strategy is invaluable.' He was about to tell her of his great admiration for that mystical factor called female intuition but stopped himself – any accusation of sexism was to be avoided. 'You're bringing in the business, my dear. By anyone's standards, you're one hell of a rainmaker!'

Her face expressionless, she threw up her hands again. 'Three weeks,' she repeated. 'Three exhausting, seventy-hour weeks.' She inhaled deeply, and closed her eyes for a moment. Suddenly, her gloom lifted. Smiling triumphantly, her eyes bright, she added, 'Fortune changes like the swish of a horse's tail.'

Quivering with exasperation, he turned away from her. 'You've been under too much pressure,' he said. 'Is London less – '

'Alien?' she finished for him. 'It introduced me to a new universe.'

'Ah – so that's why you're above it all.'

'I used only to notice the traffic here. Now I'm aware of the islands of golden tulips and daffodils in the middle of Park Avenue,' she said. 'The heart opens the mind just as the mind opens the heart.'

'Such matters are outside the realm of law,' he said impatiently. 'Your success in this case has certainly opened new horizons, and may even have changed the legal landscape.'

At the same time that Jodi was being congratulated for her brilliance as a trial attorney, Lily was opening a letter from Giles Glendenning, the country solicitor who had handled her divorce.

> Dr Challoner [she read] did not wish you to be informed of his death until after his cremation and the disposal of his ashes had taken place. He expressly requested that his cremation be unencumbered by any service of any kind whatsoever. He was, in his own words, 'anxious not to inflict any more sadness on Lily'. As you will see from the enclosed last Will and Testament, his entire estate has been bequeathed to you.

Fixated on the fact that his body had been incinerated like a lump of coal, she did not so much as glance at the enclosed legal document. She folded her arms across her chest, shut her eyes, and sat absolutely still, feeling numb, her mind turning over and over the words *what a waste, what a waste.*

Benton had tickets for Lily, Savannah and him to go to a Saturday matinee of a West End musical, but she knew she could not make herself go. After a while she phoned and, keeping her voice level, told him that Hugh had died.

'I'm sorry, Lily-bud,' he said. 'I'm sure as hell that going to the theatre is the last thing you'd like to do.'

'The very last.'

'Talk to you later then.'

She replaced the receiver in its cradle and sat motionless in the gathering darkness. She heard the phone ring, but could barely stir herself to answer it. Finally, the ringing stopped and silence returned. When it began to ring again, she took the phone off the hook and put it under a pillow. Almost at once the insistent sound of the buzzer pierced the silence. She had no alternative but to answer it.

Magsie was at the door. 'Benton Anderson doesn't want you to be alone,' she said quickly. 'He's quite right, of course. You'd better buzz me in. I'm coming up.'

She came in and gathered Lily in her arms. 'It's a blessed release, I'm sure,' she murmured.

By way of a reply Lily handed her the solicitor's letter. She waited until Magsie had read it before speaking. Then, her voice hoarse and stretched, she said, 'It's the way he disposed of himself that kills me.' Distraught, she went on and on about the barbarism of cremation.

Magsie, in turn, resorted to platitudes about respecting the wishes of the dead and the dying. And then, astonished, she heard herself say, 'Benton Anderson is in love with you.'

Lily flushed.

'How long has this been going on between you two?'

'I don't know what you're talking about – '

207

'I didn't mean to say anything about this,' Magsie said. 'I took myself by surprise. You don't have to tell me about it, but I want you to know that I know.'

Lily pressed her lips together. Her expression froze. She sat very still, statue still. Her response confirmed Magsie's suspicions. 'I began to wonder about this when he brought you home from the Daffodil Ball – I saw the way he kissed your poor, swollen cheek. I've thought about nothing but Savannah and her father for days. I realized that it must have been going on for several weeks. I remembered the frightening look of anguish in your eyes that first time you saw Savannah just before the carol concert began. And then I also remembered your unnaturally passive response when I told you of the cruel way she'd thrown Bertie in his hamster ball up in the air even though I'd warned her to be gentle with him.'

'From the very beginning you were too quick to think the worst of Savannah,' Lily burst out angrily. 'I've already told you why she did that – '

Magsie looked blank.

'You can't have forgotten, Magsie!' she exploded. 'I asked her about it and she told me about the father she'd seen in the park throwing his laughing baby in the air and then catching him – '

'Of course I haven't forgotten,' Magsie said quickly. 'The point I'm trying to make is that though I asked her to be gentle, she deliberately went ahead and did just what she wanted to do!' She leaned forward and laid her hand on Lily's arm. 'Don't let's quarrel about this, Lily,' she pleaded. 'I shouldn't have mentioned any of this – I'd cut off my right arm rather than hurt you.'

Lily covered Magsie's hand with her own. 'I know that, Magsie,' she said. 'I shouldn't have stood on my high horse.'

'Are you in love with him?'

'I don't know – '

'You don't know?' Magsie echoed.

'I can't think straight at the moment,' Lily said. 'I was so crazy about Hugh for so long.' The memory of her rampant sexual jealousy made her shudder. 'I hated him after our divorce, and then when Amanda – ' her voice trailed off. 'But I still wanted him. I still needed him, needed his body, his arms. I still thought of him as *my* husband. I convinced myself that if I hadn't taken up teaching, if I'd worked with him at his office, as he wanted me to, he wouldn't have fallen for her. We'd have been the family we were meant to be.' A quiver of grief ran through her body. 'I would not now be the mother of a dead child.'

'But Lily, you were only a mother – not an invincible deity,' Magsie said. 'As soon as we women become mothers we think we ought to be supremely powerful, so if anything goes wrong in the family, it's all our fault! I remember watching a replay of Mrs Thatcher break into tears on TV when her son went missing somewhere in Africa – she seemed to blame herself, too.'

'I think I know what you mean.'

'Does he know about Amanda?'

'I can't make myself tell him.'

'You'll find the right moment. You must.'

'So I keep telling myself,' Lily shrugged. 'I'm glad you know about Benton and me.'

'Of course you know you're in a minefield,' Magsie measured her words carefully. 'You could get badly burned.'

'It's not only risky – ' Lily's voice faltered, and a spasm twitched her face, 'it's immoral – who would think that I could be the other woman?' She raised her eyes to the ceiling, 'I stand to lose everything I care about,' she said. 'And the really awful thing is that the worst would be no more than I would actually deserve.' She went on ruefully, 'It would be cruel, but it would be just.'

'Now you're invading my territory, and talking like a superstitious peasant,' Magsie smiled. 'I'm the only one round here allowed to do that.'

'But what if anyone finds out about us?' she had asked Benton at the beginning of their affair.

'No one will ever know for sure *unless you tell them*,' he had replied with absolute certainty.

And yet, though she knew that in having been honest with Magsie she had also betrayed Benton, there was something oddly satisfying about having proved her lover right. Recently, for some inexplicable reason, she had come to accept that her relationship with him was not required to make sense. According to the laws of logic they had too little in common to fit so well. He read five newspapers a day, she read *The Times*. The only novels he had ever read had been forced upon him during school; while there was a time when she had been addicted to fiction. Indeed, the differences in their thinking, from music to travel to euthanasia, were so profound that perhaps their relationship was founded on an honouring of differences rather than a sharing of interests. True, they were both involved in Savannah, though for entirely different reasons. But there could be no comfort in this line of thought. As an antidote she concentrated instead on what she had not admitted to Magsie. The catastrophe was already upon her. It had begun the day after she saw Hugh again, when her cunningly nurtured state of self-deception had come to an end. For now she could no longer deny that however senseless, immoral or ridiculous it was, she'd been stupid enough to fall in love.

Since Benton had entered her life she had become skilled at evading hard truths. It now seemed that the wisest thing she could do was to decide not to decide on anything. Jodi had been away for three whole weeks, and eight more days remained before she was due to return. Meanwhile, it was enough to live for the moment.

Lily had turned Savannah's Saturday morning lessons at Belgrave Hall into a special treat. She always had some sort of a surprise in store, a story, a drawing, a treasure hunt. Today however, Savannah's concentration constantly wavered – she was so quiet that Lily began to wonder if she was bored. It was when the pencil slipped from her fingers that Lily knew something was gravely wrong – all colour had drained from her face, and beads of perspiration were spreading across her brow. Lily caught her head just before it fell to the desk. As she felt Savannah's head, she realized that the child was burning with a high fever. Her fingers automatically flew to her pulse – rapid, so rapid.

'Savannah, Savannah, what's the matter?' Lily asked, her voice fearful. 'Look at me, tell me what's wrong.'

But Savannah could hardly speak. 'Headache,' she said. Her head tilted to one side. The physical changes quickly intensified, her pupils were dilated and she was beginning to lose control and to seem unaware of her surroundings.

Lily's professional experience deserted her and she panicked. She might never have been a staff nurse or even a first year student. She sped downstairs to telephone Dr Jacobson, the school medical officer. She had his emergency number. Where was it? Dear God, let it be in her handbag – but she'd forgotten she'd changed handbags. She must have left it in the one she used on a daily basis. Now she charged upstairs to find it. Yes, there it was – Dr Jacobson's blessed emergency number.

Trembling, she dialled his number. 'It's Lily Lidbury,' her voice squeaked. 'Dr Jacobson? Thank God you're there.'

'What is it, Mrs Lidbury?'

'You've got to come at once to Belgrave Hall. I'm taking care of this child – her mother's away, you've got to get here immediately.'

'You're a nurse, Lily. What do you think it is?'

She burst into tears. 'Meningitis,' she said through her sobs. 'I'm so afraid, doctor.'

'I'll be with you in five minutes.'

Doctor Jacobson arrived, and twenty minutes later they were in an ambulance speeding toward the Cromwell Hospital. It was a private hospital; Savannah would have her own room. The nurses and doctors took over, and very quickly, Savannah was undergoing all the relevant diagnostic tests.

Benton met them at the hospital. He had tried to call Savannah's mother, but the Mantra Retreat had no record of a Jodi Anderson. Her cell phone was obviously out of range because it wasn't even taking messages.

'Why don't you two go down and have some coffee or something to eat?' a nurse asked sympathetically. 'She's fast asleep and we won't have the results for at least an hour.'

'Sounds like a great idea,' Benton said gratefully. He was starving; he'd missed breakfast and hadn't eaten all day.

They waited for the results of the tests in that small crowded coffee shop filled with the loud rythmical laments of a large group of Arabs, the men's heads covered with the flowing *kaffyeh*, the hooded and veiled women in their *hijabs* reminding Lily of birds of prey; and so it was that she finally came to tell him about Amanda.

Watching him wolf down a thick cheese sandwich, she wondered how he could swallow. Her mouth was dry, and her facial skin felt tight, as if it had shrunk. She could not face the terror of what was happening, what might happen. It might have been that it was because she was so terrorized by her own fear that suddenly, her eyes staring feverishly into his, she said, 'I had a little girl who died.'

'*What?*' He tugged at his hair. 'You had a little girl – do you mean a schoolgirl you were teaching?'

'No.'

'*Jesus*, Lily-bud!' he exclaimed, exasperated. 'What are you talking about? I can't say I understand – '

'My own daughter,' she began shakily. 'But I can't – it's so – so terrible that I – can't – ' Her voice keeled over. 'Unbelievably tragic – ' She broke off again.

He leaned forward and took her hand. 'I won't quiz you, Lily-bud,' he said gently. 'If you don't want to tell me about it, I'll understand.'

'I don't want to, but I must – just must – tell you.'

Benton had no idea what to say, or even what he thought.

But he said, 'I'd give anything to be able to help you, Lily-bud.'

'Her name was Amanda, and she was – ' She could not get the words out, and again stopped speaking. As if to absorb his strength, she tightened her grip on his hand. Her blue eyes were wide, fixed in unmistakable panic. 'A dog belonging to her stepmother's sister, a Rottweiler, tore her apart and – ' her voice broke, and she struggled to regain control.

He jumped up and, bending over her, tried to comfort her, but she shook her head.

'So my child died horribly.' Her hushed, lifeless voice seemed to belong to someone else. 'She was trying to rescue a rabbit – ' She looked into the middle distance and then her nerve came back to her and her eyes met and held his. 'I am unable to cry,' she said wearily.

He drew a painful breath. 'What can I say, Lily-bud? What can anyone say?'

She gave a small, helpless shrug.

'How long ago was this?'

'Fifteen years.'

'Why didn't you tell me before?'

'I couldn't bring myself to talk about it – '

Once again at a loss for words, but longing to comfort her, he said, 'You're a remarkably brave woman.'

There was a peculiar sighing silence between them. She looked down into her untouched coffee. For fifteen long years the loss of Amanda had ruled her memory. Like a titanium pin pierced into the bone after a fracture, her memory was with her as she awoke, and as she fell asleep. The shock and bewilderment might have become less wild, less violent, but the urge to rip her flesh from her bones had not entirely abated, and would only die with her.

She found herself telling him about the day she had tried to comfort an inconsolably bereaved mother whose daughter had been a Belgrave Hall student. 'She told me that it was six months since her daughter had died. She'd bumped into a friend who'd casually asked her how she was. 'A bit down today,' she'd answered truthfully. 'Still?' the friend had responded. But you see, Benton, for her, as for all mothers who've lost a child there was no *still*; it is, and always will be, ever-present.'

'I see what you mean,' he said quietly. 'I guess there are some things we – '

'I was in the middle of a Swedish massage while she was dying,' she interrupted, her voice as dry as tinder. 'I'd won a school raffle. Perhaps you remember suggesting a Swedish massage when we were in Paris?' She stood up abruptly. 'They should have the test results by now,' she said. 'Let's go back to Amanda.'

'Savannah,' he said softly.

'Sorry,' she said. 'Savannah.' She looked away, abstracted. Didn't Benton realize that Savannah's symptoms could mean a tumour of the brain?

The tests confirmed that it was a case of uncomplicated meningitis. Savannah would be given intravenous antibiotics and pain relief, and if things went smoothly she would be out of hospital within ten days.

Savannah had been in the hospital for five days and she hadn't cried once. Everyone said how brave she was, but she didn't think she was *that* brave. The truth was that she knew crying would make the headache much, much worse. She had been frightened and had been very, very sore but it was only when she saw those tears coming out her father's eyes that she had been really, really scared because he wouldn't have cried if he hadn't thought she was dying. Lily had nearly cried, too. They were all still trying to call her Mom – she could tell her Dad was angry about her mom's cell phone not working. 'Thank God you've got Lily with you,' he said over and over again. 'Luckily, she's a nurse, too.'

She felt safe with Lily. In a way it was even better having Lily than having her mom, because her mom always said she wasn't really good with kids, that's why she had Bronnie.

She wished Bronnie was with her – but even her mom would

be better than no one. Of course the nurse called Dolores came in to take her temperature, but she didn't like her; she was so thin and her hands were so bony and sharp that it felt like her fingers were made of glass. No, she didn't like Dolores, but she didn't hate her the way she hated Mrs Lidbury for being with Katie today. She hated Mrs Lidbury so much because she'd gone off to Katie's concert and left Savannah all alone even though she'd begged and begged her not to. If Mrs Lidbury loved her like she said she did, she wouldn't have gone and left her all alone in a hospital like this. *Mrs Lidbury loved Katie, not her.* She'd seen that photo taken of the two of them on the day of the Form Presentation. Well she hated Katie – she was going to stop being friends with her. Katie didn't *deserve* to have her as a friend. Katie had everything – today she had her mom *and* she had Mrs Lidbury. It wasn't fair!

Bored and lonely, she picked up the small transistor radio, one of the numerous gifts Mrs Lidbury had brought her. She turned the dial so savagely that it came off and tumbled to the floor. It was while she was searching for it under the bed that she found her father's cell phone. Good! The doctor had not yet allowed her to have a phone, so she would use this one and call Bronnie. She knew the number by heart. The phone rang and rang but there was no answer. After several attempts she decided to try her mom at her yoga retreat. Her dad must have programmed the number in – he'd done that with loads of numbers. Mrs Lidbury's number was there, too. She'd seen him get through to her that way.

She hit several keys before she found the right one.

'Mantra Retreat, good morning – how may I direct your call?'

'I'm calling from London, England for Mrs Anderson.'

'She's not here.'

'When will she be back?'

'She's not registered here.'

'She's not staying there?'

'Sorry, we have no *sanyasin* by that name here.'

Disappointed, she tried her mom's mobile again. She hit the quick-dial key, and repeated the word '*Sanyasin?*' to herself.

Suddenly her father's recorded voice filled the hospital room. '*In case you're wondering where your locket is, honey, I found it in the car.*'

Then came her own voice.

'*Gosh, Dad, thanks! I didn't know I'd lost it.*'

'*Night, honey. Sweet dreams.*'

There was a crackling for a few seconds, then a new, strangely familiar voice came on the line, as if from a distance.

'*That's one of the things I love about you, Benton – you're so thoughtful. Savannah would have been so unhappy if she thought she'd lost it.*'

It was weird – it was Mrs Lidbury's voice. Then her father again.

'*No woman ever loved me the way you love me. In fact I don't think I've ever really been loved by a woman.*' She heard her father sigh loudly and deeply. '*You're especially beautiful tonight, Lily-bud, do you know that?*'

'*Don't be so silly, Benton. I'm hardly a young girl.*'

'*Lily Lidbury with the softest, loveliest eyes in the whole world?*' A deep affectionate laugh. '*It's that tender look of yours, I guess.*'

'*Oh Benton, it's already ten past three in New York – I almost forgot my promise to remind you to call.*'

'*Thanks – I'll do that right now.*'

The voice-mail ended.

Lily-bud, she thought, her father called Mrs Lidbury Lily-bud.

She kept the phone in her hand for a long while. Then, when Dolores came in with her medications, she quickly hid the phone under the bedclothes. As soon as Dolores left she made sure it was switched off. Next, she got up and carefully placed it in her sponge bag. She did not know what she was going to do with the phone or why she was keeping it. She only knew that she was not going to give it back. Her father was always losing his phone anyway.

# CHAPTER 14

Jodi had left the Mantra Retreat in a state of high elation. She had risen at 5 a.m. to meditate, and now, two hours later, listening to Indian music as she drove along the highway that would take her back to New York, the feeling of peace seeping through her was at once comforting and energizing. Purged of so much complicated emotion, all tension had floated away, leaving her cleansed, replenished and resolute. She was going to renounce law and embrace life. She winced with shame remembering that day at Victoria Station when, drowning in self-pity, she'd wanted to walk away from herself for ever. But, like her sleeping pills, all that was history. She'd gotten her head together – the breakages of the past had been repaired, the spillages mopped up, and now her new ambition was to become a proper wife and a good mother. The kind of mother a daughter could actually like.

Like a sign from the heavens, Savannah's bitter words of a few weeks ago came back to her. *Why can't you make friends with the other moms at school? Tiffany's mom had a mom-and-daughter lunch party at the Berkeley, and I was left out.*

If she could break through to the school mothers she would break through to Savannah. But how? So what if Courtney Hunt and Verine Joseph had snubbed her? She'd be a fool to let those airheads stand in her way. *She* would give a mom-and-daughter tea party at the Ritz and, what's more, she would invite them.

And then, with startling clarity, it came to her that Savannah seemed closer to Lily Lidbury than to her. It wasn't healthy, she was sure. Forewarned is forearmed, she told herself. Somehow, whatever it took, she would take her rightful place in her daughter's life. Never one to do things by halves, this was to be as profound a change of life-style as divorce. Her supreme ambition now was to find a successful way to plead her case – she wanted Savannah to love and respect her in the way she loved and respected Lily Lidbury

She also had a vague plan to become a yoga teacher. Perhaps she could help other similarly afflicted high achievers to escape from the excesses of success? She realized she'd grown into what she'd once detested – a committed do-gooder, a fanatical seeker-after-truth treading a spiritual path.

Later, she pulled off the road to have a coffee. The cell phone that she had not been able to use in the mountains beeped to let her know it was fully charged. Good, she thought, she would use the phone. Savannah would not yet be home from school (it was 4:30 in the afternoon in London), so she would call William Hardwick. She wanted to give him advance warning of the bombshell she planned to drop at the partners' profit-share meeting, when she would announce her reasons for leaving the venerable law firm of Hardwick, Morgan and Ford. As one of the exalted few who had his private cell phone number, she could not help smiling at the thought of his reaction to her news. Exceptionally, however, his secretary, Donna Phillips, answered. 'Sorry, Jodi, Professor Hardwick is in conference – '

The moment she heard Donna's tone, Jodi tensed up. She could feel the irritation creeping back into her veins, blackening the serenity and joy of her post-retreat bliss. She and Donna had never got on. In fact the administrative staff had always given her a hard time. At least she wouldn't have to put up with them any longer.

Jodi inhaled deeply. 'I would like to speak with Professor Hardwick. It's important,' she repeated, focusing all her energy on maintaining calm.

'I just told you he's in conference. I wouldn't dream of disturbing Professor Hardwick for you or anyone else,' Donna countered.

Jodi could feel her temper rising, the bile building up inside her. No! She would not let this woman, this firm, and her *old* life-style, ruin all that she had worked so hard to achieve. She had new goals now, and new horizons.

'Thank you. Goodbye,' she said abruptly, and switched off her cell phone.

How right she was to give it all up! Shaking with rage, she pulled herself together and began to breathe in the yogic way. Disappointed, she realized she wasn't yet strong enough in her meditation practise to handle Donna with patient-loving-kindness. And right now she wanted to bask in the bliss of the retreat's afterglow for as long as she could. She continued breathing rhythmically and slowly until her serenity returned. It took longer than she'd thought. Then she called Savannah. Because she no longer took Western technology for granted, she rejoiced in the idea of sitting in a car, high in the mountains, and being able to make a phone ring six thousand miles away in London.

Opi answered.

'Hi Opi, how – '

'Savannah's in hospital,' Opi wailed. 'Meningitis.'

'Meningitis?' Jodi shrieked. 'When? How? Which hospital?'

'The Cromwell Hospital,' Opi replied. 'I got the hospital phone number.'

Jodi found herself shaking. Her heart began to beat so violently that she felt giddy. The Cromwell line was busy so she called Benton. His mobile was switched off, so she called his office. After assuring her that Savannah was recovering, Benton spared her nothing. She hadn't been registered at the Retreat, he raged; she'd been unreachable. No, she could not call Savannah – the doctor did not yet want her to have a phone. She had her passport with her, she told him, so she would drive directly to Kennedy Airport, get a plane out of there and go straight to the hospital. Savannah had really needed her mother, he fumed; everyone had understood that mobiles did not function in those godforsaken mountains, but everyone had been horrified that she hadn't at least left a forwarding number. It was obvious, she retorted, that no one had tried hard enough – she'd been at the retreat all the time. The only thing that mattered was that Savannah was getting better.

Later, when the plane was airborne, she realized that she had forgotten to let Professor Hardwick know that she had resigned from Hardwick, Morgan and Ford.

The moment Jodi reached Savannah's hospital room all her self-control deserted her. She knelt beside the bed, gently kissed her forehead, and burst into tears. Then, making a mammoth effort, she regained herself and begged her daughter to forgive her. She'd been at the retreat all the time and she couldn't understand why no one had been able to reach her.

'The lady who answered the phone over there freaked out when I called and asked for you.' Savannah told her matter-of-factly. 'She sounded like a prison wardress in that movie – '

'Oh, honey, I'm so sorry, so sorry,' Jodi began to cry again. 'You must have thought you had the most terrible mother in the whole world.'

'Don't cry, Mom,' she whispered. 'It's not your fault the lady freaked out. Please don't cry. Please! I'm going home tomorrow.'

'Oh Savannah, honey, you're so kind to me, and I love you so much and I'm going to try to be a better mom, and I'm not going to be a litigator any more.'

'You mean you won't be working? You'll stay at home like Katie's mom?'

'I've resigned,' Jodi said shakily. She paused and raised her hand to her head. 'The pain must have been terrible. You poor baby.'

Savannah made no reply. Instead, she stroked her mother's hair gently and with such tenderness that for the first time ever, Jodi experienced the touch of a daughter's love.

Now that Savannah was completely well again, Jodi looked upon her daughter's meningitis as the best thing that had ever happened to her, and perhaps to her daughter as well. During the weeks of her convalescence, like any ordinary mother and daughter, they went in for baking brownies, watching videos, paging through magazines, shopping for new clothes for both, and, all the while, discovering one another.

'Should we give a mom-and-daughter tea party?' Jodi asked one day, out of the blue, as if the idea had only just come into her head.

'That's a really cool idea, Mom,' Savannah exclaimed, rushing to hug her.

'We could design and make the invitations ourselves – '

'Gee Mom,' Savannah interrupted, jumping up and down.

'It's not good for you to get too excited,' Jodi said worriedly. 'How about we do some yogic breathing together?'

So began a companionable early morning yogic routine. But mostly it was their talk that brought them even closer. Savannah, for example, had known nothing of her mother's past – not even the names of her grandparents. She had never been told of the terrible accident that had ended their lives, or anything of the effect it had had on her mother's life. That was why she had fallen into the habit of working so hard, Jodi explained. Now, though, she was going to do her best to make up for all the time she had given to her career and not to Savannah. She explained that she had never felt as alone as when she'd had to take a subway for the first time in her life. So terrified of the crowds, of getting lost, of never finding her way out of there, she'd stood against that wall and just sobbed and sobbed.

And in recounting stories of her own childhood, and particularly of her mother's insistence on emotional control at all times, Jodi realized how seldom she gave her parents a conscious thought. Listening to the rigid organization of her mother's childhood days, Savannah learned of the unchanging weekly menus, fish on Mondays, chicken on Tuesdays, hamburgers on Wednesdays, pork chops on Thursdays, pasta on Fridays, meatloaf on Saturdays, roast beef on Sundays. Everything in her mother's household had an allotted space – though cluttered with china angels, any fractional change in an angel's position would be rectified at once, Jodi explained. She'd hated ornaments ever since, and that was why their New York apartment had been so severe, and she'd gone ahead and locked up all those china angels which were all over the house when she arrived in London, even though Savannah asked her not to. But if Savannah wanted her to, she would be happy to put them all back where they belonged.

'Oh no, Mom,' Savannah responded, 'if you don't like them then I don't like them.'

Jodi embraced her, and they held on to one another, for these days it had become easy and natural to be unashamedly loving.

The day before Savannah was to return to school she told her mother that, since she had caught up with the rest of the class, she would like to stop her Saturday morning lessons with Mrs Lidbury. Gratitude and relief ran through Jodi – she'd not realized how jealous she'd been of Lily Lidbury's role in Savannah's life.

For all that, despite the evidence of their new and easy relationship, Jodi noted with unease that Savannah's old habit of biting her nails had started up when she was in hospital.

Women were unpredictable, Benton decided. Never in a million years would he have imagined that Jodi would voluntarily give up her career and then carry on with her life as if she had never existed as a litigator. The change in the woman was extraordinary. She openly and readily admitted that she'd been less than adequate as a mother and a wife, and in so far as her former life as a litigator was relevant to the present, she only referred to it to condemn herself for having allowed it to consume her. Moreover, her bitterness toward London had turned to gratitude because, she said, she had finally met herself there, and so discovered the true path toward enlightenment.

But then last night, all these surprises, enormous as they were, had been dwarfed by her uninhibited – even blatant – sexual advance. Her energetically erotic performance had been so startling that he had even stopped pretending he was making love to Lily. Which did not mean, he hastily excused himself, that he was not madly and irrevocably in love with his Lily-bud.

Still, the sheer force of their union had been so unsettling that when he and Lily next met at Sloane Street, he broached the matter of their combined futures. Lily lost no time in telling him that though she definitely had not meant to fall in love with him, she couldn't even contemplate the possibility of his divorce. 'You have your life, Benton, and I have mine, and we have each other,' she reasoned. 'We can go on for years like this, for as long as *you* want to, in fact.'

'But I want you at my side all the time!'

'You wouldn't want a woman made miserable by guilt because she was trying to build her happiness on the sadness of a rejected wife,' Lily asserted fiercely. 'I could never do to Jodi what Jane Kale did to me!'

'I want you at my side all the time, Lily-bud,' he repeated. 'That means for ever.'

'I'm deeply, deeply flattered, Benton,' Lily said softly. 'Let's not spoil things by thinking of a future which does not yet exist. In four weeks time I'll be going to KwaZulu for two months.'

'I may not be able to stand such a long separation, Lily-bud.' He pressed his lips in to her palm. 'I need to be with you for ever.'

Unnerved by Benton's mention of the words 'for ever', Lily turned to her work for consolation. She had no sooner returned to her flat than she ran downstairs, blessing the fact that because she lived on top of the school, it was so easy to escape to the fortress of her study. There, the exacting minutiae of running a school demanded her complete concentration and banished all else from her mind. Among all the matters urgently needing a swift response, the communication from Tina Tsakiraki's lawyer took priority. She touched her cheek gingerly. It was no longer tender. Strange, the way the whole ugly incident had slid to the back of her mind. Actually, it was not so strange – Hugh had taken over. Of course she would agree to swear an affidavit on Stelios Tsakiraki's violent attack – she would do everything possible to prevent him from gaining custody of his daughter.

Next, she turned to her pending file and came upon her unmailed rejection letter to the Hunts. The letter ought to have been sent weeks ago – how could she have neglected it? She seemed to be permanently distracted – the fear of all that she was risking mingled with a delirious sense of elation. In short, she was a casualty of her own ecstasy, and as a result her precious role as headmistress was in danger.

Castigating herself for her inefficiency, she folded the letter into an envelope and addressed it. Then she raced to the letterbox and posted it. She wanted to make certain that it would be in time to make the early morning delivery.

The following week Benton called to let her know that he had three unexpected free hours – a meeting had been cancelled.

'Ah, Benton – ' she said. 'It's the wine-tasting tonight.'

'I'm dying to see you, Lily-bud,' he interrupted softly. 'I sure need you in my life.'

She wanted to tell him that she needed him too. Instead, she told him she would go to Partridges for their usual delicacies.

Lily had prepared a short list of their favourite foods, and quickly found what she wanted – tender artichoke hearts in olive oil, succulent *haricots verts* in vinaigrette, and taramasalata. Monsieur Gerrard, the amusing Frenchman who unfailingly wore a beret and who served her regularly, raised his slim carving knife and called out, 'The usual *n'est-ce pas*? Eight slices of *saumon fumé* and eight slices of prosciutto, Madame.'

'The usual,' she laughed. 'No one can slice salmon the way you do.'

'Thank you, Madame.'

Next she chose a still warm baguette, an avocado ripened to perfection and baby tomatoes on the vine. No need to buy drinks – Benton had laid in huge stocks of vintage wines and though he'd said Badoit was the Champagne of mineral waters, he'd bought several of other labels as well.

At the check-out till she told herself that she had no right to be buying delicacies for another woman's husband. She was checking her change when Annabelle Arlington, loaded with shopping, came up to her. After exchanging the usual pleasantries, they left Partridges together. Once on the pavement Annabelle immediately asked if she'd had any news of the Hunts. Lily shook her head.

'The Hunts have always had their ups and downs, as you know,' Annabelle said. 'Now she says she might be forced to go back to New York because she can't allow one daughter to go to a first rate school and not the other.'

'That makes me feel awful.'

'Courtney said that she couldn't believe what she was reading in that letter you wrote her.'

'That makes me feel even worse,' Lily said. 'But Belgrave Hall has a standard to maintain.' She shook her head. 'I wrote the letter weeks ago, but delayed sending it – I was hoping to find a way of accepting Jade.'

'Courtney was so upset, she could hardly talk about it.' Annabelle glanced at her watch. 'I've got to collect Sophie from riding. If you come with me we can talk in the car – '

Lily thanked her, explained that she had one or two chores to attend to, and they went their separate ways.

Overcome by a gust of shame and fear, Lily stopped short, as if paralysed by the realization of what her rejection had done to the Hunt family. Her mind was not on her work. She knew she was guilty of gratuitous cruelty as well as unforgivable stupidity. *I can't think straight these days. I'm making too many mistakes. Something broke in me when I first saw Savannah's uncanny resemblance to Amanda. And now I'm hopelessly locked into her father, and I'm beside myself because I'm powerless, and can't stop. And Benton doesn't even know that Savannah looks like Amanda. Today. I'll tell him today.*

But when Benton arrived, she was astonished to hear herself tearfully telling him about the way she had treated Courtney Hunt. 'I sent a letter,' she wept, 'I didn't even arrange a meeting to tell Courtney that we had rejected Jade.'

'I guess you couldn't bear to see how hurt she would be.'

'I'm not thinking straight. I've made a very, very powerful enemy.'

He was reaching into his pocket for a handkerchief for her when his mobile rang.

A sudden sense of foreboding sent a chill down Lily's spine. She felt desperately in the wrong, and had the strong feeling that Courtney already had some elaborate form of vengeance in mind.

The moment Benton ended his conversation with his secretary, she told him that she needed to return to Belgrave Hall immediately.

'You can't be serious,' he protested. 'I've only just got here!'

'I've got to write to the Hunts – '

'But you're seeing them tonight at the wine-tasting,' Benton interrupted.

'That's the whole point, ' Lily said breathlessly. 'When I see them tonight I want to tell them that a letter of acceptance is on the way to them.'

'So why the rush?'

'I want them to know that I wrote to them in advance of seeing them.'

'It makes no sense, Lily-bud, ' he said gently.

'I'm definitely in the wrong here,' Lily replied tonelessly.' And this is the only kind of damage limitation I can think of.'

Determined that her study would be a sanctuary rather the torture chamber of her own school-days, Lily had made certain that it would be as warm and as welcoming as the Sacred Convent where she went to school had been cold and forbidding. She loved this room, but she had not realized that it had also been a source of strength to her. Although she had known that she had been risking everything, she had not faced the fact that the loss of her study would bring about the total ruination of her life. It was for this reason she decided that her only salvation lay in telling the truth. She would admit that her refusal to even contemplate bending the rules had led her to the wrong decision.

After a hasty consultation with Mrs Travers who taught the Reception class it was agreed that she would cope with 25 children instead of 24.

Lily sat down to write an explanatory letter of acceptance to the Hunts. The letter went through several drafts before Lily was satisfied, and, as she had done with the previous letter, she posted it herself.

The current flowing between Lily and Benton was so strong by now, four months after they and their bodies had first met and connected, that they were afraid if they were seen together their body language would make their union as obvious to everyone else as it was to them. Accordingly, they had both decided that he would not attend the wine-tasting evening arranged by The Bees.

Actively campaigning to join The Bees, Jodi had already received permission to use this event to introduce and promote her recently formed Belgrave Hall Yoga Society. Lily had earlier approved the leaflets Jodi would be distributing this evening and there was little doubt that she would be as dynamic a committee member as she had been a litigator. Her formal proposal to Lily won instant approval and met with an equally formal reply – 'In a hectic unsettled world,' Lily wrote, 'any form of relaxation is to be welcomed.'

There was a time, before Benton had captured her soul, when Lily used to look upon this sort of school function as if she were hosting a party in her own home.

But now, following the realization of the depths of her own stupidity over the Hunts, what had promised to be an unusually pleasurable evening would now be an endurance test. Sir Mark Redwood, the wine expert who was married to one of the teachers, was a lively, well-informed man who had spent three years in France studying all aspects of the wine industry and was now continuing the well-established wine distribution business started by his grandfather. Lily was extremely fond of Mark and his wife – both she and Magsie had gone to their wedding in the country and spent the weekend in his parents' country house.

She had been so long composing her letter to the Hunts, that there was just enough time for her to change into the 1930s *café-au-lait* chiffon blouse and matching velvet jacket and trousers she had worn in Paris, and which (since Benton) made her feel intensely sexy.

After hurriedly applying her make-up, she held her high-heeled shoes in her hand, and sped down the stairs in her stockinged feet. At the bottom of the stairwell, she hastily stepped into her shoes and made her way to the school hall. Overtaken by wonder, she stopped at the threshold. The Bees had transformed the severe school hall. Trestle tables arranged in a U-shape were covered in Venetian tablecloths, and tall silver candelabras, trimmed with fresh green ivy and filled with ivory candles, brought a warmth to the chill evening. Six Steuben glasses stood in front of each place setting. The tickets, at £100 each, had been limited to fifty parents so that each one could receive individual attention from the wine expert. The wines were exceptionally good – many of the parents, believing themselves to be experienced collectors, had laid down wines for their children. Indeed, when the Hunts' wines had grown too expensive to drink, they had auctioned them off at Christie's. They had recently built an exact copy of the rustic walls and pebbled floors of a wine cellar they had seen in Burgundy, and had imported the wine and the designer as a package deal to achieve what they described as a 'genuinely authentic' effect.

As chairperson, Annabelle had been the first parent to arrive. She was holding her mobile phone when Lily greeted her, and was obviously agitated. 'Courtney just called from the car to say she wasn't sure whether she and Charles would be joining us,' she said indignantly.

'That is not good news,' Lily said. 'I've just posted her a letter telling her that we decided to accept Jade.'

'I've had to change the seating – I only hope I've got it right,' Annabelle said, gesturing toward the name-plates at each place setting. 'I've seated you beside Lady Violet and Tina Tsakiraki. Tina actually asked to be seated next to you.' Leaning forward to rest her hand for a moment on Lily's arm, she added, 'Tina's so grateful to you for what you did to Stelios at the Daffodil Ball.'

The hall began to fill. As the parents came in Lily handed them their name tags, and at the same time introduced several of them to Annabelle. She was delighted to see Tina Tsakiraki – the forthcoming custody trial certainly had not diminished her style. Her skirt clung to her; its tightness restricted her walking but caused a provocative wiggle exuding sexuality.

Jodi arrived, the floral tote bag on her shoulder bulging with leaflets on her yoga club. Lily could not help marvelling that this formerly chic woman, with butterfly clips in her unruly hair and dressed in layers of gypsy frills, was the uncompromisingly tailored litigator who had presented herself to the school less than four months earlier. The ultra-fashionable Bulgari diamond and emerald crucifix hanging around her neck mixed with ethnic necklaces disclosed that her metamorphosis was not entirely complete.

Lily felt her chest tighten and her belly churn – this was Benton's wife. A spurt of guilt hit her. Swaying, as if with vertigo, she felt compelled for a moment to shut her eyes. When she opened them, seconds later, she saw Courtney and Charles Hunt approaching. She stepped forward to welcome them and to hand them their name tags, but they ignored her outstretched hand and swept past her to greet Annabelle.

As soon as everyone was in place, Lily rose to deliver a formal welcome. 'Tonight is especially important for me, as it is for everyone who teaches at Belgrave Hall, because thanks to your generosity, all the funds of this evening are to go to the refurbishment of the staff common room – ' She paused and flung out her arms dramatically. 'I especially want to thank Mr and Mrs Charles Hunt – through their generosity we are soon to be tasting the finest French wines.'

Lily handed the microphone to Annabelle with a huge smile.

With an answering smile, Annabelle took the microphone. 'Although Courtney asked me not to, I felt I could not let this evening go by without at least mentioning how important the Hunts are to Belgrave Hall. Their great enthusiasm, organizing ability and financial assistance are invaluable. I cannot stress how much Courtney means to all of us – without her unique and inspiring leadership The Bees would not have achieved anything like as much as we have.'

She moved toward Mark Redwood to hand the microphone to him, but Courtney jumped up and snatched it from her.

'Thank you, Annabelle,' she said, in the hearty style of the experienced committee member. 'I was in two minds about coming here this evening. However, in the interests of Belgrave Hall, an English educational institution which Americans hold in such high esteem, and that is so dear to my heart, I felt compelled – and, indeed, duty-bound – to make a public statement of protest.' Looking around the room, she breathed dramatically into the microphone, and waited a long, tense moment before continuing. 'That is why I am here!'

A prickly silence fell.

Satisfied that she now had everyone's rapt attention, Courtney continued, 'For the last five years I have been delighted to focus all my energies on Belgrave Hall. To be chairperson of The Bees was a privilege as well as a pleasure – I wanted to give back to the community that had given my daughter so much. But it is impossible for me to accept a system that is so rigid in its testing procedure. A non-sibling policy rules out the close family link that should be the foundation of any educational establishment. Since receiving Mrs Lidbury's heartless letter of rejection a week ago, Jade has been to an educational psychologist. Her report is especially written for you, Mrs Lidbury. You will receive it soon, and *if* you read it, Mrs Libury, you will learn that I am not just the *super-ambitious American mom* you think I am!' she said, spitting out her words as if they were a curse. 'Academically, Jade is in the top twenty per cent of the country. Belgrave Hall has missed high achievers in the past, and, I am sure that will happen again in the future. Tara Mulock-Bentley's parents who had to face the same cruel rejection have since seen their daughter offered a scholarship to St Paul's.

'Tiffany has been very happy here and it is with great sadness that we have had to sever all our ties with Belgrave Hall. I am very angry that I have been forced to make this choice, but I am determined that my children's lives will not suffer due to actions which I believe show gross arrogance on the part of the headmistress and her staff. But Charles and I refuse to stand by and permit two little girls, who are sisters as well as friends, to be educated to become antagonists instead of allies.

'Like Mrs Lidbury's greed for virtue, her greed for fame as a stellar educator has blinded her to the realities of family life. I have no doubt that her judgment would have been more insightful if she had been a mother herself.

'I apologize for my outburst. I am sorry we cannot now spend the rest of the evening with you.'

Her face crimson, Courtney tossed her head, and swept out of the room. Charles straightened his tie, kissed Annabelle's cheeks, waved his hand in a cordial salute to the other parents and followed his wife. Neither glanced in Lily's direction –

another deliberate public snub. Managing to keep her composure, Lily smiled at Mark and nodded.

As if on cue, Mark sprang to the rescue and took the mike. 'It was, I believe, the distinguished French writer Victor Hugo who said, "God made only water, but man made wine." '

The room rang with the sound of relieved laughter. Almost at once Mark, helped by Magsie and a member of the kitchen staff, moved deftly and quickly to pour the red wine into the glasses round the candlelit tables. Eventually, two elongated hours later, the evening came to an end. Amidst laughter and thanks, the hall finally cleared; as always after a social event, Lily joined a few of the parents networking on the pavement. Returning to the hall to help Magsie, she found Jodi lighting two candles. A sharp pain passed behind her eyes. The tension headache that had begun to bite when the Hunts snubbed her turned savage; a feeling of faintness came over her and she sank into a chair and started massaging her temples.

The next moment Jodi, carrying both lighted candles, came toward her. 'This is for you, Lily,' she said solemnly, passing one of them to her.

Mystified, Lily accepted it wordlessly.

'Boy, that was bad,' Jodi sympathized, seating herself beside Lily. Handing her the second candle, she went on gravely, 'If you will study these two lighted candles in your hands, Lily, you will find that no two flames are ever alike.'

Though this was not the first time that Jodi had gone on about flames, Lily remained mute.

'You agree that no two flames are ever alike, don't you?'

Lily had no choice but to affirm this with her silence.

'In the long run the sword is always beaten by the individual spirit.' Carefully measuring her words, Jodi continued, 'You are a greatly gifted teacher, Lily, and your reputation as an exceptional educator will live on long after Courtney Hunt's outrageous exhibition is forgotten.'

'Thank you, but – '

'I know what you've done for Savannah,' Jodi interrupted. 'You've been, well, like a mother to her.'

This is too unreal to be happening, Lily thought, Jodi offering *her* comfort. At the same time she was rotten with reality and she knew it. Physically and emotionally obsessed with Benton, who was, after all, Jodi's husband, she was living a double life at full throttle, a thousand heartbeats a minute. She wished to be elsewhere, she wished to be another person. The horrible truth was that because she was so full of guilt and self-loathing Courtney Hunt could not damage her more than she was damaging herself.

'Benton is waiting for me at Mimmo,' Jodi said. 'Would you like to join us? It's our favourite restaurant – their *spaghetti vongole* is to die for.'

'It's very kind of you, Jodi,' Lily replied shakily. 'But – ' she stopped to blow out both candles. 'Most awful headache,' she mumbled, holding her hands like a poultice to her head.

The next moment Magsie was at her side. 'Are you all right, Lily?' she asked, concerned.

'It's just a headache,' Lily murmured feebly. She turned to Jodi. 'I'm afraid I'll simply have to go to bed,' she said.

'I'll say good night,' Jodi said regretfully. Then, in that ancient Hindu gesture of respect, she made a steeple of her hands, and held them against her heart. '*Namaste*,' she said, 'I salute the divinity within you, Lily.'

Magsie raised a dubious brow. 'Good night, Mrs Anderson,' she said. She turned to Lily. 'I think you should let me help you up the stairs, Lily.'

Very unusually, Lily did not argue.

As soon as they were in Lily's kitchen, Magsie set about making tea. 'Have you told Benton yet?' she asked.

'About Savannah's resemblance to Amanda?'

Magsie nodded.

'No.' Lily whispered. 'I'm afraid, I think . . . I'm *so* afraid.'

'But Lily, you've – ' Magsie began.

'This has got to stop, Magsie,' Lily interrupted. A huge sigh shook her. 'Jodi's such a good person. I don't know how I could have allowed myself to get trapped into this.' Her voice thin and jerky, she whispered, 'There is no trap so deadly as the trap you set for yourself.'

Compared with the heavy weight of Jodi's unexpected kindness, the humiliation of the night before seemed to Lily to be not only trivial but irrelevant. She was hugging herself in her study as she always did in moments of distress, listening to her voice-mail, when Tara Styles barged in, unannounced, just as she had the term before.

'As you well know, Mrs Lidbury, Jasmine has a severe allergy to nuts,' she began angrily.

'Well, of course we are aware of that – the kitchen staff have strict – '

'So can you explain why Olivia Joseph, her close friend, who has often been to our home, gave my child a *nut* biscuit after netball yesterday?' She did not wait for an answer, but rushed on, 'Jasmine was really ill, she's not at school today, and I'm here to insist that you discipline Olivia!'

'I'm sorry, I must stop you there,' Lily said coldly. 'Jasmine is nine years old – you must see that unless she can take responsibility for her own actions, she could become dangerously ill and face possible death.'

'Do you think you're telling me anything I don't know?'

'Over the years we've had several girls with acute nut allergies, and not once have they disregarded their parents' instructions to decline anything but fresh fruit from anyone. The lead has to come from home, Ms Styles. It's up to you to instruct your daughter.'

'It would seem Courtney Hunt's courageous statement last night taught you nothing,' Tara snapped. 'I don't suppose you'll be headmistress here for much longer.'

'I am confident, Ms Styles, that I will be at Belgrave Hall a great deal longer than you or your daughter.'

'How dare you! I pay good money and sacrifice so much for my daughter to be at this school,' Tara shouted. 'Courtney Hunt and I are not the only mothers who are unhappy about the way you are running the school these days. Your relationship with Savannah Anderson is – to say the very least – strange. I shall be writing to Lady Violet Anstey.'

Lily hugged herself again. Though outwardly calm, inside she felt like a volcano of surging heat on the verge of erupting into liquid fire. Naturally, Tara Styles was concerned for her daughter. 'I intend to make an announcement about this at assembly tomorrow morning,' Lily said, her voice brisk. 'All the girls will be told what happened to Jasmine. They will also be told that any girl who offers to share anything but fruit with her friends will face the threat of expulsion.'

'Thank you,' Tara said. 'Jasmine is very happy at Belgrave Hall.'

Alone in her study again, Lily rested her throbbing head in her hands. At times like this, she felt her responsibility for the lives and well-being of all the girls weigh heavily upon her. There had not, so far, been any serious accidents at the school, and she was hell-bent on keeping it that way. Tense with premonition, she reached into her desk drawer for the wooden crucifix she kept for emergencies. She surreptitiously brought it to her lips, kissed it quickly, and hurriedly hid it away again.

# CHAPTER 15

'I've got to go fetch Mrs Lidbury's handbag,' Savannah said to Katie. 'Want to come with me? Guess how many stairs there are to the top?'

'I don't know.'

'Come on, Katie, just guess!'

'More than a hundred?'

'No, silly,' Savannah giggled. 'Eighty-four.'

'That's all, only eighty-four?' Katie replied. 'I'll race you to the top.'

Taller than Katie, Savannah seized on her advantage. 'Two steps at a time?'

'Cool.'

Savannah streaked ahead, but by the sixtieth step, she suddenly tired and Katie raced past her.

'I won,' Katie exclaimed.

'I know you did,' Savannah replied, breathing heavily.

'I forgot you'd been ill,' Katie said.

'I'm OK,' a defiant Savannah responded, climbing onto the banister and seating herself. 'I dare you to sit up here next to me and look down. It's weird looking down,' she said. 'If you hold on to the banister and lean over, you'll see that it's like a dark, secret cave.'

Katie forced her gaze downward. She glimpsed the open tea chest already half-filled with gift-wrapped toys for Mrs Lidbury's sick children in Africa. The world instantly revolved giddily. 'I'm dizzy,' she moaned, raising one of her hands to her head. 'My head's going round and round.'

'Don't sit like that,' Savannah yelled. 'It's dangerous! Hold the banister!'

They heard the girls and the teachers swarming back to class from lunch. They dared not be seen sitting up there.

Turning speedily – too speedily – Savannah clambered down from the banister and in the process her body rammed against Katie, who seemed to be suddenly moving towards her. The girl went falling backward, crashing down the stairs. Katie's terrified scream mingled with the sound of her shoes and limbs hitting the edges of the steps. Finally, her body collided against the marble floor. The crash reverberated around the entire building.

A second scream ripped the air. By the time the teachers and girls reached Katie, Savannah had already galloped down the stairs and flung herself beside her. Katie lay ominously quiet, her left leg folded at an unnatural angle. Savannah's screams continued; her body jerked in powerful disjointed movements, her eyes rolled and her movements resembled the symptoms of an epileptic fit. Savannah grasped Lily's neck, dragged her close. 'It was my fault,' she sobbed, 'my fault.'

'Don't say a word to anyone,' Lily's voice rasped like a whip across Savannah's white, frightened face. 'Tell no one – not even your mother!' Her mind whirled. *If Katie dies there will be an inquest and Savannah will be accused of killing her.* 'This must be our secret,' she whispered urgently. With that, she tore herself away from Savannah, and placed her hand under Katie's chin to aid her breathing.

Savannah's screaming stopped. Lily's curt, savage instructions had the required effect and there was silence. Only a slight nod of Savannah's head showed any recognition of what was happening around her.

After telling Lily that an ambulance was on its way, Magsie led Savannah away, shielding her stricken face from the gathering crowd.

Lily continued to tilt Katie's chin upwards. Her pulse was faint and rapid, and though she knew the child was unconscious, she spoke quietly to her. This was any teacher's nightmare, and she found herself murmuring prayers she thought she could never utter again. Lily was in control but her mind was spinning – Katie's mother had chosen Belgrave Hall as a haven where she could receive an outstanding education, administered in a safe, caring environment. Her eyes did not leave Katie's face until the paramedics knelt by her side. Oxygen was administered, and her body and neck were immobilized, ready for movement to the waiting ambulance. Lily insisted on travelling with the limp body. If Katie's eyes opened she would be there to comfort her.

Lily had been at the hospital for three hours when Katie's mother arrived. She looked up sharply as she approached and moved towards her. But Harriet Ratcliffe immediately informed Lily that her presence was no longer required. Her voice was scornful as she spat out the words, 'Your care and concern are rather late in the day, Mrs Lidbury.'

Safe in her own bedroom, lying on her own bed, her mother seated on a chair beside her, Savannah refused to say how it had happened. Now that she had learned more about the skill of mothering, Jodi told herself, she knew that there were moments when, as a mother, it was vital to choose her words as carefully and as shrewdly as a litigator addressing a jury. She had been given few details – she knew only that Katie had fallen accidentally and that Savannah had been with her when she fell. But both as an attorney and as a mother she sensed an irregularity, as if some vital evidence were being suppressed. No one had told her why the two little girls had been at the top of that staircase. She would have to interrogate Savannah as gently and as expertly as she would any frightened, anxious witness.

'I guess it's exciting going up there,' she began. 'It's a very high staircase, isn't it?' She paused for a moment, and added, 'I wonder how high it is?'

'Eighty-four steps,' Savannah replied promptly.

'You've counted them yourself or did somebody tell you?'

Thanks to a combination of gentle probing and experienced acting, a few facts gradually emerged. Firstly, that Savannah knew the number of steps because her private tuition was in Mrs Lidbury's apartment. Secondly, that the top floor was out of bounds, and finally, that when Mrs Lidbury had sent Savannah to fetch her handbag, the two girls had raced one another up the stairs.

'If Mrs Lidbury asked you to go get her handbag up there, she was actually encouraging you two to break the rules, wasn't she?' Jodi asked.

Savannah did not answer.

'Well, did she ask you to go up there?' Jodi persisted.

'Stop bugging me!'

'I'm not bugging you, honey,' Jodi said. 'It's just that Mrs Lidbury has to take the blame for what happened.'

'No, it wasn't her fault,' Savannah burst out. 'It wasn't, it wasn't!'

'Then whose fault was it?'

Convulsed in misery, Savannah shook her head. Then all at once Jodi had a flicker of insight. 'I guess Mrs Lidbury wants you to keep it a secret,' she said confidingly.

Savannah nodded.

'Yours and Mrs Lidbury's special secret, right?' Jodi forced a smile. 'So special that she told you not to tell anyone. A really special secret means that you can't tell anyone – not even your mother, right?'

Savannah gnawed frantically at her nails.

Jodi made herself dismiss her mounting anger and, devoid of emotion, the logic of her legal mind took over. *Clearly, Mrs Lidbury would not have insisted on secrecy unless she believed Savannah had deliberately caused the accident. In which case, she must have concluded that if Katie did not survive, Savannah would be guilty of murder.* . . 'So when you admitted to Mrs Lidbury that it was your fault,' she went on as if this were a statement and not a question, 'she said you mustn't tell anyone.'

'It was,' Savannah sobbed. 'It was my fault.'

'But an accident is no one's fault, honey,' Jodi said. 'Everyone knows that.' Savannah looked up. 'Why don't you tell me exactly what happened?'

'No!'

'Listen, honey, I'm a lawyer as well as a mother. And I know what happens after an accident. People ask questions, and even though you're only nine years old, the police will want to ask you for details. If you don't tell them Mrs Lidbury told you to keep it a secret, they'll think you're lying. Don't you see that?'

'I won't tell them,' Savannah cried. 'I won't.'

'In that case,' Jodi's voice was cold, 'I'll simply have to tell them what you have told me.'

'I *hate* you! I wish she was my mom!' Savannah wept. 'Daddy wishes it too.' Then, like a small child, she hid her face under a pillow.

Bristling, Jodi bent to remove the pillow from her weeping daughter.

'I hate you,' Savannah shrieked. 'Daddy's in love with Mrs Lidbury and she's in love with Daddy.'

'Oh Savannah, honey,' Jodi said with an understanding smile, 'you watch too much TV and too many soaps.'

'This is not TV!' Savannah got up, strode towards her video shelf, snatched an empty video cover, and produced her father's mobile phone. She punched the voice-mail button. Benton's recorded voice entered the room. This is surreal, Jodi thought, as she heard Benton and Lily Lidbury sounding like love-stricken kids.

The recording came to an end. Too shocked for speech, Jodi said nothing.

But suddenly her maternal instinct – so long lost, so recently found – sprang to the fore with all the animal power of a mother defending her endangered young. Praying for wisdom, the great Swami's words came to her – *at the heart of victory lies perseverance.*

'Listen to me,' she said urgently.

Savannah looked up. Her unreadable eyes changed subtly. The long russet lashes curved upward, but the suspicious, almost deadened look in them belonged to a disillusioned adult rather than a child. Sensing a premature wisdom, an unexpected worldliness in her daughter, Jodi decided to be entirely frank with her. 'I'm going to talk to you as if you were an adult,' she said, adjusting her voice to a confiding tone. 'So will you listen very, very carefully to what I have to say?'

Savannah nodded.

'Do you mind if I lie down next to you?' she asked.

Without answering, Savannah moved towards the wall to make space for her, and Jodi arranged her body so that her daughter could rest her head on her shoulder. Stroking Savannah's cheek, Jodi began the opening salvo of what she believed to be the most crucial speech of her life. She explained that though she had always loved Savannah, something had gone wrong inside her head that stopped her from showing her how much she loved her, stopped her from being a good mother. Her voice calm, she said that this thing in her brain had also stopped her from showing Daddy how she loved him. It was a kind of sickness, but just like Savannah's meningitis, it had gotten better.

Suddenly and exceptionally, she followed her heart instead of her head. 'I'm very proud of you, honey, and I'll love you for ever.' Instinctively, she added, 'And even if you tell me that you'd like Mrs Lidbury to be your step-mom, I'll still love you for ever.'

Jodi felt her whole life rested on Savannah's reaction.

Astonishingly, Savannah smiled. 'What a silly mommy you are,' she flung her arms around Jodi's neck, 'Mrs Lidbury is *my teacher*,' she said emphatically.

Somehow, Jodi managed to hold back her tears, 'You're smart,' she said quietly. 'You're only a little girl, but you've taught me so much.'

Gripped by a rage more powerful than any she could remember, Jodi tried to fight her way through white-hot fury toward rational thought. Why, that sanctimonious phony, that icon of purity, that chaste headmistress with her bold, superior manner had been having if off with Benton, with her own husband, and was no better than a low-life slut. No wonder the bitch had encouraged her to go to New York so often. That old truism, the wife is the last to know, flashed into her mind, and with it the humiliating awareness that she'd been duped and outwitted. They'd made an utter fool of her. She was an experienced litigator, an expert in the detection of lies and liars, and yet she hadn't picked up the smallest hint of what was going on.

Paradoxically enough, she scarcely gave Benton a thought. Her focus was on Lily Lidbury, the headmistress, the woman whom she had come to admire and respect, to whom she had confessed her feelings of failure as a woman. Her stomach convulsed. She began to wonder when and how the affair had started, where and how often they met. She had made a tape of the conversation recorded on Benton's cell phone, and thought of listening to it again, but changed her mind. She had already heard it twice, every word had been imprinted on her heart, and there was no point in listening to it for a third time because she had already established that they had not been in a restaurant. Now if Savannah could remember when Benton had called her to tell her when she had lost her necklace, she would have a little more information to work with. She could not even begin to imagine the traumatic effect that overhearing her father's lovey-dovey talk with his girlfriend, the headmistress she idolized, must have had on the child. If ever there was an example of the monstrous abuse of trust, this was it!

In the morning, when Jodi gently raised the question, it turned out that Savannah could not remember exactly when she had lost her necklace. Jodi asked her to try to think of what she had been wearing. Although she instantly recalled wearing her long pink skirt and matching jacket, to see *Phantom of the Opera,* she could not recollect exactly when they had gone to the theatre. Perhaps, Jodi suggested, perhaps she'd kept the programme? When she was a child, she used to keep all her programmes and only got rid of them when her parents' house was sold. She had barely finished speaking when Savannah rushed off to find the programme for her. Though Jodi at once saw that the exact date was not shown, she paged through it nevertheless. It was then that she came upon a photograph of Lily and a young girl who looked like Savannah's double.

'Where did you find this, honey?' Savannah's eerie resemblance to the child was frightening. 'Mrs Lidbury gave this to you?'

Savannah blushed and looked away.

'I don't blame you for having taken this, honey,' Jodi said. 'I would have done the same thing, if I'd been you.' Turning the photograph over, she read, *Lily and Amanda, Arundel, 1989*. In the left corner, the rubber stamp read: *James Barrot, Photographer, Glenhove Road, Arundel*. 'You'd have been crazy not to take it. Where did you find it?'

'In Magsie's bedroom when I'd left the present you'd FedExed on her bed,' Savannah said.

'Ah yes, the lace collar I sent her,' Jodi almost smiled. Censoring what she should and should not say, her mind raced furiously.

'I saw the photograph and went to look at it. Then I noticed there was something sticking out at the back of the frame and when I looked closer I saw it was another copy of the same photo – so I took it.'

Lily and Amanda were wearing emerald velvet coats. Clearly, Amanda must be Lily's daughter, but she would remain silent on that one. Suddenly, thinking out loud, she asked, 'Would you like to pretend you'd never seen this photograph?'

Savannah looked puzzled.

'Do you wish you hadn't seen it?'

'Yes,' Savannah replied. 'I wish I'd never seen it.'

'I'd just like to think about all this,' Jodi said. 'Meanwhile, honey, I think I need a great big hug.'

By chance she had simultaneously discovered both the truth and the proof. She had the photographer's name and the town in which he worked. Now, armed with the cruel proof, she was equipped to decide on strategy, and go to war.

# CHAPTER 16

'She's been unconscious for sixty-six hours,' Lily said to Magsie. 'She may never regain consciousness – a vegetable, I can't – '

'It's a miracle she only broke an arm and a leg,' Magsie broke in fiercely. 'If there's already been one miracle, like as not there will be a second.'

'From your mouth to God's ear,' Lily sighed. 'Mrs Ratcliffe won't let me near Katie, and Jodi is keeping me away from Savannah. Last time I spoke to her she said Savannah was not up yet because she'd been awake all night and had only fallen asleep at six. I didn't believe her.'

'When does Benton get back from New York?'

'His last meeting is on Monday afternoon,' Lily replied listlessly. 'He'll be back on Tuesday morning.'

'You've spoken to him, of course?'

'Several times,' Lily said wearily. 'He's been out of his mind with worry about both girls.'

She rose to fill a watering can and was about to tend to her window box when the phone rang.

'It's Doctor Jacobson,' she whispered to Magsie covering the mouthpiece. Lily felt her whole body stiffen. 'Katie regained consciousness thirty minutes ago,' she repeated for Magsie's benefit.

'She's responding well to outside stimulation,' Dr Jacobson said warmly, 'and her pupils are reacting to light. She is now breathing on her own, and her pulse has dropped to normal. She's asked after Savannah, too. Mrs Lidbury, I think we can say that Katie will make a full recovery.' He gave a relieved laugh, 'I wanted to give you this wonderful news immediately.'

Lily clutched the locket at her throat, 'Bless you, doctor,' she said, 'and thank you for your understanding.'

'What did I tell you?' Magsie crowed.

But Lily was already dialling Savannah's number. 'I must tell her this minute! Doctor Jacobson said Katie was actually asking for her.'

When Jodi answered Lily swiftly reported her conversation with Dr Jacobson.

'Savannah will be so relieved and happy,' she continued enthusiastically. 'Could you call her to the phone? I'd love to be the one to give her the good news!'

'I bet you would,' Jodi said dryly. 'Why don't you come on over? It's nine-thirty now. Ten-thirty, OK?'

'It would be so much easier if you would call Savannah to the phone.'

'But what makes you think I would ever want to make anything easier for *you*?'

'I'm not – '

'You'd better come to see me,' Jodi cut in, her voice sharp. 'And you'd better make it soon.'

'I'll be there,' Lily replied.

'Good.' The phone clicked off.

Ten minutes later, showered and dressed, at 4:45 a.m. New York time Lily called Benton. Dialling his number, she recalled his first call to her, five months earlier. Curiously, it had been almost the same New York time then as it was now.

After apologizing for disturbing him she told him about Katie's recovery and before he could comment, she raced on to report Jodi's strange attitude. 'I'm afraid she suspects something, Benton.'

'If you didn't know what you know, you wouldn't be reading so much into it – '

'You mean if I didn't have a guilty conscience,' Lily corrected him. 'She knows about us.'

'Look Lily-bud, I *know* my wife and I assure you she has absolutely no idea about you and me.' His voice carried conviction; he really believed what he was saying. After all, he and Jodi had made love only four nights ago, but of course, he could not reveal anything of that to Lily. 'Believe me, Lily-bud, after you've seen her you'll call to tell me I was right.'

But Lily knew instinctively that she was going to face the most probing cross-examination of her life. Though their exchange had been brief, Jodi's tone had been distinctively confrontational. Just before she left, Lily checked her appearance in the mirror. Noting a stain on her fawn jacket, she hastily changed into a sober navy trouser suit. Then she tightened the scarlet velvet bow holding her hair back from her face, and applied a bright lipstick. The face looking back appeared composed, betraying nothing of the fear she felt that Jodi might well have the potential to annihilate the structure of her entire life. Then, on her way out, more than ordinarily aware of the sweep of the staircase, of the swift clip of her high heels, of The Bees' arrangement of purple peonies on the hall table, she shut the door of Belgrave Hall firmly behind her.

Walking more slowly than usual – there were a few minutes to spare – her heart thudding with the awareness of encroaching disaster, she straightened her back and held her head high and tried to take comfort from Benton's reassurances. But it didn't help. Now giddy with fear, she was oblivious of her surroundings. She crossed Elizabeth Street in a daze. A speeding police car, sirens blaring, slammed on its brake. Shocked, she whimpered softly, straightened her back again and pulled herself together. By the time she rang the doorbell she knew she was in control of herself.

Opi opened the door and showed her into Benton's study. 'Mrs Anderson wants you to wait here,' she said.

'Ah, so I'm to be kept waiting,' Lily thought. 'So this is how the gauntlet has been thrown.' Whatever residual doubts she had about a possible confrontation now vanished. The possibility was now a reality.

Five minutes later, the chatter of Jodi's bangles and the rustle of her white silk caftan announced her arrival. Since that brutal haircut, her hair had grown and was now a tangle of red curls. After a cold greeting she pointedly seated herself behind Benton's vast desk. 'Harriet Ratcliffe has already called to tell me about Katie's progress,' she said curtly.

'It's a great – '

'I'm sure it is,' Jodi interrupted icily. 'Those two kids had no right whatsoever to be up there.' Her stare was glassy.

Lily shifted nervously in her seat, 'I'm utterly at fault there,' she admitted.

'You certainly are!' Jodi exploded. 'Your gratuitous carelessness puts *my* daughter in a dangerously culpable position. Things are looking better for Katie now, but if she does not make it, Savannah could be guilty of murder – ' Speaking with an ominous mildness, she continued, 'That was why you told Savannah not to tell anyone – not even me, her mother – that she thought Katie's fall was her fault. You thought Savannah pushed her.'

Lily began to protest, but Jodi cut through. 'However, as you no doubt must have guessed, that is not why I wanted to see you this morning.'

'What *are* you talking about?'

'If you want to play games,' Jodi rapped out, 'I'll present you with the evidence.'

'Evidence?'

'You not only violated Savannah's trust, but had the intractable gall to think you could steal both my husband and my daughter and get away with it,' Jodi said. 'What do you have to say to that, *Mrs Challoner*?'

Lily paled visibly. 'How did you find out?'

'Why, that's simple – I couriered the fascinating information I had to W. S. Plimpton, the private investigator based in Arundel.'

Lily's hand flew to her throat.

'Of course, I wouldn't have done that if I hadn't had damning evidence to work with, would I?' Jodi said airily. 'A rhetorical question, ignore it.' She eyed Lily bitterly for a moment, scrutinizing her face, her expression. 'I guess you'd like me to tell you the *nature* of the evidence?' she said finally with a cold smile. She took Benton's mobile phone and a small tape recorder from the bottom drawer. Then she switched it on, sat back and watched Lily.

Lily could do nothing other than bite her lip and wait for the unspeakable horror of listening to her intimate, private and now public pillow talk to come to an end.

Clicking off the tape recorder, Jodi jumped up and presented her with a large manila envelope. 'Right now, Mrs Challoner,' she said bitingly, 'it would be in your best interests to open this envelope immediately.'

Lily opened it, found the mother and daughter snapshot of herself and Amanda in their identical emerald coats, and quickly replaced it. She tried to speak, but no words would come. Her mind felt as parched as her mouth. *None of this was real, none of this could be happening . . .*

'An uncanny resemblance, I grant you,' Jodi said. 'I'm truly sorry about your daughter,' she added unexpectedly.

Motionless, Lily bit even harder on her lower lip.

'Here's what *I've* decided,' Jodi began. 'It will be up to you to decide which of the two conditions to choose.' She was suddenly so angry that she had to pause to swallow, 'Either I say nothing of this to anyone, ever, and you leave London for good and, on the grounds of some suitable health problem, immediately resign as headmistress of Belgrave Hall. Or I hand all the evidence to the chairperson of the Board of Governors, Lady Violet Anstey.' She paused, and with that incalculable logic of hers, continued reasonably, 'If I take the latter option, you will, of course, face instant dismissal and for ever afterwards be known as the "disgraced former headmistress, Lily Lidbury".'

Powerless and mute, Lily sat erect in her chair.

Jodi made an impatient gesture, leapt up and marched to the other side of the desk to be closer to Lily. 'An additional condition to our agreement, *Mrs Challoner,* concerns the chief victim, my daughter, Savannah,' she said, the tilt of her head eloquently expressing a mixture of triumph and contempt. 'It's an example of the unspeakable meeting the unthinkable. I have had to go so far as to include my daughter in the negotiations, as her co-operation is essential to a fair and honourable agreement. Her undertaking to remain silent is contingent on your acceptance of *all* our conditions.'

There was a long, uneasy silence.

Jodi let out a spurt of scorn, and continued, 'Now you've heard the verdict – guilty – and the sentence – exile,' she said in her razor-sharp tone. 'I suggest we look upon this as a post-trial conference.' She shot Lily a hard look. 'Failure to accept my conditions will do untold and lasting damage to Belgrave Hall,' she said, rapping her knuckles on the desk to emphasize her point. 'I take it you agree?'

Lily managed a nod.

'Given that all verdicts have consequence, exile in your case does not equal homelessness. According to my extensive re-search, your late ex-husband has bequeathed your former marital home in Arundel to you. In addition, I'm told the orphanage in KwaZulu, where you summer, has perfectly adequate living quar-ters set aside for you.' She rapped the desk again. 'Correct me if I'm wrong.'

Lily struggled to keep her voice under control. 'You're not wrong,' she said.

Suddenly, Jodi stepped away from the desk, turned her back to Lily, and breathing deeply, proceeded to practise the Breath of Fire.

*This isn't happening,* Lily thought again. Dimly aware that the background music had switched from Balinese to Indian, she remained frozen in her seat.

The ritual was over as suddenly as it had begun. Jodi drew her chair closer to Lily. 'I stepped right back into my litigator-mode, and that pains me. I never wanted to hear myself sound like that again.' In a guarded, confidential voice, she went on, 'Let's talk woman to woman, instead of woman versus woman, shall we?'

Lily nodded.

'I was nineteen when my parents died, and I went from riches to rags. After that I forced myself to behave like a police sniffer dog on constant alert. I got so used to it that it became a habit. I forgot to be a woman. I don't think I ever tried, or even knew, how to be a wife or a mother.' She shut her eyes for a moment. 'I'd like another chance,' she said. 'It would be helpful if Benton doesn't hear about my ultimatum, or see this photograph.'

'He won't,' Lily whispered.

An involuntary spasm of pain and compassion twisted Jodi's expression. 'I'm not looking for vengeance – it's just that I need you to go away.' She slowly rose to her feet. 'Who knows, perhaps you and I could yet redeem ourselves?'

Writhing inside her own body, Lily also stood up.

The sight of Lily's stricken face stabbed Jodi's soul. She had struggled to know how to manage this awfulness – whether to attempt her new, compassionate, peaceful approach, or stick to the harsh, unrelenting and always triumphant attack-style that had served her so well in the past. It had not taken her long to decide. Though she hated herself for what she had to do, she knew instinctively that the survival of her family depended on Lily's absence.

'I wish it didn't have to be this way,' she said gravely. 'But you have ten days in which to leave Belgrave Hall.' Her voice once again clipped and curt, she added, 'I guess you know your way round this house well enough to see yourself out.'

She then looked at Lily with such penetrating intensity that, dazed and broken, Lily fled from the room and out into the street.

Late that night, Jodi returned to Benton's desk. She sat there a long while trying to figure things out. She felt none of her usual sense of triumph after the defeat of an adversary. I must have meant it when I told Lily I wasn't looking for vengeance, she thought. But the negotiation wasn't over – she still had Benton to confront, and a strategy to devise. How wrong she was to have thought that after ten years she knew her husband so well that nothing he could do would surprise her. And was she now the sort of wife who filled empty hours measuring and assessing her husband, checking his clothes and diary, brooding over minute changes in his behaviour, all on the assumption that a decline in physical intimacy was proof of infidelity? But the erotic side of their life, though always pleasant, was no more vital an aspect of their marriage than taking their vitamin supplements or their country club membership. And like all leisure activities, love-making was confined to long weekends or vacations, and there had been neither of these since they had moved to London. Priding themselves on their honesty, they recognized that they had never been troubled by a profusion of turbulent hormones.

And yet – she'd not had even the glimmering of an idea that he was involved with another woman. That it was Lily Lidbury was mind-blowing. But, if she wanted her family to survive, her anger, like her ego, would have to go on the back burner.

Benton's ego, however, was something else, and would test her negotiating skills to the limit. Because he was in the wrong, he would be on the defensive. Even if she didn't know him nearly as well as she had supposed, she was pretty certain that as a dedicated Anglophile, he must have thought he was a real star to have got his daughter's British headmistress to fall for him. But, she wondered, had Lily fallen for Benton or for Savannah's father? She needed to study the photograph of Lily and her daughter Amanda again. Her bangles jangled as she took it from the drawer. She reached for Benton's powerful magnifying glass and studied the photograph once more. It was unnerving – Savannah was Amanda's double.

She slipped the photograph into her pocket. I'll tell Benton about it, but I won't show it to him. I'll tell him I tore it up, she decided. If he sees it, he'll come to the humiliating conclusion that if he had not been Savannah's father, Lily would not as much as have looked at him.

Benton, as she knew too well, could deal with whatever life threw at him, except humiliation. She would have to handle him with kid gloves.

# CHAPTER 17

'Ah, Benton, you were asleep!' Lily exclaimed reproachfully. *He knew I was going to see Jodi – except for Amanda, this has been the most harrowing and humiliating experience of my life, and he slept through it.*

'It's 5:40 a.m. over here,' he responded. 'How did it – '

'How many mobile phones have you lost, Benton?'

'This year, or this month?' he joked. 'About two, why?'

'I think you left one at the Cromwell Hospital.'

'When Savannah was ill? That's more than likely. But – '

'Savannah found it,' Lily said. 'Actually, I'm speaking to you from Sloane Street.'

'What made you go there?'

'I needed to feel close to you, I think,' she said, sighing into the phone. 'I'm afraid I have a bit of a shock for you, Benton – ' She went on to give a detailed account of her meeting with Jodi.

'I'll be with you in about ten hours, Lily-bud,' he said. 'I'll be on the first plane out.'

'Today's Saturday and you've got that important – '

'The hell with that!' he exclaimed. 'I'll come directly to Sloane Street. Except for the airline authorities, you'll be the only person in the whole world who knows where I am.'

'I'll be right here, waiting for you,' she said. She set the telephone gently in its cradle. Then, after a few minutes, she picked it up again and called Magsie and, after letting her know where she was and not to worry because she probably would not be coming home until the following evening, she told her that Jodi knew and had proof of everything.

By now it was the middle of the morning, and she poured herself an extra stiff whisky. Then she changed into her robe, slipped Mahler's Titan into her CD player and sat back to listen, and, if possible, to think.

When your life has been torn to shreds and it's your own fault, what do you do? She let the Mahler CD play over and over again; the music suited her mood. She'd been given an ultimatum and a deadline; yet, as she saw it, there was no immediate need to make a plan. The taped phone conversation made her cringe with embarrassment, but it was the thought of its effect on Savannah that pained her most. And then it came to her that she would miss Benton far, far more than she would miss Savannah. By now she was calm enough to apply her mind to what had happened. Remembering is not the same as memorizing, she told herself. Memorizing means thinking and remembering, at least for the moment, means feeling. This morning, the whole day would be given over to remembering. The thinking part, the present and future reality, would have to begin tomorrow, which was too soon anyway.

The best antidote to thinking was remembering, she decided. It was the silly, inconsequential things – she remembered how embarrassed she'd been when he'd arrived unexpectedly and she'd nothing on under her dressing gown the first time they'd made love. She remembered their mingled scents of that night, remembered how a seeming infinity of chaste, arid years had fallen away as if they had never been. She remembered daydreaming, without any hope of reality, that the three of them – Savannah, Benton and she – might become a family. The fact that it had been an idle daydream made it all the more pleasurable – if Benton and Jodi had divorced, she would never have agreed to marry him; it was the fantasy she cherished. She remembered the night she admitted to herself that despite all her effort and against her will, she'd fallen hopelessly in love with him. She recaptured the feeling of his slow, reverent fingers caressing her, their shared laughter, the comfort of her head on his shoulder, his admiration of her very ordinary hair, his brazen adoration of her body. True, her body was still voluptuous, and even when she was celibate, she had known and rejoiced in this. She reminded herself of the days she used to try on sexy dresses clearly much too youthful for her, just for the joy of seeing the way the clothes flattered her shape. She recalled the stoicism with which some patients would accept a dreaded terminal diagnosis and for the first time felt wholly at one with them. But there was this one significant difference; they accepted their fate because they had no alternative, and Lily accepted hers not only because she had no choice, but because she believed the sentence was as just as it was cruel.

After dozing fretfully, Lily was asleep when Benton came in. She lay on the cream velvet couch. Her hair, free of its restraining bow, was strewn over a needlepoint cushion. The Mahler was still playing. He switched it off and the silence woke her. He knelt on the floor beside her and devoured her mouth. He could smell a faint, but not unpleasant whiff of whisky about her. 'Don't let's talk,' he whispered. 'For the past ten hours I've thought compulsively of making love to you.' He kissed her again. 'But I want you to be comfortable. Let's get to a proper bed.'

He led her into the bedroom and she followed willingly. Then, in a turmoil of pleasure and need, they made urgent love. Later, in the circle of their private miracle of intimacy, they began to talk about Jodi's ultimatum, and quickly turned to one another and made love again.

'I'm going to marry you,' he said over and over again.

She gently disengaged their entangled legs, slipped into her robe and explained that they could no longer put off talking things through.

'Even if Jodi had not found out,' she told him,' there could be no 'happy ever after' for us.'

'But I want to *marry* you!'

'I could never be responsible for a divorce,' she protested. 'Not after – '

'But surely,' he interjected. 'Surely you thought of the possibility of a future together?'

'A long and glorious future of snatched moments,' she said with a sad smile. 'I know of lovers who've survived more than thirty years because they kept their affair a secret. Sometimes both were married, and sometimes only one.'

'It'll *never* be over for us!' He clapped his hand to his forehead. 'But your career, Lily-bud,' he groaned. 'You've lost everything, your career, your school, your life.'

'*And* my home.'

'And your home,' he repeated. 'Oh, God, Lily-bud, what have I done to you?'

'I went into this with my eyes wide open, Benton,' she said. 'I knew what I was risking.'

'But was it worth it?'

'I don't know, my darling, I just don't know.' *I've lost everything, how can it be worth it? What a stupid question*, she thought. *But why hurt him with the painful truth?* So she looked into his eyes and lied, 'Yes, Benton, it was worth it.'

'It'll *never* be over for us,' he said again.

'Jodi does not want a divorce,' she said. 'Please, Benton, please don't let her know I told you about her ultimatum.'

'Why not?' he shot back. 'It's sheer blackmail.'

She took his hand, and rested it against her cheek. 'I can't begin to tell you how much this means to me – it will make it so much easier for me to live with myself.'

'Well, if you put it that way –' he said. 'I can't understand why it's so important to you.'

*Because if Jodi believes I kept quiet – as she asked me to – she won't show you that photograph.* 'It's a woman-to woman thing,' she said.

'How could I refuse you anything?'

Lily steered the subject towards the strategy of handling her resignation. And then, though they were certain that it wasn't – and never would be – over for them, they made love for the last time. During that all-too-brief and final hour together, they knew nothing but their greed for one another.

When she asked him, later, not to phone her, nor even try to see her, he negotiated a deal with her. He would agree, he said, but only on condition that she would definitely make contact with him on September 12, in three months' time.

'You'll be in touch with Magsie?' he asked.

'Of course.'

'Mobile phones are available in KwaZulu?'

She nodded. 'But I'm not going to call you.'

'I'll call Magsie twice a week. You'll tell her that?'

'Okay, but I'm going to ask her to promise never to give you my mobile number.'

'You drive a hard bargain, Lily-bud.'

When she finally turned to leave 515 Sloane Street, she took his robe because it had his scent, and hers because it had both their scents. He stopped her in the hallway, in front of the mirror.

He brandished her hairbrush. 'You forgot to take it,' he said.

'So I did.'

'What should I do with the rest of your things?'

'You could give them to Mrs Arbuckle.'

'Mrs Arbuckle?'

'The cleaning lady.'

'OK,' he said. 'But before you go, Lily-bud, there's just one last thing I want to do, something I've wanted to do for a long time.' While he was speaking he had been gently untying the velvet ribbon holding her hair from her face. Neither thick nor thin, her ordinary, light-brown hair fell at once to her shoulders. 'I always meant to brush it, ' he said. 'May I?'

But without waiting for an answer he began brushing it with teasing, gentle strokes. Not wishing to see her reflection in the mirror, but unable to draw away from him, she shut her eyes.

She turned and suddenly caught his wrist. 'Please, please don't let Jodi know that I told you about her ultimatum to me.' Her voice broke. 'I owe her that at least.'

'I told you I wouldn't, and I meant it,' he said.

'Thanks,' she smiled weakly. 'I'm grateful.'

'You're at the height of your beauty,' he said. 'And you are the finest person I have ever known.'

He handed her the scarlet ribbon and she quickly tied her hair back.

'I'm keeping the brush,' he said.

'You're too melodramatic, Benton.'

'I know,' he replied. 'But I can't help it.'

'I'm going now,' she said gravely. 'I'm forgetting everything – I almost forgot to give you the keys.'

She handed him the keys, and she left.

He couldn't see her home; officially he was still in New York.

There was a spacious vacancy in her heart, and though she longed to sob herself to extinction, her soul had been sucked out of her, and she had been drained dry and was destitute of tears.

Her life had become a waking nightmare of such dazzling un-reality that Lily decided to resign immediately, while she was still numb with disbelief, rather than wait out the ten days Jodi had granted her. It would have been too agonizing, like waiting for surgery, with the knowledge that there was to be no anaes-thetic.

Acutely aware that she would never mount that staircase again, Lily took the stairs very slowly. They rose in two shallow flights to the first floor, and, from there the stairs were much steeper. If over these past years she'd been up and down these stairs only six times a day, then she would have climbed at least two million steps. Strange, how facing these last terrible hours, she'd re-sorted to thinking in numbers. Because, though it was just shy of two days since Jodi had presented her with the ultimatum, she'd set her plans for her departure with military precision, and as if they'd been considered, weighed and vetted months earlier, instead of instantaneously.

In seven hours' time, at 7:30 this Monday morning, before the teachers and the children arrived, she would descend the stairs and close the door of Belgrave Hall behind her for ever. She would take no more than a small suitcase. But she was still undecided about Amanda's portrait. Magsie would willingly, if sadly, handle the rest. The bulk of her furniture had been acquired in 1870, when Belgrave Hall opened, and belonged to the school. She had time to pack those clothes she wanted to keep, and to make lists of what should be done with everything, from kitchen equipment to ornaments, photographs, books, linen, china and silver, that were to be stored or given away.

A note had been taped to her front door: *Call me at whatever time, no matter how late – when you arrive home, Magsie.* So she called Magsie and they arranged to meet for breakfast in Lily's flat at 6:30 a.m. When she put down the phone she turned her attention to the letter of resignation she was obliged to write to Lady Violet.

Dear Lady Violet,

It is with very deep regret that I am resigning as Head-mistress of Belgrave Hall. I realize that my contract necessitates a minimum of two terms' notice, but Miss Worthington is a most likeable and trustworthy deputy, who will maintain the high standard and high values for which Belgrave Hall is renowned, until a suitable applicant has been appointed.

My decision has not been taken lightly, and it is with a great deal of soul-searching that I am leaving my post forthwith. Belgrave Hall has been my life, its students my inspiration; to be Headmistress has been a privilege and an honour.

I have been diagnosed with a degenerative type of disease for which there is no specific treatment. Since receiving the news, I have been wrestling with the problem of the best and kindest way to handle this, both for the sake of the school and, I confess, for my own sake as well. It is for this reason that I have decided to go into permanent exile, and leave at once to return to Jabulani where I have spent such an important part of my life each summer. Cut off from Belgrave Hall, Jabulani is the only place where I will feel at one with nature, where I will find solace and usefulness, and where I will be able to spend the rest of my life surrounded by the love and support of genuine, decent people.

I would like to thank the governing body for their faith and trust in me, and for giving me the prodigious opportunity of playing a small role in the progress of such a wonderful centre for the education of young girls.

Change, as I have found, is often forced upon us – God moves in a mysterious way. I will cherish my years at Belgrave Hall until my final rest.

Sincerely,

Lily Lidbury

She checked the letter for any mistakes, put it in an envelope and sealed it, before placing it on the small hall table, beside the coat stand, to be given to Magsie. Once she was in the hall, she reminded herself that it would be winter in KwaZulu, so she would need a coat. She decided her raincoat would be the most useful one to take and, as she removed it from the coat-stand, she recalled her first night with Benton. She remembered the way he'd taken off his coat and hung it beside hers as if it were the most natural thing to do, as if he'd done this many times before. We are our memories, she told herself, but not now, not yet, it was too soon. There would be all the time in the world for memories. Presently, she went down to the school to clear her desk. She'd been wrong a little earlier when she'd thought that when she returned from 515 Sloane Street it was the last time she would climb those stairs.

As she had done countless times before, Lily put on the kettle to have the tea ready for Magsie. Watering the herbs in her window box for the last time, it occurred to her that she had successfully dismantled and reorganized her entire life in less than five hours. Lists had been made, letters written, and accounts paid. All the clothes she wanted were in the single suitcase she was taking to KwaZulu. It was not even a question of sending for her things later on – she was going to lead a simple life, where vintage clothes would be as unnecessary as mementos. It was for this reason that Amanda's emerald velvet coat was not in her suitcase.

Magsie arrived with a basket of Lily's favourite cheese scones. She, too, had been up all night. To explain her decision to leave immediately and permanently, Lily told her about Benton's cell phone, the photograph Savannah had stolen, the information Jodi had obtained from the private investigator in Arundel, and, finally, about the ultimatum with the ten-day deadline.

'But that's inhuman!' Magsie cried. 'You can't resign from Belgrave Hall!'

'I've accepted my fate,' Lily replied calmly. 'I believe the sentence is just and the punishment fair, and I will not appeal.'

'I'll hand in my notice,' Magsie said. 'But I won't be able to leave until the end of term.' Her chin trembled, 'You say the sentence is just. I don't agree and I never will.'

'Jodi says she wants another chance,' Lily murmured. 'I owe *myself* that, at least.' She leaned across the table and stroked Magsie's hand. 'You've been like a devoted older sister to me, Magsie. You tried often enough to warn me. I knew what I was doing. I wish I could cry, Magsie, but I can't. I'm too dry and too empty for tears.' She looked about the room. 'Everything is packed, sorted and arranged, but there will still be a lot for you to do, I'm afraid.' She threw her despairing eyes to the ceiling. 'I haven't been able to decide about Amanda's portrait, though.'

'Where are you going?' Magsie asked. 'You haven't told me, you know.'

'Haven't I?' Lily almost smiled. 'I'm returning to Jabulani to spend the summer as I always do.'

'So soon?'

Lily nodded. 'You know, Magsie, I found out something about myself.' She shook her head. 'It's too late, though.'

'It's never too late to learn,' Magsie said. 'What did you find out?'

'One of the reasons it took me so long to get over Hugh was because he was Amanda's father; and since he was so intimately responsible for her birth, the most profoundly important event of my life, I couldn't let him go. I suppose I was what the American mothers call an "emotional cripple".' A sob in her throat escaped. 'And now I have to let go of Benton,' she said. 'I'll never get over him.'

'You won't like me for saying this,' Magsie spoke slowly, shaping her words. 'But the day will come when you'll get over Benton – you'll see that your heart went to your brain.' Pursing her lips, she added, 'Lust always fades, Lily: it always does.'

But Lily continued as if she hadn't heard. 'Hugh's portrait of Amanda?'

'If you're not staying in Arundel long, you should let the portrait stay right where it is, with me,' Magsie said. 'I can always send it on to you later.'

'But the whole point, Magsie, is that nothing is to be sent to me *later*.' Lily looked at her watch. 'When I leave you, in about ten minutes, I'll be taking all I ever want to take.'

'You'll call me when you arrive, won't you?'

'I'm going to buy a mobile phone when I get there. I'll call you often,' Lily said. 'I'm not going to see or speak to Benton for at least three months.'

'He agreed to that?'

'On one condition.'

'What's that?'

'That he could call you once or twice a week. He asked me to tell you that.' A thought struck her. 'I hope you won't mind.'

'Mind? Of course I won't mind!'

'Will you come to Jabulani if I send you a ticket?'

'I'll come whenever you invite me, whether you send me a ticket or not.'

'I almost forgot to tell you about my resignation letter,' Lily said. 'I've become a magnificent liar – I told them that I had a degenerative condition; which, in a way, is what we all have.'

Lily got up and began to rinse the breakfast dishes. Magsie stopped her.

'There isn't time for that if you want to leave before school opens,' she said gently. 'Leave it all to me.'

Magsie took the small tote bag, and Lily the suitcase, and they descended the winding staircase together for the last time.

# CHAPTER 18

Lily's early arrival in KwaZulu was greeted with enthusiasm, but without curiosity. Outwardly, nothing indicated the inner turmoil tearing her apart, so no one could guess that she had returned earlier than usual this year, nor could they imagine her reasons: that she'd been compelled to flee London, and that she needed to convalesce from the catastrophe she'd inflicted on herself.

'We are indeed fortunate to have you with us,' Matron Thembi Modisani remarked after an unusually fraught afternoon.

'I'm considering giving up teaching,' Lily replied.

Matron's wise eyes brightened. 'Are you perhaps considering spending more time with us?'

'I think so,' Lily replied.

'Good,' Matron smiled. 'We have been hoping you will take over the correspondence relating to the grant we are requesting from the State Department,' she said in her careful, formal English. 'As you no doubt know, we are hoping to extend our medical facilities – Jabulani is in need of modernization.'

Formerly the colonial-styled mansion of an idealistic sugar baron, Jabulani was left to a mission station who converted it to an orphanage. By the time of Lily's first visit, Jabulani had become a centre for orphaned AIDS victims, and was both a hospital and an orphanage for about sixty children, ranging in age from newborn babies to fifteen-year-olds. Lily's tiny flat had once been a minute gatehouse. Run independently, Jabulani was one of the scandalously few South African institutions able to finance the anti-retroviral treatment that makes a significant difference to the survival rates of the children, many of whom were now chronically – rather than terminally – ill.

Completely remote, Jabulani had always seemed to Lily to be on horizonless land. When she had first seen the orphanage, in the year after Amanda's death, the spiritual dryness of the drought-stricken earth had matched her mood. There was a whiff of eternity about the place, and she had known at once that nursing such needy children in this kind of wilderness could bring a measure of sanity to her blighted life.

Jabulani saved me once, she thought now, and could save me again. All the same, she had come to depend on her telephone conversations with Magsie, and called her often, and they talked to one another as if they were not separated by thousands of miles. She had followed Benton's advice, and bought a mobile phone at Durban Airport. The very sound of Magsie's Scottish burr consoled her; it made her feel as if she were not entirely disconnected from the world in which she used to live.

'I know we had a lovely chat yesterday,' Magsie said. 'But I couldn't resist phoning. You'll never guess what Lady Violet and Miss Worthington are planning.'

'Tell me,' Lily laughed.

'They're arranging a service to pray for the restoration of your health!'

'You can't be serious!'

'I most certainly am serious,' Magsie said. 'Do you remember talking about sending a lone dove flying to the rafters at the end of a carol concert?'

'It was just a dream I had,' Lily sighed. 'Why?'

'As a tribute to your work as headmistress, Lady Violet has asked Father Milton to conclude the service with a dove flying to the rafters.'

'Oh, *Magsie!*' Lily wiped the silent tears sliding down her cheeks. 'What can I say?'

Although Lily had slipped into her nursing duties with the same ease with which the fully bilingual move between languages, her nights were another matter. Tortured by night-thoughts, sleeplessness ruled like a malevolent enemy. The resident doctor prescribed a soporific, and with the help of a drugged sleep, she was able to function as if her world had not been shattered.

But then, as a side effect of the medication, a vivid nightmare, always the same, came to taunt her. She dreamed that Savannah and Katie, each wearing their violet Belgrave Hall uniform, lay motionless in the dusty red earth at the bottom of a winding white staircase suspended from the sky. Giant white ants streamed out of the parched earth and swarmed over Savannah's face. Katie's untouched, dead face was the embodiment of purity and innocence. The same unearthly shriek that Savannah had screamed when Katie fell down the stairwell ripped through her sleep. But it was Lily's own answering scream that juddered her awake. Shivering and trembling, she gave up all hope of sleep. After six consecutive such nights she chose insomnia over nightmares, and resolved not to take sleeping pills again. But she hoarded them – you never knew when you might need them, she thought.

She felt like a refugee whose entire way of life had been confiscated, or swept away in a tsunami. She had lost everything she cared about, and yet experienced nothing like the savage pain she suffered when she lost Amanda. Instead, there was the dreadful knowledge that she had brought down her world with her own hands, and the penalty of her reckless liaison with a married man was no worse than she deserved. Nor could she help noting, with wry humour, and some regret, that catastrophic changes in her lifestyle meant that her frenzied need for Benton's body had been cut out from her just as surely as if it had been a diseased gallbladder.

But for all that, and no matter how often she ordered herself to move on, her soul still resided in Belgrave Hall. The awesome space, the bare blue skies and the scent of Africa, did nothing to appease her longing for the rhythm and ritual of her school life. She would look at her watch: at nine in the morning, she would go back to eight, when there would be the clamour of the cars dropping off the girls at the school gates, and by eight-thirty London time, she would be waiting for her beloved school bell to send the girls to their classrooms. She would imagine looking through the slatted blinds at early morning netball practice. At playtimes she would see the playground full of happy children. She missed leading her Friday morning assembly: 'Good morning girls!' and the musical chant, 'Good morning, Mrs Lidbury.'

Oh God, she thought, I miss so much of what I took for granted; the visiting old girls from all over the world, signing 'excellent' at the bottom of a school report, the contact with parents and grandparents. Life without Belgrave Hall, she acknowledged, was not one of those injustices that are part of the business of living: it was a just and earned punishment that she had visited upon herself.

When she next spoke to Magsie she learned that Benton had called twice in one day to get her mobile phone number. 'He was none too pleased when I wouldn't give it to him,' Magsie said, her voice grim.

'He's already called Jabulani,' Lily said. 'Just as well I'd made arrangements with the secretary not to call me to the phone, but to take a message.'

'Now I know why he was absolutely furious when I refused to give him your number!'

'He wasn't rude, surely?'

'I wouldn't say he was exactly charming.'

'I'm sorry about that, Magsie, but don't give in to him. He can be extremely persuasive.'

'As if I didn't know that,' Magsie's laugh was mirthless.

'I'm too angry with myself to talk to him yet, Magsie.' Lily said. 'I can't even face hearing his voice.'

'Time will help, Lily. It always does.'

If Lily had taken Benton's calls, she would have known that he was so angry with Jodi for having blackmailed her that he had decided to stay on at 515 Sloane Street, and not go home until the following evening. When he had called to tell Jodi that he'd be home within the hour, he had led her to believe that he was on his way home from Heathrow. It was ten o'clock by then, and he was certain Savannah would be in bed and asleep.

Following her advice to herself – to treat Benton with kid gloves – Jodi decided to wait for him in his study.

After she had found out about Lily, Jodi had set about examining the facts of her marriage as if she were collating evidence. Her decision to stay married astonished her. She had every reason to divorce, and she didn't need to stay married for financial reasons. If she were to divorce, it would be because she had made no effort to avoid failure. She had allowed her ambition to rule her marriage and her family as if there had been no other choice. It was too bad that Benton had fallen for Savannah's headmistress, but she could not blame him for turning to another woman; Jodi had always cared *about* him, but not *for* him.

*Once you know you have done your best*, her father used to say, *failure is not such a hardship. But you – and only you – can know whether or not you've done your best*. I didn't even try, she thought. All I want now is the chance to try.

With that in mind she began planning what she would say to Benton, and how she would say it.


Jodi heard his key in the lock, and knew he would leave his luggage in the hall, and go directly to his study. She had opened a bottle of his favourite claret, and the cookies she and Savannah had made lay in a straw basket.

Benton accepted a glass of wine, and helped himself to a cookie.

'Delicious,' he said.

'Savannah and I baked them this afternoon.'

'Looks like you're turning into a domestic goddess,' he said.

Determined not to respond to his sarcasm with sarcasm, she

went on to say what she had planned. 'How did you like the look of the living room?'

He was puzzled. 'The living room?'

It was absurd – but prudent – to be acting as if nothing had changed, she thought. But she said, 'The kelim rug and the yellow cushions.'

He remembered having noticed that the new cushions in their New York apartment were the same shade as the sun-yellow arm chairs in Sloane Street. He also remembered the time Jodi had called him in Paris when he was with Lily to tell him she'd found their all-white apartment frighteningly sterile, and had bought colourful cushions. 'We've never made love in our living room,' she had said. He had wondered, then, if she had sensed he was involved with another woman. 'The apartment looked a whole lot more homey,' he said now. 'Sort of warmer, having some colour in the place.'

'I hoped you'd like it,' she said.

It was crazy that she was behaving as if nothing out of the ordinary had happened. 'Are you planning on divorcing me?' he asked unexpectedly.

'I'm not planning on anything right now,' she said. 'But I think we both need time to calm down and come – ' her voice trailed off.

He cracked his knuckles.

'I'll wait for you, Benton.' She paused, and continued with another of her rehearsed phrases, 'I'll wait as long as I can.'

'I'll move into the guest room.'

Successfully avoiding the sarcasm that so naturally came to her lips she said, 'I thought you'd say that. The bed's been made up for you.'

They continued to live under the same roof, as if they were cousins sharing a house belonging to a benevolent aunt. As in an armed truce, they were diplomatic and well mannered, and sometimes even laughed together.

'Imagine if all this had happened while we were living and working in New York,' Jodi said one day. It was her first reference to Lily.

'As the Brits say, you'd have had my guts for garters!'

'Too true,' Jodi said. A laugh began to well up from her chest. 'I'd have had your guts for garters,' she sputtered, 'guts for garters,' she repeated again as a gust of staccato laughter shook her. It was the kind of laughter that sets others off. Benton joined in and the laughter grew louder, and then they laughed louder still, because they didn't know why they were laughing. They only stopped when Savannah came in.

'I guess you two are not getting a divorce,' she said.

'We're working things out, honey,' Jodi said.

'But why are you laughing?'

'You know what, honey,' Benton said. 'A day without a laugh is a day wasted.'

'Mrs Lidbury used to say that.'

'There are stacks of sayings like that,' Jodi said quickly to cover Benton's almost tangible embarrassment. 'Laugh and the whole world laughs with you. Cry, and you cry alone.'

Emergencies are commonplace in nursing everywhere, but that day Jabulani reminded Lily of a war zone. A teenager and her year-old daughter were admitted. The teenage mother died, and her little girl, emaciated and covered in sores, had little chance of surviving. A twelve-year-old boy who had been caring for his orphaned siblings, carried his six-year-old dying brother into the hospital. A painfully small malnourished baby boy of about two months old had been found abandoned in a dusty cardboard box on a rock-strewn sandy road. They said that every year in South Africa eighty thousand babies are born to die of AIDS contracted from infected mothers, Lily reminded herself, but the statistic did nothing to ease her anguish for this desperately ill infant.

Late that evening, it struck her that she had not thought of

Benton or Savannah for several days. On impulse she decided to call Magsie to tell her that she had been right when she told her that lust fades.

'I was just going to phone you,' Magsie said when she heard Lily's voice. 'So much news! Lady Violet told me that the Hunts are *not* moving to New York after – ' She broke off. She had not meant to mention Lady Violet.

'Does that mean that both the Hunt girls will be at Belgrave Hall next term?'

'It certainly does!' Magsie replied. 'But the really good news is that Katie's cast has been removed. Her leg has healed perfectly. The bad news is that she refuses to tell anyone why she will not touch her violin – Harriet Ratcliffe is beside herself.'

'How I wish I could talk to Katie!'

'You'd get to the bottom of it soon enough,' Magsie said. 'Hold on, I think I've had a brainwave, Lily! You could phone Katie!'

'I'll have to think about that, Magsie.'

After they rang off, Lily remembered that she'd forgotten to mention Benton.

She recognized, with a shock that quickly turned into a dull acceptance, that life without Benton and Savannah was entirely bearable. It was life without Belgrave Hall that was tough. But her nursing was an effective therapy; medical experts and journalists from all over the world frequently visited Jabulani, and her life was busy, useful and interesting. Besides, she was satisfied that despite everything that had happened, Savannah was happier now than before she came to Belgrave Hall, and took comfort from that. Lily had even stopped brooding over the last time she and Benton were at 515 Sloane Street.

In Benton's view, that bout of laughter he'd shared with Jodi had been the calm before the storm. He was letting things ride until he and Lily could get together again. His body yearned for Lily; he felt he was living in a waste of longing. He craved ecstasy – ecstasy such as he had never expected. Their affair had begun as a sort of frivolous amusement, a treat he was giving himself, the ego-boosting thrill of seducing a woman as seemingly unattainable – and as unlikely – as a headmistress. After all, Lily was hardly the trophy type. He allowed himself a smug smile – how deceptive appearances are, he thought. When they were together, they left the world behind.

As the days wore on, his fury with Jodi increased. He would never forgive her for having blackmailed Lily into going to Africa, and one day he'd find his revenge. Again and again, he would compare the two women. Familiar with the workings of investment banking, Jodi considered nothing about his career exceptional. She'd achieved as much as he had, if not more, in the corporate world. Lily found his banking world fascinating; when he was with her he felt pleased with himself, and proud of his work. It didn't come naturally to her, as it did to Jodi, to want to be equal, if not superior to him. Instead, Lily looked up to him, and made it clear that she respected his work in a way Jodi never had.

He wanted to speak to Lily; he needed to hear her voice in the same reflexive way he needed to breathe. He missed her – he felt like a schoolboy, sent to boarding school, and parted from his mother for the first time. Beyond caring whether he was treating her like a mother figure or not, he was determined to speak to her.

So far, every time he called Jabulani, he'd been unable to reach her. Six calls, six different reasons: she was dealing with an emergency, in the operating room, away visiting another clinic, admitting a new patient (twice), in Durban speaking at a fund-raising meeting.

He was going to try once more; this time he'd use a new tactic.
'I've an important message for Mrs Lidbury,' he began.
'Are you referring to Nurse Lidbury?'
'I am.'
'Hold the line, please.'

Benton's heart raced. 'Certainly.'

After a while the operator said, 'I'm sorry, sir. Nurse Lidbury is attending to an urgent emergency. May I take a message?'

He glared at the mobile in his hand, and hurled it across the room with such force that it crashed against the mirror, splintering the glass. '*Shit!*' Benton yelled. '*Shit, shit, shit!*'

His yells brought Jodi rushing in. 'What's – '

'*You bitch!*' Benton roared. '*You fucking bitch! You* gave her that ultimatum! *You* threatened to expose her if she didn't leave Britain. *You* blackmailed her into giving up her whole life!'

'But Benton – '

White with fury, he cut her off. 'What would *you* know, or care, about a fine, sensitive woman like Lily Lidbury?'

'What would *I* know?' Jodi's voice sounded like ice breaking. 'I'll show you what I know!'

She stormed out.

'I'm getting out of here!' Benton screamed into the empty room.

Jodi returned carrying the enlarged photograph of Lily and Amanda in their identical green velvet coats.

'This is what I know about a *fine, sensitive* woman like Lily Lidbury,' she said, reverting to her litigator mode. 'Clearly, Lily never showed you a photograph of her daughter, Amanda. If she had, you'd have known that it was not you, Benton Anderson, but Savannah's father she was after.' She turned to leave, but stopped at the threshold. 'Fucking you was a way of getting closer to Savannah. She must have had some fantasy that we'd divorce, you'd marry her, and she'd become Savannah's stepmother.' She sighed. 'If I didn't think she had a sick mind, I'd say she's no better than a fraudster.'

He stood up. 'You've gone too far!' He clenched his fists. 'Cut the crap, Jodi!'

'Benton,' Jodi said. 'By all the laws of logic – '

'I'm warning you, Jodi, cut the crap!'

She brandished the photograph. 'Thank God Savannah's away

on a field trip,' she said. She advanced a few steps toward him and thrust the photograph into his hand. 'For your own sake, Benton Anderson, examine this photograph. Face the facts, and the truth will stare you in the face.'

Suddenly Jodi broke into tears. Convulsed with sobs, she lay down on the carpet and gave way to the kind of weeping her self-control had never before permitted. I *trusted* her not to tell him about my ultimatum, she thought. She had believed she and Lily had reached some sort of woman-to-woman under-standing. But Lily had broken faith with her; and now there was no telling what Benton might do.

Lily had just completed dressing a toddler's emaciated arm when her mobile phone rang.

'Magsie? What's up?'

'I'm sure I'm disturbing you, but I couldn't wait to tell you,' Magsie said. 'You'll never guess what's happened! Never!'

'What *are* you talking about?'

'It's Thursday morning, isn't it?'

'Yes,' said Lily. 'Why?'

'I'll be in KwaZulu tomorrow!'

'Oh, *Magsie!*'

'Lady Violet's husband is giving me a ride on someone's private jet! They've got a company meeting in Durban, and I'll be in Africa for *three days*,' Magsie explained. 'Must go now – I've so much to do!'

'What time do you arrive? I'll be there to – '

'No need,' Magsie interrupted. 'I'm to be driven right to Jabulani – it's all been arranged. I ought to be with you by five o'clock.'

'This is too incredible – ' Lily's voice shook.

'See you *tomorrow*, Lily!'

A rush of joy surged through Lily. Flushed with excitement, she told everyone that Magsie would be with her tomorrow. They all knew about Magsie, of course, and Matron instantly decided to give her a little welcome party the day after she arrived. She suggested including two other overseas visitors to Jabulani – a Peace Corps worker and an American epidemiologist.

Benton stayed behind closed blinds for two days.

No girl or woman had ever rejected him before, and now that he'd admitted to himself that Lily was deliberately refusing to take his calls, the anger he'd felt toward Jodi evaporated beside his all-consuming rage at Lily. His rage changed to hatred, and the hatred took hold of him, and all the longing he'd felt for Lily turned to a deadly need to hurt her. He began to indulge in sado-masochistic fantasies, and envisaged the red weals he'd inflict on the soft yielding flesh of her inner thighs. Instead of aching for her, he ached to punish her. Feverishly making and rejecting plans for vengeance, his mind ran in all directions all the time, and he barely ate or slept. Finally, he called the airline company, and made a reservation to fly to South Africa. He would trick Lily into meeting him at a game lodge close to Jabulani. The bungalows there were well separated; there would be enough distance between them to guarantee complete privacy. He'd see her only once, rip her clothes off her, fuck her, and get out of there as fast as a bat out of hell.

Early, the next morning he went downstairs to his office to collect the file of personal correspondence he kept at home. He was looking for a letter of thanks from Jabulani – he needed the address. He found it at once. He was on his way back to the guest room when Jodi met him on the staircase. Unshaven and startlingly unkempt, he looked gaunt and as grey as if he were seriously ill. In spite of herself, she went up to him and laid her hand on his forehead.

'Are you OK, Benton?' she asked. 'Can I do anything for you? A cup of coffee?'

'No,' he said. 'But thanks for asking.'

Back in the guest room, he opened his file, and turned on his laptop.

He sat at the computer for a long while. When he was done he finally felt the kind of drowsiness that brings sleep.

A few hours later, he was awakened by Jodi who'd crept into his bed. 'The Swami says forgiveness is the highest virtue,' she whispered into his ear. 'Can we forgive each other?'

She drew him to her, and he discovered that she was naked.

Satisfied that everything was ready for Magsie's arrival, Lily went to her computer later than usual that evening. She expected news from the US State Department. But there was only one email waiting for her, and it was from Benton.

Dear Lily,

I've thought long and hard about you since our last meeting, and have decided to tell you what I know about the real Lily Lidbury.

I already knew that you posed as a childless widow when you were the divorced mother of a dead child. But passionate about you, and blinded by sympathy for you, I forgave you, and chose not to see that you were an imposter.

Yesterday, I saw the photograph of you and your daughter for the first time. Now I know why you behaved so dishonestly. That you deceived me is of little consequence. But that you abused and exploited my beautiful Savannah's trust simply because she resembled your own daughter, makes you too dangerous a woman to be a teacher.

About five months ago, as I recall, you called me with the excuse that you were 'slightly worried' about Savannah. I fell for that and, never dreaming you'd accept, took a chance and invited you to dinner. But you did accept and, what was more, you invited me up to see your flat. You were insatiable. I fell in love with you. In truth you used my body to reach my daughter.

I have always respected professional whores for their

honesty. You know where you are with them. It's amateurs like you who are the cheats and the liars.

And now there you are, in Africa, your reputation intact only because a lawyer (my wife) gave you an ultimatum: you could either resign as headmistress and leave the country, or the whole truth of you would be exposed, including your affair with the father (me) of a Belgrave Hall girl.

You may be one of the best lays I've ever had, but I'll always regret having known you.

Benton

Each word burned into Lily's brain. Her skin prickled, and she felt as if she'd broken out in an invisible rash. In case she was hallucinating, she read it again; and yes, it really was as cruel as it had seemed. Worse still, Benton's email had been forwarded from the general Jabulani address, and not to her private account. He'd made sure her humiliation would be both public and private. That it was an open email for everyone to read certainly hurt her, but it also stripped her of all her illusions: he was a far smaller man than she had thought. The cruel style of his underhand vengeance took her breath away: she would never have predicted that he could sink to such an act of spite.

His open email told her more about him than she had ever wanted to know. The sheer crudity of his revenge was like a bright light revealing the darker side of his character, and she understood that she had hardly known him at all. At the same time she had to face the question: had she ever *liked* him or anything he stood for? Defects that she'd deliberately ignored came to mind: how he loved watching boxing while she despised the spectators as much as the sport, and the way he wore his Franck Mueller watch over his shirt cuff. For all that, she never, never could have imagined that he could behave so despicably. How could she have misjudged him so?

To call her affair with him an obsession, she reasoned, was to diminish its magnitude, for it had been nothing less than a total loss of reason. She now understood that she'd been on the edge of madness; that she'd been in love not with him, but with what his magnificent body did to hers.

Her eyes strayed to the china box that held her stash of sleeping pills. A sudden wave of nausea overcame her, and she rushed to the bathroom to throw up.

Later, resting her head on the lavatory seat, she remembered having vomited in the same way after Jane Kale had told her that her husband was leaving her.

When there was nothing left in her stomach, she decided to take two sleeping pills – if her terrifying nightmare returned, it would be less terrifying than her present reality.

Jittery and sore-eyed from lack of sleep, Lily rose at dawn the next morning. On her way to a village store in her battered pick-up truck, she stopped to breathe in the burnt grass scent of a recent veldt fire. She imagined the rosewater fragrance that always accompanied Magsie blending in with the peculiarly African scent of dust and charred grasses she loved so well. On her way to Jabulani, Magsie would be driven through the rolling green hills of KwaZulu. She tried to guess what Magsie would make of the bleak dusty earth on which Jabulani stood. Lily found the vast plains consoling. Looking out at the limitless space, she had the sense that there was no beginning and no ending, but only an endless continuity, an infinity of space and air to which she was joined for ever.

She wondered about the kind of business that had brought Lord Anstey to Africa for only three days. No matter – it was enough that Magsie was coming.

Magsie would adore the children with their large eyes, their gleaming teeth, their sense of mischief and laughter. She would grieve for the hopelessly sick ones, but would connect with them without language in her own inimitable way.

Soon she was on the rock-strewn road to the supermarket; the nights could be cold, and she needed an extra blanket for Magsie. Her flat had recently been painted, but the furniture was rather shabby and faded. Her thoughts constantly returned to Lady Violet – not so long ago she considered her a witch, now she considered her a saint. After all it was Lady Violet who'd arranged the petition urging Magsie not to resign. And now it was Lady Violet who was sending her a living blessing in the shape of her dearest friend.

Benton's email, however, was like a threat lurking under whatever else she was thinking about. She had decided how she would reply to anyone who mentioned his email to her. 'I'm sorry you had to read such vile letter,' she'd say. 'Benton Anderson is not the man I thought he was. I can say no more than that.'

But she still had not decided how – or if – she would reply to his email.


Punctuality was as rare as twilight in KwaZulu, yet Magsie arrived at precisely the time she had said she would. Even as Lily opened the door of the jeep that had brought her, she couldn't believe that it really was Magsie who was spilling out of the door.

'I've brought Amanda's portrait,' Magsie said.

'I had a feeling you would,' Lily replied.

Then Magsie drew Lily to her, clasped her in a fierce hug, and swallowed hard. 'It took eighteen hours door-to-door, and I could do with a stiff whisky!' she announced.

'And to think I was going to give you tea and scones!'

'Scones! The last thing I expected here,' Magsie said. 'But whisky and scones will go down very well, thank you.' Once in the sitting room, she looked around. 'This room is perfect for Amanda's portrait,' she declared. 'Who'd have thought I'd be given a seat on a private jet only yesterday, and be here today, sitting with you, in your living room in Africa?'

Lily set the carefully wrapped portrait down, and propped it against the widow. 'We'll unwrap it later,' she said. She busied herself with the whisky, and handed a glass to Magsie. 'I want to hear all about your flight.'

'Later,' Magsie said. 'I'll tell you about it later.' She raised her glass, 'To Lady Violet.'

'Lady Violet,' Lily echoed.

'I suppose you're dying to hear what made her send me to you.'

'You could say so,' Lily said.

'Katie broke down and told Savannah why she won't play her violin.'

'*Won't* play? I thought the accident – '

'Harriet Ratcliffe had been abusing Katie for years. If she wasn't satisfied with the way Katie was playing, she'd make her stand naked in the bath, and hose her with ice-cold water. No bruises, nothing to show she'd been tortured.'

'*Tortured!*' Lily exclaimed. '*Impossible!*'

'Katie thought that if she were injured in an accident, and physically unable to play, the punishments would stop.' Magsie's voice dropped, 'So she used the stairwell – and Savannah – to make it look like an accident.'

'You're saying the poor child fell deliberately?'

'Yes,' Magsie said. 'I'm afraid I am.'

'Good God! Savannah blamed herself for that fall!'

'Katie begged Savannah not to tell Jodi, and she promised she wouldn't.' Magsie stopped to draw an audible breath. 'Savannah kept her word – the next morning she came to see *me*. I'd promised not to inform Jodi or any of Savannah's teachers, so I called Lady Violet. It was a brainwave, because Lady Violet took matters into her own hands and went at once to see Harriet. She pulled no punches – she simply gave Harriet the option either to see a therapist or go to prison. She's already in therapy, and it's likely that Katie will start playing again.'

'It never once crossed my mind that Katie could have fallen deliberately,' Lily muttered. 'But I *did* think – '

'I know what you mean,' Magsie said. 'Lady Violet and I also thought Savannah had pushed her.'

'Jodi thought so too!' Lily burst out. 'She as good as said so at that last terrible meeting we had.'

'What exactly *did* Jodi say?'

'She said that if Katie had not recovered, Savannah would have been guilty of murder.'

They sat silently for a while.

'I misjudged Harriet Ratcliffe,' Lily said. 'I thought she was the perfect mother to raise a prodigy.'

Lily's mouth tasted liked baked earth; and she felt dust behind her eyelids. She remembered thinking that Harriet's eyes were as hard and dry as dead leaves. She was about to say something about this when her knocker sounded. She excused herself, and crossed the room to open it. Matron, two of her small patients, and a man she'd never met before were standing on her doorstep.

'I know Magsie has only just arrived,' Matron said excitedly. 'But this is Dr Alan Feldman of the World Health Organization. He'd heard you were here, Lily, and he was in the area.' She paused. 'I think he'd better tell you the rest!'

'It's good to meet you, Mrs Lidbury,' Dr Feldman said. 'My kid sister, Lucy Feldman, went to Belgrave Hall,' he laughed. 'When I told her I'd be in KwaZulu, she said you'd left teaching to work over here. So she wanted me to say hullo to you.'

'Lucy brought her baby to see us. She was only in London for a few days, and it was wonderful to see her,' Lily said. 'Come in, and let me introduce you to my best friend, Magsie Henderson. This is our Matron, Thembi Modisane, and Dr Alan Feldman, as you must have heard. And these two little ones, Ndbanu and Thandiwe, are two of my bravest little patients. They could barely walk when they arrived here.'

'We are here to welcome you, Magsie,' Matron said. 'Lily has told us so much about you. To welcome you properly, we're having a party at the hospital to tomorrow afternoon.'

'But that's so kind of you,' Magsie said.

The smaller of the two children pointed to the portrait. 'Did you bring that big parcel on the aeroplane?'

'Yes,' Magsie replied. 'It's a picture.'

'Can we see it?'

Magsie looked questioningly at Lily.

'Let's unwrap it now,' Lily said.

'Allow me to help,' Dr Feldman said, brandishing a Swiss Army knife. 'It's seriously useful.'

Several layers of Magsie's protective wrapping were removed before the portrait emerged.

When the luminously beautiful child with the smiling, compassionate eyes was revealed, everyone gasped.

'Who's that?' one of the children asked.

'My daughter.'

'What's her name?'

'Amanda.'

'Where is she?'

'She's dead.'

'But you're still Amanda's ma?'

There was a pause.

'Yes, I'm still Amanda's ma.'

'Leave us alone for a moment, children,' Matron said, leading Lily a few steps away. 'I need to talk to Amanda's ma.' Switching to English, she made no effort to hide her disapproval. 'I've known you for well over ten years, and I never even knew you were a mother!' She shook her head and flung up her hands. 'How – or why – you could keep such a beautiful daughter a secret, I'll never know.'

'I simply could not bear to speak about it.'

Matron's eyes filled with tears. 'We've been through so much together, Lily! I thought we were *friends*.' Her voice dropped reproachfully. 'But you never trusted me.' She wheeled on her heel, and turned away.

Lily placed a restraining hand on Matron's arm. 'A dog savaged my daughter to death,' she said in a painful whisper. 'I was so *ashamed of the way she died*, that I thought I was a freak of nature.'

Matron enfolded her in her arms. 'Grief twists us in many ways,' she said. 'But a mother's grief is unquenchable.'

Lily drew away. 'I'm glad you know.' Her tone confident again, she added, 'I want *everyone* to know about Amanda.'

'That is as it should be,' Matron said. 'We should leave you now. Come and say goodbye, children,' she called out.

The children returned at once. 'Goodbye, Amanda's ma,' they chorused.

'See you tomorrow, Amanda's ma,' Dr Feldman said.

Everyone laughed.

By the end of the afternoon, the portrait was hanging on the whitewashed wall of Lily's sitting room. It's where it belongs, Lily thought. She found herself wishing that Hugh could have seen it in this setting. With a sigh of relief she realized that the bitterness and blame she'd heaped on Hugh had gone, and she'd forgiven him not only for his betrayal of her, but for the manner of Amanda's death. Lily looked into Amanda's eyes. 'I'm going to tell everyone about you.'

Later, as they stood in front of the painting, Magsie gestured toward the portrait. ' I can't take my eyes off her,' she said.

A smile lit Lily's face. 'I'll never be able to thank you enough for bringing her to me, Magsie.'

'I'd like to take photographs of her for Lady Violet,' Magsie said.

'She knows about Amanda?'

'She asked if what she'd heard about Amanda and Savannah was true. I told her it was.'

'And she knows about Benton and me?'

'I was coming to that,' Magsie said. 'Actually, that's the main reason for my being here. Courtney told Lady Violet that the real reason for your resignation was Jodi's ultimatum to you. She was appalled.'

'*Courtney!*' Lily buried her face in her hands. 'Oh my God.'

'Jodi and Courtney do yoga together,' Magsie said. 'Lady Violet was appalled not by you and Benton, but by what Jodi did to you. She called it blackmail,' Magsie added. 'Lady Violet wants you to come back to Belgrave Hall next term.'

'*What?*' Lily whispered. 'This can't be true!'

'It is true, thank God,' Magsie said. 'I'm exhausted, Lily. If I don't take a shower and get out of these sticky clothes, I think I'll pass out.'

Magsie went to take a nap before dinner, and Lily went to her computer. She knew how she would reply to Benton. Her decision came so easily that it must have been floating in her mind all day without her realizing it.

Dear Benton

Your forwarded email introduced me to the real Benton Anderson. I preferred the imposter.

I will never forget – or regret – the Benton I once knew.

Sincerely,

Lily

Outside, the wild daffodils were already in bloom. Lily fetched her mother's china pillbox from the kitchen, and poured the contents into the palm of her left hand, raising her right hand to salute the deceptively touchable African sky. She opened her left fist, studied the bundle of sleeping tablets, or, as she saw them, white blossoms of infinity, then scattered them among the daffodils.

It was the first time since Lily had left London that Benton was at his desk in his study. After his and Jodi's passionate reconciliation of the night before, he had decided to leave the guest room. That morning, Jodi had suggested that getting three tickets for a West End musical that was taking London by storm. 'Bandrika's contact can get us tickets – it'll be a kind of celebration, the three of us going to the theatre and dinner,' she said, her voice unashamedly joyous.

Now, waiting for Jodi and Savannah to join him, sipping his Scotch, he switched off the news and contemplated his email to Lily. Writing it had been a cathartic experience. Putting it all down, spewing out his rage and hate at Lily's deceit and rejection, had somehow cleansed him of the poisonous emotions that had been strangling him. He was calmer now.

He was glad of what he'd written; it had clarified his thinking. But now he felt an overwhelming rush of compassion for Lily, for the tragedy that had befallen her, and for the first time wondered how *he* would have coped if anything like that had ever happened to *his* daughter. He winced – *no*! He could not possibly even think along such lines.

He wondered if Jodi had returned the photograph of Amanda and Lily to his desk drawer. He wasn't surprised to find it. Yes, he thought, the resemblance is uncanny, eerie, unsettling. He asked himself how he would have reacted if he'd known about Amanda at the beginning of their affair. He admitted he would probably have been deeply uneasy, possibly even afraid for Savannah in case there could be a jinx on her, a terrible foreshadowing of her own destiny. He returned the photograph, face down. He'd ask Jodi if they could get rid of it – he wanted it out of their lives.

What was he doing? He was supposed to be checking the internet. When he had been up in the guest room, he'd isolated himself from the world for so long that he didn't even know what 'shows were currently on'. He hit 'Google' and at the same moment his computer flashed 'You have email'.

He hit 'read'. It was from Lily.

Even as he was reading it, he was tugging his hair and cursing out loud.

Instantaneously, he clicked 'reply'.

Oh my God, Lily, you were never meant to receive that hateful email. I hit 'send' instead of 'send later'! I didn't know it had been sent until I got your reply!

How can I apologize enough?

I wrote in a moment of bitter madness, out of an uncontrollable need to hurt you, subliminally aware that I was going to give myself time to calm down and read it over before deciding whether or not to send it.

Of course you are not an imposter. You are the finest woman I was ever lucky enough to meet.

I hope you will believe me when I say that the email was sent by mistake. I also hope you will believe – and accept – that I was raging, not *thinking*. But all that ranting brought me out of the dark cave of bilge I'd been drowning in, and now that I can think more clearly, and have a deeper understanding of your terrible, enduring grief, I find that you are an even more remarkable woman than I had thought. Your tragedy could so easily have made you bitter. Instead, your grief quickened your understanding of human pain.

The real me, and not the imposter who expressed all those unforgivable, unconscionable *emotions rather than thoughts,* wants you to know that not one word of that diatribe is true of how I feel about you. I will love, honour and respect you – from a distance – for the rest of my days.

Although you and I are now irrevocably in the past tense, the memory of my love for you will always be permanently in the present.

For all that you have done for Savannah and for me, I will be for ever grateful.

Forgive me, if you can. I know I'll never be able to forgive myself!

As ever,

Benton

Lily was on her way to put the china pill box back in the kitchen when Amanda's portrait caught her eye. She stopped still and gazed at it. 'I'm glad you're here,' she whispered. An image of the last time she had seen Savannah flashed into her mind. It was five months since she and Savannah had first met. Since then, Savannah had grown, and the shape of her nose seemed to have broadened. She was no longer Amanda's mirror image, Lily realized. She would ask Magsie if she agreed. She was checking on the chicken casserole she had prepared earlier when she heard her computer beep: 'You have email'. She returned the casserole to the oven, and then, still holding the oven glove, went to her computer. Her desk was only a few feet away from the tiny kitchen.

It was a second email from Benton.

She read it a few times, and it still didn't seem believable, so she printed it out.

Then, clutching the printout, she went into the shimmering African night again. The scent of the frangipani was strong. The children were singing, and the beautiful melody drifted over her. In a surge of gratitude she pressed the printout to her lips. 'I didn't misjudge you, Benton,' she said.

As proud as she was of Savannah for having had the sense to turn to Magsie for help, and as shocked as she was about Katie, she was thankful that the Anderson family was now safely part of her past. Now that she could return to Belgrave Hall, she was not sure if that was what she wanted. Looking up at the stars in the velvet sky it came to her that she no longer wondered what Amanda would have been like if she had lived. Mercifully, she was no longer in a naked place but at last at peace with her daughter's death.

Tomorrow, at the party, the children, the nurses, the doctors and everyone else would call her 'Amanda's ma'. The name would stick. The children of Jabulani had given her back her identity as a mother.

Rid of the shame that made her keep Amanda's life and death a secret for so long, she was finally ready for anything – even the prospect of happiness.